AN ANGEL'S DESIRE

Oh, yes, she realized. She wanted this. Lowering herself to both knees, Angeline trailed a hand inside his shirt, peering at him through slitted eyes to see that he'd tipped his head back, rapt features streaked in moonlight. His full lips gleamed, long lashes cast shadows on darkly stubbled cheeks. She placed her lips against the strong slant of his jaw, then moved along the rough whiskers toward his mouth. His tongue peeked between parted lips and she hesitated, so close they were almost touching. He leaned forward and gently captured her mouth.

Lifting her skirts, she straddled the outlaw, forcing his one knee down flat so that she sat across his lap, his clothing the only barrier between their growing desire. The movement obviously surprised him, and he could only grunt. He throbbed hotly against her, moaned in ecstasy and at last captured her in a tight embrace, as if to turn her loose would be to fall into hell itself.

Forgotten was her plan to trick him, forgotten the teasing promise of what would be his if only he would take her with him. He wanted her and she wanted him. With or without his promise to take her away.

Other *Leisure* books by Samantha Lee:
IMAGES IN SCARLET

Angel's Gold

Samantha Lee

LEISURE BOOKS   NEW YORK CITY

A LEISURE BOOK®

September 2000

Published by

Dorchester Publishing Co., Inc.
276 Fifth Avenue
New York, NY 10001

Copyright © 2000 by Velda Brotherton

ISBN 0-8439-4765-9

Printed in the United States of America.

To my dear departed friend Doug Jones,
who played a large role in my success as a writer.
His encouragement will never be forgotten.

ACKNOWLEDGMENTS

Writing this book was made much easier with the help of Pam Goodgion, who grew up in Circleville, Kansas. She loaned me family albums, stories, historical maps and pictures. Also, thanks to my brother Fred Goodgion, who took me on a tour of the cemetery and pointed out the gold mine which plays an important part in this book. I could not have written *Angel's Gold* without their valuable assistance.

Angel's Gold

Chapter One

Broom in hand Angeline peered through the doorway. A rattlesnake had coiled near the porch yesterday, but there was nothing there except a busy hen scratching in the dust. She cast a nervous eye at the dark clouds chewing at the bright azure sky, stepped into the yard and began to sweep. If she hurried she could finish the chore before the storm hit, because storm or not, John Prophet would have a fit if she didn't do her chores.

The broom straws stirred little puffs of dirt that rose into the ominous yellow air. On the ground something glittered and she bent to pick it up. A shard from the plate she'd broken last week was imbedded in the hard-packed earth, probably ground under Prophet's boot heel. He walked with such stern determination.

Stooping, she dug it out and held it in her palm, remembering how she and the other kids used to play hopscotch after chores. Mama had often joined in, lifting her skirts to reveal worn old brogans, laughing and jumping like a child.

The wind picked up, and Angeline glanced again at the threatening sky, breathed in air that smelled and tasted like the sulphur springs over at Donahue's farm.

Quickly, she drew boxes in the earth with the handle of the broom and dropped it. Just one game, a little play for all the games she'd missed since those happy times.

A quick glance at the sky told her to hurry or get caught up and blown away. Shrugging, she tossed the bit of pottery she'd just retrieved, and being careful not to

11

step in the square where it landed, hopped: two feet, left foot, left foot, right, two.

Sweat trickled down the small of her back. Prophet always made her pin up her long hair—said a woman of eighteen had no business wearing her hair down like a child. It was just another way to force her to grow up, prepare her for the terrible things he wanted to do in the secrecy of his bedroom.

Bits of dry grass exploded into a whirling dervish, danced under the long gingham dress to sting her bare legs, and whipped strands of blond hair loose from its pins. The sudden gust carried with it a scent of rain and the promise of bad weather all too common on the Kansas plains.

Game forgotten, she shaded her eyes and gazed toward Circleville, a distant cluster of buildings and trees against the horizon. John Prophet had gone to town early, to beat the storm. From the looks of that sky he wouldn't make it back. A vicious updraft sucked her breath away, then once again the air turned deadly still all around. A bad sign, the wind playing tricks like that. Not even a dust devil stirred. Her head throbbed from the pressure of the approaching storm.

It was time to get in the cellar for sure, and never mind the hopscotch. She ran for the barn, chased by a wall of black clouds that gnashed lightning teeth. A long, swaying trunk descended from its ominous underbelly, probed at the ground, came up with huge mouthfuls of trees and brush. The monster swayed to one side then another, then was sucked back into the roaring vortex.

Pulse hammering in her throat, Angeline eyed the cyclone and skittered through the open barn doors. Without taking time to shut and bar them, she raised the narrow panel flush with the hay-strewn dirt floor and tumbled inside the dark cellar. As it banged shut hoofbeats drummed overhead. John Prophet had made it back after all. She shouldered the door partway open, heard a wounded grunt and horrific shouts all but lost to the screaming wind.

That was certainly not John Prophet. He never cursed.

She peered through the crack and in the spooky gloom saw a form struggling to crawl to safety—not her husband, but someone else. A man in jeans, a dusty shirt and bandanna, long shaggy dark hair, not white like John Prophet's. Behind him a horse pranced in fear, its cream leggings flashing in the half-light. Not Prophet's black gelding either.

The unmistakable metallic smell of blood clogged her nostrils, settling on the back of her tongue with the dazzling taste of the storm. Fear crawled into her throat. It was hard to tell which frightened her more, the twister or the abrupt appearance of a stranger.

The man looked toward the opening from where she stared at him. He reached out a grubby, bloodied hand and opened his mouth, but his shout was smothered by the hellacious wind.

The walls of the barn shuddered and creaked, moaning as if in fear. Any minute it would be gobbled into the jaws of the hungry storm that had brought him scurrying for the nearest shelter.

Grimacing in pain, the man shoved forward with his good leg, advancing on his belly till he reached the narrow opening in the floor. She couldn't bring herself to slam the door in his face.

He coughed, then shouted, "Let me in, dammit, before we both get blown to Kingdom come."

Everything about the threatening voice told her to shut the door against this man, but he was a human being begging for shelter, and he sounded hurt. Angeline could not leave him to the mercy of the approaching cyclone, no matter the danger to herself. She took another step up the ladder, leaned out and grabbed him by both arms, then

13

dragged him through the opening. He thunked down into the dark hole and let out a long string of words, some of which she'd never heard. They were all definitely sinful. Her fingers clutching the inside latch, she tumbled in on top of him, the door slamming shut above with a solid thunk. They were engulfed in darkness. She landed on his middle, and he grunted raggedly and treated her to more choice language.

Despite her fear she scolded him. "Hush up talking that way. You want lightning to strike us?"

Under her, she felt damp, rough material over muscular shoulders that heaved with his every breath. In her mouth and nostrils was the odor of male sweat and dust and blood. She gasped and tasted the moldy air of the cellar. It was too dark to see, but she scrambled off him and out of his reach.

Once they were shut up together, fear for her own life set in. In a voice that trembled she spoke, the sound eerie in the underground room.

"Who are you?" The words cracked down the middle, and she thought how dumb the question was.

"A man who's damn lucky, I'd say." The reply came from between gritted teeth. There followed a wheezing breath, then, "Goddamn, it's dark down here. Who are you?"

"Please stop that!"

"What? Stop what? Hell, I'm lying here bleeding to death, a cyclone almost ripped me right off my horse, and you, woman, are ordering me around. I still didn't hear you say your name."

"I'm Angeline . . . Angeline Prophet. This is our place, and so I can tell you to stop taking the Lord's name in vain if I please. If John Prophet were to hear you, he'd whomp you up side of the head with his Bible."

"I don't know who this John the Prophet is, but he sounds biblical as hell to me. Still, I'm beholden to you

14

for the rescue. That twister chased me right into your arms. Thought I was a goner for sure." He moaned deep in his throat, then muttered.

The man knew more filthy talk than she'd ever heard.

"Who shot you? You must've done something. And didn't your folks ever teach you proper English?"

"Ah, Christ."

Angeline gasped.

"Sorry. I'm sorry as hell, I mean . . . Dangit. . . ."

"That's just as bad. Prophet says to use a substitute word you might as well say it."

"Dammit, then. Do you have any thoughts of your own, or do they all belong to this Prophet, whoever the hell he is."

"If you don't stop talking to me like that, I'm going to throw you out into the storm. Of course I have thoughts of my own. And a man who curses is not attractive to me at all."

"Well, damned if I was working to be attractive to anyone."

"You needn't worry. It won't happen."

He took in a sharp breath. "Damn those sons a bitches."

Angeline sighed deeply. It was no use. No matter what she said, this man didn't have the upbringing to use proper words in place of foul language. She supposed she'd have to deal with it, at least until the storm abated and she could send him on his way. She remembered him saying he was bleeding to death.

"Somebody shot you. Are you hurt badly?"

"I don't reckon I'll die, but it hurts like hell—if you're smart you won't ask any more dumb questions. I just might have to shut you up permanently. Do you think we could get some light in here? I could bleed to death and you'd have a corpse on your hands."

"You just said you don't think you'll die." She patted

around a bit. "I think there's some candles here somewhere."

From a grimy shelf along the wall she came up with the stub of one. While she herself also wished for light, she feared it too, for then he would be able to see her, and who knew what that might bring? Her ears literally tingled with the need to hear his every move, but he didn't stir, nor did he speak. After a while she could take the silence no longer.

"Hey, you okay?"

In reply the intruder stirred, groaning. "Hell, no. But I ain't dead."

"If I light a candle, you promise you won't shoot me?"

"I'm not gonna shoot you."

His words didn't sound much like a promise, but she couldn't stand being in the dark with him any longer. She fumbled on the shelf, found the little tin box in which Prophet kept sulphur matches, wrapped her fingers around the cool wax and lit the wick. A feeble flame revealed her visitor, lying prone, his head propped up by one arm. Eyes that glittered an eerie gold stared back at her. Cautiously she inched a little closer to get a better look. Blood soaked his pant leg just below the knee.

"You never said who shot you and why."

"Sure as hell didn't."

"You hadn't ought to talk that way. . . . Does it hurt?"

He snorted. "Not too bad."

"What'd you do?"

"Robbed the bank."

"Naw, you didn't. Sheriff would've come for Prophet."

"Not that piddly Circleville bank. Down in Topeka."

A little thrill of excitement crawled up her backbone, prickling the flesh along the back of her neck. A real live outlaw. John Prophet would have a slobbering fit. Better yet, suppose he carried her off? How exciting.

"You don't sound like an outlaw to me."

"Well, I am. You ever heard of Johnny Ringo?"

Angeline caught her breath, then giggled because that's what she always did when she was a little scared and at a loss for words.

"You hadn't ought to laugh at me, girl. Where's your pa? He this Prophet you keep talking about? Left you out here alone, did he?"

The question might have frightened her, had he not made a moaning sound again and muttered some more words she wished she hadn't heard. Thinking about John Prophet's reaction to such language, she didn't answer his question about her pa. Let him think what he wanted.

"Goddammit," the visitor exploded, scaring her half to death. "I get my hands on the bastard that shot me, I'll see him die face down in the dust. I asked you a question, girl. Where's your kin?"

At last truly afraid of this man, she moved farther into a corner of the root cellar. Thick webs clung to her hair and face, and she fingered them away, trying to be very quiet and not ask any more dumb questions, though doing so wasn't in her nature. If this man was really Johnny Ringo, he could kill her quick as a snake and never bat an eye. He might start shooting at any time. He wore a gun strapped to his hip, she'd felt it when she fell in on top of him.

"Mister Ringo, are you all right?"

There came no reply. She couldn't even hear him breathing. What if he died? And what if John Prophet got caught up by the cyclone and blown clear into Nebraska Territory and never came back? And her stuck down here with a dead man, a famous outlaw. Or better, a *live* famous outlaw. She tried on the idea and thought of how the church women would tut-tut, their eyes the size of saucers and hands fanning handkerchiefs under their noses.

Tilting her head she tried to pick up even the faintest

17

sound and thought she heard shallow breathing. She didn't know if she wished the man dead or alive, though perhaps she did wish John Prophet would get caught up and blown away. Then she wouldn't have to worry about what it was he kept wanting to do to her, his gnarly old fingers fumbling at her shirt front, finding out she'd bound her breasts tightly so he couldn't get what he wanted.

He was always saying things like, "You're eighteen now, girl" and, "How long do you think even a God-fearing man like myself can wait?" and, "It's time you performed your wifely duties before God smites you down."

She remembered him banging on her door when she'd barricaded it against him. Hammering on the planks, kicking at them, hollering, "It's a good thing I'm a Christian man, or I'd bust this door down and have you, girl."

She recalled cowering behind the bed clutching a stick of wood, in case he decided to do just that. "I'll hit you up side of the head, I will, Mr. Prophet."

Whenever she'd fend him off, his booming retort was always the same: "The Lord will smite you for this, woman."

But so far he'd always gone away after a while, slamming his door so hard the house shook. She'd sleep on the floor, crammed back in the corner where he wouldn't see her right away if he changed his mind about breaking down the door. She'd lie there, listening and clutching the bags of precious gold tight against her belly.

"Girl? You still there, girl?" Ringo said from the corner of the cellar, interrupting her thoughts.

If she didn't reply would he think she'd somehow disappeared? Probably not. He'd get mad and start thrashing around, no doubt. "Yes, I'm here."

"Can you hear the storm?"

She moved to the bottom of the steps, listening. "It's roaring pretty good out there. Hope the barn's still standing, and the house."

John Prophet had built a nice big log house last summer, to replace the little dugout they'd lived in for four years. With snakes and rats falling out of the dirt ceiling, and grass and weeds growing up there, the place had looked like part of the hillside. But the log house was just one of his tricks to get her in the mood for his disgusting advances. He'd even promised windows by winter, made of real glass. She sensed he was often sorry he'd put a door on her bedroom, though, a room which he said come next year would be for the first young'un.

"You've gone awful quiet," Ringo said.

She moved the candle slowly to get a better view of him. If he were going to kill or ravage her, he would've done it by now, wouldn't he? "You look pretty raggedy for an outlaw, especially someone like Johnny Ringo."

"Hey, I didn't say I was Ringo."

"Oh, well, I thought . . ." She broke off, appraising him closer. With a day's growth of whiskers and an unruly thick mop of auburn hair, dusty britches and scuffed boots, he looked more like a worn-out trail hand than an outlaw. But there was all that blood—and a glitter in his eye that gave her the shivers. He had wolf's eyes, gold and wild looking.

"I asked, don't you believe I robbed a bank?"

"Oh, well, sure I do. You robbed the bank, got clean away without anyone knowing it and rode in on a cyclone. And, oh, yes, you're the famous Johnny Ringo."

"You got a mouth on you, girl. And I never said that. I was aiming to tell you that he's my cousin, and in case you didn't know, he's also cousin to the Youngers—who are kin to Frank and Jesse James."

"Oh, well, then. I'm sure John Prophet will take that into account when he hauls you off to the calaboose."

"Is that your pa, this John Prophet? And he'll play thunder hauling me off anywhere."

"Want me to take a look at your leg?"

"What I want is to get out of this smelly hole, to get me

19

a drink of water and ride on. I won't bother you any more."

That was certainly a relief. "You'll want to wait till the storm passes. I'll just peek out and check." Maybe she could get him gone before her husband came home. No telling what Prophet might do.

"Give me the candle, then." He reached out, and she moved closer to hand it to him. His fingers, grubby as they were, felt strong and warm against hers.

Touching him made him real, not the make-believe specter her mind had conjured earlier. In that brief contact she sensed the pain of his wound, a tremulous fear that didn't exactly match his bravado. And suddenly she didn't want John Prophet to find this man and do him harm. She wanted him to ride off so she could always imagine him wild and free.

All the women in Prophet's church assured Angeline that she'd soon get over such romantic notions. She hoped not, because it was entertaining to indulge in fantasies in this lonely place where the only girls her own age were being sparked by young men, going to dances and pie suppers and the like.

Flustered by the way he continued to watch her, she moved away. "I'll just take a quick look. You wait here."

He laughed down in his throat. "I'll do that. I'll just wait right here."

He had a smart-alecky way about him, too.

She stepped onto the ladder and eased the trapdoor open a few inches, then listened for a moment. Rain clattered on the barn roof and a cool wind played through the open door, but the roar of the cyclone had passed. She climbed out and crossed the hay-strewn plank floor. Outside a few branches lay in the yard, a bucket she'd left on the back stoop hung from a low tree limb, and one of the old hens sat in the crook of a tree with a puzzled look on her face, feathers turned this way and that. Otherwise nothing was damaged.

Something nuzzled her shoulder and she cried out, jumping away. It was only the outlaw's horse, and with relief she scratched at the velvety nose. The poor animal looked as worn out as its owner. If John Prophet saw the strange horse, he'd know something was amiss. What could she do with it?

Quickly she unsaddled the roan, scooped some grain into a feed bucket and led the animal into the far back stall. Leaving the tack in one corner, she fetched him water and fastened the stall door. It was the best she could do for now. Perhaps later she could come up with a better solution. If he nickered or cut up, all would be lost. Hopefully, Prophet would ride in and turn his own mount out to pasture without checking any of the stalls. She couldn't worry about it with the handsome young outlaw still waiting below.

Going back to the front door, she leaned out to peer into the sky. Cold rain splattered sweetly on her face. The storm had passed, leaving patches of blue peering through breaking clouds. Licking at wet lips, Angeline remembered what the man had said about a drink, fetched a tin cup hanging on a peg and held it under a stream of water pouring from the roof.

Crossing the floor, she kicked something and saw it was a battered brown hat. She picked it up and tossed it into the cellar, then carried the water back down into the candle-lit hole. Under her rain-dampened blouse, her breasts tingled pleasantly. They'd been doing that a lot lately and she wasn't so dumb she didn't know what it meant. It was time she married, had herself a man, and created some children with him. The only problem was, she was already married—but not to a man she cared to have in her bed. She certainly didn't care to have *him* ease the tingling in her breasts. Besides, his kids would probably be as mean and ugly as him, and she'd be surrounded by nastiness.

With a sigh, she put that dilemma to rest, at least for

the moment, and called out to her visitor. "I brought you a drink."

No answer.

"Hey, you okay?"

Still no reply.

She waited till her eyes grew accustomed to the dimly lit cellar, then moved to his side and knelt there. He'd passed out, dropping the candle so that it lay on its side, the wick barely flickering. She rescued it, waited for the flame to grow, then poured a little of the water into her palm and rubbed it on his forehead. Under the grit his skin felt smooth, downy, warm.

He sucked in a breath, then made a little oh sound that puffed air onto the sensitive flesh of her inner arm.

"Be still, it's okay. I brought you some water. Can you sit up? Let me help you."

She sat beside him, propping his head on her shoulder and tipped a few sips of water into his mouth. His cheek resting against her bound breast, jaw moving ever so slightly while he drank, renewed the earlier tingling. Not wanting the feeling to go away, she held him close and concentrated on his breathing. The tingling persisted.

Jesse relaxed in the girl's embrace. He forgot the pain in his leg, forgot that he had lied to her, and forgot everything but her prairie-washed fragrance, the sweet smell of her silken hair. Girls had this smell, this feel about them that made a fellow yearn for things he knew damn well he couldn't have. Besides she was a youngster—surely of marriageable age by frontier standards, but a child nevertheless. He'd have to make tracks and be quick about it. If only that son of a bitch hadn't shot him. The bushwhackers had called him Charlie, but Charlie was dead. And what would they want with his brother anyway?

Between sips, Jesse asked, "What did you say your name is?"

She answered softly.

Had she said she was an angel? It wasn't clear. But he sure couldn't be dead, 'cause there wasn't a chance in hell he'd make it through the pearly gates and meet any angels.

An ungodly and unexpected clatter of horse's hooves hammered overhead, sifting dust down through the cracks.

The girl pulled away, letting his head drop with a thunk and sloshing water over him. "Oh, my goodness. It's John Prophet. Wait, you stay here. Be real quiet. Don't say a word. I'll be back as soon as I can, but promise me you won't come out. He'll kill you in the name of the Lord, I swear he will. Okay?"

"Yes, but—"

"No buts. Hush. I'll be back as soon as I can."

She left the cup of water, and he drank it slowly, savoring the sweet, cold flavor.

God, what an awful mess. And getting shot was not the worst of it. How did he expect to follow in Ringo's footsteps? Once, while robbing a stage, Ringo got shot and still managed to finish the holdup and ride away so fast the law didn't have a chance of catching him. If Jesse couldn't do that, how did he expect to find the men who'd hung Charlie?

Jesse closed his eyes against the pain, thought of the last day he'd seen his brother, climbing over the windowsill in the dead of night, saying how he couldn't spend another minute being beat on. And Jesse recalled begging Charlie to take him along—two boys of thirteen, thinking they were grown men.

How he'd begged, he'd made a danged fool of himself. "We're brothers. Twins. Don't go off without me. I'll never see you again."

"I ain't taking no sniveling baby along on this ride. It's going to be too rough. Hell, you cry every time old Zekial whups on you."

It had been true. He did. But not for much longer.

23

Samantha Lee

Four years later word had come to Ringo's camp that Charlie had been hanged in Missouri for bushwhacking—strung up in an old oak tree by two fellows by the name of Cross and Doolittle. Jesse hadn't found out about Charlie's death till sometime later when he joined up with Ringo's bunch.

However, a couple of years after Charlie lit out, Jesse took Zekial's leather whip away from him and made a believer out of the old man. It hadn't been hard to do, seeing as how at fifteen Jesse towered over him. He had grown strong from helping out at the local blacksmith's, too.

For a while after that he'd stayed on in the filthy one-room cabin where he and Charlie'd been raised, because it was a place to lay his head and was better than nothing. Zeke had taken them in to do hard labor after their folks had left them in front of a saloon in Fort Smith, Arkansas, when they were ten years old. The old man had never strapped Jesse again, but his damage had been done, the scars engraved on his back and in his heart.

In '63 Jesse had left to fight in the war on the side of the Johnny Rebs. He'd nearly starved to death, too, after the battle of Prairie Grove. Hungry and nearly naked he'd fetched up in Cedar Creek, Kansas, a small town in sore need of a blacksmith: a job he could do. There he'd remained until the day Johnny Ringo and his gang rode into town.

Lying on the cold, damp floor of the root cellar, the smell of aging potatoes and turnips in his nose, Jesse thought of those days with his cousin in Dodge City, and how his life had been changed: He no longer feared *any* man.

When word had come that the men who'd hung Charlie and his boys were ranging Nebraska and northeastern Kansas, he'd left Ringo's company. Charlie's killers couldn't be allowed to go free, and he'd spent his time

24

tracking them. First to Topeka, then north toward the little settlement of Circleville. He'd been looking for Cross and Doolittle; getting shot had been nothing but a dumb mistake.

How long the three men had been following him, he didn't know, but he'd spotted them the morning before they shot him. One was a giant of a man, maybe six and a half feet tall with ginger-colored hair and beard; the other two were more nondescript, average size and weight, and all dressed in worn butternuts. They were bushwhackers for sure. Confederates on the outlaw trail. And for some reason they had thought he was his twin brother, Charlie, and had wanted him alive for something. The storm had come along just in time.

Now here he was, at the mercy of a pretty, sweet-smelling girl who lived in a dream world.

He fell asleep listening for the sound of her return, the pain in his leg throbbing but no less tolerable than the ache in his empty gut.

Expressing relief and thanks to the Lord for sparing the farm, John Prophet presented Angeline with some pretties from the mercantile: a blue hair ribbon and a hand mirror so beautiful she'd gasped with delight. He'd also bought a piece of yard goods—creamy satin so smooth to the touch it almost made her cry. It was hard not to show appreciation, even though she understood the reason behind the gifts. He was buying her all over again, offering her something she desired desperately, just like he'd done to her poor father.

He draped the fabric over her chest, making sure to brush her breasts with the backs of both his hands. He got nothing for his troubles but the feel of the tightly wrapped strip of muslin binding, and moved on to encircle her tiny waist and cup her buttocks in the span of his work-worn palms.

She shuddered at his touch and smashed her legs tightly together.

He kept a good hold on her and smiled down into her face like a coyote. "You sew a pretty stitch. Thought you could make yourself a fine gown with this." He drew an open hand across her belly.

Under his touch her flesh crawled, and she gnawed at her lip. "Where would I wear a thing like that?" Deep inside she yearned for such a gown, wanted to feel it against her bare flesh. What a weak-willed girl she was.

His crafty eyes gleamed. "You could wear it for me in our marriage bed."

She held up the mirror, glancing at the way the silk lay in soft folds, shutting her eyes tight and worrying her lip some more. Would it be so bad after all? Satisfying this man who was her husband—only because he bought her—receiving in return some of the things for which she'd always yearned? How long could she fight him and win anyway?

Outside the wind kicked up, rattling against the shutters. She thought of the young man under the barn floor, the way his smooth flesh had felt under her fingertips, his wicked way of talking and staring at her, how it had excited her. Prophet leaned close, his slack lips gleaming. The smell of his breath made her flesh crawl as if worms slithered over it.

"It's time to fix supper. Are you hungry?" She pushed to get away from him, but he held her shoulders, the creamy yard goods forgotten in a heap on the floor between them.

"Oh, I'm hungry all right, for more than food. A man must be sustained by a woman in the way the Good Lord meant. He made our bodies to fit together, and it's a sin to deny me that. Don't you know that, girl? A downright sin. The Bible says a woman shall cleave unto her husband."

Miserably, she nodded. If she didn't do something

26

soon she would lose the battle and become this old man's wife in more than name. She thought of the gold she'd hoarded over the years and wondered if the outlaw lying in the root cellar would consider it good payment for taking her away from this place. The idea gave her courage, fueled hope in her otherwise hopeless soul.

With a sigh she pretended to agree with Prophet. "Yes, I suppose you're right. You have been good to me. Built me this house and took care of me all these years. But we can't do anything yet, not tonight or for a few more. You do understand, don't you?" She prayed he wouldn't ask for further explanation. Dared she mention such a thing as her monthly to this man of God?

Nose wrinkling in disgust he stepped away from her. "Good God, girl. Why didn't you say so? As soon as you're clean again there'll be no more delays, no excuses. This time next week, you'll be mine, as our Lord intended."

Tears blurred her vision as she prepared supper. Time was running out and she had little choice. She dared not flee. For a young woman alone, the dangers would be far too great. Even with gold. And it was entirely possible that if she did convince the young man hidden in the root cellar to carry her away, that it would be a worse fate than remaining here with John Prophet. She could hardly imagine that, but one never knew.

Prophet retired soon after eating, his only reminder of their agreement a shaking finger and the terrifying look of a man too long without food or water.

Placing leftover chicken, biscuits and cobbler in the warming oven, she acted as if she were going to bed, and only when Prophet's snoring grew steady from the other bedroom did she prepare rags, soap and water, tie the food into a bundle and sneak out to the barn.

A lantern hung just inside the door, but she dared not light it until she was safely underground, for fear Prophet might awake and see the glow. He'd kill them both, smite them down with religious zeal and justification. He used those words a lot and she could hear him now, bragging about such actions to all his pious friends.

The young man was asleep as she descended the ladder, but he stirred as she neared. Likely he smelled the fried chicken.

She nudged him. "You awake?"

The place was very dark and she could barely see. Angeline carried an unlit lantern, and she fumbled around in the dark lighting it, then set it on a shelf above their heads.

He rolled over, then sat up, but he didn't say anything. "I brought you something to eat and some soap and water to clean your wound. I hope the bullet's not still in it, I've never dug lead out of a man before."

"It went in, it came out. Didn't even nick the bone," the outlaw said. "I'd like to eat first, I'm starved."

"Next time, rob a store instead of a bank. You can't eat money." She angrily plopped a towel-wrapped bundle in his lap. Really, the man had no sense—or manners.

"Yeah, well, I'll remember that." He pawed out a chicken leg and went to work on it. She'd brought biscuits soaked in butter, a bowl of apple cobbler and a quart jar filled with milk. And the man looked for a while as if he had died and gone to heaven.

Dear God, the man was hungry, apparently clear down to the bottom of his soul. Angeline saw that hunger in his eyes, and it seemed very deep indeed. Yet, propped up against a dirt wall in a stinky old root cellar with a bullet in his leg, the young outlaw gave her a smile.

Despite his gratitude, the man's hunger shamed Angeline, made her sorry she'd waited so long to bring the food to him. But tonight had been particularly hard, perhaps the worst yet.

She wondered, as she watched the young outlaw gobble her offering, if she should tell him about the gold and how she'd come by it, or keep her mouth shut until she convinced him to take her along. Surely he'd be grateful enough for her saving his life, without the added temptation of gold.

Still, if all else failed, she'd gladly offer him the hoarded nuggets to get her out of this place and far away from Prophet.

Chapter Two

With the leavings of the outlaw's supper set aside, Angeline reluctantly tackled the next task.

"I brought soap and water to clean that wound."

She could hardly speak above a whisper. This was a daring thing she was about to do, something so personal she couldn't quite imagine she'd actually be able to do it. He'd have to remove his britches. She hadn't even seen Prophet without britches.

Swallowing hard, she said, "You'll have to take off your pants. I'll turn my back."

He laughed and she scowled, but said nothing. Behind her he grunted and swore under his breath, moaned and scuffled about.

"Well, I got 'em undone, but I can't get 'em off without some help," he finally said, and she could tell he was mad at himself. "Couldn't we maybe just push up the cloth far enough to get at it?"

She held up the lantern to take a look, hope growing. That would be the ideal solution. Setting the light nearby, she took hold of the bloody pant leg, then tried to shove it up over his calf.

He hissed between his teeth, stiffened, and breathed out, "Goddamn."

"Hurts too much?" She'd become so engrossed in her task, she forgot to scold him for cursing. With a great sigh, she moved to help him pull down the pants. She gripped the material, her knuckles touching bare skin at his waist.

"If you could lift your . . . ah, your . . ."

"Butt? My butt?" he supplied and did so, hands planted on either side. "Damn, I never knew a bullet could hurt so much."

"Don't be such a baby. You'd think they'd cut off your foot or something."

"Well, by God, I've been shot."

She yanked hard, felt the pants coming off. They skinned past his thighs, over his knees and into a bunch at the tops of his boots.

"You're going to have to take off your boots."

"I think you'd better do it."

He sounded winded, and she knew she'd hurt him, though he hadn't cried out again.

Kneeling there at his feet, trying not to even glance at his lean, muscular thighs and certainly not at anything above them, she whispered, "Oh, dear God, I'm sorry. I'm so sorry."

"Just take off the goddamned boots. God don't care how sorry you are about what you're doing."

"Shut up. You're a wicked man, I don't even know why I'm helping you."

"Well, girl, I really don't either. It's not been my experience to find anyone willing to help. Why don't I just pull these pants back on and crawl out of here. What'd you do with my horse, anyway?"

Indignation filled her throat. "No, I can do it. I'm sorry. I'm going to take the boot off the hurt leg first and get it over with. You ready?"

He sucked in a ragged breath. "Go."

She'd pulled off boots for men plenty of times. For her father and her brothers and Prophet. On her knees she straddled the leg, then took the boot heel in both hands. "Ready, set—"

"Goddammit, go," he shouted, and she did.

A sound like that of an animal rolled from his throat,

31

like he just couldn't help it, but then he went limp and still. He had passed out. Quickly, she removed the other boot and finished removing the pants before he could come around and be hurt any more. She'd wash the blood out of them while he slept.

The bullet had punctured the fatty part of his calf and exited on the other side. He'd been right. If it grazed the bone, she'd have been surprised. Bleeding so much had probably cleaned out a lot of poison, but she bathed the wound over and over in her pan of hot soapy water. If it became infected he'd die, and the man would never go to a doctor. Whatever she did for him here was all that would be done. How she knew that she wasn't certain, but it was a fact.

"Dear God, help him, and me too," she murmured.

"Amen," he replied. "You about through torturing me?"

His voice startled her. "I thought you were out."

"Guess I was. What's it look like?"

"What? Your bony old leg or the wound?" She felt a sense of relief that lightened her mood.

"That's not funny."

"If I had legs like yours, I wouldn't think it was funny either."

"You can stop wiping around on that any time. Unless you just enjoy playing with my leg."

She jerked away. He had nice skin, firm and warm over tight muscles, and it made her mad that he came so close to reading her thoughts. She plopped the bloody rag into the crimson water. "I brought something to bandage it with, so if you'll just be patient another minute, I'll through. Your pants are soaked in blood. I can take them outside and clean them up with water from the rain barrel if you can wait."

Angeline gazed down into the man's face. He'd relaxed some, his determined jaw line softened, the grim lips filled out. Long dark lashes shadowed the smudges under his wide-set eyes. A finely sculpted nose and full lips lent softness to the otherwise craggy face. His eyes closed for a moment, but when they popped open, she saw they truly were as gold as winter wheat after it ripened, and flecked with rich brown. Earlier she'd thought the color had been reflections of lantern light. She'd never seen human eyes quite that color.

"Oh, I guess I can hang around a while longer," he said.

Her strong fingers ministering to him actually sent rivers of delight into Jesse's groin. In spite of the pain of his wound, it was a most pleasant sensation, having her bathe his leg, then pat it dry and wrap the bandage round and round, tying it gently. Her soft gentle fingers trailed across his skin until he shuddered with delight. He didn't remember a woman ever seeing to him. If his mother once had, Zeke's brutal treatment had erased the memory.

He must have fallen asleep, for she awoke him when she returned with his pants.

Her presence startled him, and he blinked his eyes, for a moment wholly disoriented. Then—oh, yes, he was being tended to by an angel. Dropping to her knees, she touched his shoulder.

"Don't worry, it's just me. I brought your pants. They're wet, but I'm afraid to hang them anywhere to dry. Prophet might see them. Why don't you wait till morning to put them on?"

Jesse nodded and licked dry lips. He couldn't have replied to the girl if he'd been on fire. And indeed, certain parts of him felt like they might be. Her hand remained on his shoulder, like a brand. Taking a deep breath, he inhaled her essence and gazed at her. She was so beautiful, with the lamplight playing over her gentle features, an artist might have drawn her—the perfect woman. She had a wide forehead over high cheekbones, azure blue eyes shaped like almonds, a tiny upturned nose and a squared-off chin that was determined as hell. He closed his eyes, implanting her vision in his brain to carry along when he rode away, which he would do very soon. He dared not stay here feeling this way.

Being in her presence produced strange sensations, like drinking hot coffee on a brittle cold morning with the cup warming his cold hands; or putting hot, tired feet in a snow-melt creek; or relaxing in a soft bed after a long, hard day in the saddle. God, he was going crazy. If he didn't get gone come morning, he'd be in deep trouble.

While immersed in such soothing thoughts sleepiness again overtook him. He was way too tired to keep thinking about this girl or anything else except getting the hell out of there. He didn't have time for such nonsense. Sometimes, though, a man got so blamed needy he could hardly set his saddle. And having a woman was damn soothing to the soul. But he sure as hell didn't expect a woman to ever love him when he didn't care anything at all about himself.

He heard his angel gather up everything, but the light of the lantern remained. He heard her say, "You can keep that. I'll bring you something to eat in the morning whenever I can."

"I'm obliged," he said in a voice that was slurred with drowsiness.

Her footsteps sounded and he heard her climb the steps. After the door clicked shut, Jesse relaxed on the floor. For the first time in memory, he slept with a full belly and an oddly contented heart.

The next morning, as Angeline went about her chores, she thought about the man hiding under the floor of the barn. And once again seriously considered the possibility of hiding him till he was healed and then leaving with him.

At the kitchen window she watched as John Prophet went into the barn. There was nothing she could do but

34

wait. If he found the horse, he'd search till he found its owner. A man whose name she didn't even know. But after a while Prophet came out carrying his tool bag. He whistled up Duke, saddled him and rode off across the east field.

He hadn't come near her this morning, even to touch her hand. She was suddenly glad that some men were that way about women during their monthlies. It wouldn't keep him away long, though, and the next time no locked door would stop him. She had four or five days, a week at the most, before she would be, in his words, "clean" enough for him to touch.

In that length of time she had to convince the man hiding out in the barn that she was worth carrying off. He didn't seem suited to the role of knight in shining armor, like the fairy tales mama used to read out loud. But she had helped him, perhaps he would consider it payback to help her. She hoped so.

With John Prophet out of sight, she finished kneading a rubbery mound of bread dough and left it resting on the table while she carried breakfast out to her prisoner. She thought of him that way, now, as if he were imprisoned and couldn't get away until she said so.

After one quick glance in all directions, she stepped into the gloom of the barn and swung the door closed behind her. Sunlight shone through cracks in the walls to trace long golden lines across the hay-strewn floor. A hen, interrupted on her nest, clucked a question, then hopped down to peck at stray grain scattered about. Angeline moved toward the cellar, saw that it stood open, and at the same moment the man spoke from out of the shadows. His gruff voice startled her.

"That sure smells good."

"What are you doing out here?"

"I couldn't stay down there any longer. Had to get out and move about, or this leg'll stiffen up on me." He

35

emerged into the bars of light and limped carefully toward her. He was wearing his pants, but hadn't put on his boots. His gray socks had a hole that let one big toe stick out.

"And what if John Prophet caught you?"

He shrugged, lifting a corner of the cup towel she'd spread over the plate, and eyed scrambled eggs, half a dozen thick strips of bacon and two buttered biscuits.

"Here," she said, and held out a steaming cup of coffee. She hoped he would appreciate this.

Jesse literally snatched the plate and cup, backing up to perch on a rough-hewn bench near the back of the barn. "You're a wonderment." Spoken hesitantly, the words were unfamiliar on his tongue. He seldom spoke compliments and they came hard.

"I hope you remember that," she retorted in a tone he didn't quite understand.

He set the cup aside, shoveling eggs into his mouth with the fork she'd provided, then alternately fingered up a strip of bacon and a biscuit, or sipped at the coffee. He didn't think much more about what she'd said, though it did sound a bit ominous. Like in the end he'd pay big for her hospitality. She let him finish eating, though, before saying more, all the while standing in front of him, her hands clasped behind her back, rocking on her feet like a little kid.

He washed down the last delicious bite with coffee, licked grease from every fingertip and handed her back the utensils.

"I want you to take me with you when you go," she said, just like that, no explanation or anything, and then she waited for him to reply.

He got the feeling she thought he couldn't say no, that it simply wasn't possible for him to deny her request. For a long moment he couldn't think what to say. Of course, it was no. A firm "hell, no." But gazing at her, seeing the hope in those sky-blue eyes that looked like they'd been washed by the rains of yesterday's storm, he bit back that harsh reply and attempted a less hurtful remark. What the hell had gotten into him, anyway, that he cared what she thought or how she felt?

"You don't want to go off with me. I'm nothing but a no-account outlaw. Someone's always chasing or shooting at me." He pointed at the wounded leg.

"Oh, yes I do. I'd rather be shot at than stay here. You don't know." She broke off, and he understood why her eyes looked rain-washed. Tears overflowed and ran down her cheeks, but she made not a sound nor did she move to wipe them away.

"Your pa beats you?" Hell, he knew all about that, and it would be even worse for a delicate little thing like this than it'd been for him and Charlie.

"He's not my pa. Stop calling him that. He's my husband. And no, he doesn't beat me. He's just . . . mean, that's all. And old."

Husband? The word exploded around him, hammering at his brain, filling the silent confines of the barn. That withered up old geezer? Amazed, Jesse waited for her reply to stop bouncing around like ricocheting bullets. Hell, he couldn't have said anything if he'd had to, she'd caught him so unawares.

She said nothing, though, and it was only when, in the back of the barn, his horse nickered and broke the stillness, that Jesse asked a question.

"Why in God's name did you marry an old man like him? A pretty little thing like you."

Tears poured down her cheeks and the girl swiped at them with clenched fists. He suddenly wanted to take her in his arms, an urge that made his gut ache worse than hunger pangs.

"Will you take me with you? I can't stay here with him

37

another minute. If I do he's going to . . . He says it's time I . . . If he touches me I'll kill myself, I swear I will."

"You mean he hasn't . . . You haven't . . . ? God. How old are you, girl?"

Drawing herself up to her full five and a half feet, she rasped, "I turned eighteen this spring. And I truly do wish you'd stop calling me girl."

Miserable, Jesse crammed his hands down in his pockets. "And how long have you . . . and he . . . ?"

He had to lean forward to hear her reply. "Five years this summer."

"But why? Good God in heaven, why?"

When she answered it was in a monotone, as if she were retelling something she'd memorized and it had nothing to do with her.

"After the war Pa wanted to move west, and so we started out. But things got bad, real bad. The babies were starving, all the food was gone and we had nothing. Even the oxen died. When we got here, he met John Prophet, who wanted more land—and if he was married he could get it. Homesteading, you only get so much, you know? And so he offered to outfit Pa so they could continue west. Pa didn't want Kansas land, he wanted to go on to California or Oregon."

"And he sold you?" Jesse swallowed thickly against the pain in his chest. "Your own pa?" Not much worse than his folks, who'd abandoned him and Charlie when they were ten. Just up and run off without their boys.

Her reply was hurried. "I said it was okay. I didn't want the kids to starve because of me. I thought I could run away, you know? But when I got to thinking about it, I didn't know where to go."

"There must've been something else your pa could have done."

She shook her head. "Lots of people were hungry then, right after the war. And anyway, John Prophet has been kind to me. He's a religious man, a deacon in the church in Circleville. Strict but fair. And as long as all I had to do was the womanly chores, which I'd been used to at home anyway, it wasn't bad. But then he . . . his hands . . . his eyes . . . I can't do that, not with him."

"He wants you in his bed," Jesse said woodenly.

"Please help me. I don't know what to do. He has his land now, he can remarry, too."

This girl had been reduced to asking a total stranger. Jesse couldn't help but remember the times he'd searched in vain for some bit of kindness from strangers, someone to protect him from Zeke's vicious beatings, and found none. He'd been told not to exaggerate, that Zekial Forster was a good man, hadn't he taken in two orphaned boys to raise? Besides, spare the rod, spoil the child.

And because there had been no help, Charlie had gone bad. So bad he was hanged by some no better than himself. And Jesse figured he was no better either, when you got right down to it—killing being in his blood and all.

He didn't know what to say to her. He couldn't help her. He had absolutely no responsibility to do so. Even if he did there was simply no way he could take her along on his thundering ride toward hell—for once he killed the men who'd hanged his brother, he'd be hanged as well. She'd be better off with the old man. Here she had a roof, food, clothing and eventually maybe some babies she could love. After all, John Prophet didn't beat her, and plenty of folks were mean. The old man just wanted what he considered his marriage rights. Who could blame him for that? She was, after all, his wife. She did belong to him. Bought and paid for. And what was she worried about, anyway? Lots had it plenty worse.

"I can't help you," he finally told her, unable to meet her gaze, staring down at his scuffed boots. He was ashamed of his own weakness, his inability to do what was right, then furious at himself for feeling that way. He didn't owe this girl. He didn't owe anybody a damned thing.

At his words, anger replaced Angeline's despair. "You're nothing but a coward. I knew you weren't an outlaw when you came here, or you'd have thrown me on your horse and rode off with me. You're just some lowly sneak thief who got himself shot for pilfering. I'm sorry I even helped you, I should have let you bleed to death."

Warming to the challenge, he said sharply, "This isn't a fairy tale, girl—and I was hardly bleeding to death."

Deep inside she knew he was not obliged to carry her off. Besides, she hadn't really expected him to say yes right away. It would take some persuading. What she had to do was keep him from leaving until she'd had time to change his mind.

She took a step forward, willing him to meet her gaze until he did. "But you were hurt and I helped you. That should count for something."

"I might figure the only reason you did that was to leave me obligated. And it doesn't matter anyway. Some men would've killed you soon as looked at you, even after you helped them. Don't you see, that's how it is, and you have no business out there running loose 'cause you don't understand that. You're a romantic. Why, I'll bet you read dime novels every chance you get. Probably still believe in fairy tales."

"John Prophet won't let me read anything but the Bible; he says it's a waste of time and evil besides."

"But you would if you could."

"I should be able to read whatever I want, without anyone saying different. That's what I'm trying to tell you."

He looked torn, pausing for a moment and staring into her eyes. Then he shrugged his shoulders. "I know what you're telling me," he said softly, "I just can't do anything about it. I have to ride on. There's something I have to do, and I can't take you with me. That's all. I'm sorry for your troubles, I truly am. But I've got to go now, before your John Prophet comes back."

"Then damn you. Damn you to hell and back." She'd never uttered such curses, but they felt right and just on her tongue. He deserved them. All the same she waited for God to strike her dead.

Without blinking, the outlaw said softly, "It's already been done, girl." Then he moved toward the stall where she'd penned his roan.

From outside came the slow clip-clop of hoofbeats, a horse approaching in no big rush.

She grabbed his arm. "It's Prophet. Hide, quick. Hurry." She dragged him back to the hole in the floor and guided him down into his tiny prison, away from the stall where his horse waited to carry him to freedom. It was a weak effort, she knew, but worth a try. Quickly, she shoved the breakfast dishes out of sight into a loose pile of hay and dropped to her knees to search for the hen's nest. She came up with a warm egg and, with it in her palm like an offering, turned to face Prophet when he swung open the big wide door.

Making a pocket in her apron, she continued the pretense of searching for eggs, her insides trembling so badly she thought he might see and know her secret.

Prophet grunted a greeting and dropped the horse's reins to the ground. "Git on inside and fix my dinner. I want to plow the west field this afternoon. Fence was down toward Tremaine's, and I like to never got it fixed. His cows'd be eating my crop before it got a good start. Never saw hide nor hair of him. You'd a thought he'd a lent a hand, but like the others he thinks if a feller's gonna raise crops it's his lookout to keep them fenced away from cattle. I ought to get Brother Blaine to speak on that at Sunday's service."

Without waiting for her to reply, he started across the

41

barn to the tack room where he kept the harnessing for the mules. He stopped midway, booted feet dangerously near the cellar door. "Need anything from down here for dinner?" He bent over, put a hand on the pull latch.

The fragile eggshell crushed inside her apron. "No, uh, no. That's okay. I have plenty in the house."

"Well, then git to it. Don't keep me waiting. And next time, you might gather those eggs early of a morning, so you don't have to be lollygagging out here when you ought to be cooking and baking."

"Yes, yes I will." She didn't want to leave Prophet in the barn with the outlaw hiding under him, but had no choice. Dear God, suppose he found the man or his horse? The outlaw still hadn't told her his name, and he might be about to die. All she knew was he was a first cousin to Johnny Ringo, the notorious outlaw—if that hadn't been a lie just like his story about robbing the bank in Topeka. Prophet would've surely mentioned it. That kind of news always spread like wildfire.

For a brief moment she imagined riding free with an outlaw gang, doing whatever she wanted when she wanted. Answering to no one, and most especially John Prophet.

Tonight, after Prophet was tucked safely in bed, she intended to find out what this man's name was, where he was from and where he was going. And somehow, some-way, she must convince him to take her out of here. She would make another trip to the gold mine, salvage a few more ounces from the veins that ran like fingers along the walls of the mine down on Elk Creek. If all else failed, she'd offer it to him to take her along. Surely if he cared about nothing else, gold would persuade him.

The thought made her tremble, for if he knew her secret, might he just break into the house while they were asleep, kill both her and John Prophet and make off with it?

For five years she'd salvaged the precious nuggets as she could find them, sneaking off whenever she could. Her hoard of tiny bags had increased at a steady rate. Long ago, when she'd first sneaked into the mine, it had been her plan to take some gold and run away, but as she grew up and learned the wicked ways of the world, the idea of going alone frightened her. She might be as innocent and naive as the outlaw suggested, but she knew that a young woman had little chance of survival on her own. And she also knew that gold would significantly improve her chances, if it didn't get her throat cut. She'd continued sneaking in and improving her hoard. Now, only as a last resort would she offer her stash to this man. She had to be sure she could trust him.

Soon after dark a huge rosy moon slipped above the horizon, making it easy to see, but also putting her in grave danger of being seen. Thank goodness for John Prophet's abnormal fear of night air that kept the windows shuttered. Even so, after she left the cellar she would have to be extra careful approaching the mine. Often a guard stood watch, but often he dozed off by midnight or so. Still a bright night increased the danger of being caught.

The last time she'd accompanied Prophet to town there'd been talk about shutting down the mine. It wasn't producing in enough quantity to pay for all the work it took. Maybe they'd already done so, and there would be no more guards. Would they have boarded over the entrance, making it impossible for her to get inside? If they quit mining, there would soon be none for her either.

Once inside the barn, Angeline called out softly, "You here?" The outlaw had probably come out of the hole in the ground again.

Sure enough, he whispered back, "Over here, looking at the moon."

He sat on the floor beneath a window in a puddle of

43

golden light, his injured leg stuck straight out, the other knee raised. Chin in hand, elbow propped on the knee, he stared outside. She supposed he couldn't bring himself to look at her. His dark hair was damp, curled along the nape of his neck, his face clean.

He hadn't already left, so maybe there was still hope. With one finger she touched a wet curl, experiencing a welling of emotion.

He shifted and glanced quickly at her. "I hope you don't mind, I cleaned up in the rain barrel out back after it got dark."

She imagined him rising in the shadows, bare chest gleaming while he washed face, neck, underarms. She shivered, then tried to speak normally and stick to her agenda, but the vision stuck in her mind, cavorted there. Gruffly, without answering his implied question, she said, "I want to know your name."

"Why does it matter? I'm leaving in a little while. Beautiful night to ride the trail."

"Tonight?" She felt betrayed, as if he had broken a promise, but that was nonsense, wasn't it?

"Yep. Time I moved on. Longer I stay, more chance *he'll* find me and I'd have to kill him. Neither of us needs that kind of trouble."

"I thought you'd—"

"What? Change my mind?" He turned, and in the moonlight she saw a feral glimmer in his golden eyes.

"Well, when I saw you were still here, yes, I thought . . ." She moved closer to him and touched his shoulder. "Please, tell me your name." Beneath her fingers the tight muscles quivered.

"Jesse." It was all he said, but she read a plea there; he wanted something more.

She heard him swallow, and pressed the advantage she sensed. "Like Jesse James?"

"Yeah. Like that." He shifted away from her touch but only a little.

Refusing to let him get away with that, she took another step, brushing a thigh against his arm. He felt warm, hard, damp from his rain-barrel bath. Her breasts tingled and she dragged in a breath, grateful she'd removed their hateful binding before coming to him. She could do it if she had to, seduce him like the common whores Prophet often railed about. It would be so much better than letting John Prophet take her. With this man she might actually . . .

"Jesse," she whispered and ran fingers through his glossy auburn hair. The smell of hay hung thick in the air, stirred by an evening wind that carried on it the tang of freshly broken soil. She suddenly felt overpowered by the new-washed maleness of him.

For an instant he leaned his head against her, turned so that his breath penetrated the fabric of her dress, heating her own rising desire.

Oh, yes, she realized. She wanted this. Wanted it beyond any plan to trick him, to make him need her badly enough he would give in to her pleas in return for her favors.

She cupped Jesse's head between her palms, held him there for a moment as her passion mounted, its drumming the plucking of a taut string deep inside her. It held a rhythm ancient as time itself.

Lowering herself to both knees, she trailed a hand inside his shirt, peering at him through slitted eyes to see that he'd tipped his head back, rapt features streaked in moonlight. His full lips gleamed, long lashes cast shadows on darkly stubbled cheeks. She placed her lips against the strong slant of his jaw, then moved along the rough whiskers toward his mouth. His tongue peeked between parted lips and she hesitated, so close they were almost touching.

He leaned forward and gently captured her mouth. His lips were like smooth silk, moist and sweet. A tiny groan rolled from deep down in his throat and he rubbed a thumb tenderly along the flesh at the base of her neck, spread a palm gently over her unbound breast. The touch seared like fire and sent shudders through her. She leaned into the cupped hand, her nipple hardening.

Her firm, warm breast filled his hand, and she exulted in feeling it both unbound and handled so deliciously. For a long moment he simply held her, exploring the taut nipple, sending bolts of desire electrifying her entire body.

Lifting her skirts, she straddled the outlaw, forcing his one knee down flat so that she sat across his lap, his clothing the only barrier between their growing desire. The movement obviously surprised him, and he could only grunt. He throbbed hotly against her, moaned in ecstasy and at last captured her in a tight embrace, as if to turn her loose would be to fall into hell itself.

After a moment, he whispered, "We can't do this," but didn't let go.

Wiggling against the pulsing hardness between his legs, she said, "Yes, yes we can."

"And then what?" He nibbled at the lobe of her ear, sending shivers of delight through her.

Sensing his growing need, she rocked from side to side and felt an imminent explosion growing within herself.

He gasped, sucked at her throat. Then he paused, obviously torn. His hands encircled her waist, lifting her a bit, but she struggled and he froze.

"Ah, God, Angel. Stop this before we can't."

"Take me with you, please." She nibbled at his ear. Ripples of sparkling desire shot through her. No wonder this was considered evil by Prophet and the rest. She wanted his hands on her breasts again, and settled for rubbing them against his chest.

Forgotten was her plan to trick him, forgotten the teasing promise of what would be his if only he would take her with him. He wanted her and she wanted him. With or without his promise to take her away. The desire increased until she had to satisfy it, and she reached between them, fumbling at the buttons of his pants. She had never seen a man, not like she was about to see him, to feel him. About to have him inside her. But with this man, it felt more right than anything she'd ever known.

But suddenly, he grew taut and cold. "You're just trying to get out of here. You're just like . . ." The rest was muffled as the outlaw locked his fingers around her upper arms, lifted her and literally tossed her into the mound of hay nearby. Awkwardly gaining his feet, he loomed over her. Looking up into his mask of fury, terror filled Angeline's heart. A terror that strangled her passion.

She backpedaled, scrambled to get out of his reach, uttering little ohs that even to her own ears sounded like those of a wounded animal.

For a beat, he stared at her, breathing raggedly. Then he looked hurt. "Damn you, girl," he muttered.

In her haste to put distance between them, Angeline had kicked his wounded leg, and she heard him gasp in pain. He rolled away from her, then lay there quietly. She took that moment to escape.

Chapter Three

Fists clenched at her sides, Angeline leaned against the barn door for a moment. Her anger had faded to disappointment. Jesse had guessed at her motive and had every right to be furious with her. There was no way she could explain that what had begun as a childish game to get her way had bloomed into true passion. Her wicked attempt to trick him had turned on her, awakening a heated yearning within her own heart. But he wanted no part of her.

She leaned on the door for a moment. The wind rippled the fabric of her blouse over taut nipples, reminding her of his touch. Dear Lord, what a sensation: his strong hands, velvety smooth lips, and the hardness of male flesh pressed against her.

Brushing strands of hair from cheeks moist with perspiration, she headed for Elk Creek and the mine. Over the past five years the dust and nuggets she'd come up with had filled two dozen small bags, safe against the day she would leave Prophet. Even anticipation of any gold she might find this night did not stop her reeling emotions. She ached for Jesse's touch.

The road underfoot, muddied by recent storms, was rutted with wagon tracks and churned by horses' hooves. Nevertheless, she could almost walk it in her sleep. Off to her left cottonwoods marked the banks of Elk Creek as it flowed east for a while, then swung north to skirt Circleville. At the edge of town she crossed the railroad tracks and headed north on Front Street. The night was warm, the wind steady, the sky clear and lit by a silvery moon.

Walking briskly along the moonlit, deserted street, the night wind kissing her cheeks, Angeline thought with longing of her mama and papa and infant siblings. Loneliness for her family had never left her mind, but now she missed Mama more than ever, for she had no one except herself.

Guided by a lacy veil of moonlight, she continued along the path. Her head spun with plans. She would return and offer to pay Jesse in gold to accompany her away from Prophet. Straightforward and up front. It hadn't been right to even consider garnering his favors with her body. He could use gold, surely. And that would make it honorable for them both. It would be a business deal—and they would be together.

The church steeple cut darkly into the sky to slice the moon in half. Across the creek the dark mouth of the mine yawned. She approached with stealth, but to her surprise no guard stood watch. Perhaps the rumor that had circulated at church was true and they were going to shut it down. Carefully, she picked her way along the narrow gauge track, slipping around the railcar parked in the gaping black mouth. From behind a rock in a shallow cavity she fetched a pan, a beat-up old bucket, and the stub of a candle. Taking a match from her skirt pocket, she lit the wick. In the wavering light, she moved toward the back of the main cavern and the latest work of the miners. Laboriously she hauled a bucketload of scrapings down to the creek bank. There she dumped the bits of broken rocks and sand into the pan, dipped it into the water and swirled the contents around and around so the valuable, heavier gold could separate.

While she worked, the moon crept across the sky, cold beams of light dancing like fireflies along the surface of the crystalline water. She washed through the battered vessel several times with no luck, then spied the gleam of three small nuggets no larger than the end of her little finger. From her pocket she took a bag and dropped the precious gold into it. Calculating how much time she had by the moon's movement, she worked on, occasionally picking a precious small find from the settlings. Surely there would be enough gold in all her bags to tempt Jesse to carry her far away from this place. Remembering his brief but tender caress, his soft, luscious mouth nibbling at hers, she shivered.

To the east the sky glowed a pearlescent silver when she finally sneaked wearily into the house, stashed her treasure, undressed and crawled into bed. She'd have to rise soon for today was laundry day. If all went well, by the time Prophet came home he would find the bushes hung with sheets and towels and his britches, and she and Jesse would be long gone. He would have to get some other foolish woman to scrub his clothes until her knuckles burned. Tears wet her pillow, but she managed to fall asleep for a few hours.

When Angeline awoke, it was to find John Prophet regarding her in the predawn light. He fingered a strand of hair from her lips, traced the fine shape of her mouth.

"Angeline, get up. It's too late to be lying abed." His voice was gruff, and he gripped her arm with fingers strengthened by hard labor. He spoke louder. "Get up, wife. Where's my breakfast? The older you get the worse you behave. No wife of mine will lay abed after dawn."

Fear overcame Angeline's initial sleepy confusion as she stared up into Prophet's flushed features. Had she hidden away the gold before falling asleep? Where was Jesse? Had he gone already?

"What is wrong with you?" Prophet yelled, and dragged her from the bed by one arm, fingers gripping her flesh so tightly she yelped.

His face nearly purple, her husband hauled her across the room, plucked a dress from its hook on the wall and flung both her and the garment to the floor. "Put your clothes on and get to work. Stop being such a laggard. God abhors laggards. I told you that more than once."

She kicked both feet and her heel caught his shin. It couldn't have hurt him any more than it did her. Pain streaked up her leg.

He looked hurt for a moment, then roared and hit her, his open palm catching her across the temple and rattling her brain. Fists clenched and features drawn into an evil mask, he loomed over her, huge and terrifying.

"I try to give you everything, and this is how you repay me?"

Fear clogged Angeline's throat until she could barely breathe. He had never hit her before. Had his frustration built to a head? She didn't want him to be unhappy, but she simply did not want to be his wife. If only he could understand. Feet churning against the slick pine board floor, she tried to get away, screaming when he took a few quick steps toward her.

In the barn Jesse had just tightened the cinch around Buck's middle when he heard Angel's scream and the old man's shouts.

She'd said he didn't beat her, but something sure as hell was going on in the house. He hobbled to the door, cracked it open and listened. She cried out once again, then all was quiet. He palmed the butt of his pistol, moved into the barnyard and, without thinking about it, loped up the steps and into the house. It was like setting fire to his leg. Vision blurring, he followed the sounds of sobbing and stepped through the door to see Angeline cringing in the corner of the room, Prophet bent over her. His hand was raised.

Jesse yanked the Colt from its holster and started to thumb the hammer back to shoot the old bastard, then thought better of it. He thunked him across the back of his head instead. Prophet crumpled to the floor in a heap, one arm flopped across Angeline.

He was even older than Jesse had imagined. No wonder she wanted to escape. He could've easily been her grandfather. White-headed old coot. He should've shot him and been done with it. Jesse shoved the inert form aside, holstered his weapon and reached to help the girl to her feet. She slapped out at him, kicking out and making mewling sounds.

"Hey, hey, young'un. It's me, Jesse. Let me help you up from there."

When she stopped fighting, he gently took her arm. As she struggled to her feet, the ripped gown fell away from one shoulder. A rosy nipple peeked out at him and he couldn't help but stare, remembering that firm, full breast cupped in his hand the night before.

Blushing, she tried to cover the bare flesh with hands that trembled so much that it pained him. He averted his eyes, so angry he cursed and kicked the helpless old man.

"No, don't," she cried, tugging at his sleeve.

He turned toward her, fingered the red marks on her face. "I thought you said he doesn't beat you. I ought to have shot him."

She nodded her head up and down, then shook it back and forth. He knew exactly how she felt. She alternated between wanting to die herself and wishing her tormentor dead. That was something he knew all about.

He knelt beside her, reaching out. "Don't worry, it's okay. Get dressed."

"We can't go off and leave him—leave him like this."

"How in hell can you say that?"

"No, no, listen. You have no idea. If he comes to and finds me gone he'll move heaven and earth to find me. He'll track us down and kill you and drag me back. He has power you can't imagine."

Jesse gazed at her. "But how did you expect to ever leave, then?"

Her teary eyes clouded. "I don't know, I guess I didn't

really think it out. I was going to leave while he was gone, just not be here when he returned. I guess I thought . . . Maybe I can tell him he slipped and fell, hit his head."

Jesse grabbed at the out, knowing he would regret it, but all the same convinced he had to get away before this beauty wrapped him up in her web. Yet he couldn't help making an attempt to change her mind. "Just get dressed and I'll take you somewhere safe. Surely there's someone, somewhere."

Shaking her head, she took his arm, her firm grip frantic. "No, listen. He's never hit me before. He's only mad because I won't give him what he wants."

Jesse scowled. Echoes of his own youthful guilt, lived with for so long, bounced around in his head. "It's not your fault that he hit you."

"Yes, no. I mean, I don't know." Then she seemed to realize what he'd offered. She brightened. "Okay, that's what we'll do, run away—but tonight, after he goes to sleep. That way, we'll have a good head start. He won't know I'm gone for hours and maybe we can get far enough away that he won't find us. He could come to any time. We wouldn't get two miles down the road before he'd have a posse after us."

Jesse actually backed away from her. Dammit, he'd lost control of the situation by making the suggestion to take her to safety. He hadn't meant to. He ought to ride off and leave her alone. No one had ever helped him, why should he help her? Besides, having a woman along wasn't a good idea. How was he supposed to track his brother's killers with a woman along? He was damned, and it was unfair to bring anyone to hell with him.

"Okay," he said instead, as if he had no control over his own tongue at all. "You go get a pan of water and start bathing his face and crying, like you're afraid he's dead. You've got to convince him that he fell and knocked himself silly. If he figures out that I'm here, we're lost. I'll have to kill him. You understand that? I *will* kill him if I have to, Angel. I know that won't be best for either of us, but it's what I'll do."

She nodded, her eyes big and blue and trusting, leaking tears. For a moment she gave him a look like that's what she wanted, then she turned.

He wished like hell she'd quit looking at him with that pleading gaze. Goddammit, how had he got in such a fix? "Go on, do what I said. Hurry, before he comes to." He left before she could argue.

Angel listened to Jesse limp across the wooden floor, pass through the kitchen and out the back door, closing it gently.

In the ensuing silence, she poured water into the bowl on the dresser and knelt beside John Prophet, shaking so hard she could scarcely hold the cloth to his forehead. After a while his eyes rolled and opened.

Without giving him a chance to gather his thoughts and recall what had happened, she said, "Thank goodness you're all right. When you tripped and fell I thought you'd killed yourself. Are you okay?" She swiped at his face some more, until he finally shoved at her hand.

"Fell? I don't remember falling."

"Well, you did. Must have fallen over . . ." Quickly she glanced around, and saw one of her shoes lying in the floor. ". . . over my shoe. Took a hard knock on the side of the dresser. You've got a real goose egg there." She fingered the knot above his ear where Jesse had hit him with the gun butt.

Prophet winced, pushing her hand away to touch the place for himself. She couldn't tell if he actually believed her or if he couldn't remember enough to disbelieve her.

"I'll get dressed and fix your breakfast. Why don't you lie down for a while?" She knew she was babbling, but she couldn't help it.

He squinted his metallic eyes and gave her a long stare, like he couldn't quite figure out what was going on.

"Let me help you up," she said, wrapping both hands around his arm.

"Git off me, woman. I can get up by myself. I'm hungry. Call me when breakfast is ready."

She nodded and tried to appear humble. "I'll get dressed."

While she prepared biscuits and gravy, ham and eggs and coffee, she didn't glance once toward the barn. Suppose Jesse decided to ride away? She wouldn't much blame him. He didn't need to get involved in her troubles. Probably had plenty of his own. Why hadn't she told him about the gold?

Her face throbbed where Prophet had hit her, and both arms were sore from the harsh grip of his strong fingers.

Watching her morose husband gulp down his breakfast, hope grew that she and Jesse would actually escape as soon as it got dark. The idea excited her, but it frightened her, too. Prophet would see it in her face, he surely would.

"Today's wash day," he said when he'd finished the last of his meal. "Make sure you scrub those collars till they're clean. You know how I abhor dirty collars on my Sunday shirts."

She nodded, keeping her eyes down. Relief coursed through her when he rose, took his hat off the hook by the door and tromped out. He didn't tell her where he was going and she didn't ask.

Jesse waited until Prophet set out across the field, then led Buck from the barn. Once the man was out of sight, he rode to a grove of trees on a rise on the opposite side of the house. *Angel.* Sitting astride the roan he watched the slight girl hoist bucket after brimming bucket from the well and fill a huge black iron kettle in the yard. She

55

lit a fire under it and soon smoke trailed through the morning breeze.

He smelled the wood burning and fresh-turned earth and the sweetness of honeysuckle twisting up a tree trunk nearby. And on his hands and in his shirt, her tangy musk lingered, but surely only in his mind. Memories remained of her across his lap, her head bent so her golden hair tickled his cheek. And of that damned old man beating her. If not for that, he'd have been gone last night. Hell and damnation.

He would have to be careful to quickly take her away somewhere and leave her—ride away so fast he wouldn't be caught in a tangle of desire. It was a place he had no business being. She'd learn soon enough what he was really like, and she'd know she didn't need his kind any more than she needed Prophet.

His vow to find the no-accounts who had hung his brother, to get them at all costs, had kept him alive through the worst of times. His need for vengeance had eventually become his only reason for living. But watching Angel, other emotions flickered into existence—feelings he'd never experienced, and along with them came an unexpected desire to protect another living human being. Where had such a thing come from? He'd had enough to do keeping himself alive.

The bitter hatred nourished by Zeke's whip left little room for anything else. When Charlie had fled, leaving him alone, he had dreamed of actually killing that crazy old man for what he'd done to his brother, to the both of them. They were twins, and had only each other, and Charlie's leaving had torn Jesse's heart, mortally wounded his soul. Those wounds had never healed, but Angel eased the pain.

"Blamed fool," he muttered. She needed him, that was all, and was willing to do anything to get him.

Buck twisted an ear. "I wasn't talking to you, horse,"

Jesse muttered. If he weren't such an idiot he'd light out this minute; if he hadn't come along he would never have known of her troubles, and she would have been forced to face them like everyone else. Alone. But despite the truth of that, he found he couldn't go and leave her. It would haunt him for the rest of his days, and there was enough horror bouncing around in his head without that. He'd just get her out, that's all. And then he'd be done with her.

His horse shifted from one hind leg to the other, anxious to be on the move again.

Jesse laid a hand on his neck. "Not just yet, ol' boy, not just yet."

Buck lifted his nose, whinnying into the wind. Off in the distance another horse answered and Jesse whirled to have a look. Someone out there was watching. He shaded his eyes, scanning the rolling horizon. For an instant he thought he caught movement at the fringe of his vision, but it was gone. Was someone watching him watch Angel?

Nothing moved, and after a while, he grew as restless as Buck. The injured leg had begun to ache by the time Angel finished the wash and spread the wet clothing over bushes alongside the yard. Still Jesse remained where he was—watching. Waiting. He'd take her away tonight, and probably be damned for it, but it couldn't be helped. Memories of that lost, small boy he'd been, alone and crying in the night, wouldn't allow anything else.

Prophet didn't show up for dinner, though Angeline had put a pot of leftover stew on to heat and wrapped the breakfast biscuits in a warm towel for him. She went back outside to empty the wash water, tilting the heavy kettle over to drain, then ran to the barn to throw out some grain to the chickens and search for eggs.

It was hauntingly quiet inside the hulking structure, and she listened for the sound of Jesse's voice, fearing he had left without her. Moving through stacks of loose hay, she checked all the favorite nesting spots, then stepped into the shadowy back stall where Penny, her favorite hen, usually left a daily offering. She feared Jesse had gone.

"I wondered when you'd come," he said from the far corner.

With a startled little "oh" she dropped the eggs bundled in her apron. Of all the things she might have said, nothing came out. She stood there shaking, surprised by tears of relief.

"Sorry, I didn't mean to scare you."

"No. Yes, I thought . . ."

"You're crying."

"No . . . yes . . . I mean—"

"You mean you're crying. I'm sorry he hurt you. I should have protected you."

She heard the catch in his throat and wondered at it. "It's okay. You did all you could. And you didn't leave."

He moved toward her, laying a hand on her arm. His movements were tentative and she was pleasantly surprised by the breathlessness he seemed to be suffering.

A bright shiver surged through her, and she hooked her other arm around his neck, burying her nose in the warmth of his skin. Feeling oddly protective, he held her for a long while. She cried a little, but then stopped. His shirt was wet and hot where she'd laid her head.

"No one has the right to beat on someone," he said, the words sounding harsh and ugly. He moved one hand up her back and into her long hair, touching her gently as if to calm a skittish animal.

"He promised my father I'd be brought up with discipline, treated like a child of his own."

"And now he wants to take you to his bed? That's hardly like you were his child. That's sick, Angel."

"I'm his wife," she whispered.

He wouldn't have heard her had her mouth not been against him, she spoke so low.

"That's bull. You're no more his wife than you are mine. You can't buy and sell human beings, Angel—and I'm sorry, but your father was *wrong* to sell you."

"I agreed to it. I couldn't let the little ones starve, could I?"

"It wasn't your place to be responsible for that. It was your father's."

She didn't answer, saw the futility of arguing with him. But it didn't change her mind. "I was young and didn't know I would have to be his real wife," she said in a small voice. "It was like playing house until . . ."

Jesse shuddered with pity. "Some men can get downright mean when a woman deprives them of what they think is rightly theirs. Still he had no right to hit you."

"And what about you, Jesse. Do you ever get mean?"

His fingers kneaded her scalp gently, and he was quiet for a long while. Then, he lowered his head so that his lips were against her temple.

"Oh, yes, I do. I could easily have killed Prophet for what he did to you today."

"But you didn't." She began to tremble, fear riding through her like a fever. "He'd kill us both if you tried anything. I saw that in his eyes today and wondered why I never noticed his mean streak before. Oh, Jesse, why do we have to grow up? Why can't we stay little?"

"We grow up so we can protect ourselves," he said.

Holding her in his arms, Jesse knew down in his heart that he would not permit John Prophet to touch the girl again, even though, as she said, it could mean bad trouble.

"I'll take you somewhere safe, but if he comes after us, I don't care what you say. I'll stop him, however I have to." He was truly going to take her with him and not just saying so to make her feel better.

Jesse released Angel abruptly and moved to the window, scanned the plains. No sign of Prophet. She came up

59

behind him, touched his back, making his skin tingle. What was he doing, letting her get inside him like this?

"Are you hungry? I made some stew last night and have it on the stove. And there's biscuits left from breakfast."

"Yeah, yes, I could eat. Sounds good."

She moved toward the door.

"Angel, be careful. Don't let him catch you bringing me food."

"No, I won't."

As she crossed the yard, one of the barn cats twined itself between her legs and she stooped to pick it up.

Jesse stood in the doorway and watched her pet the cat, looking so much like a child. The brilliant gold of the setting sun gleamed in her hair, and he remembered her pale thighs when that old man had her down on the floor; and the firm, full breast she'd covered so quickly. Youthful she might be, but the woman in her had emerged before the child had been allowed to live. He could not stand the thought of John Prophet putting his hands on her, much less climbing into her bed. In a few short hours he had gone from not giving a damn about anything to being willing to protect this girl with his life. He wasn't sure how that had happened. He settled in to wait.

Prophet didn't return until long after dark. Jesse heard the steady clop of horse hooves, and scurried into his hiding place. Angel would come to him after the lamps went out and the house grew dark and quiet. They would sneak away into the dark, still night, leaving the old man sleeping soundly. And when he awoke they would be so far away he'd never catch them. Never. And God help him, then what would Jesse do with her?

Thinking about that old bastard hitting her made him furious again. It was all he could do to keep from going into the house, jamming the barrel of his revolver in the man's ear and blowing his head off. If he pretended the man was Zeke, killing him would be easy. And he practically was Zeke, wasn't he?

Angeline sat across the table from her husband, and picked at a bowl of steaming stew while he wolfed his down. The kitchen smelled of clean laundry and fragrant meat and vegetables, but was too warm from the dying fire in the cookstove. They didn't talk.

After he went to bed she sat in the dark for a long while, waiting for the sound of snoring. When it came at last, she sneaked from the house with her scant belongings and her gold, wrapped in two small bundles.

The moon had not yet risen and it was black as pitch outside as she picked her way slowly across the yard. As she stepped through the barn door, she bumped into Jesse, who was hovering just inside.

"I was afraid he'd done something to you," he said.

"No, it took him a while to fall asleep." Slanting a glance up at him, she asked, "Are you afraid?"

Jesse rubbed the butt of his pistol, but shook his head. "No, not for myself."

She turned away then, but as she did, she thought she felt him reach out to touch her. Did he feel the same desire for her that she did him? But when she spun back toward him, his face was stoic. A little confused, she made her way toward the door.

Out in the open, Prophet's house gazed at them in inky silence.

"You can ride behind me," Jesse said in a low voice. "Buck'll carry us both easy if we don't push him. Maybe we can get you a mount later."

She nodded, waiting nervously. Leather creaked as he climbed into the saddle. Goose bumps rose along her arms, and she thought she heard a footfall in the darkness. Behind her, the shadow of man and horse maneuvered awkwardly, but then there was something else. She started to turn, but there appeared a man—then two, then three, like specters in the night. A screech left her throat, and terror swelled in her chest like knots of fire.

Behind her Jesse cursed, but she didn't turn. The looming figures held her in a trance from which she couldn't move.

A gruff command. "Rest easy, Cole. We'll kill her."

A gun barrel glimmered, eyes caught starlight. Though she could not see Jesse's face in the shadows she reached out for him, heard the ominous click of a hammer thumbed back.

"Don't Jesse, he's got a gun," she hissed in a voice that cracked.

"Fine advice, Jesse," the voice mimicked. "The little lady's right. And I don't think either of you want the old man to wake up. Do you? It'd be best, Cole, if you two just come along with us."

Angeline moved closer to Jesse, tensing against him.

He stepped away. "No, leave her. I'll go with you," Jesse said.

The one in charge chuckled. "Like her a lot, then, do you, Cole?" Without waiting for a reply he spoke to his men. "Grab her and let's be on our way. We've spent enough time here." Then to Jesse, he said, "You going upright or across the saddle?"

Huge arms like trees encircled Angeline's waist and she was lifted off the ground and deposited behind a saddle. She didn't scream or make a sound. Things were bad enough, but if Prophet woke up they'd kill him, and maybe her and Jesse as well. As long as she and Jesse were alive they all had a chance.

Jesse must have mounted, for no more words were spoken and they rode out, her captor leading the way. Mouth dry and heart hammering, she clung to the belt of the huge man in front of her. She was escaping her prison, but in a horrible way she had never imagined.

Chapter Four

For hours the outlaws and their captors rode through the
night, making little conversation. The moon hung high,
its glow broken up by intermittent clouds. Angeline could
no longer feel her numbed fingers, but the leader called a
halt in time to keep her from losing her grip and sliding
off the horse. He appeared to be in charge, and he also
seemed to know Jesse—though he insisted on calling him
Charlie.

"We'll rest the horses for a few hours," he said. "Get
some shut-eye. Me and Charlie here have to talk. When
he tells us what we want to know, we'll move out."

Jesse grunted. "You may think I'm Charlie, but I can
set you straight about that. Charlie's dead. I'm his brother
Jesse."

The man haw-hawed into the darkness and dismounted. "Yeah, and if I believe that you'll sell me a
plantation complete with slaves and a beautiful mistress."

"We're twins, you asshole."

"Now that there's a good story. Fletch, help this fella
down."

"You got it, Rawley." The large, ginger-haired man dismounted and dragged Jesse out of the saddle. He landed
on his wounded leg, stumbling to both knees with a muffled grunt. Fletch hauled off and kicked him.

Angeline shouted, "Stop that," and hammered on the
big man's back.

He cursed, then grabbed her arm and slung her down
beside Jesse.

She crawled to his side and touched him. "You okay?"

"Fine. I'm fine," he growled. He guided her hand down to the cool butt of his gun, still in its holster. In their haste to leave, the men hadn't disarmed him.

She had no idea why he hadn't used the gun on the trail, but took it now and quickly tucked it into the waistline of her skirt, bunching the tail of her blouse over it.

"Watch me and use it," Jesse whispered. "You can do that, can't you?"

Fear muted her tongue, but she nodded vigorously as the big man jerked her up and shoved her forward.

"Git over yonder in them woods, girl. You'n me's gonna have some fun."

"Leave her alone," Jesse shouted. "I'll tell you what you want to know."

Rawley nudged him hard with the toe of his boot. "You're in no position to bargain. Fletch will do what he pleases. . . . He's big enough to, ain't he?"

All three laughed and Angeline shuddered in the grip of the giant. In the light from the moon, she watched Jesse for a sign. If she didn't use the gun quick, this monster would do much worse things to her than Prophet had ever dreamed.

Struggling to his hands and knees, Jesse said, "He lays one finger on her, and you can kill me before I'll talk. And if you think I can't take what you have in mind, guess again."

"Fletch, not now," Rawley decided without raising his voice.

The big man shrugged, and let go of Angeline. Her trembling legs almost dumped her to the ground.

The other fellow, a nondescript man with a balding head and potbelly spoke in a deceptively soft voice. "Let's build a fire and make some coffee."

"Not tonight. That old fart might have woke up and be out looking for this 'un, though it's doubtful he even knows what hit him. Fletch here thumped him pretty hard. Man don't know his own strength." They all enjoyed the comment, then stopped laughing as soon as Rawley went on.

"When he does come to he'll likely be on our trail. Probably should'a killed the old codger, but that'd meant a posse. Besides, we need to be on our way to getting the gold, huh, Charlie." He gave another boot to Jesse's ribs.

Though the kicks must be doing damage, Jesse did little more than grunt. "Yeah, sure. Just leave her be, that's all. Turn her loose, let her go back. She won't say anything."

Again, the men hee-hawed.

Rawley knelt beside Jesse, who had managed to sit up. "Let's have ourselves a talk. Cake, you and Fletch lead the horses down to that stream, water 'em, then put 'em out on the grass. Me'n ol' Charlie here are gonna get reacquainted. He appears not to remember us, and that's a shame, ain't it, boys?"

Cake and Fletch chuckled, then did as they were bid, following an animal trail into the umber shadows.

Angeline moved closer to Jesse, and the man called Rawley, who had him by the shirt collar, dragged him to his feet. Jesse had both hands on his knees, and he took deep breaths, shaking his head. He appeared to be hurt. She took another few steps, aiming to help him, but before she could, he butted Rawley in the belly.

The surprised man let out a whoof and staggered backward, Jesse grappling for a good hold. Both tumbled to the ground. They rolled around, grunting and clawing at each other. Through the bushes and into the darkness of the woods they fought, then she heard a sickening crunch. She fumbled the heavy gun from beneath her blouse and held it in both hands. She pointed it at the spot where they'd disappeared.

Brush crackled and rattled and out staggered a figure—it was dragging another. She pulled the hammer back, the click ominous in the suddenly quiet night.

"Hsst, it's me. Jesse. Come on."

He grabbed the pistol barrel from her and let down the

cocked hammer, then took her hand and hustled into the woods. They circled in the direction Cake and Fletch had taken the horses. If the two had heard, they would come back, probably on the trail they'd taken to the stream. Angeline stumbled along behind him, through thickets, dodging low-hanging limbs. It was hard to keep up. The way Jesse moved he hadn't been hurt near as bad as he'd pretended, though that terrible Rawley had kicked him hard.

Why was he headed *for* the two men instead of running in the opposite direction and safety? *And why was he dragging the other man along?*

She had no time to ask, for he pulled up short, signaling her to be quiet. He dropped the unconscious Rawley and listened. The whisper of running water formed a backdrop for the conversation of the outlaws, who had hunkered on the edge of the stream watching the horses drink. Gesturing for her to remain there, he crept into the moon-washed clearing.

"Stand up real slow and unbuckle those weapons," he said.

"What in thunder . . . ?" Cake shouted.

Fletch rose to his full six and a half feet and roared like a cornered bear. Jesse let off one shot and the big man grabbed his shoulder, then took a few steps toward Jesse.

From the woods, Angeline watched in horror as Jesse thumbed the hammer once more. "Another step and I put one between your eyes. Even you won't get up from that."

Fletch must have believed him, for he halted. The blood from his wound gleamed black in the moonlight.

"Now, both of you do as I said and drop your gun belts on the ground. Fletch, I want you on your knees, where you stand. Then you—Cake? Is that your name?—I want you to bring those horses over here to me." Without turning to look in her direction, Jesse called, "Angel, come on out here."

Cake gaped, grumbled, "You damn well know my name, Charlie."

Jesse took another shot, cutting rock at his feet. "Move, now. I don't want to have to kill you, but I will."

Cake fetched the horses and, keeping his distance, held out the reins.

"Now, both of you, take off your boots and clothes."

Fletch bellowed "What?" and lurched as if to stand.

"I've got four rounds in here. I won't waste any more," Jesse said. He pointed the revolver at the big man's head. "Now, sit down on the ground, get out of those boots and undress. Put your clothes all in a bundle. Get to it."

Cake cursed under his breath, but Fletch continued to shout his displeasure. "You leave us naked out here without horses, and I'll hunt you down and strip your hide off in little bitty pieces."

Off came his boots, and he threw them toward Jesse.

"You'll have to find me first. Besides, it appears to me you were already in a mood to strip off my hide."

Angeline watched in amazement as the men did his bidding, taking off everything down to their underdrawers. Rawley had awoken and he followed orders as well, though angrily. If she hadn't been so frightened she would have giggled at the sight of grown men in ragged BVDs, socks and hats.

Jesse called out. "Angel, fetch their clothes and bring 'em here. Don't go near either of them and don't get between me and them. Come around behind me."

She did as he said, rolling the clothing and trying not to gag at the stench. These men could do with a wash, britches and all.

"Boots too, Angel. Tie 'em all on one of the horses. And when you've done that, mount up and take the reins of the others."

Rawley gestured angrily. "You leaving us here without

our horses? I lay hands on you, I don't care if you do know where the Confederate gold is hid, I'll kill you and it'll take me days, maybe a week. You'll be glad enough to tell me all about it 'fore you die."

"I say we rush him now," the giant ginger-haired man roared. "He can't shoot us all."

"You're first," Jesse said, and pointed the gun at Fletch. "Go ahead, boys. Rush me. See who dies first."

"Aw, hell. There'll be another time," Fletch said.

Cake regarded the situation with dead eyes. "I can get him, Rawley, 'fore he can get us. Let him shoot Fletch. Hell, it won't kill him. He's strong."

"Son of a bitch," Fletch shouted.

"Calm down, boys," Rawley said. "Charlie, you cheated us once, hiding that gold so we couldn't find it. Hell, man—we helped you steal it, put our lives on the line, and you do us this way? I figured at first you'd been caught, and that was the reason you didn't come back after you left to hide the wagon. Then I hear you've been cutting up in Nebraska, shooting folks. Some said you went to prison, others said you was hung. Didn't know what to believe, thought for sure you was dead. The Charlie I knew wouldn't cheat on his pals."

"The Charlie I know would," Cake said. "You always was too trusting. I told you all along to watch that lying sneak thief. It was us found out about Shelby's men turning and lighting out with the wagon 'fore he left Texas for Mexico. Me and Fletch, we knew the route they planned to use to take the gold to Canada—not Charlie. And still you let him light out with it, leaving us to cover our tracks. Mop up after he shot them three rebs. This boy always did have you in his spell, Rawley, dadblame it."

The words made little sense to Angeline, who listened as she tied the bundle of dirty clothes on the long-legged bay horse Fletch rode. Jesse killing? She didn't believe it. If it were so, then why was he going to let these three men

go? Men who threatened his very life? Was he this mysterious Charlie they spoke of? They at least thought so.

She chose the buttermilk mare Cake rode, and gathered
the reins of the others. "You coming?"

"Go on, I'll catch up."

"Want me to leave Buck for you?"

When Jesse didn't reply, she cast him a quick look. He
had collected the men's gun belts, draped them over one
arm and stood staring as the three argued.

Was he going to kill them after all? "Jesse? Come on. I
don't want to go by myself."

Ignoring her, Jesse mulled over what the men had said,
tried to make some sense of it. Shelby? Jo Shelby? The
Confederate general from Missouri who had ridden off to
Mexico with his troops rather than surrender when the
war ended? What did he have to do with Charlie and
stolen gold? Charlie, like their cousins the James boys,
had ridden with Quantrill. And it was said Quantrill had
trailed along with Shelby for a spell.

"Jesse, come on," Angel shouted, fright tinging her
voice.

At last yanked from his reverie, Jesse backed off from
the three indignant, barefoot and unarmed men. If they
ever caught up to him, there'd be hell to pay, but he didn't
see how they could. He'd be long gone before they could
get anywhere to get horses, clothes and guns. The idea of
killing them had entered his mind, but he couldn't do it.
The only killing he'd ever done was in the war, and he
hadn't liked that. Not one bit.

Mounting Buck, he cursed himself for a fool. How did
he expect to ever be an outlaw if he couldn't kill anyone?
It was just plain stupid. But his brother Charlie had killed,
according to these men. Together they'd shot three rebel
officers and stolen a wagonload of gold. No wonder they
had hanged Charlie. What had he done with that gold?

He joined an impatient Angel. For several minutes they rode in silence, both deep in their own thoughts.

Finally, she spoke. "Is your name Charlie?"

"No."

"Why do they think it is?"

Jesse thought about that question, wanting to clam up like he usually did when someone trod too close to his secrets. Was there any reason for him to tell her?

"I have a right to know if you're a killer, don't I?" she asked.

He glanced at her, the night's shadows making a crazy quilt design of moonlight over her features. "I guess you do." Still it took a few more minutes before he could speak. He began by talking about Charlie, about how close they were and how one always knew what the other was up to, about the birthmark like a tiny paw print just below Charlie's belly button, the only physical difference between them.

By the time he finished telling her about Zeke and the beatings, they had put a lot of miles between them and their assailants. The moon had slipped silently across the sky and hung in front of them as they rode on west— away from Circleville and John Prophet.

Angeline glanced at Jesse, unable to make out his expression as he finished speaking. Escape was in her grasp at last. But with what kind of man?

"It must have been terrible," she said. There were worse things than living with a man like John Prophet. That didn't make her life seem any the better, but knowing it gave her a new perspective to consider.

"Worse for Charlie than for me, I reckon. Or else he was much braver than me. I couldn't leave, was too much a coward—and he knew it, so he left without me. Almost killed me when he did. I still miss him, still keep hoping one day I'll look up and he'll be standing there."

70

"I know. I still miss my family, too. My sisters, Ma and Pa." She paused, then said, "The two of us, we are alone but together."

When he made no comment, she watched him ride, back straight, head tilted to study the trail that shone pale in the moonlight.

"Can they follow us?"

"Nope, but John Prophet can. Question is, will he?"

"Oh, yes. He will. Those men made sure of that. He has friends. The sheriff and others, they'll come with him and try to catch us. We'll have to cover our trail somehow."

After another prolonged silence, he said her name, softly, with a question implied.

She answered and waited a while longer for his next words.

"Did he . . . I mean, uh . . . have you . . . been in his bed?"

"No, he thought I was having my monthly." She stopped abruptly, amazed that she could speak of such a personal thing to this man she hardly knew.

"Smart."

"How do you know I'm not?"

"We were . . . well, uh . . . pretty close recently. I would have known. Your husband's not real smart—not where women are concerned, leastways."

"And just how did you get so smart?"

He chuckled. It broke the tension and she relaxed a bit. It was a while before she realized he hadn't answered her question.

As dawn gleamed across the sky at their backs, he called a halt to rest and water the horses.

"You think he's coming?" she asked, glancing nervously over her shoulder before dismounting.

"Even if he was, we've got a good lead on him. We can't ride these horses to death."

"You aim to keep the other two?"

Samantha Lee

"For a while. Reckon we ought to get rid of them before we get too close to Abilene. I heard Wild Bill Hickok is running a tight town there, and we don't want anything calling his attention to us."

Her heart tripped and her spirits raised. "Before we get to Abilene?" she asked. He was taking her with him, at least for a while.

When he didn't answer, but led the horses to the small stream that marked the place he chose to stop, she trailed after him. Bone-tired, she flopped to the grass at the water's edge. He busied himself refilling all the canteens on the four horses, then carried one to her, limping badly.

Eagerly she took it and drank deeply. The water was cold and bright tasting, like gold nuggets when she touched them to her tongue. Jesse's roan still carried her two bundles and she glanced at them to reassure herself that her stash was safe.

That reminded her of the story of the stolen gold.

"Jesse? Do you think that story about the Confederate gold is true?"

He lowered the canteen and refilled it, bending awkwardly to accommodate his stiff leg. "I don't know, but I reckon it is. Quite a story for rough men like them to make up, wouldn't you say?"

Growing impatient with his wandering around, she patted the grass next to her. "Come sit with me for a minute, rest that wound before we have to ride. You're worse than a maggot in hot ashes."

He chuckled. "Charlie used to say that."

"So did my pa."

He gazed down at her, then did her bidding, stretching the sore leg out.

"It's getting better, I can tell," she said.

"Yeah. You did a good job. I never thanked you proper for that."

"No need, you brought me with you. That's payment enough."

72

"Didn't realize you did it for payment."

"I didn't," she snapped, angry with him for turning her words on her.

"Sorry."

She plucked a blade of grass, stretched it between flattened thumbs and blew across it, making a sharp, burry sound. One of the horses raised a head from grazing, nickered and stared at them for a moment. Pink-tinged morning light turned dark shadows into distinct objects: a cottonwood, the animals, Jesse's broad-shouldered form.

He plucked himself a blade and created his own noise to blend with hers. Both laughed and had a contest, shredding several thick green leaves before calling it a draw. Buck sauntered over and butted Jesse's back with his velvet nose.

"He's telling us to quiet down," Angeline said. "Like we were kids and him our pa."

Jesse stared at her for a long moment, then he reached for her hand that still held the grass and touched it to his lips. He had soft, warm, moist lips, and his tongue darted out for a taste of her skin.

Hope swelled within her, sweet and unexpected as honeydew on a spring morning. He gazed at her with eyes sparked by golden fire.

Suddenly, he leaned forward to take her mouth with his. In the presence of a growing desire, all fear faded. Her fingers wound through his thick hair, and she returned the kiss.

He pushed her backward so they lay in the grass, his body covering hers, his heart beating against hers, his need throbbing in rhythm with her own.

Spanning her waist, he spread long fingers beneath the loose tail of the blouse, caressing her warm, bare flesh. He lowered his mouth into the vee at her throat.

She locked both arms around him, thinking to keep him there forever, wanting to rip off her clothes, then his, and make love as the sun burst over the horizon. How could a man make her feel like this? So new, so fresh, so needy of his slightest touch?

"Angel," he murmured against the swell of her breast. "You are my angel."

His breath heated her passion, sending a pounding ache to her breasts and loins. This was love, this desire, and she bathed in its glory as long rays of hot sun spilled through the grass, flowing over them and into the water, its heat as intense as her need for him.

Jesse stirred and moaned. "Oh, dear God, Angel. I don't know what to do about this."

Wide-eyed, she gazed at the bulge in his britches. "I'd think you would."

He closed his eyes and took a deep breath. "That's just it. I want you so badly, but I know better. You're so young and sweet, innocent. What do I do, take you and ride on as if nothing happened? I can't do that. And I can't stay with you."

"Take me with you. You said we'd be in Abilene. *You* said it."

"But not you and me, Angel. We can't...." He brushed at the line of her jaw with a thumb, gazing into her eyes. His own were haunted with despair.

Then he was gone, leaving her there almost as if he had drifted off on a sunbeam. Tears leaked from her eyes and she stared into the empty distance.

Back at the homestead, Prophet raced from Angeline's room, searched through the house, and ran to the barn. He was frantic. Enraged. Shaking his fists at God in his heaven, he lifted the cellar door when he didn't find a sign of her elsewhere, shouting into the empty cavern. There came no reply.

In the middle of the floor he saw something white. He stumbled down there, then picked it up. A candle lay nearby, in the square of light from the open door. He held the rag, then ran to the barn door. Blood stained it. Somebody had been hiding out down here. Lying in wait for the right time to take his beloved Angeline. What did this mean?

Tears of rage burned his eyes, but he brushed them away on a shirtsleeve. Out in the barnyard, fresh horse droppings told a dreadful story, and he circled the disturbed earth until he found the tracks of four horses headed off to the southwest. Someone had stolen her! Taken advantage of her sweet nature and took her right from under his nose. Making tight fists he pounded at his own thighs. If they hurt her he'd see them hanged.

"God, do not forsake me now," he shouted at the sky.

Mind whirling he whistled up his black gelding, saddled him quickly and raced off toward town to get up a posse.

In Circleville, outside the sheriff's office, a dozen or so townsfolk milled about while he sat on the magnificent black, white hair blowing in the wind.

He was a pious man, by God. The women would pray for him while the men took up arms to aid their brother in Christ. He shouted all this in a voice wild with fury.

Sheriff Oursler now stood at his side, having sent those willing to join the posse after their mounts and arms.

"Who were they?" Oursler asked. "Did you see them? Did they say anything?"

"Must've broke into her room in the night, gagged her, tied her up and took her off. I know she wouldnt've gone without a fight and there's no sign of one. I never heard her yell. They rapped me upside of the head as I slept."

He buried his face in both hands for an instant, then regained control. Anger ruled, casting aside the grief, at least for the time being. He'd raised, loved and cared for Angeline. He'd anticipated a long happy marriage. He'd waited, by God, like a man should, for her to be ready.

"Why you reckon they took her?" someone asked.

Prophet shuddered. "Why does any dastardly varmint steal a beautiful woman? Reckon we ought to contact the sheriff down in Topeka, see if there's a wanted out on them. Four of 'em, unless they brought an extra horse for—"

Several armed men rode up in a flurry of shouts.

"Let's git after them before they ride clear out of the county," one shouted.

Prophet quieted them down with the wave of a hand. "Fellas, be careful. I don't want no shooting to get my little girl hurt, you understand? I want her back in one piece, alive and pretty as ever. That clear? Once she's free of them, do as you please. In fact, it looks to me like it's coming up to be a fine day for a hanging, don't it to you?"

The trail proved easy to follow once they left the farm. Prophet stopped only occasionally to study the terrain and make doubly sure four horses still cut tracks through the lush grass.

After all he'd done for that little gal and her near-starving family, how could she be taken from him like this? Questioning God's motives wasn't part of his belief, but this loss was a hard thing to swallow. He loved her so much he couldn't hardly stand her holding him off at arm's length like she did. She put him some in mind of Becky, the love of his youth who lay buried in the churchyard back in Ohio. Just thinking about her brought tears to his eyes. Set to be married, they'd been, when the fever had taken her. They'd both been so young and full of dreams.

He'd run off and fought in that awful war just trying to get himself killed so he could join her in heaven. By the time it was over, of course, he'd seen all kinds of hell, and knew he wanted to live. It was then that he'd spotted Angeline, a skinny little thing with eyes blue as cornflowers and a wishful look on her sweet face that made his heart turn over. At that very moment, he'd known he had to have her. That she was the child he and Becky never had, and would one day be the wife Becky never had a chance to be. God would surely forgive him for raising up this child to become his wife. He had seen to her every need, loved her like a father and would now like a husband. Surely such a thing could not be a sin.

The past couple of years, after Angeline began to turn from child to woman, had been the most difficult of his life. God had sorely tempted him with her lush beauty, but he'd kept his hands to himself. He wasn't, after all, a lustful man. But he did have strong and urgent needs. The Good Lord had seen to that. And he wanted children before he grew too old to sire them. He would get Angeline back, one way or another, for he saw little chance of finding himself another woman out here in this wilderness where they were scarce as snake's feet. Oh, there were some widow women in town, but they were ugly and wrinkled, set in their ways—worn out.

Narrowing his eyes, he stared toward the horizon. By God, he shouldn't have to go in search of no woman, for didn't he have himself a wife, legal in the eyes of both man and God? He'd get her back and string up those outlaws that stole her out from under his nose. And if any one of them so much as touched her, Prophet would see to it the man pleaded on hands and knees for death before he'd finally grant it.

He gouged Duke with his heels, picking up the pace. "Come on, men, let's ride. They've got a head start on us, and I sure don't want to give them time to hurt my Angeline. One hundred dollars, cash money, to the man who brings her back to me without a hair on her head harmed."

Shouting with excitement, several of the riders raced out ahead, whipping at their horses flanks.

Chapter Five

Jesse and Angeline rode steadily all day, stopping only to rest, water and feed the horses. They ate sparsely of the food she'd wrapped in one of her packs. Though he held back to save the horses, she consistently moved out ahead as if demons were on their trail. Sometimes she wasn't aware that she was prodding the buttermilk, until Jesse caught at the bridle and slowed her.

"It's like I can feel him coming. I won't go back, Jesse. I won't. Not after what he's done. Being his prisoner was bad enough, but having him come at me like that, and knowing I couldn't stop him . . ." Her voice caught.

How well he understood. "Don't worry, we'll get away. Even if he came to right away, it'll be dawn before he scouts up a posse. A man like him, he won't come alone, I'd wager."

He glanced at Angel. Damn the man, and damn her for being so needy. He didn't want to feel protective of her, there was no place for it. Hardened hearts held no compassion. But when he looked at her, he couldn't help but feel sorry. Dark smudges lay under eyes bright with fear, as if she'd been to hell and back—as if she expected at any moment to be sent there again.

It was a look he had seen on Charlie's face enough times, and he figured his own had carried it too. Other than his own reflection in still pools of water, the only glimpse he ever got of himself was in the face of his twin. The two of them had been the same until the dark got Charlie, took over his mind and turned him inside out.

Charlie had been so crazed that he almost killed Zeke, who had probably wished more than once since then that he had died instead of been crippled like he was. Charlie had beat him so bad it had made Jesse sick to his stomach, so bad that Jesse'd eventually even pulled his brother off the old man. Sometimes he thought he ought to've helped kill the abusive bastard. If Prophet caught up to them, Jesse wouldn't make the same mistake.

More than once, in the hellish caverns of his own mind, Jesse had imagined himself finishing the job Charlie had started on that horrible day. But staring at the helpless old man, he never could, then or later. That was why he'd finally taken off, ending the torture for both himself and Zeke. But it had left him without purpose, adrift.

It wasn't until once, running with Ringo, Jesse had come up against a man who mistook him for Charlie, a man who fled screaming from the sight of what he thought was a dead man walking, that he regained it. For it was then that Jesse learned those fellows had strung Charlie up without a trial, without mercy of any kind.

Cross and Doolittle. Their names had become a curse. The worst of it was, Charlie probably had done what they hung him for, and then some. But that didn't matter to Jesse. Blood was blood. He had the names of the men involved, knew what they looked like. One was tall with strawberry red hair, the other stocky and so ugly women turned away in disgust. When he caught up to them they would pay for hanging Charlie.

The terrible thoughts rode with him like monsters; he couldn't banish them from his mind. Never would till the deed was done. Despite his vows a small voice mocked him. *You're no killer, and you never will be.*

He shoved the devilish thoughts to the back of his mind. To take Angel's mind off her fear, he talked to her about traveling across the prairie without going in circles

79

or getting lost. He pointed out landmarks to go by, and told her how at night the big dipper and the bright north star always let you know directions. He explained how cooks on trail drives pointed the tongue of the cook wagon toward the north star before bedding down at night so they'd know what direction to go come morning.

"You can always tell where you're headed if you find the north star," he told her.

When she didn't reply he thought she probably hadn't even heard his story. He reined the roan closer just as the buttermilk stumbled. Angel slipped to one side, and would have fallen if he hadn't caught her arm. They would soon have to stop, hide out somewhere. She and the horses could use the rest. With a groan he massaged a kink in his back and rode on.

Some time later he reined in the animals, dismounted and gazed at the wet ground. The churned tracks of their passing stretched out behind them like signposts through the bluestem grass. How in God's name were they going to escape without leaving a trace? He had to come up with something, or the posse would catch them before the day was out.

The lush grass grew from spongy soil, and there weren't many rocks. Off to the left trees marked what might be a stream. He cocked his head and in the silence of early morning heard the lullaby of rolling water. If they could somehow get in the creek bed without leaving telltale tracks, then follow it a ways before taking cover, they just might have a chance.

Headed toward the stream, he gazed back at the signs they left behind. There was no chance they could fool the posse. The men in pursuit probably weren't expert trackers, but anyone could follow four horses crossing the rain-soaked Kansas plains. Unless they could manage to fly through the air their trail would be visible to even a half-blind tracker.

"Angel, wait here a minute," he said, and led the extra horses back along the trail they'd made. He had an idea which just might throw off the posse, at least for a while.

Looping the reins of the two animals over the pommels, he slapped each harshly on the rump and shouted at them. Both took off, heading back to the northwest. How far or how long they'd run, he had no idea, but they made a trail through the grass that might fool their followers.

Satisfied he'd done what he could for the time being, he rejoined Angel at the edge of the rain-swollen creek. Ahead somewhere, there might be a place where they could leave the water and mislead the posse further.

Because of recent storms the meandering stream ran high on its banks. The horses didn't go easily into the roiling water, clambering in up to their bellies, eyes rolling.

The docile little mare settled first, following along behind the gelding, nose almost touching his sweaty flank. Buck remained jittery, tossing his head, going stiff like he might buck any time. Jesse held him in with locked knees and gentle hands, so intent in the task, he jerked to attention when the sun sank below the horizon, sucking the afternoon heat along with it. There was no time to enjoy the sight or embrace the coming night. He had to get them to a shelter of some kind, and soon.

She could no longer feel her feet soaked by the cold water, but her buttocks and inner thighs ached sorely from the long ride. She yearned to lie down somewhere and sleep. Her eyes drifted shut and she saw Prophet's evil expression when he'd stood over her, arm upraised to strike. She would not, could not, give up. Ignoring the discomfort she clung harder with her knees and straightened her back. In spite of Jesse's promises, she feared the worst if Prophet caught them. The more she thought of the man touching her—his body forcing her to do

81

unspeakable things, big rough hand striking her when she didn't obey—the more she knew that she would not go back with him if he caught them. Death was preferable.

Suddenly, the buttermilk jigged to a stop, and she opened her eyes to see Jesse dismounting. With a stiff gait he led them out of the water onto a rocky embankment and limped to her side. Dusk blurred their surroundings, made of the plains a dark, frightening place with great ghostly trees waving bony fingers at the stars.

"You can get down now, Angel." He held out his arms.

Much as she tried, she couldn't move her legs from their grip on the mare's sides. Staring down at the man who would catch her, she yearned to be in his arms. Safe, protected. He encircled her waist with strong hands and eased her from her mount's back. Flowing like thick honey into his arms she rested in his strong embrace, but pins and needles shot through her legs.

She rested her head against his shoulder, and thought how good he smelled with the heat of the sun clinging to his wild hair and honeysuckle sweetening the night air. How soothing his strong arms were around her, and the steady thrum of his heart assured her. At that moment she would have followed him into the fires of hell without hesitation. All he would have to do was hold her hand. They were alive, both of them, and young and free.

She felt him rearrange her in his arms, his hard muscles feeling delicious beneath her own tender flesh. He sighed, then, and tilted his head so that his lips touched the pulse at her temple. "Can you walk?"

Dizzy and fatigued, she took a moment to respond to his question. She didn't want him to take his arms away, or move off where she couldn't feel his breath or hear his heartbeat. Her own thudded as she tested first one foot then the other, then nodded. She would make it.

Giving her a serious look, he pointed. "Yonder, see that outcropping, all those trees? I'm taking you over there on foot. We're gonna be real careful and not leave prints, find something to step on. It's rocky, the clumps of grass thick. Go easy. There's enough light to see the ground. Once you're settled in, I'll come back the same way and ride out to lay a false trail while you sleep."

Panic smothered her, and Angeline had to fight to breathe. She grabbed his arm. "You're leaving me alone?" She bit off the question; it made her sound like a baby. She had to let Jesse handle things, trust him. There was no one else. He knew what he was doing. But was she being naive? He'd claimed he would leave her. Suppose he rode off and didn't return, innocently taking her bags of gold that were stuffed in one of his saddlebags? Where would she go and what would she do, alone and without even the gold to pay her way?

"We've no choice, Angel. I'll be back as soon as I can, but if you don't rest and get some sleep, you'll not make it another day."

"What about you?"

He looked around nervously. "We don't have time to discuss this or argue about it or take a goddamned vote. I know what I'm doing. I've gone without sleep and food before. Now get moving, and be careful. I'll walk behind in case you leave any sign."

She raised her head and glared at him. "Don't worry, I won't. I can do this as good as you can. But I want my stuff out of the saddlebags."

"I'll get it. Go on, now."

Lifting her skirts, she carefully picked her way across the wide meadow that stretched between them and the outcropping. It looked to be nearly a quarter of a mile of open prairie they would have to cross, but the ground was high and had drained well.

She pretended she was playing hopscotch, checking

out her next jump before making it, wavering on first one foot then the other until she could take another step, without leaving so much as a faint mark in the soil.

Jesse watched her for a while, amazed that she had summoned enough strength to go on. Then he snubbed the horses to a low-hanging branch where they could browse on green leaves, and tugged one of the canteens and her bundle from the saddlebags.

The false signs he'd made might not fool an expert tracker, but he figured no one riding with the posse would have sharp enough eyes to pick up the true trail. Pray God the posse was thrown off by his earlier trick and were far behind. He didn't want them finding her when he left—or him. He could still be in Abilene come nightfall if he rode hard.

What of the girl when he didn't return? What of this beautiful girl called Angel? He didn't give a damn. He couldn't.

She'd awaken and find her way to a nearby spread. They'd take her in, maybe protect her even if John Prophet figured out where she was. Jesse wasn't responsible for everyone that hurt, just because he knew what it was like. He also knew what it was like to reach out for help and get none, to do it all on his own. That had only made him stronger, though. He had survived because of that strength. She would do the same.

All the same, deep down inside, he hated like hell to leave her, and when it came to doing so, found himself trying to come up with a better solution. She looked so forlorn, hair bedraggled by the wind, skirts muddied, a slight swelling along the side of her face where Prophet had smacked her. All Jesse wanted to do was take her in his arms and lie beside her in the leaves. To hold her close while she slept. Maybe he'd doze off himself. But there was no time, none at all. And he couldn't tarry. It would only make things harder for both of them if he even considered taking her with him.

He approached where she had settled. Together they raked dry leaves into a bed in the lee of a large rock surrounded by underbrush and several scrubby trees. Angeline fell on her knees on the makeshift bed, glancing up at him with such a wretched look that he almost changed his plan. Instead, he backed off a few steps to put some space between them. He *had* to leave her, had to go.

"Let me go out a ways, see if you can be spotted, then I'll be gone." His voice cracked, but he managed to go on. "You'll be safe here as long as you don't make any noise or poke your nose out."

Shivering, she hugged herself and didn't look up at him. "When will you be back?"

"By sunup," he lied, to make sure she wouldn't wander off in the dark in search of him.

That she didn't look at him again suited Jesse just fine, for he wouldn't have been able to meet her eyes.

"You'll be okay. Get some sleep. There's food, some water." He gestured toward the bundle and canteen he'd taken from the saddlebags—wanted like hell to touch her one final time, but didn't dare.

"Take some of the food I brought," she said, and untied the corners of the cup towel. She looked around then, a bit frantically Jesse thought, but then gave him a resigned look. He'd left all of her belongings, hadn't he? She held out a biscuit and a chunk of bacon for him. Why was her hand trembling? Did she know he wasn't coming back?

Emotion thickened his throat until he could scarcely speak. "You keep it, I'm fine. I have to go." He backed out of the thicket and was gone before she could make him change his mind.

He hated like hell to do this to her, but she had no business with him. Hell, he wouldn't even have ridden into her life if it hadn't been for that cyclone and those damned bushwhackers. If not for that he'd already be in Abilene and she'd be home with John Prophet. Neither ever knowing about the other.

Going off with Jesse would put her in more danger than she faced alone. If there'd been any way, he'd have left her the buttermilk, but having two horses was the only way to lay a convincing trail away from her. He'd done what he could for her. Besides, all she had to do was keep walking till she saw the lights of a homestead. There'd be more than a few, somewhere out there on the prairie. She'd be okay, she was young and smart and strong.

Besides, he wasn't her keeper.

He rode on into the night. The moon rose off to his left, casting wavering shadows across the wind-swept grass and a lonely man fleeing relentlessly into the night.

Angeline nodded, watching Jesse grow smaller in the closing dusk. He hesitated, raising a hand, then turned and was gone. A man riding away, taking with him her only means of escape. He hadn't given her back the bag with her clothing—or the gold.

Suppose he never came back? A breeze rustled through the trees, tousling her hair and cooling her cheeks. Somewhere a night bird called, then hushed. All she could hear was her own breathing, and after a while something wiggling through her bed of leaves.

For a long time she remained there on her knees, the biscuit and bacon in one hand. Then she began to nibble at first one, then the other. After a while she lay back, the odor of damp earth thick in her nostrils. Curled up in the leaves, she thought she might never fall asleep. She worried about Jesse not coming back, then about the gold, then herself and Prophet, all in a vicious circle that kept her awake despite the deep exhaustion. Her ears strained at every sound, mostly the comings and goings of small critters that made their home around the outcropping. At last she closed her eyes, yielding to the cry of her aching bones, and slept.

She awakened lying in puddles of warm sunlight, for a moment having no idea where she was. Some part of her expected to hear Prophet moving around in the other room. No matter how she tried, he always managed to rise of a morning before her. A breeze rattled the branches above, reminding her of the previous night's journey, Jesse hiding her away just at sundown and riding off. She sat up, rubbed at her eyes, and listened to the sounds of the day. There came the distinctive call of the meadowlark, and bobwhites whistling to each other.

Jesse wasn't coming back. If he had been, he would've been there already. No, she would never see him again. Not today, not ever.

For a long while she huddled there, unsure what to do.

At last anger replaced dismay. Damn him, anyway. Damn him to hell and back. Still, wishes in that direction would do little good; she'd never had much pull with Prophet's God, and knew no other. Everyone had deserted her, left her to her own devices, of which she had few.

Despite a growing fear that she might die out here on the plains, lost and alone, she reached for the bundles Jesse had taken from the saddlebags. And then she remembered.

Jesse had taken her gold. He'd ridden off with her gold and the horses, and left her to fend for herself, as if they'd never meant anything to each other. It had been a trick, rescuing her from Prophet, a trick just to get his hands on the little bags of valuable ore. But how had he known about them? He'd probably searched her room while she was doing the wash—or maybe it had been that night she went to the mine after he'd pushed her away as if he had

Samantha Lee

no use at all for her. He'd let her think he didn't care, then
stolen her gold. But if that were true why hadn't he just
taken the bags and ridden away when he found them?
Why would he cook up this elaborate plan of escape? It
didn't make sense. And the rest. Suddenly she blanched.
What of those three disgusting men? What if they found
her? She had to face it. Jesse or Charlie Cole, whoever he
was, had said he was a coward, and now he'd proved it.

What she had to do was something besides sit there
feeling sorry for herself and bemoaning something she
couldn't change. Lips set in grim determination, she
crawled from the hideaway, dragging her small parcel of
food and the canteen. Standing, she stared up into the sky.
The sun climbed high, pointed out the way they had
come, and she turned her back to it, fixing a distant grove
of trees as her first landmark so she wouldn't walk in circles. At least Jesse had taught her that much. And somewhere west and south of here was Abilene. If she had to
go that far, then she would. But surely she would run
across a settlement before then. A road or trail she could
follow. Somewhere down there was the Kaw River.
Maybe she'd come to a homesteader's cabin where she
could ask directions.

She would show both Prophet and Jesse Cole.

Setting her back to the sun she moved out. At first she
walked much too fast, muttering under her breath in
anger, but the pace soon tired her and she relaxed into an
easy rhythm, remembering the way Jesse had conserved
the horses' energy. Occasionally she sipped from her canteen, but never took too much for she feared dying of
thirst as much as anything. There would be streams
where she could drink her fill and renew her supply—
perhaps a well or spring or windmill, too, but she dare not
count on that.

By evening she had covered a lot of miles, and began
to search for a place to hide and sleep. Surely thanks to

Jesse, the posse had not caught up to her, but they could still crisscross the country and might accidently come upon her. She couldn't take that chance.

For three nights she used the north star to make her way south, always veering to the west. If she kept doing that, even if she missed Abilene, she'd come to the Chisholm Trail and then have a route to follow. She'd heard folks at Prophet's church talk about it, and now was glad she'd gone.

Though she ate sparingly, the food ran out. When she stopped the evening of the third day, she had nothing to eat. She drank from a small creek, then crawled into thick underbrush along its banks to sleep, her belly growling.

She'd been hungry before Prophet came along and made his deal with her father, but those days were only a dim memory. Still, she vowed that being lost, alone and hungry would not defeat her, for she was free. But if she ever laid eyes on Jesse Cole again, she'd be sure to let him know what a rotten no-account skunk he really was. She held on to that anger; it would keep her strong.

Upon awakening, she lay for a while watching the water flow and imagining the aroma of bacon frying and biscuits baking. Calmly she considered starving to death. One day someone would stumble across her bones, bleached white by the wind and sun and rain. Prophet would never know what had become of her, and soon wouldn't even care. Nor would her family hear of her fate. Such a forlorn thought brought tears to her eyes, but she swiped them away with doubled fists, washed hands and face in the cold water and crawled out of her hideaway.

The sun lifted over the horizon, so soon she should leave. Perhaps today she'd find a homestead at last. It seemed she had been walking forever. She couldn't have guessed how desolate the plains were, had imagined settlers living everywhere—soddies with grass growing on their roofs, children romping in the chicken-scratched yards, an old milk cow munching nearby.

Sitting beside the creek, skin and head itching as if they crawled with vermin, she decided to bathe before she continued on. In three days she had seen no one, not even an Indian, so there was no danger of being seen herself. Quickly she kicked out of her shoes, shucked off her torn dress and shredded stockings and waded into the cold water. Wouldn't Prophet have a fit, her out in the open before God and everybody, naked as the day she was born. The idea gave her a thrill.

Without soap, the bath might be less than perfect, but she scrubbed as best she could, using what was left of her dress to scrub the worst of the filth from her dirty skin. Dousing her head she rubbed at her scalp harshly. Teeth chattering, she finally waded out of the water and was struggling to put on the wet, torn dress when she heard a noise nearby. If she didn't know better, she'd think someone had giggled.

Ragged material clutched to her breasts, she called out. "Who is that?"

There came another series of giggles, then three Indian squaws and two small girl children appeared out of the shadows. She and Prophet had dealt with their share of curious Indians, some more frightening than others. These appeared to pose no threat, unless of course their men were nearby, of which there was no sign. That didn't mean anything, though. Indians seldom let their women and children travel alone, but they often allowed them to approach white people first. She studied their attire; leggings, long sweeping coatlike dresses open at the front, intricate beadwork. One of the younger women carried a child and she had opened her dress to bare breasts so the child could nurse more easily. They were probably Kansa from the Kaw nation, or Pottowatamie or Kickapoo; those were the names she'd heard Prophet mention most frequently.

Holding the hand of a petite and quite lovely girl child, the youngest of the three women stepped forward, pointed at Angeline's tattered dress and laughed behind her hand.

"Yeah, I know. But it's all I have," Angeline grumbled. "Maybe you could let me have one of yours." Turning her back she quickly donned her dress.

When she faced them again, four magnificent braves stood behind the women, their bare chests gleaming in the late afternoon sun, hair cropped into stiff brushes on top of their heads.

They too wore leggings, and an older one had a red blanket wrapped around his shoulders as if he were cold. None of them were laughing. Her heart flip-flopped, but she stood her ground. She squared her shoulders as they approached.

Jesse estimated he'd ridden sixty miles or so in the three long days since he'd left Angel. He'd crossed the Kaw River late the evening of the second day and camped for the night on its southern bank. The night before he'd shot a rabbit and roasted it before dark, putting out the fire to keep from being spotted. Merely a precaution, for he had no fear of the posse now. Figuring he was far out of Prophet's territory, he observed only the normal precautions of any man on the trail. Tonight he noodled a catfish lazing in the shallows and cooked and ate the sweet white meat, sucking the bones clean. After the fire burned itself out, he adjusted his saddle, lay down with his head resting on it and stared up at the stars.

Once more, as in the previous days and nights, the face of the young woman he'd deserted intruded upon his thoughts. He ought to feel good, out here on the open plains with no one to vex him. But he'd not figured on her haunting him. Sometimes she would speak out in the middle of the night until he awoke, expecting to see her sitting nearby pointing an accusing glare at him. He'd never before been so bothered by thoughts of a particular woman. Oh, he had a natural appetite and occasionally satisfied it, but that was different, more of a physical need that had nothing to do with his mind. This was different, and he'd made a mistake with her, looking deep into her eyes to search out her hidden passions. Now he couldn't rid himself of memories of the innocence he'd found there, of her touch, her smell, of the melodious soothing sound of her voice.

"Get away and leave me be," he grumbled, and pawed at his saddlebags, trying to arrange them into a sort of pillow. He felt strange, unfamiliar lumps in one, and opened it. Rolled up inside Angel's cloth were a dozen small drawstring bags. He balanced one in the palm of his hand, hefting it. It was heavy for its size. Fingering it open, he sprinkled out what felt like tiny rocks.

Excitement swelled in his chest and he scooted closer to the glowing coals, laying a few dry pieces of wood on the fire. In the light of the dancing flames, he gazed down in awe and dismay at a handful of sparkling gold.

Chapter Six

Elbows tucked against her sides, Angeline held herself stiff and scarcely breathed while the Indian women walked a tight circle around her. They smelled of wood smoke and wild flowers and a pungent aroma she couldn't place. It made her hungrier and her belly growled loudly. The children laughed.

The braves were tall and rawboned and carried weapons, probably for a hunt. They appeared peaceful enough, though stern dark eyes showed no amusement as they gazed beyond her, arms folded over their chests. There'd been no sign of an encampment. She'd heard many plains Indians lived in mud huts or hogans, but when they traveled they put up hastily constructed wigwams, different from the mammoth, intricately built teepee of the Sioux. These dwellings were simply brush that was covered temporarily by skins.

The oldest of the women clapped her hands smartly, jerking Angeline from her reverie. The others stopped their assessment of her to gaze upon their elder. She said something in a tone of command and two of the young women clamped Angeline by the upper arms and began to drag her away.

The children laughed and cheered. Obviously they were amused. She was not. The stoic braves watched her struggle and smiled behind their hands.

She fought her captors, trying to jerk away. "Stop, I don't want to go with you. Leave me alone."

It did no good. They were set on taking her somewhere. She only hoped they weren't going to stake her to an anthill or something equally terrifying. Surely these women would not allow the men to do something awful, like ravage her. Not where the children could see. But they were, after all, savages. Terror ripped through her, and she struggled harder. The older woman shouted a command into her face, the harshness of the words freezing her heart. The children stopped running around and shouting with glee; they grew quite somber and trailed along in silence as the group moved through the trees along the creek. Soon they broke out into a small meadow surrounded by a thick growth of cottonwood. There the Indians had set up their camp. Several wigwams formed a loose circle around a large fire pit. Racks of meat strips dried in the heat of a fire, their fragrance pungent in the air. A small herd of horses grazed in the lush grass. More men, women and children greeted the party, some pinching at Angeline's skin and tugging at her tangled hair while they chattered excitedly among themselves.

To her dismay, the two women ripped the remains of the dress from her body. Still, fear of what they intended to do made being naked a minor consideration. They tossed her to the ground, backed away and formed a circle. The women appeared to be in charge, but all the men gathered to watch and comment without actually entering into the game.

Crouching in the dust, the bright sunlight pounding down on her bare skin, Angeline felt like an animal about to be butchered. Her mouth dried so she couldn't swallow, her heart beating in her ears like hammered gongs.

Why didn't they do it and get it over with? Chop her into bits or burn her at the stake or beat her senseless. Anything but this. Afraid to look at any of them, she kept her eyes downcast.

A pair of moccasined feet shuffled into her field of

vision, then hands grasped her shoulders and dragged her to a standing position. She cringed, refusing to look at the woman, who was the very one who had led her capture.

The woman held out a skin of some kind, folded over her arms, and offered it. "You wear this."

When Angeline didn't take the gift, the woman punched her solidly in the chest with a fist, then spoke in an accented English so melodic it sounded like words to a song. "You must not go about without proper clothes." The gentle tone belied her actions, and once again she offered the gift.

This time Angeline took it, and saw that it was a buckskin dress, pale as cream and soft as butter. The woman draped it against her bare, dusty body, and signed she should put it on. Blue and red beads formed a colorful and complicated design on the bodice. The Indian woman lost her patience, yanking the garment away and lifting her arms high. Angeline matched the gesture, and the woman dropped the dress over her head. It flowed along her skin like water, caressing her breasts and belly and thighs, its fringed hem settling softly halfway between her knees and ankles.

Around the circle, women and children cheered and clapped while the men looked on. Another younger woman approached and held out a pair of moccasins in the same creamy color. Standing on one foot then the other, Angeline slipped them on. As she straightened, the fragrance of the tanned skin wafted about her, sweeter and more delicate than the leather of saddles. It too smelled of wood smoke. Both the dress and moccasins had been worn and she wondered who had given up their clothes for her, a stranger.

Tears standing in her eyes, she met the dark-eyed gaze of the girl who had given her the moccasins, then thanked her and the older woman. The girl smiled, touching the tangled mass of Angeline's golden hair, then her own

95

sleek black braids, and made a brushing motion with her hands. Angeline nodded, taking her offered hand and followed her to a wigwam. They sat on the ground outside the opening and the girl began to work through her hair with a lovely tortoiseshell comb. It took a while to remove all the tangles.

Before long they were laughing together, sharing stories with sign and simple words. The girl spoke some English and some French. Neither could pronounce the other's name, so they shortened them to something they could say and became Twana and Lina. Angeline learned that Twana was soon to marry an older brave who had lost his wife to a fever. The young man she loved was very angry about this, and had begged her to run away with him—a thing she could not do because it would destroy her father's honor.

Angeline sympathized. She told the girl she had fled an older husband and then been deserted by a young, handsome man. It took very little language for both to decide that men were not trustworthy, young or old, and a girl had to be very careful to whom she gave her heart.

Angeline remained with the them for two days while the men hunted buffalo. It was women's work to butcher, skin and prepare the meat they brought in. The elder woman, Silent Deer, taught her how to scrape the buffalo hides, but it was dismal, dirty and disgusting work. Angeline enjoyed most learning to string together patterns of intricate beadwork while sitting around the fire after the day's chores were done.

Sometimes in the evening they played games, boys and girls joining together in a friendly jostling kicking match to gain ownership of a gourd and kick it over a line drawn in the dust. Angeline wanted to play, but it was discouraged for young women, Twana told her.

After spending a day and night with the group—the Kaws, she learned—she realized how very poor they were. They were supposed to remain on their reservation near Council Grove, but had very little to eat without these hunting parties. Buffalo were growing more scarce as well, as was all game since the coming of the white man. The children were thin, some sickly. They lived mostly on buffalo meat and what roots, bark and berries they could find in the woods.

The tribe feared the day they would be sent to the Indian territory to the south. She listened to them speak—the old man, Hard Heart, and the younger Lone Coyote and Blue Moon Face, and others whose names she didn't understand. They spoke of how the white man had gobbled all the land for himself so that the Kaw were left with only a very small portion. With the railroads expanding, rails would soon cut the plains like steel ribbons, and the buffalo and other game would be gone.

She heard that stinking buffalo hides in piles the size of white man's houses waited alongside the railroad tracks in Dodge City for shipment, much of the meat left to rot in the prairie sun. It would not be long now before the white man finished off the Indian by starving him to death. The talk brought Angeline much sorrow.

On the morning of the third day it was time for the Indians to move on in search of more game. Angeline and Twana bade each other good-bye, and Angeline gave her new friend a bead necklace she had painstakingly fashioned. In return, Twana pressed into her hand the exquisite comb.

"For your pretty gold hair," she said with a smile that seemed almost sad.

For Twana to have given her such a gift brought even more sadness to Angeline's heart, but she knew to refuse would dishonor their friendship. She stood in the clearing long after the trailing line of Indians moved out of sight beyond the rise to the north. Twana was the first real friend she had ever made, and she would likely never see her again.

With remorse Angeline turned, picked up her bundle of

food, water and gifts, and headed for the trail that would take her to Abilene. The Kansa knew of the cow town from which railroad cars loaded with cattle departed each day and had directed her in the right direction.

She felt more secure now in her travels, for surely after all this time Prophet had given up in his pursuit. Nothing would lead him to guess she would go to Abilene. Topeka was much closer and more civilized. But Jesse had spoken often of heading for Abilene, and he had her gold. She would find him and he would give it back to her, even if she had to take a club to him.

Jesse tussled fiercely with his conscience. His cousin Johnny Ringo would have taken this gold and lit out, not sparing a thought for who it belonged to. All the men he'd ever known or admired would not have hesitated to make that choice. They all knew they were bad and acted accordingly. Jesse had always thought he was bad, but often had a hard time proving it to himself. He thought about that for a long while.

He remembered watching Angel play hopscotch, drawing boxes in the hen-scratched yard dust, her merry tones of laughter pealing like tiny bells blowing in the hot Kansas wind. Like a man dying of thirst gapes at a water hole, he'd watched her brush an escaped golden lock of hair off her sweaty cheek. Watched until his eyes teared with the intensity of it. Or perhaps he had cried because he could never have her or anyone like her.

Studying the handful of glittering gold dust, he thought of how she had cared for, comforted and embraced him. *Him*, a total stranger. He had to try to find her and give back the gold, see that she was safe. He would double back on his trail, then cut cross-country toward the place where he'd left her. From there he could follow her tiny footprints in the mud, unless it rained again. Sooner or later he'd catch up to her.

So, not fifteen miles out of Abilene he turned back, and actually found himself whistling as he rode, leading the buttermilk mare for Angel to ride when he found her. So intent was he on his noble quest that he didn't see the mounted man who waited in the shadow of a large oak tree beside the trail. It was Jezebel that spied the strange horse. She showed her teeth in a loud whicker.

Too late, Jesse reined up, then hunkered down to kick Buck into a full gallop back the way he had come. The man had a .44 pointed right at him, and let off a shot that whizzed past his ear, cutting flesh and sending a warm trickle of blood down his neck.

Jesse slapped leather instinctively, but the man's curt command stopped him.

"Name's Hickok. I'm a U.S. marshal, boy. Draw that gun, it'll be the last thing you remember. Toss it to the ground and climb down nice and easy. Don't mind a bit if I shoot you."

Cursing himself for a fool, Jesse did as bidden. He didn't know if he hoped the man was truly a lawman or a lying thief. Either way he'd probably take Angel's gold, and either way the fellow might put a bullet in him. Lawmen and outlaws weren't too far separated out here. But surely Wild Bill Hickok wasn't a back shooter.

Once on the ground, Jesse checked out the famous lawman. A well-built man in yellow buckskins, he had two pistols belted over his long fringed shirt. He wore a wide-brimmed hat and had long, yellow hair that touched his shoulders. His eyes were bright blue and flashed an intelligent humor.

"I heard you was out," Hickok said.

With no idea what he was talking about, Jesse kept his silence. He had a horse that wasn't his, and could easily be hanged.

The fellow nodded. "Mount up, then. We're riding into Abilene."

Doing as he was ordered, Jesse continued to say nothing while the lawman took his Colt and lashed his wrists to the pommel of Buck's saddle. Gathering the reins he mounted up and off they went, the buttermilk trailing along.

As they rounded a curve in the road, Jesse spotted up ahead the figure of a woman dressed in buckskins, her hair gleaming golden in the afternoon sunlight. Moccasin-clad feet kicked up dust as she walked briskly along the side of the trail. When they drew near she turned to watch them, and he saw with some surprise who it was.

Angel! Dread that the lawman would lump them both together overpowered his delight at finding her. He shook his head when her eyes lit on him, and hoped she'd get the message. She glared fit to kill.

The lawman touched the brim of his hat. "Howdy, ma'am. Where you going?"

"Nowhere," she replied, and continued to glare at Jesse.

"Must be going somewhere, or else why're you traipsing down the road in this heat?"

"I like to walk, that's why. You going to arrest me for that?"

"Nope. Thought if you were on your way to Abilene, you might as well ride this fine buttermilk mare this feller seems to have."

Jesse shot a quick glance at the lawman. Did Hickok know about the posse out of Circleville? He sure didn't act like it.

Angel stared up at Wild Bill. "He under arrest?"

"Yep, reckon he is. But that shouldn't stop you from taking advantage of a free ride. I'm William Hickok, ma'am, U.S. marshal." He took off his hat, tipped his head so his long curls bobbed, then put it back on. "I can guarantee your safety."

"Humph. I guess you're someone famous."

The man chuckled. "Could be I am, ma'am. Don't ever read much about myself, myself." He laughed heartily.

Angeline continued to stare at Jesse, without even the ghost of a smile.

Uncomfortably, he shifted in the saddle. "Could you two cut short this palavering so we could be on our way? It ain't exactly enjoyable being tied to a saddle."

She sent Jesse an impish grin. "Is this owlhoot real bad?"

His heart sank. She was going to do him in, maybe even have him arrested for stealing her gold. Hell, what was he thinking? He was already under arrest. How much worse could it get?

Hickok interrupted his train of thought. "This man is a bank robber and killer, ma'am. You'd do well to keep your distance. Just mount up there. Sorry I can't give you a hand."

Bank robber? Killer? Jesse gaped at Wild Bill. "Just who the hell do you think I am? I never robbed a bank in my life and I sure never killed anyone."

Angeline gazed at him. "What about the bank in Topeka? You said . . ."

"Dammit, that's a lie."

"Shut up, son. You know this feller?" Hickok asked.

"Uh, no, sir. I was just funning with him. He really robs banks and kills people? You know this for a fact?"

"Oh, yes, ma'am. Got a wanted poster and all. Spitting image, can't be anyone else. Hell . . ." He touched the hat brim, mumbled, "Excuse me, ma'am," then went on. "He no more'n got out of prison back east till he was back at his old tricks. Robbing and killing. I got me a real bad 'un. Now mount up so we can get out of this sun."

Hickok visibly enjoyed the show of legs when Angel made a running leap onto the mare's back. Jesse wanted to rap him one upside of his head, but was hardly in a position to do so.

Jesse saw Angel, now mounted, glance back toward him. "Oh, don't you worry, sheriff. I never listen to outlaws and the like."

"Marshal, miss. Not sheriff."

She nodded, but didn't say anything further, just continued to stare at Jesse as they rode on toward Abilene. He felt her eyes boring holes in his back. She'd never believe now that he'd been going to give her back the gold. Well, what the hell did he care anyway? He had worse troubles.

Angeline wasn't quite sure how to handle the situation. If the marshal put Jesse in jail, he was apt to find her bags of gold and confiscate them. She hated to think that Jesse might be a thief and killer, but managed to maintain her outward composure. Inside her emotions remained in a turmoil.

This man had snatched her out from under Prophet's cruel hand, and gone on to rescue her from those other awful men. Of course, they were after him in the first place, so maybe he felt a bit guilty about that. But he had taken her gold. And that just wasn't decent.

They reached the Kansas cow town toward evening. At the outskirts a sign declared. *No guns in Abilene. See Marshal Smith*. The name had been scratched out and Hickok scrawled below. Someone had shot a couple of holes through the center of the letter A. Ahead stores cast long shadows across the churned-up road. A glimmer of excitement filled Angeline at being in this notorious place. Even in a remote town like Circleville, everyone knew about Abilene. The destination of the Chisholm Trail, the growing settlement offered bawdy entertainment to the cow hands who drove the tens of thousands of cattle up from Texas to be shipped by train to the markets back east. It was known to be wilder than Hays or Dodge City.

After the marshal tied the horses to the hitching rail out front of the rustic jail, Angeline slid off the mare and picked her way through the mud to boards spread in front of the row of buildings. Warily she watched the marshal untie Jesse and lead him into the jail. He had left the saddlebags hanging over Buck's back. She could hardly believe her luck, and ducked quickly under the rail, laying her hand on the leather. She was fixing to pull the bags off and run when Hickok's voice came from the doorway.

"Just fetch them in here if you don't mind, missy. Probably got his last loot in there."

For a moment she froze, not daring to even glance in the marshal's direction. If she did, he'd see what she planned written plain on her face. Instead she yanked off the heavy bags, flung them across her shoulder and took off running. Heart hammering, she shoved through a crowd of reeling cowboys and past the batwing doors into a saloon. Inside it was so dark she stumbled around tables and ran into patrons on her way to the back in search of a door. Frantic, for she expected any minute that a huge hand would descend and grab her up by the nape of the neck, she dropped to all fours and crawled through leather-clad legs. The heavy bags slipped off her shoulder to drag along the rough floorboards.

Above her, men stepped aside, some laughing, others cursing, but for the most part they let her be. Finally she came up against a wall and began working her way along it. There must be a door there somewhere. At last her searching fingers felt the jamb, she reached upward to the latch and released it. Tumbling through, she shoved the door shut behind her, only to discover she wasn't outside, but inside a dark, windowless room. And from nearby came masculine grunts and moans and an occasional feminine cry. A bed creaked, and dry husks crackled. Someone was in bed, and in the middle of the day. Two someones, from the sound of it. And they were . . . either enjoying themselves or suffering enormously.

She hunkered back against the closed door. Hands over her ears, she rocked back and forth, eyes squinched tightly shut until the action reached its crescendo and ceased.

Judging by the way she'd felt during her brief encounter with Jesse, sex might make people feel that good. Or maybe they were each putting on for the sake of the other. No matter, she doubted either of the participants would be happy to find her there. She had to get out before she was discovered and tossed out, probably right into the arms of that marshal. She caressed the leather bags. Her gold was safe, all she had to do was sneak out of town without being caught. She needed to find someone who would sell her a horse and be on her way. She would be free at last.

The heavy breathing across the room settled down. The woman murmured something Angeline couldn't make out and the man laughed. They were getting out of bed. They'd find her!

Glumly Jesse stared through the bars of his cell, which didn't even have a window. In one corner a cowboy slept off a drunk, snorting in his sleep. Another sat on the floor, knees drawn up, head between his hands. The place smelled like a hog sty. And he saw little chance of getting out of there except to be led to the gallows. Bank robbery and murder. Prophet had a long reach indeed. And what had happened to Angel? He'd heard Hickok shout at her, then, because he had Jesse to deal with, the lawman had reluctantly locked him in the cell before running back out in the street.

God, he hoped she had found her gold and got away. He'd brought her nothing but trouble. It didn't make him feel better to know he'd warned her.

Hickok came back after what seemed like hours, and

headed right for the cell, fury darkening his eyes. "You no-account. The two of you was in cahoots. What'd you have in them saddlebags, the money you stole from Dodge last month?"

Jesse let out a sigh of relief. Angel had the gold. Now, if he could talk himself out of this. "Marshal, I haven't been in Dodge in years. Who puts me there?"

Hickok yanked a folded poster off his desk, smoothed the creases and jammed it up against the bars. "This does. You saying this ain't you?"

Speechless, Jesse stared at the likeness, read the description that mentioned the strange color of his eyes, then rubbed at the thin scar that ran across the bridge of his nose and above the right brow.

The marshal watched the gesture, looked back at the drawing. "Could'a got that since this was done."

Grabbing the bars, Jesse stuck his nose through to give Hickok a good look. "This look new to you? I've had it since I was a whelp. My old man liked to knock me around, busted this open when I was no more'n ten or eleven."

"Only your word for that," Hickok muttered, but Jesse could tell he was thinking hard. "Besides, who could look this much like you 'cept you?"

Fear crawled up Jesse's spine. Who indeed? Who but his brother Charlie?

Angeline skedaddled back through the saloon in much the same way she had entered, only this time she was pursued by a half-naked screeching woman and a barefoot man pulling on his pants. All around her punchers shouted and laughed in delight at the sight of her scurrying through the crowd pursued by a naked whore.

"What'd she do, Lula, steal yore man?"

"Run, young'un, if you value yore hide."

"Next time, Lula, make sure who you got in yore crib."

The taunts followed them through the swinging doors

and out into the center of the muddy street, where Lula gave up wading ankle deep mud in favor of taking high ground, screeching and waving her arms about.

Before the marshal could come out to see what all the hubbub was about, Angeline scampered into the first alley she came to. After a few minutes everyone went back to their business, and though the street remained noisy, it was obviously the normal way of things in this untamed town.

In a few minutes she crept out to the front of the building that backed up to the Alamo Saloon and faced another street that fronted on the railroad tracks. A sign out front proclaimed Novelty Theatre. It seemed this town had everything. But she wouldn't have a chance to take advantage. If she wasn't careful she might become as much a wanted criminal as Jesse Cole.

Scampering along the side street, she stationed herself behind the jail where she could watch what the marshal did with Buck and Jezebel, who were still tied to the hitching rail out front. She didn't intend to walk out of town if she could ride. Might as well steal a horse that was already stolen. What could they do to her, anyway? No more than hang her. If she tried to buy a horse they'd likely tell the marshal and she'd be caught, anyway. Best to wait till dark and take the gentle buttermilk mare.

Hickok came out a while later and led the horses to the livery stable across the way, remaining inside a while, then came out and strolled down the street, thumbs hooked in his belt. He strutted like he owned the town, and she guessed he did. She watched as he approached two armed men and lit into them loud enough for her to pick up a few of the shouted words. The men put up a fight, but Marshal Hickok laid one out with the barrel of his revolver, and disarmed them both.

Illegal weapons bundled against his chest he disappeared into the Alamo, one of the countless saloons along Texas Street. The man still standing helped his friend to his feet and they followed the marshal through the swinging doors. Now, it seemed, they would all share a drink and a few laughs together as if nothing had ever happened.

Dusk had darkened the alleyway, and so she sneaked into the shadowy street. Lamps were lit as darkness crept across the prairie to engulf the town. She glanced toward the jail. Had Hickok left someone there to guard the prisoners? Why did it matter, anyway? She was going to get out of this place, fast as she could.

But Jesse was in there, locked up, and she couldn't imagine that he had murdered anybody. He'd had a chance to kill Prophet and hadn't, had even let those mangy outlaws go. But he had taken her gold, she reminded herself. She wasn't sure what to think, but despite his desertion a few days ago, she could hardly bear to think of him behind bars. His sad eyes hid plenty of secrets, but she didn't think he was a thief and a killer. Look how he had treated her when he could have taken advantage of her desperation. She shuddered to think what could have happened to her—and even Prophet—had he been really bad.

But he had deserted her! What a dilemma she faced.

Quickly she glanced one last time in the direction of the saloon where Hickok had disappeared, then made up her mind and slipped across to the jail. It was gloomy inside, the desk up front empty. A gaping door led into a back room, and probably the cells. She headed for it, still afraid there might be a deputy about. The stench of the windowless cells sickened her. If there was a deputy, he wouldn't be in there. She took a chance and hissed Jesse's name.

There was no answer right away, so she spoke aloud.

A voice answered. "Yeah, here. Who's that?"

"It's Angeline. Jesse, are you in here?"

"Course I am. Where the hell else would I be? Question is, what're you doing here? You ought to be miles away by now."

"Don't know it. But I couldn't . . . I mean, I had to . . . I couldn't leave you here to hang."

His sigh swam to her through the murk. "Did you find the keys?"

"No, I didn't look. I wasn't sure . . ."

He was silent as she trailed off, but when she didn't continue, he spoke up. "You weren't sure I'm not a killer? Well, I'm not."

"You could be lying to me."

"Then why the hell did you come back, Angel? To gloat?"

"No, of course not."

"I reckon if you're not going to get me out of here, you'd best be going before Hickok comes back and flings you in here with me. I don't think you'd like that too much, Angel. It stinks in here, and I'm not alone."

"I can tell it stinks." She paused, then thought again about backing away and fleeing into the night like a wild thing. "Jesse?"

"You still here?"

"Jesse, promise me you didn't kill anyone. Swear it by the Bible."

"Jesus Christ, Angel."

"Don't, Jesse. Don't talk like that."

"Ah, Christ. Get out of here, Angel. Leave now. You and I, we don't have any business together. Let them hang me and be done with it. It's all bad blood, anyway. None of us are any account, don't you know that? Now get out of here before you get caught. Ride that little buttermilk out of here and don't look back."

"Swear you didn't kill anyone."

"You are the most stubborn . . . Okay, Angel, I swear I never have killed anyone except in the war, and for what it's worth, I never robbed anyone either. I was lying to you before about the bank in Topeka."

She swallowed hard. How could she decide what to believe? He lied, then he didn't, then he did again.

"Oh, Jesse." She moved to the cell bars, wrapping her fingers around his where they clutched the iron for dear life. And the moment she touched him, knew she was going to set him free.

"I'll be right back, Jesse. Wait right here."

"Where would I go?" he asked, then gave a sound like a chuckle. She couldn't tell if he was amused or sad.

In the outer office, she searched the top of the desk. In the growing darkness she had to feel her way along. No keys. She opened a drawer, scrabbled quickly through the contents. Nothing.

A voice she didn't recognize said from the darkness of the cells. "They're hanging on a peg over on your right as you come in."

She could barely make out anything in the room.

"Angel, it might be a good idea to hurry." It was the same voice that had told her where to find the keys. Somebody else was in there with Jesse, and he wanted out too. She was suddenly very afraid. What was she doing, putting herself in such a dangerous position?

Her fingers lit on a nail, then the ring and a huge skeleton key, and it was too late to back out. She held Jesse's freedom in her hands and would never forgive herself if she deserted him now. Even if he rode off and left her once again, she had to let him go. Could not be responsible for him being hanged.

Quickly she moved into the dark, felt around for the keyhole and poked at it with the long metal key. From outside she heard footsteps approaching along the boardwalk. She froze until they moved past the front of the jail, then struggled to unlock the door. Finally the inner works clicked and turned. She stumbled back as the door swung open.

"Hurry, let's get out of here before . . ."

It was the man who'd directed her to the key, but he didn't get to finish, for someone came in the front door and slammed it shut. The marshal had returned, just in time to catch them.

Chapter Seven

At the sound of someone entering the sheriff's office, Jesse grabbed Angel and yanked her into the cell, shoving her behind him.

"Don't say a word." He carefully eased the door closed and pulled the key out, dropping it into his boot. Then he took a deep breath, shuddering against the distraction of her warm breasts pressing against his back.

In the other room, a match scratched and a lamp flared, its weak glow trickling into the cell. The other prisoner hunched outside the bars in the narrow walkway, hugging the wall where dark shadows played with the flickering light. If Hickok, or whoever was out there, came in, all hell would break loose. They were suspended between freedom and capture, and one wrong move could get them killed.

A rivulet of sweat ran down the small of Jesse's back. Against him, Angel trembled, breathed raggedly. He concentrated on the hard-edged outline of the saddlebag pressing into his shoulder blade, ignored the steady beat of her heart, her firm breasts rising and falling. She had her gold. They were square. But first they had to get out of this place with their hides intact, make it to the livery, and find the horses and ride faster than the hail of bullets that would chase them. It was all pretty hopeless. Damn, he had to get her out of this.

Why the hell had she done such a stupid thing as come back for him after what he'd done to her? Didn't she know you had to take care of yourself first? No one else

110

was going to do it. Before he could consider his next move, the prisoner outside the cell made one of his own.

Faster than a snake striking, the cowboy barreled through the door into the lighted front room with a whoop and a holler that must have taken Hickok totally by surprise, for after a short scuffle, the cowboy shouted, "Y'all get yore tails moving and do whatever it is you was about to do, 'cause I'm gone from this place. I'm going back to Texas where a man can have a little fun without going to the hoosegow."

The fading of his racing footsteps removed their doubts.

Jesse dragged Angel from the cell, hesitating only long enough to grab up his pistol and another from the desk top. A quick glance at Hickok, crumpled in the corner out cold, and they were gone.

Outside Angel yanked him in the right direction. "Horses are over there in the livery. Come on."

They hurried up Texas Street, sneaking through the splatter of light from the windows of the Alamo Saloon and keeping to the shadows. Once inside the stable, he pressed up against the wall, listening while he quickly strapped on his Colt and stuck the extra pistol down in his belt. There was no hoopla yet, just the noisy hilarity of cowboys having good times in the saloons that lined the street. Wherever they were going, they'd better do it and quick. It was just a matter of time before Hickok came to and put out the word. Their lives wouldn't be worth a plug nickel then.

Inside the dark barn, Angel grabbed his hand. "In here." They slid into a stall alongside the mare. The gelding poked his head over the next stanchion and whinnied at Jesse. Saddles hung over the head-high dividing rail. After mounting up they hesitated only a moment in the doorway, then he nudged Buck and headed for the shortest way out of town, west past the jail and away from the

111

Chisholm. They'd head south later, cut the trail at some point. The cowboys in those saloons up and down Texas Street were itching to have some fun, and chasing him and Angel would qualify.

Crouched along their mounts' withers, they thundered past the jail and around the slight curve that led through a stream. Out of the water and on they rode, into the moonless, starless night. Far to the southwest lightning flashed and thunder rumbled. The horses galloped on, breath chuffing, bodies lathered in sweat.

After some time Jesse sensed his huge gelding slowing, knew the mare with her shorter reach would soon give out completely. They had to stop, but first they had to get off this road. If a posse were after them, they'd search every barn, house and shed that might offer shelter. Ahead the hulking shadows of trees meant a river, and not one of those measly little creeks either. The road dropped along the bank. He reined up and shouted at Angel, who did the same.

On the banks of the river a storm overtook them, and in a flash of light her wide eyes stared at him out of a pale, frightened face. Circling wind lifted her hair in a crazy snake dance.

"We'll follow the river. Rain's coming, it'll wash away our tracks." He dug in his heels to lead the way. The mare would follow, even if Angel grew too tired to urge her on. The buttermilk liked this old proud-cut gelding.

Above their heads cottonwood leaves chattered in the rain-sweetened wind, their great limbs swaying and creaking. He hoped one didn't come crashing down. From the low-hanging clouds streaks of lightning cracked like demon's whips. Hair stood out on his arms and the air smelled of the devil himself. An elongated rumble shook the very earth beneath their feet, setting loose torrents of rain. They had to get off this slippery riverbank and to shelter. Soon. But he saw noplace to go.

And so on they rode, hunched against the driving rain, cold and soaked to the bone.

Angeline clung to her mare, thighs and knees aching with the effort. The buckskin dress Twana had given her weighed heavily on her shoulders. She could barely make out the horse and rider ahead. Jezebel slipped in the mud, then scrambled for her footing and regained it. Alongside the narrow path the rushing water chewed great chunks from the bank and threatened to swallow them up.

She swiped water from her eyes, squinting through the trees. Surely someone lived along here somewhere. There must be a barn or an abandoned soddy or shack, anything where they could get in out of the storm. They saw nothing for what seemed like forever. The rain continued to come down, though the lightning and thunder had abated some. A brilliant flash revealed what looked like a small group of houses or structures of some kind in the distance. In the ensuing blackness they vanished. Had she really seen anything? She shouted at Jesse, but her voice was lost to the storm. Staring at the spot, she waited for another flash. When it came she made out a cluster of houses but no lights. There were either no windows or everyone was in bed.

Urging Jezebel forward, she caught up with Jesse, shouting at him again and again, until he finally heard. She pointed. "Over there, see?"

He reined in and both stared. After some time he said, "Must be the Kansa Indians. We ought to be getting close to Council Grove, and their reservation's around here."

"Let's go there, get out of this rain."

"Are you crazy? Why should they help us?"

"They will, Jesse. Come on."

Before he could stop her, she prodded the buttermilk up the slope and across the rain-swept meadow where she could better make out what appeared to be small stone

113

houses. White man's work, surely. Horses whickered from a nearby corral. Through the piercing wind and rain came the thin cry of a baby. Outside one of the buildings, she slid weakly from her horse and approached the dwelling before Jesse could stop her. With both fists she hammered on the door.

After a while someone came, pulling it open a crack. A dark eye gleamed there.

"Are you family of Twana? Is Blue Moon Face here, or Hard Heart? Have they returned from the hunt? I'm Lina, Twana's friend. Can we come in? We're cold and wet."

All she could see was the shine of a face, dark, wide-set eyes. It seemed like a long while before the door swung inward.

"Angel, our horses. Ask what we should do with them." Jesse's voice reflected a bone-tired weariness.

While they waited for a decision from inside, the lightning and thunder slid off to the northeast and the rain let up some. A tousle-haired young man stepped through the doorway, pointing toward the corral without a word. Angeline took the saddlebags off Jezebel, glaring at Jesse. She wasn't about to turn him loose alone with the gold again. He'd probably ride off like he had before. With a shrug Jesse rode toward the corral, leading the buttermilk.

While he was gone she spoke briefly to the young man, and learned that the hunting party had not yet returned. Several family members had roused, anxious to hear news of them. Jesse returned to stand in the open door, rain-soaked and exhausted. The need for news outweighed any reluctance the Kansa might have had to admit these white people, and so they allowed them entry. Some of the family members, like the hunting party, spoke a smattering of French and English, as well as their own tongue. Though conversing with them was difficult, it wasn't impossible.

114

A small fire burned in the center of the room, its smoke rising through a draft hole they'd knocked in the roof of the white man's house. It was almost too warm inside, with a dozen or more people gathered there.

After Angeline told them all she knew of the hunting party, the eldest woman of the family showed her and Jesse a buffalo robe spread in a narrow space on the floor. It would be their bed for the rest of the night. She signed that Angeline should remove her buckskin dress and drape it near the fire so it could dry, then pointed at Jesse's wet shirt and indicated he should take it off.

Angeline wanted to object about the sleeping arrangements, but was too weary to do so. She could have slept propped in a corner with a bear for company if that had been the only option. Her shoulders drooped with the weight of the drenched buckskin, and her skin itched. Taking it off posed a problem, for she wore nothing under it. Perhaps she could get a blanket. The old woman finally understood and fetched her one.

"Turn around," Angeline said to Jesse. He had removed his shirt, but was tussling with the woman, who seemed to think she could remove his wet pants.

"Tell her I don't want to take off my pants, Angel."

"You tell her, you can talk as well as I."

"She's not listening." He cupped the woman's hands in his to stop her fingers from working at the buttons of his fly. "No, I'm fine this way," he said.

Taking pity on his plight, Angeline touched the woman's shoulder. "Help me, please?"

The woman finally left Jesse to his own devices and held the blanket to shield Angeline while she removed her wet buckskin dress, no mean feat. She was panting by the time she managed the task, and meekly submitted to being wrapped in the red blanket. She didn't think she could stand upright much longer and yearned to sink down onto the buffalo robe. Finally, she did so.

* * *

By the time Jesse lay down by Angel's side, everyone had settled down once more to finish out the night's sleep. He sprawled on his back, head propped on one arm. Angel's nearness prodded at him, and he tried not to think of her naked under her blanket. His wet pants clung uncomfortably to his legs, and after a few more minutes he quietly unfastened them and slipped them off, pulling a corner of the robe over his own nakedness. The fire had gone out and it was black as nine kinds of pitch in the crowded house.

Sometime during the night Angel turned over and draped one arm over his bare chest. The act brought him awake abruptly. Someone had rekindled the fire and it flickered, casting dancing fingers of light over her breasts and pale belly that had been bared in her sleep. He gazed at her for a long time, then tentatively brushed a finger over the satiny skin of her neck.

She was so beautiful, and so at his mercy. He licked his lips and thought of tasting the tantalizing flesh, trailing fingers over the mound of her breast. In a rush of passion such as he'd never known, he wanted her. But he'd seen her playing like a child, listened to her speak of childish desires not yet satisfied. He wanted her to have that life. His desires were simply wickedness compared to what this beautiful innocent girl truly needed.

He hated the way she made him feel, for he could love her so easily. Lying beside Angel, even the search for his brother's killers paled in importance. For a bittersweet moment he cupped one firm breast tenderly in his palm, his eyes closed to snatch at a dream of something he would never have.

She stirred, and he jerked his hand from the rosy nipple, gone rigid under his touch. To his dismay she moved closer, snuggling her head against him and sighing, her breath warm on his skin. Her leg slipped upward, flesh

116

brushing flesh, and her knee cradled at the root of his unbidden desire. He bit his lip, closed his eyes and brought himself under control.

It was no easy task, but he wasn't, after all, an animal. And she was the sweetest, most precious thing he had ever known. He would die before he hurt her, kill before he let anyone else do her harm. The idea that he could ever feel that way about any human being was beyond his comprehension. It terrorized him in a way not even the threat of death could. He intended to get far away from her—and as quickly as possible. He closed his eyes, allowing for a brief while longer the impossible dream.

Angeline awoke snuggled against Jesse, the red blanket draped over her arm and his chest. Her bare leg curved across his naked thigh, and the buffalo skin covered them both from the waist down. Against her sleep-warmed body, his flesh felt firm, the muscles hard. She was afraid to move. If she awoke him, what would he do? His chest twitched under her hand and he shifted, turned a little toward her so that an expelled breath fanned her cheek. An exquisite feeling erupted in the pit of her stomach. He put a leg over her, entwining them together. Against her stomach, his manhood pulsed like a heartbeat. She drew in a jagged breath. What would it be like, to have him inside her? The mystifying throbbing he evoked enticed her.

He appeared to be asleep, breathed as if he were. But a part of him was alert. She wanted to touch him there in that mysterious place, but was afraid.

He made a small sound down in his throat and opened his eyes, then unwound in quick jerks that separated them, and threw back the buffalo robe. For an instant she caught sight of his nakedness. He was magnificent and quite frightening. She couldn't help but stare.

Then the moment passed and both scrambled to cover

themselves, to look away, to stammer. She hated that he no longer slept coiled around her, and wondered if he felt the same.

Standing a few feet away, a small boy gazed somberly at them. His presence startled Angel. How long he'd been there she had no idea.

"Good morning," she stammered to the child.

She had slept the night with a man. Naked. Had he done anything to her? Would she know? Surely she would have awakened if he'd tried anything.

"Good morning," Jesse grumbled, like he thought her words were meant for him. He didn't look at her and she was glad, for if he had she didn't know what she would have said or done.

The boy continued to stare in silence, not in the least perturbed by their state of undress. Quickly, she wrapped herself in the blanket.

Everyone else had risen, rolled their night robes and left the dwelling. The child sucked on his finger, then pointed at the fire.

There on a stone sat a bowl filled with some sort of gruel, maybe pemmican or something similar, obviously left for the two of them. The child indicated the food again, and stood guard as if it might get away.

"—Jesse?"

"—Angel?"

They spoke at the same time, and he let her finish.

"Did you . . . ? Did we . . . ?" She clamped fingers over her lips.

"Yes?"

"Yes, we did? Oh, no. Why, did you . . . ?"

"No! Of course not. Don't you think you'd know?"

She wanted to say yes, but she wasn't sure. She hoped that she would be too ecstatic to remain sleeping should he make love to her, but how could she know? When she glanced his way, he had swiveled to pull on his pants. She gazed at his backbone and the mounds of his buttocks resting on the buffalo robe. Then he stood, giving her a quick view of more bare skin before tugging his pants up around his waist. When he turned, the fly was unbuttoned at the top. Coils of dark hair spilled in a narrow line down the flat belly. She couldn't help dropping her gaze to where that line pointed. Scowling, he adjusted himself with one hand, then did the buttons up, all the while watching her.

Speechless, she stared, then uttered a breathless little sound. Her heart fluttered, a flush crept up her throat where she continued to clutch the red blanket.

"What?" His golden eyes regarded her through lowered brows and his thick auburn hair was mussed from sleeping. Muscles rippled across his shoulders and upper arms when he put on his shirt, which had dried beside the fire.

The small boy watched with wide eyes as Jesse picked up the bowl of food and held it out to Angel.

With a foolish grin Angel dipped in two fingers and scooped up the mix. "Thanks. I'm starved."

The child watched raptly while she chewed the stuff. It tasted musty and a little bitter. "Are you hungry?" she asked the boy.

Jesse took some, then chewed with an odd expression and handed the child the bowl.

He snatched it, scraping the gruel directly into his mouth. He paused, once, darting a look at Angeline and Jesse, then continued ravenously, gulping down every bite then licking the inside of the bowl. After that he licked his fingers.

Jesse swallowed noisily, made a face. "The poor little fellow's sure hungry to eat *that* stuff."

"They all must be."

Jesse's expression as he watched the child brought a lump to her throat. Something or someone had broken his heart, perhaps his spirit, and it was badly in need of mending. Even as she realized this, she felt incapable of doing so herself. To get her mind off the odd emotions, she glanced around. The interior of the house contained an odd mixture of Indian and white man's furnishings. Though there were no beds and mattresses, there was a work table with a few utensils. They cooked over the open fire on the dirt floor.

The little boy turned and ran outside, leaving the door standing open to a sunny day.

Jesse led the way from the house, which smelled of poverty and the odor of too many bodies. "How did you know they'd take us in?"

"I wasn't sure, but I met up with a small hunting party, and a young girl befriended me, gave me these." She indicated the buckskin dress she now wore instead of the red blanket, as well as the intricately beaded moccasins and the tortoiseshell comb twisted in her hair. "She told me they were Kansa, and so I thought they might give us shelter."

Jesse shook his head at her innocence. He had to cut loose from this girl as soon as possible. Who else would just simply assume that a tribe of Indians might assist them? All he wanted to do was fetch the horses and ride out. But Angel had other ideas. She headed toward a young mother sitting outside another stone house, a fussing child at her breast. Impatiently, he watched as she knelt to talk to the woman. They talked for perhaps four or five minutes before Angel returned.

"We need to ride into town."

"What for? What we need is to light out before that Hickok fellow catches up to us. He'd like to put us both somewhere and throw away the key. Hell, he'd like even more to hang me."

Angel glanced around, and for the first time Jesse took a good look at the Kansa village. Obviously, white men had built the small stone houses here on the reservation. They were crowded rather close together. A few scraggly chickens scratched listlessly in the dirt yards, a couple of bony dogs ranged, and some poorly clothed children played. Everyone went about their business without energy or joy.

"They're hungry, Jesse. That mother doesn't eat and so her baby isn't getting what he needs. I want to go back to town and buy some food for these people. It's the least we can do. They took us in. Strangers."

"Believe me, Angel, they won't thank you. How's that going to look to them? A white woman giving them charity. It'll make them angry."

She whirled on him. "Maybe the men, Jesse, but not her. No mother is too proud to feed her child, no matter how she has to do it."

"Maybe. What're you going to use to buy this food? Your precious gold?"

She stared at him, then nodded angrily. "That's exactly what I'm going to use. What good is it otherwise?"

"Angel, listen to me. This isn't a good idea. These men will be very angry with you."

"I don't care. I can't help it. Are you going with me or not? Doesn't matter to me, one way or the other."

"Dammit, Angel. I'm going with you. Of course I am."

"Well, then. Come on."

She flounced away from him, and he couldn't help but grin at the determined set of her shoulders as she walked briskly toward the corral. She would, by her very actions, cause him to remain involved, make him care in spite of himself. These Indians were doomed; what possible good could it do to bring them some food?

At the general store in the town of Council Grove, Angeline purchased several cones of dark sugar, bags of flour, cornmeal, and beans, a heavy slab of side meat and a dozen cans of milk, then added coffee and tobacco for

121

the men. While the clerk fetched and wrapped her purchases she found some red and blue ribbon. On the counter in a large glass jar were some hard candies, and she had the clerk fill a sack.

Jesse looked on with a frown. What would the poor little tykes do when that ran out? Better if they never had it, as to get a taste of something they knew damn well they'd never have again. But he kept silent. It wouldn't do any good to tell her. He'd already tried. For someone so young, Angeline sure had developed her a stubborn streak. It wasn't his place to break it. Instead, while the clerk weighed out the gold she presented, he carried the sacks out to the horses.

On their way out of town, he told her grumpily, "You ought to be using some of that gold to buy us . . . I mean yourself some supplies. Might buy some underwear. I noticed you're sadly lacking in that department. And some blankets to put under these saddles. And the buttermilk's bridle is a sorry outfit. It doesn't bother me, but it'd make it easier for you to ride. This must be hell on your . . . uh, well, you know, your legs and all, hiking that dress up, and nothing between your delicate skin and that greasy old leather."

"I swear, Jesse Cole, if you won't say just about anything that comes to your mouth. I never knew a man would bring up a woman's unmentionables like that. I'll have you know there's not one woman in ten in this country that would bother with underwear. All those highfalutin women back east might think wearing all that frilly stuff is smart, but we don't. As for riding this horse . . . well," she lowered her gaze, then smiled resignedly. "I could use something between me and the saddle. It is a might uncomfortable." She turned the horse around.

Less than an hour later, they mounted up once again, but this time each had a blanket spread under the well-worn saddles, and a new bridle for the buttermilk. Plus they carried food supplies of their own.

Angel's Gold

They spoke little on the ride back to the reservation.

Angeline reined up in front of the house where the young mother lived, rapped on the door, and signaled Jesse to bring the supplies. He did so, placing both gunnysacks next to her and taking a few steps back.

The woman opened the door still holding her fussing child. A tall, rangy brave, bare to the waist but wearing leggings, approached from across the way.

Watching him out of the corner of her eye, Angeline gestured to the supplies. "I brought some food for you . . . for the baby. To make bread."

Bending over, Angeline hefted out the cloth bag of flour, another of cornmeal.

The woman's dark eyes darted from the offerings to Angeline's face, then over her shoulder to the brave.

He roughly pushed past Angeline, almost knocking her off the tiny porch, and spoke harshly to the woman, then turned abruptly and swept one arm in a wide gesture.

"Go. Out. Leave."

Angel ducked and Jesse, thinking the man was going to hit her, stepped between them.

She tugged at his sleeve. "No, it's all right. He's just upset. Let me talk to him."

"Oh, he's upset all right. Angel, I warned you."

The brave reached down, yanking up the sack as if it weighed nothing, and dumped the remainder of the contents out in the dusty yard. Cans of milk bounced through the dirt. He kicked at the other sack, then shouted something harsh, first at Angeline then at the woman with the baby.

"Wait, look," Angeline cried, and grabbed up the package of tobacco. "I brought *you* something, too. See, tobacco." She sniffed and pantomimed smoking a pipe. "And coffee." Scrabbling around, she came up with the red Arbuckle coffee sack.

She knelt there, looking up at the scowling Indian

brave, her heart beating so hard in her throat she could scarcely breathe. But she didn't back down, because behind him, in the doorway, stood the woman and her hungry child, tears making tracks down her flat cheeks. She had not uttered one word since the brave approached. This was her husband, Angeline supposed.

He stepped off the porch, then took the tobacco and sniffed it.

"To thank you for your people's kindness to us last night," Angeline said in a steady voice, though inside she trembled so badly she was afraid her legs would give way and dump her on the ground. She gestured from her chest in an outward motion toward him. "Thank you for helping us. Share with the others."

"You're welcome," he said gruffly. "I understand the white man's tongue, but never his motives."

She bowed her head. "Often the white woman's tongue speaks a different truth than the white man's."

There was a long silence, then he grunted and began to pick up the scattered packages of food. "Not only the white woman's. All women. We thank you, and offer our hospitality."

"I wish I spoke your tongue as well as you speak mine," Angeline said. "We would be glad to join you for breakfast and coffee, wouldn't we, Jesse?"

She cocked her head in his direction, but didn't exactly look at him, afraid she would stick out her tongue in an I-told-you-so gesture.

"Oh, yes, indeed, we would."

The tone of his voice told her how he felt about the proceedings. She stifled a chuckle. It was no time to get involved in one of their disagreements.

Inside the gloomy house they introduced themselves, and were told that the couple, who were husband and wife, were Horse Keeper and Genevieve—she being the daughter of a French trader and his Kansa wife.

The Kansa were no more than six hundred strong now, the brave explained, and would soon go to the Indian Territory to the south. Soon they would disappear, he told them matter-of-factly, then stared somberly at his wife and child and did not look back at his white visitors.

Angeline knew that, by bringing the food, they had only prolonged the inevitable for a short time, and she wished she could do more. Before they left she stuffed a small pouch of gold in among the sacks of flour and meal, then followed Jesse to the corral. From there they mounted up and rode from the impoverished village. Once again, she felt foolish about the pity in her heart for her own circumstances.

Chapter Eight

Angeline watched Jesse in silence as they rode from the village of the doomed Kaw. His jaw clenched, he stared straight ahead, no sign of sympathy in his expression. What had gotten into his soul that had so hardened him? Why couldn't he open himself to emotions? He was alone, fighting whatever awful thoughts filled his mind and heart, and that's the way he wanted it.

He must have sensed her watching him, for he turned and said in a flat voice, "Everybody suffers, Angel, everybody dies. It's the way of things. You'll only be miserable if you don't face up to that, look out for yourself."

"How can you be so harsh, so unfeeling?"

"It's how I've survived." He looked away.

Along about noon, with the sun high in the sky, Jesse called for a break near a clear stream surrounded by lush grass. Sitting beside the water they ate sparingly while the horses drank and grazed in the deep shade along the bank, their teeth tearing and chomping at their own meal.

The long silence got on her nerves, but Jesse didn't seem ready to carry on a conversation. He lay on his back, arms crossed beneath his head, and didn't look at her when she asked, "Do you think they're still after you?"

After a long pause, he replied, "Someone's always after me, might as well be them as anyone."

"I mean, tracking us now, this minute."

Jesse laughed, but it wasn't a happy sound. "No tracking to do after that rain washed everything away."

The prairie wind continued to blow, howling through the cottonwood trees.

Angel's Gold

"Where will you go?" she finally asked.

"I'm not sure. Dodge, maybe. Had it in my mind to inquire after some men while I was in Abilene, but that didn't work out too good. Sure wish I knew more about who Hickok thought I was."

Angeline glanced quickly at him. "We could find out."

"I can't show my face around there again."

"We could change your looks, or better, I could change mine. Go in and nose around, see what I can find out."

"Why would you want to do that?"

She sat up, then leaned over him, forcing him to meet her gaze. "You're the most irritating man I've ever met. I want to help you."

Patches of sunlight flashed in his eyes, the color of the gold she carried. Disbelief crossed his handsome features. "I don't understand what you hope to get out of this. You think I'm going to do something for you? I've already told you I'm not taking you with me."

She looked all around, then back at him. "I'm already with you, Jesse."

"Not by my doing," he mumbled. He looked vaguely uncomfortable.

"Oh, come on. Let me see what I can find out. He'll never know I'm in town, and if he does I can talk my way out of it. I'll say I don't know you, never did. He'll believe me."

"No. We're too far away to go back. Besides you're going to stay at the next place we come to. You can use that gold to buy passage on a stage, to go wherever you want. I'm heading back toward Circleville. Those men know something about my brother and I need to find them, to learn what it is."

"Jesse, they'll kill you. They almost did once before. Why do you have to go back *there*?" She wanted to argue with him about leaving her, going someplace where she dared not follow, but saw the futility of that.

"I've been thinking a lot about what they said. Maybe

127

my brother's not really dead. And if he isn't, I have to find him. He's the only family I have, surely you understand that. As for the gold, they could've made that up."

"Then why is Hickok looking for your brother?"

"Said he killed some people. I don't know."

"Just like he thought you killed someone."

He darted a quick glance at her that made her nervous. "I didn't, though."

"Well, maybe he didn't either. Maybe you shouldn't be so angry at him. Maybe he didn't do anything."

Sighing, Jesse sat up and stared into the distance. How could anyone always see the good and never the bad? If only he could believe she might be right, but he'd seen the look on Charlie's face the night he beat Zeke nearly to death. If Jesse hadn't stopped him, Charlie would have killed the old man. It wasn't much of a jump to suppose he had killed those renegade Confederate soldiers to get his hands on a wagonload of gold. And if he had, what had he done with it? And why in the world hadn't he already got it? Though, maybe he had, and those men didn't even know it. Charlie and the gold could be long gone.

"Jesse?"

Angel stood over him, the noon sunlight haloing her loose hair. An ache stirred in his groin, warning him of trouble to come, and he forgot all about Charlie. He swallowed thickly, rolled over and stood with a slight grimace. His damn leg still bothered him some, but the pain brought him to his senses.

"Yeah, we'd better be on our way. I can leave you at the next homestead or put you on a stage in the next town. Up to you."

When she didn't reply he turned to take a furtive look. She was so young, so beautiful, even in her sorrow and despair.

Cursing himself for a fool, he said, "Well, what's your

128

answer?" His voice sounded gruff, even to him, but that was for the best. Kindness had no place here.

Her azure eyes sparkled with unshed tears. "I don't know where to go."

The helplessness made him feel pity and that made him angry. He wanted to tell her to go home. To shout at her, "*Go back where you're safe, where you have food and clothing and a roof over your head. Where nobody is chasing you, where nobody like me can get their sinful hands on you and turn your life sour.*" But he didn't. Instead, he just nodded.

"Well, hell, come on. Let's ride. We'll come up with something." He dragged his gaze from the grateful look she gave him. Just the kind of thing he didn't want to deal with at all. Her gratitude.

It was a long way to Circleville, and he aimed to make the trip alone. Anyway, she couldn't go back there, and that settled that. Prophet would have her in a minute.

Charlie rode west on Grant Street, past the hulk of what looked to be a big school of some kind, standing black and silent in the moonless night. Past the churches and the Circleville bank. There he paused and let the horse stand for a long while in the center of the dirt road while he pondered all the possibilities.

He liked to ride into a strange town at night. It gave him a chance to look things over without being observed. The rinky-dink bank offered definite possibilities even if the place was an end of nowhere town. What in hell had Jesse come *here* for? But he was here, or at least had been. He sensed him, just like when they were kids and played that silly game of hide-and-seek. One never could hide from the other.

It had been a long ride from the prison in Albany, New York, where he'd served six years for mayhem. All he'd done was ride into every saloon in Ellsworth, wahoo

129

them old boys and shoot a few holes in the ceiling. Maybe they'd made up that mayhem charge. Anyhow, they put him away, and coming back he'd made a few detours to fill his pockets with money. Ill-gotten gains, the law called it. Or maybe just more mayhem.

And then, when he had finally crossed the border into Kansas, worn out, thirsty and in bad need of a woman, the first place he'd stopped, he found out his brother was kicking around this part of the state. Talked some in his sleep to a whore he'd been with. Jesse always was a weird kid.

Poor, helpless Jesse. He ought to've taken him along in the first place, toughened him up to the life. Together, they'd have been the scourge of Kansas and Missouri, just like the James brothers. Old cousin Jesse and his brother Frank was sure tearing up Ned all over the border. Once reunited, Charlie and Jesse Cole could do the same. Maybe even best them, who could tell?

A thrill of excitement prickled at his skin. Coming here was dangerous as hell, him being wanted in Abilene. He'd seen the posters in Topeka, didn't look much like him, except for that business about the eyes. You'd have thought it wouldn't make much difference in Kansas. Wasn't much law here, but there was enough to run him down and really hang him this time.

He moved on through town and crossed Elk Creek. There he rode into a grove of trees and made camp for the remainder of the night. In the morning he would find Jesse or learn where he'd gone. Apprehension lay coiled in his stomach like a nervous rattler, but he could hardly wait to be reunited with his twin. What an expression old Jesse would have on his face when he learned Charlie was alive, if somebody hadn't told him already.

Early the next morning, he rode back into town. A place like this likely had it some weak-livered sheriff. Surely they couldn't afford much.

He reined in at the general store where he tied his

mount and went inside. His sweet tooth was killing him, and if he didn't get some horehound candy soon, he'd go mad. Wonder if they had a wanted poster of him here, like just about every other place he'd been? And what about Jesse? If they still looked the spitting image of each other, his brother might be hiding out or in jail already. Let these folks get a good look at him, Charlie thought, and he'd soon know something about his twin.

The gloomy interior of the mercantile rendered him almost blind for a few seconds until his eyes could adjust. A potbellied man stood behind the counter, wearing a white apron. Charlie had him measure out a nickel's worth of candy, then studied the enormous pile and nodded with anticipation that nearly made him drool. That ought to do him a while. He held out the nickel between grubby fingers, but as the clerk reached to take it the bell jangled on the front door. The man's eyes nearly bugged out of his head, and Charlie whirled, his hand going for the gun he'd stolen down in Topeka a few days earlier.

"Do it and you're a dead man," a stern voice said. A heavyset old man wearing a badge pointed a .44 at Charlie's gut. And he looked like he could shoot him with little effort. Nervous lawmen were the worst, they were apt to pull off a shot even if you didn't do anything stupid.

Charlie spread his hands out at his sides. Didn't matter much if the old geezer locked him up. There wasn't a jail made in any hick town he couldn't bust out of. He might be crazy, but he wasn't stupid enough to get shot when he didn't have to.

A white-haired man he'd barely noticed earlier out on the street hovered just behind the sheriff.

"That's him," he said, pointing a bony finger.

"Looks a good deal like him."

"You're blamed right. That's the vermin on that wanted poster in your office. Probably one of the men that stole

131

my Angeline, too. Make him tell you where she is, sheriff, before I beat him half to death."

"Now, Mr. Prophet, you don't want to do a thing like that. We don't know he took your wife. You, son, you stand easy. Pull your gun out and lay it there on the counter."

In disbelief Charlie eyed the lawman, the familiar glint in the eye, the twitch of the fingers on a trigger that might be touchy as hell. This old fart could well shoot him without even meaning to. He did as he was told. He'd been right. The whole state was after him.

Charlie Cole was out of prison and back in Kansas. By now everyone knew he hadn't been hanged. All bets were off and he would be made to pay for the killings five years ago. Sure as hell, though, he didn't know nothing about snatching some old man's wife. The possibility that Jesse'd been up to no good came and went. The old fart was blowing smoke, pissed cause his woman had run off. Likely hot to blame it on the first man they arrested. Unless he'd changed a lot, his twin wouldn't have ever desired to steal some woman, and even if he did he wouldn't have the guts.

As Charlie walked across the street ahead of the sheriff and the crazy-acting old man, he experienced a rare twinge of regret for what he'd done to his brother. He didn't give a damn about the old man or what had happened to him and his kin, but Jesse, well that was another story, and he'd come all this way to make it up to him somehow, someway. The only way he could think of doing that was to let him in on the gold, though, if and when he ever found him. But first, he had to get out of this little spot of trouble.

Once they settled in for the night, Angeline lay wide awake for a long while. She'd spent so much of her youth roaming around while Prophet slept, that she found it difficult to sleep nights and would often doze for several hours during the day, rocked by the gentle movement of the buttermilk mare. They'd ridden a roundabout route back toward Circleville without coming across a homestead. The country was so vast that even though thousands of settlers were moving west on the Santa Fe and Oregon trails, settlements were still few and far between. As they rode, out of necessity they stayed away from commonly traveled routes that would just naturally lead to a house or town. It would take a while before they reached Prophet's stomping grounds, but she dared not go there. She feared Jesse would leave her soon, no matter where he had to dump her.

In the stillness, embraced by the songs of night creatures, she wrapped up in the blanket and slipped from camp, through the sheltering trees onto the open plain. Gazing upward, she let the wrap slip from her shoulders into a shadowy puddle around her feet. Stars spread like shattered glass across the dark sky. There was no moon to pale their shine, and she reached up a hand that glowed ghostlike in the light. Some appeared close enough to pluck and she imagined doing so, gathering them in her arms, a bouquet of forever.

The air was filled with the scent of meadow grass and wildflowers and the nearby creek, along with the musky smell of the horses and the dying campfire. She'd bathed in the cold water soon after dusk and later heard Jesse doing the same. She'd wanted to peek at him naked, but resisted the temptation.

He'd made it so very clear that he didn't want anything to do with her, that she dared not nurture the feelings that grew stronger within her every day. They were feelings she must deny, because he would leave her soon and she'd never see him again.

Jesse awoke with a start, one hand raised to block the leather strap Zeke swung. He panted, wiping perspiration from his forehead, and sat up. You'd think a grown man

133

could control such a childish reaction, he berated himself. How long would he be haunted?

He glanced toward Angel's bedroll, then moved on hands and knees for a closer look. It was empty! His heart raced. Dear God, where was she?

Barefooted, he moved about the perimeter of the camp without finding her. Heart in his mouth, he finished a second complete circle. Confusion boggled his mind. He should be relieved to have her run off, but not knowing what happened to her was unendurable.

At last, he spotted her through the trees, a dark silhouette in the starlight, reaching for the sky and swaying slowly like a graceful dancer. His throat nearly closed from the sight of her naked body in the act of some kind of dreamy worship. He glanced back at the camp, expecting to see both himself and Angel in the bedrolls asleep, for surely this was a dream.

But no one lay beside the dying fire, and when he searched the plains once more Angel continued her graceful dance. He moved carefully toward her, making no noise in the wet leaves. The soft ground muted his approach so she didn't hear him, and only realized he was there when she pivoted in his direction.

Frozen, she gazed toward him, arms still uplifted, hands like delicate white birds suspended in the night. Shadows and starlight played over her exquisite body, the delicate mounds of her breasts shining silver. A shimmering trail touched the softness of her belly, drifted briefly into darkness, then slipped down her legs, slightly spread for the dance.

Sure that she was an illusion and him still dreaming, Jesse closed his eyes, shook his head then took another peek. She remained poised like a marble statue. Then she reached toward him and called his name sweetly. Beckoned.

Mesmerized, he moved toward her, capturing her hand.

It was so small and soft and cool in his. He lifted the palm to his mouth, tasted the pure flesh with the tip of his tongue, and knew he was lost. This dream, so much better than the nightmares, enclosed him in a bright light that warmed his cold heart.

With gentle fingertips she massaged his temples, appearing to float into the circle of his essence, staggering him. He wrapped her in his arms, gathering her close as if she were precious and fragile; clung to her to keep her from disappearing into nothingness; lifted her effortlessly against his trembling body. With a joyous heart he sank to his knees in the aromatic grass and lay her there, spread out like a delicious banquet. His moist lips brushed each nipple, the hollow of her throat, the flat of her tummy, while his fingertips followed in tender caresses. Her hands were trembling, but she reached under his shirt and traced the skin over his stomach.

In breathtaking silence, he continued his exploration, each kiss more deliberate, until at last he found her mouth.

That first meeting of their lips consumed him, and Angeline opened her eyes in wonderment. Stars reeled across the sky leaving trails that lit up the night. Her beauty captivated him. She moaned and he made a sound down in his throat that echoed her desire. His intense need swirled almost out of control as Angeline pulled him down to lie beside her; they curled as one together, limbs entwined.

His fingers brushed through her long hair, wove silken webs, captured his dreams, then gave them back to him like a gift. Could this be? Loving this woman, lying in her arms, drinking her sweetness? He took her breath and held it within himself, as if he had never drawn air before. Dazzling as the stars above, life-giving. He could not have this. It was too much; it could not last.

She caressed his lips, eyes, the flesh of his desire, her

fingers light as butterflies, demanding as the whisper of prairie winds. He rose to her, nearly exploding with a passion so new and bright and intense as to threaten his sanity. And he could not go back to what was—would die with the sheer agony of it, refused to believe he could not keep what she offered.

For another instant he held her so close their flesh briefly joined and became one. Then he released her, enclosing her hands in his and laying them over her breasts. A sadness filled him, the taste bittersweet. For a brief time he had loved and been loved, and he knew it would be even harder for him to survive without it, now that he knew its wonder. The memory might one day destroy him. Tears rolled from his eyes and he hid them in the darkness, then turned from her, rose and walked away. No one would ever see him weep.

Not a word passed between them. The sound of her forlorn crying followed him back to camp, where he crawled in the bedroll. It was, after all, only a dream. He could do nothing about it.

Chapter Nine

She had slept far into the morning, as if she would never awaken, and Jesse dared not go near her. Not after last night. So he broke camp, strapped on Buck's rig and, carrying the mare's saddle, led the horses through her tall grass. At a great distance, he glanced over his shoulder toward her small, still form. Every fiber in his being wanted to race over, take her to his heart and never let go. His dark, evil side urged him to mount up and ride off, put her memory away in a deep hole where it could never escape—down there with all the other ghosts he couldn't face.

But he could not do that, either. For some reason he might never fathom, he knew if he did that she would haunt him forever with those accusing blue eyes. It was one thing to deal with memories of Zeke and a bitter childhood, quite another to desert her and have to live with that guilt.

They had to get a move on. With a heavy heart he left the horses and walked to the unmoving shrouded figure. Sometime during the night she had wrapped herself up like a cocoon. A mass of golden curls spilled from the blanket. He would shout her awake without touching her or meeting her gaze.

She had rolled up her dress and placed it and the moccasins on a nearby log, and he picked them up, holding them against his beating heart and imagining her in them, sensing her there. Glancing down at the tightly wrapped bundle, he used her full name for the first time since the devil's whirlwind had chased him into her life. He would call her Angel no more, though that fit her so well.

He called out several times before she stirred, threw one arm wide, and uncovered herself. Blades of grass clung to one firm, bare breast. Oddly abashed, he turned his back, leaving her for safer ground.

Weary and sad, Angeline climbed out of the darkness. Something about the previous night filled her with remorse, and when she looked up and saw Jesse standing a good distance away, gazing out across the prairie, she wanted to go to him so they could touch. But he left her no time.

Before she had time to awaken properly, he told her his plans. "You can catch a stage at Junction City, before we get too close to Circleville. No one will know us there."

"I was afraid you'd leave," she noted, her voice smoky with sleep.

He shrugged and held out her dress, bundled around the moccasins, and kept his eyes pointed at the ground. "I said I'd see you to safety."

Quickly she covered herself, but when she started to rise, approach him and take her clothing, he let it drop to the ground and retreated to the waiting horses. There he remained while she dressed, and each time she glanced his way he was staring out across the prairie. She might not have existed.

Except he hadn't deserted her. That was something.

Every moment of the previous night hovered crystal clear in her memory. He had found tenderness within himself—she had seen it in his eyes. Now he felt embarrassed, or perhaps angry, she wasn't sure which. As for herself, she wasn't at all surprised by her own feelings, for she had known they were there, lurking beneath the surface of each lonely day she lived. They held the promise of a priceless gift yet to come, but one which seemed unreachable. If she and Jesse had consummated their feelings the night before, he would be bound to her forever, in spite of his feelings to the contrary. Perhaps he felt that was a trap she had baited with great care.

After dressing she handed him the blanket and he spread it on the mare's back, saddling the horse and carefully placing the bags that contained Angel's gold. She looked long and hard at him, but he refused to return the favor. Hitching her dress high on her thighs, she mounted without any help, then rode into the sunrise, keeping it a bit to her right so she was headed in the appropriate direction. How much longer dared she remain with a man on a mindless quest to get himself killed, even if she did care for him?

He hung back for a while, but when she approached the Republican River surrounded by thick growths of trees he hurried to catch up. Side by side they stared at the raging water, muddy and treacherous. Storms had made it treacherous, much deeper than when she had crossed it after leaving the Kansa hunting party.

"How deep do you think it is?" Angeline asked, not really expecting an answer because he hadn't talked much all day.

For a while he studied the terrain in both directions, checking out the far banks to the S-curve where the wide stream bent out of sight. "Stay here and I'll see if I can find a safer place to cross."

The buttermilk grew nervous watching the water and tossed her head, doing a little backward dance—probably remembering the storm and fording the Elk. Dismounting, Angeline led the animal in tight circles, talking to her until she settled down. She didn't much blame the mare, for the idea of fording that river spooked her too.

After a while Jesse returned. "Down yonder it widens out but looks a mite shallower. Might be easier to cross. Can you swim?"

"Swim? No."

139

"Too bad. Well, best then if we let the horses do the swimming if there is any to be done, and just hang on. Don't turn loose, you'll be okay."

Fear filled her. Would he let her drown without a second thought? Lifting her chin she followed, not bothering to climb back on the buttermilk. By the time they reached the crossing he'd chosen, her legs trembled so badly she could hardly walk. The roar of the river filled the air, like a hungry beast that senses it's about to be fed.

Jesse checked the cinches on both animals. "They can swim. You can't. Grab hold and don't let go."

Miserably she nodded and followed him. Buck snorted and kicked out, startling her mare, who backed up a ways and reared, pawing air high above Angeline's head. Jesse snatched Jezebel's reins, settling her.

"Stick your arm through here," he said, indicating the stirrup. "And don't let go. She'll see you safe on the other side, just hang on tight and pray."

Without waiting for a reply, he led Buck into the raging water. The buttermilk tossed her head, screamed into the air and launched herself after the other horse. Angeline matched the horse's scream, but had little time to dread the crossing before she was plunged into the frothing eddies.

As the bottom disappeared from under her feet, she kicked and clung to the swimming horse. Water filled her mouth and nose and she gagged, sputtering, and tried to keep her head high. She would no sooner get a breath of air than another wave would swamp her. The current sucked at her, trying to pry her loose from the stirrup. Her locked arm burned like it might be jerked from her body, so violently did the river toss her about.

The buttermilk swam on, undaunted in her pursuit of Buck, who it appeared was more than halfway across. Something was wrong, though. Buck appeared to be moving away from them rather than getting closer. Frantically, she kicked her feet, shouting at the mare. They were being washed with the current, heading for the curve in the river. Her valiant little horse kept swimming, but the harder she worked, the farther downstream they were dragged.

The last Angeline saw of Jesse and Buck, they had moved onto the far shore, a gentle slope that compared badly with the steep bank beyond the curve. There both sides were steep, heavily covered with brush and trees that leaned into whirlpools of debris. A tumbling log narrowly missed hitting them.

The buttermilk was tiring, breathing harshly in her effort to reach shore, and Angeline considered turning loose and fending for herself. But she couldn't swim, didn't even know what to do. She would go under and die, and the thought brought a black dread. In all her short life, she'd never pondered the possibility of actually dying. It was terrifying.

But she had a decision to make. Stay with the floundering mare or strike out on her own. She eased her arm loose from the stirrup, but continued to hang on with both hands a moment longer.

"Dear God, help me," she prayed. Then she held her breath and let go.

But at that precise instant the mare stumbled. Her feet had struck bottom!

Pawing to grab hold, Angeline went under, surfaced, and felt the fender slide through her fingers. The mare heaved its shoulders out of the water, found purchase with its back feet and scrambled through the mud, slipping and sliding. Frantically Angeline clawed at the saddle, and finally managed to grasp the dangling stirrup and hang on.

She looked up and saw Buck and Jesse on the high bank. The mare would never get up there. It was too high! Much too high!

"Let go, Angel. Let her go. I'll get you." She barely heard his shout above the roar of the river.

He slid down the muddy embankment and into the waist-deep water, grabbing her about the middle, and she saw that he had a rope tied to Buck's pommel and looped under his arms.

He dragged them both out, slithering and sliding through the black mud and shouting at Buck to back off. Sorrowfully, Angeline watched the valiant little buttermilk mare wash on down the river, its head high, feet still working.

Jesse deposited her on her hands and knees, and covered in mud, she dragged in great mouthfuls of air. Coughing, choking and spitting out river water, she mourned the loss of the mare. Please, she prayed, let the horse get out farther along.

Next to her, Angeline saw Jesse lying on his back gasping for breath, gazing up into the sky.

At last he sat up, then wiped a cupped hand down across his face. It left a great smear of black mud behind. Then he gazed at her, covered from head to toe in the gooey stuff.

She raised her head to meet his stare. His eyes glittered out of the mess like he still felt pretty annoyed about her causing so much trouble, and she suppressed a giggle.

"What's funny?"

"You're all muddy."

"I wonder why? Look at yourself."

The beautiful buckskin dress looked more like lumpy chocolate than pure cream. She wondered if the slime would ever come off. Her arms and legs were streaked as well. But they all worked, every finger and toe, hand and foot. She could even breathe again.

Relief coursed through her. They were alive—battered and filthy, but alive. Once again she laughed, then crawled to him, wiping a finger down his cheek and held it out. A great blob of soggy black river silt hung there. She rubbed fingertips over his lips to clean them. His gaze captured hers.

He slipped his fingers through her muddy hair, entwining them at the back of her neck, and then pulled her close. His breath fanned her skin, still chilly from the cold river water, and she leaned into a kiss that tasted at once gritty and smooth.

Covered in mud, they rolled into the grass, locked in an embrace that sent shivers through her. Or was it just the cold? His body, wrapped around hers, radiated an intense heat, and she soon grew warm.

Jesse slid both hands down her hips and over her thighs, and he found the hem of the wet dress and peeled it upward, turning her over to tug her bottom half free. Then he went to work pulling the buckskin off over her head. He said absolutely nothing, just grunted once in a while with the effort.

Afraid she'd break the spell, Angeline uttered not a sound, but complied with his efforts in every way she could, raising her arms to allow easier undressing.

The afternoon sun scarcely touched them in this thicket of growth alongside the river. She could scarcely make out his features, masked as they were, but the shine in his golden eyes set her on fire.

Her handsome protector tossed the dress aside and ran his hands down the length of her, slowing to rub mud from each erect nipple with the tips of his thumbs, then moving on. At last his fingertips spanned the swell of her hips, his thumbs resting at the base of her stomach, rotating and exploring. She could see his desire. Her skin felt wet and slick as an otter's, and that made the touch of his hands that much more powerful.

She was on her knees before him, her arms still upheld as if reaching for the heavens, eyes closed, awaiting whatever it was he would do with her. Jesse lowered his mouth to hers, and Angeline wrapped around him, moaning with pleasure. Suddenly, passion seemed to wholly overtake him and he threw her to the ground, tore at his pants to free himself, then poised astraddle of her.

Gazing up at him, Angeline felt a flicker of fear. But despite it, she caressed him with gentle hands, not knowing what else to do. Her soft touch seemed to drain some of the savagery that had overwhelmed him.

He collapsed beside her, one arm lying over her stomach, and she felt that he was trembling. "Angel, I'm sorry, so sorry."

Hushing him, she cuddled close, pressed fingertips to his temple, lips to his cheek.

"I would never hurt you," he told her after a few moments had passed.

"I know."

"But I frightened you."

She nodded but kept silent, wrapped in his warm arms.

"This is why you mustn't stay with me, Angel."

She stiffened but didn't pull away. "This would seem a good reason for us to stay together. The way we feel about each other."

"But it isn't. We have bad blood, my family. We're all born to raise hell and die doing it."

"That's stuff and nonsense." Though her words sounded childish, she stuck to them.

The chuckle her reply brought obviously surprised him as much as it did her, and for the moment, she simply enjoyed it.

After a while resting in his arms, she asked, "How did your mother and father have you without making love?"

"They didn't. Of course, they didn't. What a foolish thing to ask."

"Well, you don't want to make love to me because of your family's bad blood. Why did they think it would be okay?"

"How the hell should I know? Too stupid to give a damn, I guess."

The harsh reply made her shudder. Bad blood, he'd said. It was true that under certain circumstances he quickly became another person. Worse, she never knew when to expect it.

He went on, voice dull, like he had memorized the story and omitted all emotion. "Our parents left us. They didn't want us in the first place. We were an accident, Charlie and I, and they threw us away. You think I want to do that to a kid?"

"No, of course not. So, we wouldn't do that. If we had children we'd love them with all our hearts and souls."

"I don't think I could. Love someone, I mean."

"You love me." She spoke simply, for she believed it was true.

"Dammit, what makes you think that? I've never said so." He released her, then sat up and hugged his knees with both arms, eyes hard and bright.

"You do love me, Jesse Cole, and I can prove it."

"How could you prove a thing like that?" He appeared so angry with her that she didn't know if she should continue. Yet she couldn't stop, forging ahead because she sensed that her very life depended upon it.

"Easy. You saved my life and wouldn't let go even when we both could have drowned. Why would you do that for someone you didn't love—put your own life in jeopardy? You're tough and stubborn, but softhearted."

He glared at her. "Hah! Hah! Softhearted?"

A tiny smile curled her lips. "Protest all you want. I don't care. I'm on to you."

If Jesse never looked at her again, everything would be okay. Every time he so much as glanced her way, nothing good came of it. Or perhaps all that came of it was good,

145

and that he couldn't handle. She'd cast some kind of spell over him, and though he hadn't drowned in the river, he sure as hell could drown in the depths of her shimmering blue gaze. And if he let himself go down, he'd never come up; he'd be lost forever.

There she was, naked, all covered in mud lying in the grass smiling at him like he was some kind of a great man. What did he have to do to convince her otherwise?

Standing, putting his clothing back together, he spoke harshly. "Goddammit, you're going home. Right now, before this goes any further."

That did it. She scrambled to her feet, eyes flashing blue icicles. "You can't make me unless you're going to tie me up, so don't start this again."

"That, Angel, is a hell of an idea."

Hands on bare hips, she backed away. "You wouldn't dare."

Raising his shoulders, he sighed. "No, I wouldn't."

"So much for your bad blood," she sneered. Then, like a child, Angeline stuck out her tongue, grabbed up her muddy dress and ran off through the woods toward Buck, who had moved away to graze and give them privacy.

She and Jesse rode downstream for a long while, looking for the buttermilk, but never found her. Angeline cried against his back as they traveled along the shore, mile after mile, without spotting the mare.

"She's dead and gone, because of me," she finally whispered into the fabric of his stiff, dirty shirt.

"It was the river done it, not you. Don't be foolish, and for God's sake stop crying. Nothing lives forever. No sense in crying over it."

After a while she stopped, but she kept her cheek against him and both arms around his waist. Buck moved at a leisurely pace, for Jesse wouldn't run him with both himself and Angeline on his back.

* * *

They arrived in the small settlement of Cody Grove late that night, looking as much like vagrants as was possible. The place had no law, just a few buildings, some shacks and soddies where families lived, and a natural spring where an enterprising young businessman had erected a bathhouse. The proprietor did not allow mixed bathing, though, so Jesse let Angel go first. Sometime later, their clothes and skin scrubbed, they ate beans and steak at the only eating place, a saloon with planks suspended between two whiskey barrels for a bar and a dirt floor. Angel handed over more of her gold in payment for the food, and they bedded down outside town in a grove of cottonwood because there was no boarding house or hotel.

"In the morning," Jesse said, "we'll find a place for you in town. Someone will be looking for a girl willing to work, you'll see. I've got to go on, Angel, you see that."

She nodded. She wouldn't fight him any more. He seemed to surely believe that was the only thing either of them could do. Still, in her heart, she knew that somehow, someway, she would follow him when he left.

That night he slept as far away from her as possible, and though she intended not to shut her eyes for one moment, for fear he would sneak off and leave her, she fell into an exhausted sleep.

But apparently, bad dreams paid Jesse a midnight visit, for he leaped from under a nightmare, the young child he'd once been crying out in anguish. Awake and bewildered, Angel crept to his side and wrapped her arms around him. He shook so hard she could scarcely hold on, but hold on she did, and finally he rested his head on her shoulder and quieted. His breathing eased, and he allowed her to try and chase away his demons.

Yet with hands meant to ease his torment, Angeline felt the ridges of scars on Jesse's back. She'd felt them before

147

Samantha Lee

but hadn't asked how he got them. She couldn't help but wonder who had beaten him and why.

Men like him, living the kind of life he did, came up against all kinds of dangerous situations. But that he had been whipped until it left scars seemed surprising, even for his lifestyle. It would take some pretty strong and determined men to put Jesse Cole in a situation where they could beat him. Perhaps that was what had caused his night terrors. She continued to hold him until he quieted.

With Jesse in her arms, Angeline felt safe. Even though they had stripped naked to allow their clothing time to dry, she felt natural in his arms. His warm hard muscles were pressed against hers, burning into her, and she felt his arousal behind her. Still, he was fighting it, so she would too. After a long time, Angeline's desire began to fade to exhaustion, and she lay, her back spooned against him. She fell asleep with him holding her, as if it were the most natural thing in the world.

Charlie watched an elderly man shuffle past the single cell he and some drunken sodbuster shared in the Circleville lockup. The place he'd been put by that hick sheriff Oursler. A homely little gal dressed in faded homespun had brought supper about an hour earlier, slabs of fried beef and beans and biscuits. Charlie ate all of his and most of the sodbuster's, who was a little green around the gills.

A combination of whiskey and the stench of the bucket in the corner was enough to turn almost anybody's stomach, but Charlie had seen and smelled worse. If he'd learned anything riding with Quantrill when he was just a young buck, it was to eat what you could get and sleep when it was safe—but never unstrap your gun or take off your boots.

He peered toward the old codger the sheriff had sent in to watch the place while he went home for some shut-eye. If the man was a deputy, he'd eat his left sock. He

148

didn't even wear a gun. Charlie's was in the bottom right-hand drawer of the desk in the corner, he'd seen Oursler put it there.

The old man raised shaggy brows in his direction, but didn't come close. Charlie moved his mouth without saying anything, and the old man cupped an ear.

"Cain't hear you, son." He took a couple of tentative steps forward.

Charlie mouthed some more.

"Heh? Speak up, boy. I don't hear so good." Another few steps.

He could almost reach out and grab the old fart.

Clutching his stomach as if it pained him, Charlie opened his mouth.

The deputy must have thought he'd gone stone cold deaf by this time. He moved within reach, and Charlie had him. Jerking the fragile arm so hard a bone snapped, he slammed the screeching man backward against the bars.

His neck broke with as little effort as the arm, and as the old man sagged lifelessly to the floor, Charlie hooked the key ring off his belt loop. With a quick glance toward the sleeping farmer, he unlocked the cell door, shoved the inert body aside and went for his gun.

He knew where his brother was now, knew it as certain as if Jesse had left him a note. The talk he'd overheard between Sheriff Oursler and that Prophet fella about tracking him to the cattle trail was enough; he knew where his brother would go, and he knew why.

Within five minutes Charlie Cole was riding southwest toward Abilene, catching up with Jesse. He could feel his brother in his heart and in his head. And he would see him soon.

Arms held Angeline snugly when she awoke. She lay very still for a moment, orienting herself to the roar of the river and the cottonwood's song in the prairie wind, that and the sweet smell of honeysuckle. Memories of the night before returned, of what had put her in Jesse's arms in the first place. She lifted the hand that lay across her hip, then wiggled free of his embrace and sat up. When she turned, Jesse's golden eyes gazed at her, troubled but steady.

Quickly, she looked away. They lay in the shelter of trees, the open prairie to one side, the engorged river on the other. Her dress and his clothes were spread on some nearby bushes and a campfire let off feeble tendrils of smoke. She remembered being naked with him, kissing, touching . . . she tingled at the thought. Had they . . . ? No, what, she had recalled was from the day before, when they'd climbed from near death in the river and ended in each other's arms covered in mud. Last night he'd been cool, and following his lead, so had she, until he'd awoken her by screaming out in terror. She glanced over at him.

Blinking those incredible eyes, Jesse rolled over and hooked his pants from a nearby bush, nonchalant. "Sorry I disturbed you. Did you get any more sleep?" Without waiting for an answer, he pulled the pants on, keeping his back turned.

She tried not to look at the flash of his bare behind, but didn't succeed. His broad, bronzed back, with its brutal crisscross of white scars, rippled when he buttoned up and eased into his shirt. "Are they dry?" Her voice crackled and she cleared her throat.

"Yep, good and dry." His voice was a bit hoarse, too. He was running his fingers over the buckskin. "This wind'll dry anything." He tossed it to her and she slipped it over her head, stood to smooth the buttery deer hide down over her hips and thighs. It was not much the worse for wear, considering.

"We ought to sleep in our clothes from now on," he said sharply.

"If we can keep them dry," she remarked with a pertness she didn't feel. Maybe she could cheer him up, get his mind off leaving her. He *had* said "from now on." Her heart leaped with hope. Yesterday he'd talked of leaving her in Cody Grove. Maybe he'd changed his mind.

"Want to eat before we go into town?"

"We don't have much left. Maybe we can buy some supplies there. The store might have a few things."

He shot her a sharp glance. "I'll probably go on to Topeka, buy my supplies there."

Her throat closed. "But I thought maybe I could go with you. Cody Grove isn't very big. I'd have a better chance in a town like Topeka."

"Angel, how many times must we go through this? You can't go with me." He hefted Buck's saddle from their bedroll, whistling up his hobbled horse and beginning to ready it for the trip.

She ran after him. "Aren't you even going to make coffee?"

"Nope."

She touched his arm, felt a tremor and his muscles tense. She would not cry. Angeline took a deep breath and swallowed two or three times. Tears burned her eyes but she blinked them back.

"All right. Leave me here, go on over to Topeka where everyone is looking to shoot you on sight. Get yourself killed, I don't care. Ride on out, don't even wonder what happened to me. But you will, Jesse, you know you will. You love me, you just don't know it yet. Maybe when you finally do, it'll be too late. What if I died and you didn't even know it? You'd be sorry then." The childlike statement was out before she could stop it.

He whirled on her. "Don't say that, don't even think it. Dammit, Angel, I can't take you and that's that. Even if I did love you, especially if I loved you. You can't go. I won't do that to you. Find a home, be safe and happy. Have babies and enjoy a house and family and friends.

151

What do you think you'd have with me? Nothing. Less than nothing. You'd have hell, that's what. Now get ready."

Furious and at a loss for words, she whirled, but he called out.

Quivering, she turned, hope flickering like a tiny candle flame fighting the wind. No one had ever called her Angel, and she would never allow anyone else to do so. Not ever again.

"Don't forget your gold," he said, then concentrated on Buck's girth strap, back as rigidly set as if he'd been built of rock.

The flame of her hope went out.

Jesse had his back to her, working on the cinch, settling everything just so when he felt the presence. It was reaching out to him, calling his name. He whirled and peered up the trail, then back down the way they'd come. Nothing. Nobody.

It was a voice he hadn't heard in more than ten years, calling him little brother. He knew it, knew it like his own. Hell, it was his own.

"Charlie?" he whispered, gazing up the trail toward Cody Grove.

Of course no one answered. It had been a stupid trick of the wind, or wishful thinking. If Charlie was out there why hadn't anyone seen him?

He stopped dead still, one hand lying on Buck's quivering withers. Someone *had* seen him. Those men had thought he was Charlie, and Wild Bill Hickok did as well. Because of his eyes, too. No one in the world has eyes like a wolf, like a predator, a killer; no one but Jesse and Charlie Cole. Jesse didn't know why he hadn't seen it before: His brother *was* alive.

"Are we playing hide-'n'-seek, Charlie?" He didn't know he'd spoken the question until Angeline called out:

152

Angel's Gold

"What, Jesse? Who you talking to?"

"No one, Angel. I'm not talking to anyone. Just thinking out loud."

They rode into town in silence, him wishing she didn't have to hold on so tightly, pressing her firm, luscious breasts against his back, wrapping her arms around his waist. And with her gripping his hips for balance, her hands resting so tantalizingly close to the part of him that she made ache, he wished things were different . . . that she would never have to let him go.

Chapter Ten

The man in the Cody Grove general store, a lanky fellow with a shock of graying hair, rubbed at his chin in concentration.

"I don't reckon they's anyone in town who needs them a woman to do for 'em. We're only about ten families. There's me and my wife to run the store. Not enough business to need help. Then there's Lem and Ida Franklin. They got eleven kids and that's enough help for anyone. Ol' Burke runs the gristmill and his son Wilbur has the blacksmith shop. Marv owns the saloon, his daughter Dina does the cooking and bartending when he's in his cups. Nope, sorry about that. They just ain't no work in Cody Grove—not even for keep. Folks around here do well to feed their own."

Angeline stood beside Jesse, giving him a smug look.

"What about a stage, one run through here?"

The storekeeper fashioned a gap-toothed smile. "Young fella, ain't no stage goes through here. Why, I reckon you'd have to go all the way down toward Topeka to find a stage run. You might get a feeder out of Council Grove. I ain't too sure about that, though. Haven't been out of Cody for ten years or more myself. We get a freight wagon in with goods once a month or so, and that's about it." He scratched through his scraggly hair, shook his head in amusement.

"Well, would the freighter ever give a ride to anyone? Angel here, she needs to go . . . another way than I'm traveling. I'd sure appreciate it if you could—"

154

"My idea would be that you take her on with you till you get somewhere with more promise. She might starve here." He eyed her as if considering something, tempted, then shook his head and chuckled.

Jesse didn't look amused.

Angeline tugged on his sleeve. "Let's buy us some supplies and go on, Jesse."

"How far is it to Topeka?" he asked the smiling store-keeper.

"I don't have a notion. Reckon it might be a four-or five-day ride if you hustle and don't run into trouble."

"And Circleville?"

Angeline stared at him evilly.

"Never heard of it."

Jesse nodded, turning to her. "Tell the man what supplies we need, and make sure and get some coffee. I'll fetch the gold to pay him."

Her heart swelled and she wanted to throw her arms around his neck, but instead, she simply smiled sweetly.

Jesse had told her that paying for supplies with gold often as not was taken pretty calmly. Merchants would rather have it than just about anything else, and they were leery of paper money, even after the war had been over all this time. The storekeeper packaged the order, and she asked for two cans of peaches, an extravagance in which she had not indulged since leaving home. Prophet used to buy them for her, and she'd always hated to let him know how much she appreciated it.

The storekeeper wiped the dust from the top of the cans with a corner of his apron. "Not much call around here for these, most folk cain't afford the price, but I keep a few on hand just the same. Too bad me and the missus never took a likin' to store-bought peaches, or we'd indulge." He chortled again, obviously thinking he was a pretty funny fellow.

Dragging out a black iron scale, he chose a small

round weight, placed it on the flat tray and trickled gold into the pear-shaped brass pan until the two balanced. Angel saw that Jesse remained in the background, checking out some of the offerings in the scantily stocked general store. She wondered if he had any money at all and thought about buying him a new pair of britches, but decided not to mention it. His mood was pretty foul and no man liked the idea of a woman paying his way, even if his knees did poke out of his pant legs.

Without speaking he plucked up the packages of supplies and stalked out the door, leaving her to tag along behind. She waited while he adjusted the packs across the horse's withers. He mounted up and reached down to take her hand, kicking free of the stirrup so she could place her foot there and climb on behind him.

She accepted his anger. He'd wanted to be rid of her, resented having to take her any farther, and she wasn't about to make matters any worse by chattering on like a ninny. But as they rode mile after mile and minutes grew into hours she could stand the silence no longer.

"I'm sorry," she finally muttered, though wished she could have sounded more contrite.

"About what?"

"No stage and not being able—"

"Not your fault."

"No, indeed it isn't, but you're acting like it is. Maybe I ought to climb down and walk off into the wilderness, let some bear or something eat me."

"Good God, Angel, there aren't any bears out here."

"Well, or something."

When he didn't answer, she went on. "Where you taking me, Topeka?"

"No, it's too far back to Circleville going that direction. I'm cutting across, following that Indian trail we came down on."

"But I can't go back."

He only said, "We'll think of something."

She gnawed at her lip. "Why are you going back there? What if those awful men are hanging around still?"

"I'm sure they are. I *hope* they are."

"Heavens. Why?"

"Because I think they can help me find my brother Charlie."

Flabbergasted, she didn't reply right away. Was he crazy? They thought *he* was Charlie, and would kill him once they found out what they wanted to know from him. She was beginning to wonder if there really was a Charlie at all. Maybe Jesse had done all those things and changed his name. It was possible, wasn't it?

"Jesse?"

"Hmm?"

"What are you going to do if you do find your brother?"

"I don't know what you mean."

"Well, if he is alive and he did kill those Confederate soldiers and steal that gold, then he could go to jail or even get himself hung. If he's caught. What are you going to do if you find him?"

"Well, I sure as hell ain't gonna turn him in. What kind of brother do you think I am?"

She'd annoyed him even more, so she tried to think of some way to change the subject.

"I sure do miss the little buttermilk mare. She was so sweet."

"Me too, and I think poor old Buck misses her too."

"If I'm too heavy I can walk awhile, I don't mind."

Jesse reined in the gelding. "Tell you what, Angel. Let's both walk, it'll stretch our legs and give Buck a rest."

He kicked free of the stirrup and threw a leg forward over the cantle, sliding to the ground and raising his arms to catch her when she did the same. He no longer showed any sign of pain from his leg wound.

157

Samantha Lee

Feet on the ground, she pressed against him and locked both arms firmly around the back of his neck. His body felt so good, the hard muscles cradling her breasts and stomach and thighs. Lips grimly set, he spanned her waist and placed her at arms length, then took a quick step backward to put more space between them. But his eyes locked on hers as if he couldn't entirely let her go, and she held the stare, waiting for him to break it first.

Beyond him, a group of Indians moved within her view without a sound of warning. No footfalls along the trail, no murmured conversation. They were suddenly just there, appearing as if from some other place or time.

She and Twana spotted each other almost at once. *Kansa!* The two ran to hug, laughing and dancing round and round and holding hands. This unexpected meeting almost made up for the bad feelings between her and Jesse.

"Where are you going?" she asked the young Indian woman.

"Home, back to the reservation. We haven't done well on the hunt." She gestured toward the pack animals and the paltry load of smoked meat. "We had hoped to kill more buffalo to carry home fresh meat, but found few. The white men have slaughtered most of them." Twana glanced at Jesse. "And where are you going?"

Angeline lowered her head. "I don't know. I'm afraid I'm going back home."

Twana hugged her. "You have chosen an honorable thing."

"No, not really. I have no choice."

Eyebrows raised, Twana replied, "There is always a choice. Yet what we choose is sometimes difficult to taste . . . swallow?"

"And you, do you return to honor your father's wishes?"

"Yes. It is my destiny."

158

"I thought you said we had a choice."

"You twist my words, friend. I could choose another path, true—but I do not feel that to be what should be. I must honor my father . . . my people . . . myself, and so I do what I know is right."

"Right?" Angeline stared across the way at Jesse. He was engaged in conversation with two of the Kansa men. "How can you know what is right?"

Twana doubled her fist and placed it between her breasts, then touched her temple. "What is here and here."

Angeline touched her own chest. "That's my trouble. What is here battles with what is here." She pointed at her head. "And I don't know which one to listen to."

"You love this man?" Twana gestured.

Miserably, Angeline nodded. "But he says he doesn't love me. I think he does, it's just that he is on a path that may lead him to kill someone, and he can't see anything beyond that. Worse, I'm afraid he'll die."

"But you can carry your love with you, here, no matter what happens." Again the young Indian woman indicated her chest. "It will never die as long as you carry him in your heart. That is something."

Anger built in Angeline. "You mean only have him in my dreams? What kind of life is that?"

"Perhaps the best one we will ever have." The sadness reflected in Twana's chocolate-brown eyes nearly broke Angeline's heart.

A brave known as Lone Coyote shouted something out and Twana jerked around. She nodded, then, and touched Angeline. "It is time for us to go."

"When will you marry?"

"As soon as we return."

Angeline grabbed her arm. "Run away with the man you love! How can we put anything before love? In the end it's all we'll have, and if we give it up, what then?"

159

"I can't, I won't. It would dishonor my father, my clan. How could I love him and know I had hurt all the others I love? I have made my choice. But I wish you well in making yours."

"And you too," Angeline said, and kissed Twana's cheek, salty with tears. How could anyone be so dreadfully unhappy and still go ahead with the very thing that caused their unhappiness? She had a sudden thought and called out to the girl. "Wait just a minute. I have a wedding present for you."

Quickly she dug out one of her precious bags of gold. From a distance, she saw Jesse staring at them, but she placed the bag in Twana's hand. He had no say in this. "Put this away. You may need it one day. Keep it your secret."

"What is it?"

"Never mind, just keep it safe. It's very valuable in the white man's world."

Twana gave her a fast hug. "I will treasure this always."

"We'll meet again. I can tell." Raising a hand, Angeline continued to wave until the small band moved out of sight.

Watching the Kansa trail away with their meager kill, she mulled over what Twana had said about honor and duty and choices. To remain with Jesse when he didn't want her made no sense, but to return to Prophet didn't either. Yet if Jesse wouldn't have her . . .

She knew nothing else, had no way to care for herself on her own in this wild and dangerous country. If she treated him with respect, Prophet would surely care for her and see she had the things she needed. He had before. It wasn't so bad a life, now that she had witnessed some of the alternatives. She had a feeling she was growing up.

All the next day they rode with few breaks, and Angeline seemed nervous, put off by the growing closeness of Prophet and her old home. Jesse would not discuss their

A Special Offer For Leisure Historical Romance Readers Only!

Get Four FREE* Romance Novels

A $21.96 Value!

Thrill to the most sensual, adventure-filled Historical Romances on the market today…

FROM  LEISURE BOOKS

As a home subscriber to the Leisure Historical Romance Book Club, you'll enjoy the best in today's BRAND-NEW Historical Romance fiction. For over twenty-five years, Leisure Books has brought you the award-winning, high-quality authors you know and love to read. Each Leisure Historical Romance will sweep you away to a world of high adventure…and intimate romance. Discover for yourself all the passion and excitement millions of readers thrill to each and every month.

SAVE AT LEAST *$5.00* EACH TIME YOU BU

Each month, the Leisure Histori Romance Book Club brings you four bra new titles from Leisure Books, Ameri foremost publisher of Historical Romano EACH PACKAGE WILL SAVE YOU AT LEA $5.00 FROM THE BOOKSTORE PRICE! A you'll never miss a new title with our con nient home delivery service.

Here's how we do it. Each package carry a 10-DAY EXAMINATION privilege. the end of that time, if you decide to ke your books, simply pay the low invoice pr of $16.96 ($17.75 US in Canada), no sh ping or handling charges added*. HO DELIVERY IS ALWAYS FREE*. With tod top Historical Romance novels selling $5.99 and higher, our price SAVES YOU LEAST $5.00 with each shipment.

AND YOUR FIRST FOUR-BOOK SHIPMENT IS TOTALLY FR

IT'S A BARGAIN YOU CAN'T BEAT! A Super $21.96 Value!

LEISURE BOOKS A Division of Dorchester Publishing Co., Inc.

GET YOUR 4 FREE* BOOKS NOW— A $21.96 VALUE!

Mail the Free* Book Certificate Today!

4 FREE* BOOKS 🐾 A $21.96 VALUE

Free *Books Certificate*

YES! I want to subscribe to the Leisure Historical Romance Book Club. Please send me my **4 FREE* BOOKS**. Then each month I'll receive the four newest Leisure Historical Romance selections to Preview for 10 days. If I decide to keep them, I will pay the Special Member's Only discounted price of just $4.24 each, a total of $16.96 ($17.75 US in Canada). This is a SAVINGS OF AT LEAST $5.00 off the bookstore price. There are no shipping, handling, or other charges*. There is no minimum number of books I must buy and I may cancel the program at any time. In any case, the **4 FREE*** BOOKS are mine to keep—A BIG $21.96 Value!

*In Canada, add $5.00 shipping and handling per order for first shipment. For all subsequent shipments to Canada, the cost of membership is $17.75 US, which includes $7.75 shipping and handling per month.[All payments must be made in US dollars]

Name _____

Address _____

City _____

State _____ *Country* _____ *Zip* _____

Telephone _____

Signature _____

If under 18, Parent or Guardian must sign. Terms, prices and conditions subject to change. Subscription subject to acceptance. Leisure Books reserves the right to reject any order or cancel any subscription.

Get Four Books Totally
F R E E* —
A $21.96 Value!

(Tear Here and Mail Your FREE* Book Card Today!)

PLEASE RUSH
MY FOUR FREE*
BOOKS TO ME
RIGHT AWAY!

Leisure Historical Romance Book Club
P.O. Box 6613
Edison, NJ 08818-6613

situation, or the wisdom of returning to Circleville. He rode as if in a fog.

Every moment he sensed Charlie's presence. It was a feeling he could not begin to explain, not even to himself, like when they were children and played hide-and-seek. He had always known right where he was. He remembered once, Charlie crouching behind a fallen log, and himself walking right to him, as if he could see through the thick tree. It was like Charlie had tapped him on the shoulder, saying, "I'm here, look closer, I'm here."

By the time Jesse found a place to camp for the night, he felt like he could reach out and touch his brother, the essence of him being hung nearby, thick and elusive as the smoke from the fire. Jesse grew restless, and took a long walk to try to get nearer his twin, leaving Angel on her own.

Bone-weary, he finally returned without seeing any sign of Charlie. He would need to sleep if they were to make good time the next day. Beside the fire he found his supper plate sitting on a rock, and nearby a can of peaches, half-eaten. He scraped the cold beans out on the ground for the night critters and, taking up a spoon, sat cross-legged near to the dying flames to scoop up the sweet fruit. Where had Angel found these?

Each bite was cool as the night air, the delicious juice reminding him of the taste of her lips, the slippery fruit as tantalizing as her smooth flesh. He shook that image away, angry that she had invaded his thoughts at all. Despite all efforts to do otherwise, his glance moved toward her bedroll. She lay without cover, the hem of the buckskin dress hiked up around her thighs. Her hair, which she'd taken to wearing in braids during the daytime, was spread loose around her head like a crinkled fan of gold.

Unable to tear his gaze from her, he spooned up another golden peach half, laid it on his tongue and closed his lips around it. In its honeyed flavor he tasted

Angel again, imagined her satiny skin under his fingertips, smelling the wild flower fragrance that surrounded
her. The winds of night carried the aroma of ripening
grass, the moist earth, the sharp tang of the deep woods
and the smoke off the burning birch and oak. Also of the
peaches and Angel. He turned up the can and drank the
syrup, then set it carefully beside the empty plate.

Suddenly nothing else existed. With an urgency he
thought might well kill him, he wanted the woman who
lay asleep on the other side of the campfire.

But he had to deny himself that luxury, and did so with
a rage born of his painful past.

He would take her back where she belonged, find
Charlie and be on his way. In the end she would be grateful. She swore she loved him, but what did she know at
her age? Even if she did, now she would have the memory of that love without the pain of what would surely
come after, its dissolution. He turned and tried to sleep.

Before dawn, Angeline awakened to something soft rubbing across her shoulder. There came a chuffing noise,
and moist hot breath flowing over the nape of her neck, a
deep-throated whicker. She came fully alert.

It was Jezebel, the buttermilk mare. She'd come back!

Shouting with joy, she cupped the animal's dear face,
kissed its velvety nose. Coming to her feet, she inspected
every inch of the animal's mud-covered body. The saddle, nearly as scruffy as the animal herself, drooped to
one side, and Angeline removed it and the bridle.

"Poor little thing," she murmured in the horse's ear.
Jezebel tossed her head, snorting. Joy filled Angeline.
"Oh, I'm so glad I didn't drown you."

With her roaming hands, she found a few cuts that
were already healing, and she checked them closely to
make sure no bot flies had laid eggs that would hatch into
worms and eat away the little mare's flesh.

162

"Had yourself quite an adventure, didn't you?" Jezebel tossed her head. "Bet you don't want to go swimming anytime soon." Angeline chuckled with happiness, again kissing the velvety muzzle. "Well, neither do I."

In the lavender dawn she and the mare cavorted from the camp and out across the meadow. Occasionally she stopped to once more rub noses with the buttermilk. A gust of morning wind caught her hair, tossing the palomino's mane and tail.

Jesse rose up from the bedroll, rubbing his eyes. He was just starting toward the woods to answer a call of nature, when he spotted a horse and girl silhouetted on the open prairie by the glow of early morning. In awe he stood and stared at them, a hum of desire buried so deep in his stomach he could never ease it. Streaks of pale sunlight fingered through the girl's hair, streaked the mane and tail of the buttermilk, turning them the same color of gold. In that moment he knew he would never feel precisely this way about anyone again.

His heart, his very being, literally ached with love for her. It was so potent that for the first time in his life he knew an emotion stronger than the anger that had dwelled so long in his soul.

He had never felt love like this before, clean and without reserve. Even his feelings for his brother weren't so pure. To love someone as he did her, meant he cared more for her than for himself. But that meant he had to save her from himself, from Charlie. If he kept her near him, he would get her killed, or put her in a situation that could cause her great harm.

Though the idea of her living with Prophet was abhorrent, he had to convince her to go back to the man. At least she would be safe there. At least, safer than what could happen to her if she stayed with him.

Turning from the sight of her bathed in the golden

dawn, a vision that would be forever branded in his mind and on his heart, he busied himself building a breakfast fire.

Soon Angeline came back to camp, her mare following along like a puppy. "Look, she came home."

"I see. That's good." He feared his voice would break if he said more, so he continued to tend the fire.

"Good? That's great! I thought she was dead." She turned to the horse. "I thought you were dead." Unable to contain her joy, she threw her arms around the buttermilk's neck and laughed with delight.

"Looks like she could use a bath," Jesse said. "Is she hurt?"

"No. Just a few cuts, but they look okay. Oh, isn't it wonderful?"

"Indeed it is. Now you'll be able to ride home."

He watched as Angeline froze, then turned from the mare. This had to be faced. Now. As much as he hated to send her away, he must. And he could see in her eyes that she understood.

"I will go, Jesse, but I want you to tell me something first."

He gazed at her, wary.

"Tell me the truth. Tell me you love me so I'll have that much of you with me always."

He raised his shoulders and felt tears come to his eyes. Then he held out his arms to her and she went into them.

"Oh, yes. I love you, Angel. With all my heart and soul, if I have such a thing. If I could, I would carry us both far away where no harm would ever come to you, but we both know I can't."

She laid gentle fingers over his lips. "Hush. We can't help what is. I will always love you, and I'll keep you with me."

Moving her hand aside, he lowered his mouth to hers.

drinking of her sweetness, and felt a passion so pure and bright it couldn't be contained in this world or the next. Deep within his being, joy uncurled, stretching through every fiber of his being. To love her, to be loved, denied all the ugliness in his world—swept it away, at least for the moment. He would not think of a time without her, for never again would that be. In his heart and mind and soul, he would carry her forever.

Gathering her into his arms, he carried her to the bedroll and lay her there, lowering himself gently beside her. There he held her until the sunlight grew hot and brilliant and the wind rose to sing in the trees. It was a ballad of their love, a song that had no words but carried the meaning of the ages.

He wanted to take her for his own, to be the one who showed her what it was like to be worshiped, adored. To open her to love. But he had to send her back to Prophet untouched. She had left her husband a virgin and she must return to him the same way if she were to have a contented life.

Jesse sighed and released her, then rose to fill the coffeepot with water. He watched as she lay for a moment longer, seemingly enraptured, then he went about his tasks. He scraped out a bed of coals and snuggled the pot into the flames. Then, pulling the drawstring on the Arbuckle coffee bag, he dumped some in and fitted on the lid. All the time, he concentrated on his tasks, not looking at her or speaking another word. But, in his heart, was the beauty her love had uncovered.

"Jesse, I'm ready to go home, but I think I should go alone. If Prophet or anyone else sees you with me, they'll only think the worst. They could kill you."

"No. I won't let you ride there alone. Those three yahoos could still be on the prowl. Besides, I'm headed for Circleville to find Charlie. I'll take you in sight of the farm, then go on my way."

She glanced up at him, setting her mouth in a determined line.

He held up a hand. "Best I can do, Angel. Take it or leave it."

"They're going to kill you there. What makes you think your brother's there anyway? It's just plain stupid, what you're doing." Her eyes filling, she voiced a lingering, childish desire, though she knew it was foolish. "Oh, Jesse, let's go out west where nobody knows us. You can rob trains or banks, or whatever, just like your cousins. I'll help you, I will. Anything to be with you." She actually stomped her foot, kicking up puffs of dust.

"Listen to yourself, Angel. You can't be an outlaw, you'd be even worse at it than I am. Girls don't become outlaws."

"What about—"

He held up a hand. "Enough. I've listened to all I'm going to. As soon as we eat and drink some coffee, we're on our way. We've got a few days' ride and I don't intend to listen to this all the way. You go with me or you stay here. But if you go you keep still about this nonsense. I won't be tempted by what I can't have, and you shouldn't either. You have no idea what you're talking about."

"You can't tell me what I can talk about or what I can do! And I'm not a child you can boss around either," she said angrily.

He whirled, consumed by desire for her and knowing what was right. "No damn wonder you exasperated John Prophet. You're stubborn as any mule I've ever run across."

Clamping her lips tightly together, and giving him a look that spoke volumes, Angel ran off into the woods. The buttermilk trailed along, obviously so overjoyed to see Angeline she couldn't let her out of sight.

Jesse marveled at how one day the girl could be a grown woman, facing life with good sense, and the next

166

revert back to living the childhood she'd never had. He understood her better than he wanted to, for there were times when he missed the boyhood he'd never had, wondered what it would have been like to shoot marbles or play ball. But such yearnings were foolishness, and she would one day learn that for herself.

Prophet would soon take it out of her, that joyous childlike nature that she had retained. She had almost lost it when Jesse had first seen her. Prophet would turn her into a proper wife, a lady.

It was too bad, in a way. Jesse didn't want to imagine her a dour-faced old woman with bitter regret lining her face. But it was better than seeing her face down in the dust with a bullet in her back. He clamped down the horrible thought. Decisions had been made, on both their parts. He supposed it might be natural that they would each have second thoughts, but nevertheless, the deed was all but done. He was taking her home, no matter what. They were just now getting everything out of their systems.

Off and on all that day, he felt a nervousness he couldn't shake. Shadows played on the edge of his vision. Once he thought he saw riders off in the distance, gaining on them. And to make it even worse, it seemed Charlie's presence moved closer and closer. The excitement of seeing his brother once again paled against the pain of losing Angel. And amidst it all lurked a black dread he couldn't explain or understand.

It was early morning. Charlie Cole sat his horse on a rise, studying the country that spread out in all directions. There he lingered for a long spell, gazing out across the prairie, looking for Jesse. His brother was out there, somewhere close by. Lines of thick trees followed low cuts where creeks ran. A rider in there couldn't be seen. Beyond the rolling hills the grassy plains flattened out, ran smooth and unbroken to the horizon.

167

In the distance, two riders appeared as if from a hole in the earth, startling him even though he knew they were coming. One sat a long-legged roan with white leggings, the other rode a smaller, light-colored horse—a palomino, what punchers often called a buttermilk.

The smaller one might be a boy or a woman. He couldn't tell from this distance.

The larger one he knew instantly, even though he couldn't see the face or make out the hair color. It was his twin. The knowledge was in his gut and around his heart; it embraced his mind. Charlie was watching Jesse Cole, his twin brother, whom he hadn't seen since they were lads of thirteen when he'd beat Zeke unconscious and lit out, leaving Jesse behind, bawling like the baby he'd been.

If anything in Charlie's life filled him with regret, that one act did. The killings or the "mayhem" or any of the other things he'd done to man or beast, none bothered him like deserting his brother. Now, at last he would have a chance to make it up to him.

By nightfall, they would come close enough to shout a greeting to each other. He tried to imagine what Jesse would do, how he would act and what he would say, but couldn't.

Angeline waited until Jesse's breathing told her he slept before she quietly rose. Fetching her mare's saddle and bridle, she found her grazing nearby and readied her for her trip. She glanced at the saddlebags where her gold was hidden, then one last time at Jesse.

He lay on his back, his arms flung wide, as if he had fallen asleep staring up at the stars. Both had slept fully clothed and far apart since their mutual admission of love, for they dared not do otherwise.

Still, what would he do when he awoke and found her gone? He would be furious, she knew, but she would not be responsible for him being caught, accused as the one who had stolen her away in the dark of night. She could tell Prophet it had been those three bandits, for they were truly the culprits. Let everyone in the west look for them. Jesse's name or description would never cross her lips. Only in her dreams would she allow him to remain real. No one in Circleville would ever know he existed.

Carefully she crept to his side to look upon him one final time. In the dark of night she couldn't make out his face, just the shape of it, but in her heart and mind she would always carry memories of him, of the ecstasy of being held against his warm, strong chest; his sensuous lips on hers; the passionate glance of his golden eyes. Picking up the saddlebags she quickly took out one bag of gold and laid it next to him. He might need it for something. If she had a piece of paper she would have written that she was going home so he'd know for sure and not be worried. She settled for taking up a stick and writing in the dust. *I've gone home. Love Angel.*

Without looking back she tiptoed to her mare, mounted up and rode off slowly so he wouldn't hear and awaken. Tears streaked her cheeks but she held her head high. This would be the last time any man ever caused her to cry.

Chapter Eleven

Jesse rolled over and awoke with a start, as if he'd heard something, though he had no idea what. The still air rang with the songs of night, but nothing else. A deep melancholy dwelt deep within. Tomorrow he would lose Angel forever. The decision had been made, but he hadn't expected to be filled with such overwhelming unhappiness.

After a while he knew he wouldn't go back to sleep, so he sat up, stretched, then ran fingers through his hair and climbed to his feet. Across from the glowing bed of coals, where Angel's bedroll should be, was nothing but flat ground. Even in the dark he could tell she wasn't there. Frantic, he went in search of the horses. He found Buck hipshot and asleep, his head hanging low, but no sign of the mare. The pale glow of the quarter moon cast great mysterious shadows in the distance. Nothing stirred that could be Angel.

Dear God, what had happened to her? Back at the camp he checked for her things, but found the saddlebags and her pack gone. She hadn't been forcefully taken; she had methodically picked up all her belongings including the precious gold. She'd left on her own, but where to? And how would he find her? He couldn't track her till morning, not even then if she had taken the well-traveled trail they'd been following. It would lead to Olsburg, then meander to the northeast toward Circleville, Holton and beyond, clean to Nebraska.

Or had she gone the other way, been lying to him all

along? Had she only been saying what he wanted to hear so she would have this chance to run in the opposite direction? Perhaps she had never intended to return to Prophet.

Now, he had two choices. Go back the way they'd come, assuming she was headed west to Dodge, or keep going toward Circleville. What would she do? Much as she'd hated the idea of returning to Prophet, she'd agreed to do so, and it made good sense—at least to him. It did make sense, even though all he'd wanted to do was grab her up and run to the ends of the earth where no one would ever find them.

Standing barefoot in the middle of the trail, looking first one direction and then the other, knowledge of Charlie's presence tapped at his shoulder, like a ghost too long ignored.

But Angel was alone out there somewhere, and above all Jesse had to find her. First he'd go back the way they'd come, pushing Buck hard. She couldn't have been gone more than a couple of hours. He'd catch her quickly. If not, he'd come back this way and ride hell bent for leather toward Circleville to make sure she was safely back home. He couldn't abandon Angel, Charlie would have to wait.

In the pale light, Jesse fumbled around, saddling the bay, gathering his belongings, and it wasn't until he shook out his bedroll that he found the bag of gold. With tears in his eyes he held it tightly in his fist. She'd left it for him.

Dear God, he had to find her. And when he did they would ride away *together*. No more foolishness about Charlie or being an outlaw. All that was over. He'd encircle her in his arms and love her forever. They could go west, far, far west. With the gold they could make their way easily, find a place to settle down. Have a decent, normal life. Away from Charlie and Prophet and their pasts.

171

He itched to get underway, to catch up with her and tell her the news. They would get married, be happy. He had to catch her before she went back to that old man. Jesse suddenly found himself praying that she had run away instead.

Leaping on Buck, he took to the trail, urging the gelding into a gallop back in the direction from which he'd come the previous day. It would be just like her to head out on her own and not go back home. Hopefully, he knew her that well.

When he didn't catch up with Angel by dawn, Jesse took a shortcut back to Olsburg that would cut off a good ten miles of traveling, and possibly put him ahead of her unless she was moving real fast. It was a little-used trail, but marked well enough not to slow him down. A wagon might not be able to maneuver the narrow trace, and Jesse would have to ford the Big Blue River, but he could make good time on horseback. Once in Olsburg it would be a straight, easy shot to Circleville.

Obviously she was headed in that direction. She had better sense than to take off cross-country. By noon he had made good time and the river crossing lay behind him. If she hadn't ridden through Olsburg he'd wait there for her, tell her she didn't have to go home to Prophet. She could come with him.

Thoughts of Charlie lurked like a viper coiled beneath a rock. He knew it was there, heard its rattle, but first he had to take care of Angel.

At Olsburg, a fellow behind the counter in the general store said he'd seen a woman such as Jesse described. "Rode through not even an hour ahead of you. Astraddle of a palomino and didn't even slow down. Wouldn't have noticed her but I was sweeping mud off the boardwalk when she rode by. A white girl in Indian garb ain't something we see too much. I even remarked on it to Martha. She's the wife."

Anxious to be on his way, Jesse shifted from one foot to the other. "I thank you, sir."

The man scratched his cheek and stared at Jesse. "Strangest thing, young fella."

His mind already on catching up with Angel, Jesse only half paid attention. He wanted out of this place fast. "Yeah, what's that?" he asked.

"You look jest like a feller that went through here not ten minutes ago. I don't usually pay too much attention, but he cut up a ruckus with ol' Mr. Nebert, who has this bad habit of wandering around in the middle of the road when he's stewed to the gills. This young feller, like I said, come near to running poor old Nebert down. I went to the old drunk's aid, so I was looking right up into this feller's face. Scruffy it was, but had eyes like . . ." The storekeep stared pointedly into Jesse's face. "Never seen eyes that color. Odd they'd be two of you within such a short space of time, come rambling through little ol' Olsburg. Off the main track like we are, that is."

Jesse ground his teeth. Good God, that had to be Charlie! And he was trailing Angel. How? Why? It didn't make sense. Surely it was purely a coincidence. Or was it? He recalled sensing Charlie, wondered how long he'd been following them. And now he was following Angel?

A shudder rode through him. "I thank you kindly, sir. I have to be on my way."

The old man talked him out the door and to his horse, arm raised as if to indicate his latest point, even as Jesse mounted up.

He took to the road once more, not sparing Buck, despite the lather foaming from beneath his saddle and cinch. Jesse's heart wouldn't sit still after that. It galloped in his chest like a penned mustang. Charlie? And he was after Angel. How in hell had that happened? She was in danger, but like the other feelings concerning his brother, he couldn't have said how he knew. Charlie was up to no good, and Angel was right in the middle of it.

Angeline rested on the edge of the creek, her bare feet dangling in the cold water. Jezebel stood in the water too, as if her own feet hurt. She smiled a bit at the mare's antics. Since catching up with them after the river incident, she had acted more like a pet hound than a riding horse. She kept a wary eye on Angeline, followed her around and never let her out of sight.

The two of them weren't but a few yards off the trail, so she heard the rider coming before he moved into sight. Brushing loosened strands of hair back out of her eyes, she recognized the familiar roan gelding, Jesse on his back, spurring him on much too fast.

She stood, raised a hand and shouted. But by that time he was past her.

Jesse never ran Buck that hard. Never. What in the world was going on? Had he heard news of his brother and taken out after him?

She hollered again and made her way to the road, limping over the rough ground in her bare feet. For a moment she thought he'd gone on, not even glanced in her direction, but then she heard him coming back, Buck chuffing loudly.

He dismounted on the run and caught her up in his arms, whirling her around.

"Jesse, what is it?" Without waiting for an answer, she hugged him close and squealed. Stubble scratched her face and she saw he hadn't shaved, but she didn't care.

He'd come after her, they were together. Could it be he wanted her? Otherwise what was he doing here?

"Oh, Angel. Thank God I found you. Have you seen Charlie?"

Her heart thudded in disappointment. This was all

about Charlie. "No, of course not. I thought you'd come after me."

She wanted to cry, to strike out at him, to scream her frustration into the evening sky.

He gazed down into her face. "I did. I came after you, but someone saw Charlie following you. I was afraid for you."

"Why?"

"Well . . . you're alone, and I didn't know what he might do. . . . I don't know him any more. Or maybe I'm afraid I do. Why would he be following you? I was terrified when I woke up and found you gone. Why did you do that? I was going to take you home. You didn't need to run away. At first I thought you were going someplace else and I wasted precious time searching."

"I left you a note. But, I meant, why would Charlie be following me?"

"I don't know why he would be following you. A note? No, I didn't see a note."

"In the dust."

"In the dust?" He chuckled, wrapped her up once again to hug her so tightly she grunted. "Only you, Angel, would do that. It was dark when I woke up and found you gone. How could I read a note in the dust?"

"I didn't have any paper."

He kissed her jaw line, laughed, then nibbled at her ear and laughed some more. "My dear, sweet Angel. I thought I'd lost you. I was afraid it was too late."

His amusement was contagious and she laughed too. "You came after me," she finally said.

"Indeed I did."

"Why? You said."

"Never mind what I said. I was a fool. I love you and we need to be together. Somehow, we'll figure this all out."

"What about Charlie?"

"What about him?"

"He's your brother, don't you need to find him, set things right?"

"Nope. What I need—all I need—is you. Now and forever. That is, if you still love me."

Finally his message got through to her. Giddy with delight, she kissed his mouth, his nose, both eyes and tugged at his hair and ears. "I love you, Jesse Cole. But what are we going to do?"

"Danged if I know, but we'll get along. You've got gold and we can go somewhere and make a fresh start. I'm strong and not too dumb. I've apprenticed blacksmithing, I can do that, or something else. No bank robbing, though. You want to homestead a farm, or live in town, or go to California and see the ocean? I don't care. Say something and I'm ready."

"I have to go back to Prophet."

The words sobered both of them into a brief silence.

"We're married," she finally said so low he almost couldn't hear. "I don't suppose I can just go off without setting that straight."

Jesse nodded. "You mean, get a divorce?"

"I guess. It's only right, isn't it?"

"Doesn't matter to me. I don't want you spending another night in his house, giving him a chance to . . . well, you know. And he hit you, he might try that again. I don't know what I was thinking before. It's not a good idea for you to go back there."

"I could talk to the sheriff, find out how to do it. The judge comes around . . . I guess we'd have to wait for him to do it properly."

"Or we can just leave. He'll never find us, never know what you're doing. No one but us will ever know. You said Prophet has a lot of influence in town. Suppose the sheriff drags you back to him, all legal and everything?"

"I guess he could, but surely he wouldn't dare do that. My mama would never, ever forgive me if I just ran off from him. I promised."

Jesse sighed from way down deep. "Angel, your mama allowed you to be sold to a man old enough to be your grandpa, sold like a slave, and you worry about her forgiveness? I don't understand."

She placed both hands flat against his chest, then looked up into his pleading eyes. "I know it doesn't make sense to you, but I vowed, I promised. If I go back on that, if I just sneak away into the night, it wouldn't be right. Mama and Papa trusted me to do what was right."

"They *sold* you!" Jesse encircled her wrists, pleaded with her. "How can you owe them anything? Only a few days ago you were ready to run off with me, become outlaws."

Miserably, she shrugged. "I know, but it isn't right, and you know it. All I know is I have to make it right before we can be happy. Besides, it's against the law to be married to more than one man, and I want to be married to you. I want us to live together forever and have babies and . . ."

His arms came around her again, and he held her close. "I do too. I never thought I would say that, but I do too."

"Well, then?" she asked after a while. It was so wonderful to be in his arms, to know he loved her, that she could hardly contain herself. Yet the way she had come to feel about her abandoning John Prophet would stand in the way of their happiness.

"Okay," he said after a long while. "But let me ride into town alone. They don't know me there; no one saw me out at your place. Let me find out where Prophet is and what mood he and the sheriff are in about your kidnapping. Feel the way a bit before you go in. That old man could drag you home, lock you up and it wouldn't be against the law. What *is* against the law is you being with me. They'll arrest me for kidnapping you if we're together."

She kissed him, long and deep, then trailed her fingers through his dusty hair. "Go tomorrow," she said huskily.

"There's a fine place to camp right down there on the creek. We can bathe and . . . and . . ."

He picked her up and carried her off the trail and along the creek bank. Jezebel, who had been nuzzling Buck since the reunion, tagged along, followed by the gelding. The two seemed to have taken up where they had left off.

With the setting of the sun, streaks of copper and pink clouds brightened the evening sky. The wind that had blown much of the day settled to a gentle breeze, and they lay in each other's arms, content to simply hold each other and speak their dreams aloud. Once she was free, they would be together forever.

Jesse touched her cheek with his thumb. "So young, so innocent. You could be hurt so easily, Angel. God, how glad I am I didn't let you go back to that old man. Heaven only knows what he would have put you through."

"Mama told me having a man would hurt, but I had to bear it, for it would be my duty to satisfy the needs of my husband. That I should never enjoy it for a minute. But what you and I do—oh, I do so enjoy that."

"I never want to hurt you, Angel. If I could die to prevent that, I would."

They kissed for a long while, exploring with tongue and lips in an almost lazy fashion. He nibbled at her earlobes, and shivers shot through her, raising goose bumps all over her body. He sucked at her throat, kissing her breasts thoroughly until desire made her delirious.

Raising from one nipple, he grinned in a lopsided way. "What do you think of your mother's advice now?"

"I think she was afraid I'd find out how much fun this is." She gasped and pushed his mouth back where it had been. He chuckled against its erect tip.

"But this isn't all there is to it, Angel. There's more, but that may hurt you a little. We'll wait, though. I don't want you to think that we're sinning."

The last was spoken in a teasing manner, but she sensed the kernel of truth hidden behind his manner.

"You mean, until I divorce Prophet."

"If you wish. It's up to you. The way I feel, you've never been married to the man, not really. But it's how you feel that counts. I can wait. I don't want to and it won't be easy, but I can." The last was spoken with a sense of resignation to a terrible fate. Then he laughed and she knew everything was truly all right between them.

When they first met he had so seldom laughed. He'd never teased, and was curt and angry most of the time. Now that they were back together at last, he seemed almost a different person, though still the same in ways that counted; his strength and deeply ingrained sense of morals remained. She was pleased to realize that she liked this Jesse very much. Though she had loved him almost from the moment they met, there were times when she'd feared him. That had been confusing.

"I think it's time we had a cold bath; maybe that'll cool me off some," he said, grabbing her hand and pulling her out of their nest in the grass.

Together they waded into the creek and washed each other. Jesse complained that the cold water really wasn't helping much after all, and that she should be careful how she rubbed and where. They were a long time at their bath before retiring into a common bedroll for the night.

The next morning, after a scant breakfast of jerky and hard biscuits, Jesse left her in camp. Soon, very soon, they would be together forever.

Before he set off for town, he said, "Promise you won't follow me or run off somewhere. And stay out of sight if anyone comes along," he said, kissing her for the third time.

"I promise. Don't worry. And you be careful too. Don't say too much to Sheriff Oursler or he might take you for my kidnapper. Please, please be careful." Holding on to him fiercely, she almost begged him to forget it, but knew she had to do the honorable thing. Twana had made her realize that.

"I really think maybe the storekeeper was wrong about Charlie. He should be around somewhere. If he truly was following you, why didn't he show up when I did? But all the same, stay well out of sight." He kissed her one last time on the tip of her nose, closed each eye with his lips, then hugged her tight. "I love you, Angel. Love you, love you." He couldn't say it enough now that he knew it to be true.

"I love you too, Jesse. Always and forever. Don't worry about me."

Nodding, he reluctantly let her go and mounted up.

He no longer favored the leg that she had doctored a while back. She waved him out of sight, then went back to the camp they had set up around the bend of the creek and out of sight of the road.

It wasn't far to Circleville, but Jesse was nervous about leaving her, even for a short while. Yet he saw no alternative. Besides, there had been no sign of Charlie. If his brother was around, he'd have made an appearance by now.

He urged Buck to move out. "You rested last night, old fella, so let's go." He reached town fairly quickly.

In front of the sheriff's office, he dismounted and tied Buck to the hitching rail. The horse immediately dropped his nose into the watering trough.

Jesse pushed the door open and stepped inside to a greeting that all but stopped his heart.

The bald man was sitting with his feet up, but he slapped leather and thudded himself upright, scattering stuff all over the desk. Despite his awkward behavior, he managed to point the ominous black eye of a .44 at Jesse.

"Well, I'll be blamed if the fox ain't walked right into the henhouse."

Not sure yet what was going on, Jesse tried to remain

calm, even though his insides quivered. No man liked the barrel of a gun staring him in the face. He managed a querulous, "What's up?"

"Don't you even look like you're gonna move, or I'll blow a hole in you they can see through," the sheriff said.

"What's going on?" A gut feeling told Jesse to draw his gun or run, but he was afraid the old man would shoot him at the least provocation.

The sheriff must have sensed his instinct. "Rest easy, son. Take off that gun belt and hand it over here and don't you even twitch. It would be easier on everyone if I just shot you right here, so all I need is the slightest excuse. Might do it anyway, considering what you done to poor ol' Max."

"What'd I do? I've never been here before." Despite his denial, Jesse went to work unbuckling the gun belt, then carefully deposited it on top of the cluttered desk between him and the lawman. He had a terrible feeling Charlie had been and gone, and gotten him into deep trouble.

"You killed my helpless old deputy, and you're gonna pay for that—along with all your other crimes. You'll probably be hung by sunrise if the word gets around. Otherwise, we'll wait till the judge comes and holds your trial, *then* we'll hang you. Either way, this time you ain't getting out of this jail, I aim to see to that."

The night before, Charlie had camped a good ways off the main trail, probably a mile from his brother's fire. He'd been right in following the girl after he'd heard that sheriff give her description; she'd led him right back to his brother. But when it came right down to facing up to Jesse, he'd had second thoughts.

Wait till morning, he thought. A fresh day, then just ride in casual as you please. What difference could one more night make? What would he say? How would Jesse react? Did he still feel bad about being deserted?

When the girl had come riding by in the middle of the night, he'd hidden in a puny growth of plum bushes to watch, not sure until then if it was Jesse or someone else. She didn't spot him, though, seeing as how the moon hadn't risen yet. It was only a quarter moon anyhow. A man on the run always knew the phases of the moon. And he never let himself fall into a deep sleep. One ear always had to be cocked.

As her horse meandered past, he got a good look. It was Jesse's woman, of that he was sure. Charlie despised the female of the species. Hell, he even liked Yankees better'n women, and he hated them sons a bitches. But this was the one who'd been riding with his brother. He sure didn't want to get off on the wrong foot with Jesse after all this time. So he hunkered there watching her ride on by. Whatever was going on, he'd do well to stay out of it and not rile his brother.

It was amazing how women seemed to glow in the dark, their skin and eyes and hair fairly gleaming. Another of their false attractions. Good thing she was lighting out; she probably took old Jesse for all he had. Teach him a good lesson, that would. And the two of them could be alone, then, like he'd planned.

Finding Jesse's camp empty added to his confusion. Where had his brother got to? Would it be best if he followed the girl? Jesse didn't seem to ever get too far away from her. There was one thing about him and his brother: Following his instincts always worked out. When he figured Jesse would do something, the boy always did. His brother would meet up with this girl, sooner or later, and he would be close by.

He almost rode up on her when she stopped at the creek, and had to backtrack where he could wait and watch. He'd heard the thundering hoofbeats of Jesse's roan, galloping full tilt soon after the girl stopped. They hadn't budged since, and had even built them a fire come dark. He settled in to wait.

When the sun came up, Charlie left his camp and rode along the trail, keeping an eye out. He could put it off no longer. It was time he and his brother met up.

He'd almost missed her, off the road and hidden up the creek like she was. If it hadn't of been for catching sight of the palomino eating grass along the water's edge, he'd have ridden on past.

Cautiously Charlie dismounted and led his horse a ways up the bank, and sure enough, there she was. They'd camped around a curve so as not to be visible from the road. Neither Jesse nor his roan were in sight. The girl sat on an old log, her bare feet hanging in the water, head leaned back to let the sun shine on her face. She hadn't heard him.

Her eyes were closed, and she hummed softly, a tune that caught at his heart stirring a bittersweet memory. He shook off the brief pleasure. A man'd be a damned fool to go all soft over a pretty woman singing a song in the early-morning light. But God, even he who hated women could see why Jesse had fallen for this one. Her skin was kissed to a peachy hue by sunshine that lit her hair like spun gold. A woman like this was made to trick a man, to eat him up inside and spit him out. He'd soon see Jesse free of her wily ways.

She must have heard him then, for she stopped singing and straightened, looking right at him.

Angeline's surprise at her first view of the stranger was outweighed by a fear that grew in her belly, giving her the shakes so she could hardly breathe. He was Jesse with whiskers, Jesse with dirty hair—Jesse, only not. She couldn't put a finger on what it was that terrified her so about him. It was as if he were Jesse with all the good missing, replaced by something evil.

The man whipped his hat off. He saw right away he had scared her, and apparently didn't want that. She could tell, because he immediately assumed a less menacing expression.

183

"Sorry to bother you, ma'am. My name is Charlie Cole. I think you know my brother, Jesse, and I've been looking for him for a mighty long time. Can you tell me, ma'am, where might he be?"

Angeline glanced over her shoulder, searching for a way out. This man was terrifying. She slid off the log and put it between him and her.

He held out a hand to soothe her, but it didn't work. "Don't be afraid," he said. "I don't aim to hurt you. I would never hurt anybody that was a friend of Jesse's. Just tell me where I might find him. Is he here?"

Glancing around, he saw she was probably alone. She cursed her foul luck that Jesse's brother had appeared when he wasn't around to protect her.

Angeline tilted her head and studied Charlie. In color he had Jesse's eyes, but they were wild like some animal eyeing its prey. A wolf, perhaps. This was not a man to be fooled with. She decided to tell him the truth. Jesse would be pleased to see him, and he could handle this brother of his. And she stood in his way, she had a bad feeling about what might happen.

"He went . . ." Her voice broke, she cleared her throat and tried again. "He rode in to Circleville."

Charlie stared at her. Hard. "Ah, Christ. Hell." He slammed his hat to the ground. "Woman, you telling me the truth?"

More frightened than ever, she could only nod. Let him give her half a chance and she'd run, hide in the brush along the creek.

"Well, that tears it. He'll be in jail by now and hung by morning."

She lost all desire to run. What was this man saying? How did he know such a thing?

"You sure that's where he's at? Circleville?"

"Yes, I am." Anger at the implication of his question overrode her fear. "Why would they want to hang Jesse?

184

He hasn't done anything. He didn't even have anything to do with kidnapping me. He was saving me. Even Prophet wouldn't let them hang him for that. Would he?"

"I don't know much about a prophet, but they'll sure hang ol' Jesse if he rides into Circleville. And it'll be for something I done. Dammit, I come back to make things up to him, and here I go and get him in more trouble."

He picked up the hat, captured the dangling reins of his horse and climbed aboard. "I'll just have to ride in and get him out, is all."

"Wait, wait. I'm coming with you."

"The hell you are."

She stopped cold in her tracks. This one wouldn't be played with. Not at all like Jesse, he probably would tie her up to a tree to keep her from tagging along. So instead of insisting, she waited until he rode out of sight, then quickly put on her moccasins, saddled her mare and went after him.

If she stayed out of sight, things would be okay. And there was absolutely no way she would stay behind when Jesse's life was at stake.

Chapter Twelve

The mare, hard put to catch up with Charlie and his lean mount, stretched her legs and gave her all. The road passed within a half a mile of Prophet's farm, her home for five years, but she spared it not the slightest glance. It might as well not have existed except as a threat to her happiness with Jesse—a man who could at that very moment be in jeopardy. On she rode, hunched low in the saddle while the little buttermilk galloped. Only a mile to go, but she had to be careful to not ride into town in the open. Prophet, or someone who sympathized with his loss, might see her. If she were found out, she would be of no help.

At the outskirts of Circleville she forded Elk Creek and guided the mare into a growth of thick trees along its bank. Dismounting she tied her mount where it could reach water and grass and started toward the jail on foot. Wearing the buckskin, her hair in braids, face darkened by the sun, she might not be recognizable as the young woman in calico who had disappeared a few weeks previously. The real danger would be in meeting someone face to face, and that she hoped to avoid.

What would Charlie have done when he got to town? She wished he'd let her come. The two of them might have come up with a workable plan. This way, whatever they did separately might only make matters worse. He was here somewhere, doing no telling what.

Hugging the shadows along the east side of Lincoln Street, she moved cautiously toward her objective. The town was quiet this time of the morning with only a few riders and fewer residents walking about. At the intersection with Grant, she waited a long while before scuttling across and back into the shadows. As she neared Nuzman's Mercantile, she slipped into an alleyway where she could keep an eye on the front entrance of the jail.

There was no sign of Charlie or any trouble he might have caused. It was a normal weekday morning. Come Saturday the town would throng with people, but today only a few went about their business. It didn't matter what day it was, though, Jesse was probably in jail for a murder his brother had committed, and it was up to her and Charlie to get him out. Somehow.

Even as she breathed a sigh of relief that he hadn't ridden in, guns blazing, she caught movement out of the corner of her eye, a shadow that crept from the doorway behind her. Who was it? There was no place to run, and with her heart hammering in her throat, she cast around for a weapon. Something, anything she could use to defend herself. The shape spoke before she could bolt and run.

"That you, girl? It's me, Charlie. I told you not to follow me."

She didn't bother to reply. What could she say with her heart in her mouth?

"Okay, so you did what you wanted," he said. "No big surprise. Now that you're here, I guess we'll go in after Jesse together, but you'd do well to stay out of the way. Where's your horse?"

"Back at Elk Creek. Where's yours?"

"Yonder, at the end of the alleyway. Where you reckon they put Jesse's?"

"Over at the livery, I'd guess."

Charlie remained quiet for a minute. Standing so close to this twin of the man she loved raised the hairs on her neck. It was eerie to look at him, to see Jesse there and realize this man was a killer, several times over.

187

His golden eyes fastened on her. "Can you find him?"

She'd lost his train of thought. "Who?"

"The horse, dammit. Don't play the dense, helpless little woman. You came along, I expect you to do what's necessary."

Shivering, she hugged herself against his fury. "Yes, I can try."

"I'll need him in back of the jail in ten minutes. Can you do that?"

"How will I know ten minutes?"

Charlie hissed a string of curses. "Make a guess. Just get the damned horse over to the jail as quick as you can without getting caught."

She nodded. "What'll you do?"

"You don't need to know," the man said, and pulled his pistol. He rolled the cylinder to see if it was fully loaded and let it hang at his side. "Git a move on, now!"

She hurried to the street, then glanced back at him. He waved the gun barrel at her.

Tears of anger and fear blurred her vision and she swiped them away with the back of a hand. If Charlie got Jesse killed she'd see he hung for what he'd already done, and without a qualm. Damn him for ruining Jesse's life—and maybe hers too.

Peering around the corner, she waited for a lone man to pass by, then slipped out into the deep shade cast by the buildings and worked her way toward the livery stables. If Buck wasn't there, she'd simply take one of the other horses. This was no time to be a good, honest citizen, not with Jesse's life at stake.

After what seemed an eternity, she sneaked through the open doorway into the silent livery. The aroma of hay and horses greeted her. The morning sun that filled the street left the buildings on this side in shadow, and it was hard to see anything for a while. She hoped that the proprietor was occupied, though he wasn't the kind to figure out what was going on. As she recalled, the poor man wasn't much smarter than the animals he cared for, a boy in a huge, awkward man's body. He loved horses and didn't mind cleaning up after them. He was a perfect employee for the Oursler family, who owned the stables and several other businesses in town as well as a huge farm on the north side.

He shuffled toward her, large hay rake in hand. "Mornin', ma'am."

"Morning, Doolin. I came for that roan gelding, the one with white leggings. The sheriff sent me."

"Oh, yeah. I'll get him."

"Uh, could you saddle him?"

Doolin stopped, scratched his head and studied her. She smiled sweetly.

Finally he nodded. "Uh-huh. I can do that too."

"Thank you."

"You're welcome, ma'am." Nodding again, as if satisfied with himself, Doolin fetched Buck, slipped the bit in his mouth and the bridle over his ears, spread the blanket and threw on the saddle, then pulled the girth tight, each movement so slow and deliberate that Angeline almost exploded with the need to move. She had to get out of there before someone came in, before Charlie started something over at the jail and she got trapped in the middle of it.

She knew better than to say anything to Doolin about hurrying, for that would distract the poor man from the chore and he'd be a long time getting back to it.

Her anxious glance stumbled over an anvil just inside the door. Lying beside it was a hammer and chisel. If Jesse were chained, they'd need something to cut him free.

Outside, several people strolled by while Doolin slowly finished his chore. She imagined Prophet walking right up to her, taking her arm and dragging her home, everyone in town standing by and watching, doing nothing. Even poor, dumb Doolin.

And Jesse over there in jail waiting to be hanged.

Another quick glance over her shoulder, and fear ate a great hole in her belly. Dear God, couldn't the man hurry?

She shifted, took a few steps toward him, then captured Buck's dangling reins. *Move, get out of here now!*

Doolin finished cinching the latigo and turned to her with a wide grin. "There, ma'am. He's ready to go."

"Yes, yes. Thank you so much." She clucked her tongue at Buck and led him toward the front door. Beside the anvil, she stooped, hefted the tools and slung them through the stirrup to let the gelding carry their weight. Doolin said nothing.

Taking a deep breath, she walked out onto the street with the horse, acting as if she belonged there. There was nothing for it but to go in plain sight to the alleyway that led to the back of the jail. Now would be the time where she might get caught. Everyone must know about her kidnapping. Let even one of them see her and they would raise such a cry, she'd never escape, let alone get the horse to where Jesse could get away.

She would settle for his escape, she knew, if it came to a choice.

"Oh, please, let him get away," she said to the gelding. "Carry my Jesse away."

Buck nickered and trotted along beside her, his ears perked forward. Something was up and he was eager to be part of it. "You're a fine horse, Buck. Real fine."

Balancing the heavy tools, she leaned against his neck, head down, and made for the alley. Once off the street, she began to run, terrified that her ten minutes were up and that any minute Charlie would come flying out of the jail with Jesse, guns blazing, and find no way to escape.

At the back of the small building, all was quiet. Had they caught Charlie and put him in a cell with Jesse? Were they even now trying to figure out which one of these identical men had pulled off the killings? Or would they hang them both and be done with it?

She stood there only an instant before Charlie led his horse up to join her from the other end of the alley. He handed her the reins and she showed him the tools, her heart settling down a bit in her chest.

He nodded with surprised satisfaction. "A handled chisel and hammer. Smarter'n I thought you were, girl. If he's chained we're liable to need those. Hold the horses, and be ready for us to come out." He gestured toward the back door of the jail. "You'll ride double with Jesse and we'll head out toward Elk Creek, pick up your mount and be gone. Got it?"

"Yes, but what're you going to do in there? Not kill someone."

"If I have to, I will. I'm getting my brother out, anyway it takes."

She set her jaw, grinding her teeth so hard they ached. There had to be a better way than more bloodshed.

As Charlie made to leave she grabbed his sleeve. "Let me go inside first. Try to get him out."

"Don't be a fool. How you gonna get him out? That's about as stupid as I'd expect from the likes of you. You're nothing but a ragamuffin."

He jerked away and was gone before she could say another word.

Hobbled by chains Jesse took tiny steps back and forth across the small cell. What a mess, and him with no way to get in touch with Angel. What would she do when he didn't return? Come after him? Dear God, he hoped not. Prophet would have her in the blink of an eye if she did. He prayed she'd go free and nothing bad would happen to her. He tried to imagine a noose around his own neck, choked as if it were already there and stumbled around the small cell. To his body it was as if to sit would be to give up.

The sheriff's office and jail were one open room, not like the one in Abilene, so he saw Charlie pass by the

191

window that opened into the alleyway, his gun raised. Hope curled upward in his throat. He hopped to the cell bars, then watched as his brother eased through the door.

Charlie took one look at the condition the man had left Jesse in and cursed. "Good to see you, brother. Where're the keys?"

"Sheriff went to eat breakfast, took them with him. My God, Charlie."

"Yeah. Well, hell. We gotta hurry, get you out of there."

Jesse shrugged, and held out his hands to show the shackles on his wrists. "I can't ride like this—can't hardly walk."

"Don't worry about that. I get you out of that cell, we'll toss you over the saddle like a tow sack if we have to. I'm getting you out of here."

Jesse studied the harsh features of his long-lost brother, so glad to see him that his chest tightened. Life had treated him bad. There was no joy in the man's squinting eyes, lined by the fury of his ways; no mirth around the full lips so like his own but stuck in a permanent scowl.

He watched Charlie ransack the desk. "What are you gonna do?"

"Find something to pick that lock. Get you outta there before that old fool comes back and I have to kill him too."

Jesse swallowed hard. "You killed that deputy, didn't you?"

"Hell, yes, they were gonna string me up. What'd you expect?" He stopped, and came up with a narrow-bladed knife. "This oughta do."

Kneeling on the floor at the cell door, Charlie worked for a few seconds at the large key hole. "These things ain't very complicated inside. You just gotta know what you're looking for. Got out of Dodge jail by picking the lock from your side. Not so easy as this." He screwed up his mouth, fiddling around a bit more. Then there was a loud click. The door swung open.

. "Come on, out back. That whore's waiting with your horse."

"A whore? Where'd you get a whore, and why?"

"Hell, brother, you tell me. You're the one traveling with her."

Angel, a whore? Jesse wanted to slug his brother, but he was so glad she was safe he let it go. Charlie nearly dragged him to the front door, then stuck his head out to take a quick look. "Okay, go, go. Around the corner to your right."

Jesse hobbled as quickly as he could, jumped off the boardwalk and shuffled into the alley where Angel stood, holding Buck's reins. Her eyes lit and she cried out his name.

Charlie hissed at her. "Keep it down, you want the whole town out here?"

By that time, though, she was hugging Jesse around the neck, tears of joy wetting his skin and shirt. His cruel iron shackles were surely poking into her skin.

Charlie pulled her away. "No time for that. He can't ride this way and we can't take the time to bust 'em here. Someone might hear, or that fool sheriff might come back. I'm gonna throw him across the saddle; you'll ride behind me. Now, do what I say and don't stop to talk."

Brutally Angel found herself shoved toward Charlie's long-legged bay. The outlaw bent, folding his brother over his shoulder and backed up to Buck. Awkwardly, Jesse managed to pull himself across the saddle, belly down, as Charlie crouched to slide out from under. Then he gave Jesse another shove to balance him. The chains rattled in the still morning air. Charlie mounted and Angel handed up the tools, then hurriedly leaped up behind him. He didn't help her, and she was left grabbing hold as the bay moved off down the alley.

They took the back way, following the alley past several nearly deserted residential streets. It was slow going because Jesse couldn't hold on and they dared not gallop or even canter. Angel clung to Charlie's waist, though she seemed reluctant to make any other contact.

"We have to break those chains off him," Charlie said when they arrived in the shelter of trees where Angel had left her mare.

The palomino raised her head, then nickered at Buck and stomped. She wanted to be free. Angel slid off the horse's backside and ran to Jesse. It had to hurt, riding that far hanging over a saddle, wrists and ankles shackled. She tried to help him off. Charlie came up behind, grabbing Jesse's belt and hoisting him easily to the ground.

"Good to see you, little brother," he told Jesse, and that was that. No hugging or back slapping.

Angel rubbed Jesse's shoulders, his arms, stood on tiptoe and kissed him. He dropped chained wrists over her head and shoulders to hold her close. Against her ear his heart beat a fast rhythm, and she was surprised to feel him trembling.

"I thought I'd never see you again," he said in her ear. "They were going to hang me."

"For something *he* did," she said, glancing at Charlie.

"Well, I guess so. But it's okay, we got away."

"You two can stop that now. If we don't get you out of those chains and ride out of here, we'll all be in jail."

"I know a place we can hide. No one will find us and we can rest up the horses, decide what we're going to do next. We can get Jesse out of those chains, too. It's real close by and no one goes there since they closed down the mine."

Charlie studied her, then Jesse, who nodded. "Where Angel?"

"The old gold mine, it's just up the creek a ways. It's shut down. We can lead the horses in the water, they'll never be able to track us. They'll sure think we rode off."

"Aw, that's a load of guff. Whoever heard of a gold mine in Kansas?" Charlie said.

"Well, there is one." She was going to say more, about going there and finding the gold, but Charlie would probably steal it all and ride off, mean as he was, so she shut up.

"Let her show us, Charlie, it'll give us some breathing space while they're out chasing their tails looking for us."

"Hell, no."

Jesse took her hand. "You do what you want, I'm going with her."

"After I risked my life to get you out of there, you'd side with a whore against me?"

Jesse stiffened. "That's the second time you've called Angel a whore. Do it again, I'll clean your plow."

"Ho, ho, ho. Little crybaby grew up, did he? Okay, show us your dadblamed gold mine. But I'm not saying I'll stay. I come to get you, brother, but I got bigger plans than hiding like cowards in a played-out mine."

Taking a deep breath, Angel grabbed up Jezebel's reins and led her into the shallow creek. Jesse followed, taking shuffling steps to accommodate his chains. Bringing up the rear, Charlie brushed out their tracks with a tree branch, then moved into the water.

The opening to the mine lay in a high bank above the creek. Someone had run off with the cart that had been used to haul out the gold-veined rocks. The roof of the cavelike entrance was just high enough to allow the nervous horses inside. For a ways, light splashed the floor and walls and picked up an occasional wink of gold. Farther in it grew quite dark. Hanging on the wall was a coal oil lantern, likely the last, and Charlie took it down and lit it.

"How far back does it go?" he asked, his voice echoing eerily.

"A ways," Angel said. "The veins petered out and so they finally shut it down. Just a few weeks ago."

"Never knew Kansas had any gold mines. Course I do know where there's a fortune in gold."

Angel shivered at the smug tone in Charlie's voice, like someone coaxing a rabbit out of hiding so he could put a bullet in it. Still she didn't react any further to his statement, nor did Jesse. His chains rattled over the rock floor as they moved deeper into the mine. Behind them the entrance shrunk into a small, faraway hole. Shining the dim light, Charlie spied a broken-off slab of rock.

"Here, brother. Let's get you out of those."

Jesse laid his wrists so that the chain was drawn tight over the surface of the rock. Placing the cutting edge of the chisel in the riveted slot of the shackles, Charlie came down hard on the flat end with the heavy hammer and the iron cuff popped loose.

"Wowee," Charlie shouted. "Wowee, wowee," echoed back at them.

They stood there for a moment, almost afraid someone had heard.

When nothing happened, Charlie whispered, "Good thing they used wrought iron. We'd a been all day getting you loose from steel." He freed the other wrist, then instructed Jesse to lie down and prop his legs up on the rock. All the shackles and chains soon lay on the floor.

Angel watched from a distance. Charlie tossed the evidence back into the darkness with a clatter that made her ears ring.

Jesse sprung to his feet, pounding his brother on the back, then wrapping him in a bear hug. "How you been? My God, how you been?"

Pushing him away, Charlie growled. "I been in prison, how you think I been? Well, now what do we do?"

Jesse went to Angel, touched her. "I'm sorry about this, honey. Real sorry. Everything'll be okay, once we get out of this country."

The flame of the lantern reflected a sadness in his eyes. Charlie had hurt him, and Angeline wanted to soothe that hurt. He reached out and she went into his arms, and

196

exchanged kisses with him. He nibbled an ear while she licked at the base of his throat. His tongue followed her jaw line and she kissed his chin.

"It wasn't your fault. I love you, Jesse. I thought you were going to hang,.and I wanted to die."

Charlie took the lantern off its hook. "If that's all you two can do, I'm going exploring. See how far back this goes and what's here. We don't want to be trapped in here with no way out."

After his brother left, Jesse cleared some of the rubble from the floor and he and Angel sat there wrapped in each other's arms. They had come so close to losing each other; she never wanted to let him go again. They weren't safe, and both of them knew it. They had to go somewhere far, far away. There was no way to pursue her divorce now. With a sigh, Angeline snuggled into his arms.

Later that evening, after Angel fell asleep with her head in his lap, Jesse remembered Charlie's talk about gold. When his brother returned, he asked him about it.

"Oh, so you are interested in something besides that little—"

"Watch your mouth, Charlie. I'm not the sniveling baby brother you left behind."

"And I don't suppose you've ever forgiven me for *that* either."

Jesse studied his twin in the dim light. "I don't guess I have, but when I heard you'd been hung I set out to catch the cowards that did it and see they paid. So I guess I care a little bit about you."

"Cross and Doolittle? I made that story up. Thought if the law believed I was dead they'd quit hounding me. It didn't work, though. I went to prison anyway, even though they didn't put it all together for a spell. Hell, I couldn't behave myself long enough to make anyone believe I was dead."

"Killing Zeke over and over again, huh, Charlie?"

"Shoot. Ain't as complicated as that. Just having me a little fun, just a little fun."

"Well, it's not a life I want. Me and Angel, we're going to get married and have kids—a normal life."

Charlie snorted. "After what happened today? Better not count on it. You just escaped a hanging party. They'll be after you big time."

"But they thought I was you."

The mine echoed with Charlie's laughter. It gave Jesse the chills. "And they will again."

Angel stirred and Jesse smoothed her hair. He had to protect her, make sure no one hurt her, not even himself.

"Why'd you latch on to her? Don't you know you can get that anywhere you go?"

Jesse studied his twin's unforgiving expression, and remembered it hadn't been too long ago he'd felt the same. Maybe all Charlie needed was someone to love him. Then he thought about all his brother had done and knew it was too late for that sort of redemption—or any sort, for that matter. Charlie was alive, not hanged at all, and that released Jesse from any need for revenge. He and Angel could move on, could get out of this place and go west where no one knew him. Maybe they could go far enough away, they could build a marriage that no one would ever challenge.

He glanced down into Angeline's angelic sleeping features and felt the grip of powerful emotions. They were stronger even than any ties he might have to this brother, this man who cared so little for himself or anyone else.

Charlie played idly in the rocks on the floor, then glanced up, and in the lantern light Jesse caught a glimpse of that young boy who had suffered so much, who so many times had taken a beating to protect him. The vision came and went so quickly he wondered if it had really been there. But it made him doubt his earlier thoughts. He owed Charlie a lot.

His brother spoke. "Jesse, I came back for you. You asked about the gold? Well, I know where there's a wagonload, ripe for the taking. You and me . . ." He paused, gesturing toward Angel. "Her if you have to. All we need to do is go get it. No one will ever come looking for it."

Without thinking, Jesse scoffed. "Yeah, you and hundreds of others. Don't you know better than to believe stories of lost gold? What'd you do, buy a map?" Then he thought again. Was this what those men had meant?

Charlie grinned. "It's not that way at all. I know where it is. Me and three others, we took it, back at the end of the war, and only I know where it's hid."

Jesse shifted on the hard rocks, and in his lap Angel pursed her lips, smiling in her sleep. He wanted to kiss her, hold her tight, make love to her. Instead he met his brother's brutal, cold stare. It was the look of a stone-cold killer. Those three bushwhackers had been telling the truth after all. A shudder rocked Jesse to the core.

The sooner he and Angel got away from Charlie, the better. But escape from family might be easier planned than carried out.

Chapter Thirteen

Jesse thought Charlie would never sleep, almost nodding off himself before his brother finally began to snore. He waited a while longer, then placed a hand over Angel's mouth and gently shook her awake. Her eyes that widened with fear quickly calmed.

He held a finger to his lips and signaled her to get up. In the pale glow of the lantern they crept to their waiting horses. Leading them, they made their way to the mouth of the cave. Hooves clinked on the rocks strewn about the floor, the echoes sending shivers down his spine.

What would Charlie do if he awoke and caught them sneaking off? Jesse hated to leave his brother, but for Angel's safety as well as his own, they had to separate themselves from him. His hatred and way of life would get them both killed.

Once outside the mine, they mounted up. Their animals moved off slowly, picking their way along the creek bank and into the water. Dusk embraced them in pinks and golds and purples. Off to the southwest enormous thunderheads boiled into the rainbow-hued sky. They would have to hurry to reach shelter before the storm broke. It looked like a vicious one. Perhaps it might be wise to delay their escape, to remain safe and dry in the mine.

As if reading his thoughts, Angel eyed the threatening sky. "Maybe we should've stayed there."

Only hesitating a moment, Jesse made up his mind. "No, Charlie scares me. Much as I love him, we can't take that chance." He didn't tell her he feared for her

200

safety if they remained with his brother. And he couldn't voice the sadness that filled him. It was almost as if the old Charlie had died.

"Where are we going?"

"Anywhere you want," he said, and reached out. She nudged Jezebel close, placing her hand in Jesse's, and they rode side by side, the rhythmic movement of the horses rocking them into a false security.

Not long before full dark, with lightning illuminating the heavy-bellied clouds overhead, Jesse spotted a deserted soddy. Its roof was grown over with tall wheat grasses, its door gaped and its shutterless windows stared at them like empty eyes. Sensing no pursuit from his brother, he suggested they bed down for the night. Charlie would soon awake and know that Jesse had deserted him.

The wind freshened, though it still smelled of sulphur and dust and the approaching rain. Lightning played tag amid the wicked clouds above, and thunder rumbled and rolled while the ground trembled. Unsaddling the horses, they left them in the lee of a mud wall that had at one time been an animal shed of some sort. Poor shelter, but a summer rain wouldn't hurt the animals and there was plenty of grass.

Inside the soddy they spread their bedrolls and saddles, and Angel unpacked the last of their food supplies. At one end of the twelve-foot-square room was a mud and straw fireplace, but they had no use for it. It wouldn't do to have their smoke spotted. They would eat a cold meal and be thankful for what they had.

Angel handed Jesse a large portion of the remaining deer jerky and stuck the end of the last piece in her mouth. It tasted sweet and salty. "Do you think he'll follow us?"

"I don't know. It'll depend on his mood, I guess." For a while he gnawed on the hard, smoky meat, not saying anything until she spoke.

"Are you sorry . . . about Charlie, I mean?"

"Some, but it's for the best. What I'm really sorry about is the way he is. When we were kids I knew he was different, but we got along. It was like I kept him from being too crazy and he kept me from being too cowardly. We were good for each other, I reckon." He shrugged. "Now, I don't know if I could control his urges."

She couldn't imagine Jesse ever being a coward, and thought he might be too harsh on himself. But she didn't say so. In companionable silence, they chewed on the jerky while the storm raged outside. Finishing hers off and licking her fingers, she took out the last can of peaches. He remembered eating the others alone, when he'd returned to camp to find the can sitting open beside the fire and her already asleep. This time she was with him, and that made him smile.

He took out his barlow knife, thumbed the blade open and rammed the sharp point into the can lid. Patiently he hacked around the top, then carefully turned the sharp metal up to get at the fruit. He speared a half with the knife point and held it out. She leaned forward and took the sweet morsel between her lips. Lightning flashed outside, lighting the gleam of juices on her lips. He bent to take a taste. Laughing, mouth to mouth they shared the bite of fruit, then another and another, their hunger for each other growing as wild as the weather.

Afire with longing, Jesse shoved the can aside, grabbed Angeline's shoulders and kissed her deeply. The last vestiges of remorse for his brother faded from his mind when she responded eagerly to his advances. The clamoring storm echoed their furor as they strained toward the pinnacle of their desire.

He wanted her totally, completely, and sensed she felt the same. Did they dare consummate their love while she still belonged to another man? In all probability she always would legally be Prophet's wife. There was no safe way out of the unfair situation.

Her fingers flitted over him like butterflies upon a flower. She touched his burning flesh with tender eagerness, tasting, pulling away to move to another, sweeter spot.

Under her ministrations the buttons of his shirt fell open. She pushed it apart, kissing the base of his throat and trailing down his bare chest to the belt at his waist. Her tongue warm and moist, her lips nipping and demanding, she drove him to new heights of passion. He could scarcely deny himself, and imagined throwing her down and taking her with total abandon.

Outside, the rain drove against the walls in noisy cascades, lightning danced and thunder rolled. A rain-kissed breeze darted through the windows, cooling their flesh but not their ardor.

In the darkness of the storm he held himself in check, relishing her hands at his belt, tugging, working at the buckle until she finally loosened it. For a moment he let her set the pace. He would not force her. She had never known a man and he wanted her first time to be pleasurable. If not tonight, then soon. It was her choice. They had time, and this delightful play encompassed him in an exquisite joy. This was a new experience with a woman he truly cared deeply for.

She twisted open each button in his stiff jeans' fabric, taking her time and kissing each inch of bare skin as it was uncovered. A burning desire blossomed within him, growing in intensity until he could hold back no longer. Raising his hips, he helped her pull down the pants, took her hands and guided them to his throbbing arousal. The gentle touch, turned fierce by her own desire, drove him into a frenzy. He felt like baying to the heavens.

Outside the storm roared in its climax. Rain whipped through the windows to soak their perspiring bodies. The walls shuddered.

Cupping his hands on the outside of her thighs, he

pushed up her buckskin dress, encircled her bare hips, and rubbed his thumbs over her smooth belly and down to the hot mound of her sex. He lifted her to straddle his lap. By only shifting a bit, he could be inside her. Crazy with the need to do so, he lifted her hands away, sliding her forward until their needful bare flesh touched with the shock of a bolt of lightning. Together they cried out.

At the sound of her voice he drew back. He didn't want to hurt her, no matter how much he wanted this. He thought he might burst with the need of her, and he held her close while the ecstatic agony peaked and subsided. Release left him exhausted and terribly dissatisfied. He would not be able to hold back again, he feared. The next time there would be no stopping short of fulfillment for them both.

Coiled against him, she panted. "It didn't hurt like you said it would."

He took a deep breath, thought about what she'd said, and willed himself to relax. It had hurt plenty, but there was a strange sort of satisfaction in caring more for her than for himself. After a moment, he could reply. "We didn't do anything, Angel. Not yet. We were just having some fun, enjoying ourselves. I didn't . . . I mean, we . . . didn't finish."

He knew no other way to say it to her. He would have to teach her everything she was to know about sex and making love, and he didn't want to do it wrong, to make her afraid or ashamed of the way she felt. And most of all he didn't want to hurt her.

"Oh, but it felt so good. Up inside of me, I mean. Like . . . like a little heart there pounding thousands of times a minute."

In the darkness he caressed her with trembling fingers. "It is a little heart, my sweet. And I hope I can always make it pound like that. When the time comes I'll be very gentle with you. When a man gets to needing a woman so badly, he sometimes isn't as careful as he should be, sometimes he hurts her with his blind passion. Sadly, it's the way we're made. I promise to be very careful with you." He made the vow with his eyes closed, and hoped to God he could keep it.

She was quiet for a long while, then softly, she said, "I like it when you want me so much you can't help yourself. Is it bad to like that?"

He laughed, holding her close, and willed his semi-aroused flesh to calm itself. "No, Angel, that isn't bad." If anticipation was half the fun of the doing, then their first time would be about as enjoyable as anyone had ever known.

"When will we do it, then? I thought you loved me and we were going away together. Doesn't that mean we can do it now? We can never go back and get my divorce from Prophet, not now. They would surely catch you and hang you."

"There will be a time when we're both truly ready."

She ran her hand teasingly over the bulge between his legs. "It seems you're always ready."

"And if you don't quit doing that I'll be more than ready."

"I thought I was ready tonight."

"Me too, but . . . well, let's work at it some more. It'll be easier for you if I . . . well, don't just plunge right in, if you know what I mean."

She didn't, but by this time had decided that whatever Jesse said was the gospel truth, something she could abide by. He would never lie to her or let her down, would always protect her and be with her. She only hoped that they would soon fulfill their love.

As the storm rumbled on past and faded into the distance, they slept in each other's arms. The hush of its passing soon filled with the lilting serenades of thousands of night creatures.

* * *

Jesse and Angel rode into the small town of James Crossing two days later. Named for the intersection of trails, it offered several choices. With Circleville behind them to the north, they could go east to Holton; south to St. Mary's Mission on the banks of the Kansas or Kaw River where they'd hit the trail to Dodge and points west; or west across the Pottawatamie Reservation, eventually crossing the Big Blue River before turning south where they could hit the trail to Dodge. Though more remote and less settled, the western route appealed to Jesse.

Anybody with good sense would travel the more populated trail south and then take the more heavily traveled route along the Kansas River. That would be what Charlie might think too.

Since Jesse had never taken either route, when they arrived at James Crossing, he questioned several folks. At the blacksmith shop, where he took the horses to be shoed for the long trip, he talked to a freighter having repairs made on a wheel at the blacksmith shop.

The freighter, a bearded man who was lean as a rail, was eager to talk. "The route through the reservation is safe enough, but danged barren. There's water, though you ought to take plenty of canteens. It's tall grass country. You might even see some buffaler, though they're getting scarce as snakes' teeth."

"What about the Indians?"

"Aw, they're half-starved and know their time is come and gone. Mostly, if you run across any, you won't be a-scared. It's pity you'll be feeling. Take some sugar and lard along, they'll be happy."

"I'm still not sure we wouldn't be safer going the other way."

The lean freighter spit a long strand of tobacco juice into the hay-strewn mud. "Maybe, but renegades and bushwhackers prefer the better traveled trail. Richer pickin's, I expect. If I was a-goin' that southern route, I'd fall in with other travelers. There's safety in groups of folks together."

Jesse thanked the man, shook hands and told the farrier he'd be over at the saloon while the man finished the shoeing and feeding of the horses. He'd be back for them directly.

With Jesse absorbed in his tasks, Angeline found the general mercantile and went in to replenish their supplies for the long trek west. As much as she liked the buckskin dress Twana had given her, she needed something more practical.

She bought a pair of bloomers—the only pair in stock—and a skirt which she would shorten using the needle, thread and scissors she also purchased. She had seen many of the pioneer women wearing the blouse-legged bloomers under short skirts, claiming such garb enabled them to get around with a good deal of modesty, climbing in and out of wagons and traipsing around the wilderness. Though most did not ride astraddle, Angeline did, and she had a hunch such an outfit would be much more comfortable on horseback than the buckskin.

She also bought Jesse a new pair of jeans pants, searching for those with the longest legs she could find. If they didn't quite fit around the waist he could cinch them up with the leather belt he wore. Having had her arms around that narrow waist on several occasions, she thought herself a good judge of its size. Two blouses, two shirts and two pairs of stockings finished the clothing list. The weather was turning hot and she had a feeling they would wear fewer clothes when alone. She inspected some boots and brogans, but left them where they sat. Before winter would be time enough to buy new shoes.

At the notions counter, she spotted a mirror with mother-of-pearl inset into the handle, and picked it up to glance at herself.

Reflected in the glass at her shoulder was the lovely, heart-shaped face of another woman, lips and cheeks rouged a bright red. She smiled and turned to see a girl with bare shoulders and full bosom, blushing pink nipples partially revealed. In her upswept black hair was pinned a bright bauble that flashed in rays of sunlight drifting through the windows.

A fancy woman. The first she'd ever seen.

"Sorry, I didn't mean to bother you. You going to buy that?" Older than she'd first appeared, the woman spoke with a southern drawl, her dark eyes luminous and sad.

Angeline held the mirror out to her and shook her head. "It'd just get broke where we're going. You want it?"

"Might as well. I like pretties and why else do what I do but to buy them." The statement, in no way a question, had a sharp edge to it. She tilted her head, examining Angeline from head to toe. "Where you coming from, honey?"

Immediately wary, Angeline said, "Oh, just up north. We're going . . . I mean, I guess we'll head south."

"Oh, sweetie, you don't want to do that unless your man's got himself a big gun. That trail is rife with the worst outlaws you can imagine."

Angeline only nodded. She didn't want anyone knowing where they were going, even if this woman appeared harmless. She might remember them later and talk about where they went.

Two women dressed in faded calico entered the store, glanced toward Angeline and the fancy woman, then sniffed and made a point to swish their skirts as they turned away.

The girl she was talking to lifted her chin, and Angeline touched her hand. There she saw a wicked bruise encircling the delicate wrist, prints that looked as if someone had grabbed her there, hard.

"Don't pay attention to them. I've seen that before.

Back where I come from some women are so uppity they can't hit their mouths with a fork for holding their noses so high in the air."

The girl chuckled and looked at her with wary gratitude. "My name's Sally, what's yours?"

Without thinking, Angeline told her, then wished she had bitten her tongue. She had to be more careful if they were to keep Charlie, John Prophet or even Sheriff Oursler from finding them.

"Well, it's nice to meet someone human," Sally said. "I have to get my things and go back to the saloon. Reb doesn't look kindly on us taking time off."

Angeline bid her good-bye and continued shopping. With her purchases neatly stacked inside the door, she ran into the street to find Jesse. As she looked to the north, she noticed three riders rounding the curve into town. One, a tall, ginger-haired giant stopped her heart. Racing onto the boardwalk, she hid in the shadows while the men passed. The big one glanced her way, but didn't see her. She saw him, though, and her suspicions were confirmed. He was the giant Jesse had so thoroughly thrashed and left along with his friends on the riverbank naked and without mounts. These men had called Jesse by his brother's name and insisted he take them to the gold. Gold she now knew Charlie Cole had stolen.

She had to find Jesse, warn him. Yet she dared not kick up a fuss. The men probably would make a stop here, for it was a long way between settlements on the plains. Dear Lord, suppose they found her and Jesse?

Slowly, she stuck her head around the corner to see where they went. Down at the end of the street, they reined up at the saloon, tied their mounts and disappeared inside—hopefully only to drink and not to ask questions. Several people had no doubt noticed her and Jesse, and would be more than glad to talk for the price of booze.

Once they were in the saloon she ran across to the

blacksmith shop. Missing Jesse there, she hurried to the livery. She inquired about a pack horse there, or perhaps a mule. She found mules came too dear and settled for a broad-chested, big footed gelding the man was willing to part with for the largest of nuggets in one of her bags.

The man threw in a ration of feed for the three animals to supplement the grass they would find along the trail. The animals would be expected to work hard in the days to come and deserved grain along the way. Glancing once more toward the saloon to see the men's horses still tied out front, she led the pack horse back to the mercantile, wondering once again where Jesse had gotten to.

In the saloon, Jesse sat midway along the bar, nothing but rough oak planks laid across empty whiskey barrels, when Rawley, Cake and Fletch came busting through the door. Hands wrapped around a beaded glass of cold brew, he nearly squeezed it into splinters when he saw them. Thankfully they didn't see him.

How in hell had they followed him? Or was it pure coincidence? He had a hard time believing in that, it just didn't seem possible. No, they had picked up his trail somewhere, somehow, and now he and Angel would have to lose them. Damn, what a mess, and Charlie no doubt was on their back trail as well. Too bad he couldn't sic these three on the true culprit and force Charlie to share the gold that these men had no doubt helped him steal. Maybe that would get them out of his and Angel's hair. They had enough troubles without this, what with wanted posters for Charlie everywhere and no one able to tell Jesse from his brother.

At the moment, though, his main concern was to get out of the saloon before they saw him. He touched the butt of his Colt, but knew he didn't want to start a gun battle. The war had been enough for him, and he wasn't like his cousin Johnny Ringo, no matter his fears of bad blood. All he'd do was get himself killed. Eyes on his opponents, he downed the last of his beer and glanced toward the back of the saloon. Most of these places had a second entrance where deliveries were made and where the fancy girls could come and go without wading through customers. If he could sneak quietly out the back, he'd find Angel and they'd get out of town without being spotted.

Angeline moved down the alley behind the saloon, recalling that the girl she'd met at the mercantile worked there pleasuring men who paid her. It was hard for Angeline to imagine such a thing. As much as she liked Jesse holding her and kissing her and all those other things he did, she couldn't imagine catering in that way to nasty, drunken men, and different ones each night, too. Sally probably didn't like it much, but had no choice. It was a fine example of what happened to a woman alone in the west.

The back door stood partly open and she slipped inside. For an instant she was struck blind, coming in out of the bright sunlight. Someone ducked through a hanging curtain to her right and she saw it was a fancy woman with very few clothes on, her lips, cheeks and eyes painted. Much like Sally, but not her.

"Excuse me, but do you know Sally?" she asked the girl, who turned weary eyes on her.

"Who wants her?"

"I do, well, I mean, I'm really looking for a friend, and I thought she might have seen him."

The girl threw back her head and laughed harshly. "Honey, you lose your man to Sally, you might as well give him up for gone."

As the girl laughed, Sally came through the curtain, adjusting the top of her dress, an angry red brand along the top of her breasts. She peered toward them, and Angeline thought she might burst into tears at any moment.

211

But her eyes cleared when she spotted Angeline. "Honey, is that you? What're you doing in this hellhole?"

Angeline couldn't take her eyes off the angry mark on Sally's pale skin. "I can't find my man. I've looked everywhere; he must be in there." She nodded toward the front of the building. "And I'm afraid to go in. There are some men . . . I mean, they can't see me . . . I don't—"

Sally held up a hand, interrupting her stammering excuses. "Never mind, I'll take a look. What does he look like?"

"He's real tall and handsome."

Sally guffawed, the tone raw. "Well, honey, what man ain't?"

"He has hair like mahogany wood and golden eyes."

Squinting, Sally frowned. "Golden eyes?"

"Yeah. You can't miss him."

"I'd think not. You stay here, I'll go in and take a look around, bring him back here with me if he's in there."

With a knot in her throat, Angeline nodded. She waited in the narrow, dark hallway outside the room where the fancy women plied their trade. From inside she could hear grunts and yelps, moans and whimpers that made her flesh crawl. She'd heard them before and knew what was going on.

A few moments later, Angel heard his voice. He was following Sally into the back. "Now, look here, honey. You're pretty and all, but I've got me a girl and I—"

"Oh, Jesse," Angel said, and grabbed him from behind.

"I take it this is your guy," Sally said, voice carrying a certain amount of envy. "He is handsome." She tweaked his cheek and laughed.

Sweet relief filled Angeline. "Oh, Jesse, this is my friend, Sally. Sally, this is my . . . this is Jesse."

Puzzled, Jesse nodded at the other woman. His expression said that Angeline made the darndest friends.

"Oh, Jesse, I was so afraid. I didn't know where you were, and when I saw those men . . . Did you see?"

He spoke at the same time. "—I couldn't get out without going past them, and so . . ."

Both cut off their speech and hugged.

"You two need a place to stay, and I know of one," Sally said.

"Why would you do that? You don't know us or what we might have done," Jesse said in a voice Angeline found too harsh.

She squeezed his hand and frowned. He had the sense to appear sheepish. "Sorry," he mumbled.

Sally seemed not to mind, though, or perhaps she was used to being spoken to in such a way. Her dark eyes remained focused on Angel, as if they were long-lost friends.

"I have a little place outside town, but on Saturday nights I'm never there till Sunday morning. You can use it, get a good night's sleep. Maybe whoever's after you will have left by then, or given up finding you here."

Angel took her hand. Sleeping in a bed would be wonderful. "Oh, that's sweet. But I don't know. Maybe we ought to just ride out, get as far as we can." She looked to Jesse for agreement.

"Nonsense," Sally said, taking charge as if she were a mother hen and they her brood. Fingering deep in the cleft of her bosom, she produced a key. She gave them directions to the cabin, then winked. "There's a nice bed too— That's one thing I can never skimp on. Now, be off before they go back out on the street. Get a move on. Don't worry about anything. When I come out in the morning, I can let you know what your friends are up to. Come on, young man, show them to me before you leave."

Jesse went with her, peering into the gloom of the saloon and pointing out the giant Fletch, and his companions Cake and Rawley. "They are bad ones."

"I've been taking care of myself with worse than them since you were a baby," Sally said. "Leave them in my care and get on out while you can."

Jesse found himself liking the woman, who, on closer inspection, he saw was a good ten years older than he'd thought. She must be coming up on forty. Soon she would be out of here, homeless and jobless. How did women get themselves into such predicaments? He shuddered to think that Angel might have fared no better had she succeeded in running away.

They thanked Sally once more, then slipped off down the alley and across to the livery where they fetched their horses, stopping by the mercantile to pick up their supplies. Then they headed toward Sally's cabin. Never once did Jesse take his eyes off the door of the saloon. If those three yahoos had come out, he would've had no choice but to try and gun them down in the street.

The hairs on the back of his neck rose and wavered in the evening breeze as they rode out of town.

The three men weren't their only problem. Jesse could sense that Charlie was coming.

Chapter Fourteen

The sun had set by the time Angeline and Jesse arrived at the hidden lane to Sally's cabin. Jesse had been particularly nervous during the entire ride, glancing over his shoulder constantly. His uneasiness was catching, and she soon found herself doing the same.

After a quick circle of the small house, he visibly relaxed. "Looks good."

It took a while to unpack and store everything in the sparsely furnished single room, but finally it was done. Jesse led the horses off to find grass and water. When he returned, Angeline announced her need for a bath, scratching an itch under her dirty buckskins. Her skin felt as if it were crawling with vermin.

Interrupted in visions of the two of them having a home like this—making love in the narrow bed or on the rug before a roaring fire, or various other imaginative locales—Jesse grinned sheepishly.

"It's out back. I hobbled the horses across the creek in a little meadow. No one can see them from the trail. There's a path from the house down to a rock-lined basin." Once more he grinned and scratched under his arm. "I could use a bath myself. How about if I join you?"

When she looked up she glimpsed a devilish twinkle in his eyes, briefly reflected by the pearlescent glow of evening coming through the window.

She dug around in their purchases, and came up with the sweet-smelling soap. "Well, I suppose that would be all right, as long as you don't look. My mother taught me not to let a man look upon my bare body."

"Not ever?" He grabbed at her but missed as she darted from the cabin. Their laughter filled the air with sweetness and light, and the joyful sound entwined like the honeysuckle vines that hung thickly from the trees.

Through the high branches, patches of sky shimmered a farewell to the day. Under their feet the ground grew dark, the path nearly invisible.

"I hope we don't get lost," she said, and took his hand. It felt warm and powerful wrapped around hers. "Oh, Jesse, suppose there are snakes."

"Probably are. You know how they like water. Oh, the snakes come out at night, what a fright," he sang, "To bite you, oh, yes they do."

"Oh, keep that up and you'll scare all the varmints away—including the meanest snake crawling."

"Thank you very much."

"You're quite welcome. And I thank you for clearing out all the living creatures for at least ten square miles."

"Oh, well. Glad to do it. I'm at your beck and call."

They quickly reached the sloping bank and a large hollowed rock that formed a natural bathtub in a still pool. Sparse evening light lay over its surface like liquid silver.

"Look, you can see the bottom. It looks wonderful." Without hesitation, Angeline sat down and took off her moccasins, then rose and peeled her dress off over her head.

A cool breeze licked at her warm flesh, and goose bumps crawled along her arms and legs. She hugged herself.

Standing above her, Jesse gazed in awe at her dark silhouette against the water dancing at her feet. Caught up in her beauty he'd forgotten to take off his own clothes.

She raised her head, turned so that her up-tilted breasts formed tempting shadows, and reached out. "Well? Aren't you coming in?"

He swallowed so loudly that he looked around to see

216

where the noise came from, and it felt as if his heart were trying to beat itself to death against his rib cage. Desire for her infused him and made him dumb. He opened his mouth to reply, but nothing came from his dry throat but a husky caw.

God, how he wanted her. Not just in the passion of this moment, but forever. He wanted to wake up every morning for the rest of his life and see her dear face, its sweet innocent smile, and the flash of her azure eyes. He needed to feel the touch of her mouth on his, run his hands through the rumpled golden hair that seemed to go everywhere but where she put it.

But was happiness truly possible? Someone would soon catch up to them, destroy all their dreams. They'd seen those three men in town, outlaws who weren't likely to give up.

But what would be wrong with capturing happiness, even if only for a brief moment? Angel and he could share that. Soon, he would be caught and probably killed, either by the law or one of those greedy bastards chasing his brother. But wasn't it their right to know happiness? Wasn't it his right?

Not that long ago she herself had practically begged him to make love to her. And fool that he was, he'd backed off. Well, that wouldn't happen tonight. Everything was just right. The warm velvety night, the balmy wind, an audience of stars just beginning to twinkle, the song of the flowing water. It was all so very perfect.

He unbuttoned his shirt with fingers that felt like tree stumps. They were big and fat, and stiff as another part of his anatomy since watching her disrobe.

A squeal frightened him and he started for her with his shirt half off. "What? What's wrong? You okay?"

"Yes. The water's cold, that's all."

He saw she had waded in the pool up to her knees. "Be careful, that may be deeper th—" The warning didn't all get out before she went under without a sound, loose hair

217

floating out around arms that chopped awkwardly at the surface. Without hesitation he jumped to her aid, catching her under the arms and lifting her effortlessly. She hung there looking half-drowned. Though she couldn't have been under more than a few seconds, she choked and gasped and coughed something awful.

Holding her at arm's length—he couldn't help but notice how her firm breasts floated on the surface—he regarded her with a quizzical expression. "It keeps me hopping, rescuing you from drowning. Remind me to teach you to swim next chance we get."

She spewed and sputtered, peering through strands of wet hair plastered over her face. "Just because a person can swim doesn't make that person superior," she said.

"Oh, little miss prim and proper. I'll teach you superiority." He pulled her close and she wound her arms around his neck.

He staggered and almost lost his footing on the slick rocks. In water up to his neck, he couldn't do much but hang on to her. Moving toward the rim of the tub, he touched a shelf of rock under the surface and deposited her there. "Now, stay put while I get out of these clothes. And don't make me rescue you twice in one night or I won't be responsible for what happens."

Arms propped on either side, she leaned back and tilted a look at him that almost made him forget his own name. "Is that another one of your false promises?"

Her posture drew his gaze to her breasts, gleaming in the starlight. He bent forward and hungrily kissed first one, then the other.

"There, that ought to hold you," he said in a voice that quavered. God, he felt like grabbing her and . . . and . . . the throbbing in his sex had grown exquisite, torturous, as if he'd been plunged first in fire, then in ice.

It was getting too dark for him to see. He had to get out of his clothes, get into the water, take her in his arms. On the bank, with some effort he dragged off his wet boots and clothing, then left them in a pile and leaped into the water with a howl and a splash. Angel screeched and one of their horses whinnied from somewhere nearby.

Paddling to her, clamping her legs with both hands, Jesse whispered, "Be quiet, be quiet. Someone might hear us."

"Me be quiet? You nearly swamped me."

Lazily, he floated, gazing at the luscious curves of her young body. For a long while he found great satisfaction in simply drinking in her beauty while moving his hands over the smooth flesh of her calves and thighs. He took his time, enjoying each touch, each sensation. But he knew that another part of his body wouldn't be content with that for long. It wanted more, throbbed for release.

She lathered the soap and wiped slick suds down over his stomach.

He groaned, moving her hands lower. His body had risen to the occasion quite nicely, despite the cold water.

"Better give that to me or this is going to be over before it starts." He took the bar, then rubbed it between his palms and washed her back, concentrating mightily on the immediate task at hand. Starting with her hair he wet and sudsed it thoroughly, then leaned her backward over his arm and rinsed out the fragrant bubbles. Next he massaged the hollows of her collarbone and smooth shoulders. She was right, the soap was sweet-smelling, like roses or lilacs, something vague he could barely remember from childhood.

Her skin felt slippery as satin, better even; it was so smooth he couldn't come up with anything to compare. When she raised her arms, he washed under them, then slid his hands beneath the water, tracing along her ribs to her small waist and past the gentle curve of her hips.

Encircling her with his arms, he stroked her flat belly. When his touch strayed lower, she leaned back against him, encouraging him. Cupping one hand over his, she guided him to her most secret warmth.

Gasping, he slipped his fingers within her, but there he stopped. He sensed the barrier of her virginity, the gate he would have to open.

"Angel, Angel," he whispered against her cheek. "I don't want to hurt you."

Unexpectedly, she turned so they faced each other, his fingers slipping out.

"My turn," Angeline whispered and took the soap. She rubbed it between her palms. This time she wouldn't let him stop.

Her body tingling all over from his ministrations, she washed his chest, teasing the curly dark hairs into circles. Stopping at his waist, she left him moaning with expectancy and moved to tenderly wash his wrists. They had been rubbed raw by his shackles. Then she moved her hands up to his broad, muscular shoulders.

The scars on his back felt like strips of leather under her fingers, and she shuddered, kissing him quickly several times to drive away the visions of him being beaten. She moved on to lathering his hair.

He leaned forward as if to take her in his arms, but she held him off and continued her chore of bathing him, teasing him. She massaged one earlobe, then the other, probing inside each one with a small finger.

"My mother told me never to put anything smaller than my elbow in my ear," she said. "But I'm being very careful."

"And very deliberate."

"Slow? You mean I'm slow?"

"Oh, God, yes."

"Do you like it?"

"I . . . yes . . . I . . . No. It's a little love, a little hate."

"Oh? What about this."

Without warning she cupped her soap-slick hands around his erect member.

From down in his throat came a guttural cry, a half moan, half growl. The sound affected her, too, and she thought she might burst from within, her need for him grew so strong. The little heart between her legs pulsed till she feared it might explode. With a gasp of desire, she guided him inside her, easing the tip of him in and savoring the feeling of him beginning to stretch his way inside of her. Then, with determination, she raised her legs and locked them tightly around his waist.

Something inside of her burst with a sharp pain, but it turned to ecstasy as he slipped deeper into her. It seemed he stroked the core of her soul. His hands locked around her hips, he gently, exquisitely, explored the depths of her being, igniting a raging desire that burned away the ache of his intrusion. Her head back she held on as he thrust within her, mind reaching for stars that cavorted through the darkness like dancing fireflies.

Embraced by the night wind, a cool mist off the water that whistled through the leaves of the cottonwood, Angeline let herself be swept away in a rhythm of desire, love and hope. Higher and higher she rode, letting him swirl her into the heavens with the power of his touch.

At the apex of her ecstasy, she felt him shudder. He cried out then and held her so tightly against him she caught her breath, holding it while her world tumbled apart.

After a moment, his mouth buried in her shoulder, he said, "Are you okay? I didn't hurt you? I don't want to hurt you. Angel, say something. Do something."

"I love you, Jesse Cole," she whispered, and she cupped his head in both hands.

They played in the water then until their fingers and toes were wrinkled. Touching, kissing and exploring, Angel and Jesse spent the night inventing new ways to enjoy the age-old joining of man and woman. At last, when the night sky had begun to lighten with morning,

221

they made their way to the cabin. There they collapsed on the narrow bed, wrapped in each other's arms.

Usually Sally walked home in the early-morning light. A mere mile or two, and it gave her a chance to rid herself of the stink of the hole where she worked. This Sunday, sore from a beating by a man who looked exactly like the man she'd lent her cabin to, she took a carriage left at the livery for the use of all the women who sold their favors in the saloon. It had been a gift from one of their well-endowed admirers who got his kicks in very strange ways, but for which he was extremely grateful. He often left expensive gifts for the girls who indulged him; the carriage had been one of them.

Every inch of her body objected as she rode along toward the safety of her home. The man who had beaten her had pretended to be hunting his other self, but if he was in truth the same one with Angel, then the girl could be in danger. On the other hand, if he had told the truth, then the other two needed to know he hunted them. What a vicious man. She had thought he would kill her, but by the time he had finished, she had wondered if she cared.

Fearful that he might be lying in wait to intercept and follow her, she used extreme caution, stopping at the turnoff and studying every direction before steering the carriage down the left fork. The sun had slipped above the horizon, pouring a bright golden light over the land, but clumps of trees could easily hide all sorts of creatures in their deep shadows. Slowly, she approached the lane that led to her hidden cabin. There was still no sign of movement in any direction. Nothing but birdsong floated on the brisk wind.

Her mare's hooves thudded softly in the rich earth. From up ahead a horse cried out a greeting. The mare returned it, dancing an impatient two-step.

"Whoa," Sally said, but couldn't hold back her eager

horse. Her arms ached so from being gripped and twisted last night, and it was all she could do to hold the reins.

Inside the cabin, Jesse heard Buck whinnying and rolled over to listen. Were he and the buttermilk mare having some fun? The second cry convinced him otherwise. It had come from up the lane toward the main road.

Someone was coming!

He shook Angel, told her to dress and, gun in hand, darted to the window to peer cautiously outside. It was the woman from the saloon, in a fancy buggy. She was doing well to keep the animal under control, and he hurried out to give her a hand.

When he got there, he got a good look at Sally. Her eyes were swollen nearly shut, a smashed lip had ballooned to twice its normal size, and blood was smeared along one temple. Running to her aid, he caught her as she fell from the seat into his arms.

He carried her inside. There he laid her upon the bed.

Angel, who had quickly put on the darndest garb he'd ever seen—some kind of long pants gathered at the ankles and a skirt that didn't even come to her knees—was buttoning on a plain white shirt. Her eyes widened at the sight of the beaten saloon girl.

"My goodness, what happened?"

"I don't know. We'll have to ask. Looks like someone beat the hell out of her."

Angel had long since given up improving Jesse's speech, and he was grateful she didn't even flinch at his cursing. Truly, he did try to curtail it, but sometimes the words slipped out when he got excited or upset.

Sally moaned and rolled her head toward them. Obviously she could barely see through the slits of her swollen eyes. How she had gotten out here without collapsing, Jesse had no idea.

Gazing at Angel, then at Jesse, the woman's face crinkled and tears poured over the battered cheeks.

Angel dropped to her knees beside her and took her hand. "What happened? Who did this to you?"

Sally stared past Angel at Jesse. When she spoke, the words were a jumble of sounds that Jesse could scarcely make out, but Angel must have because she asked him to step outside for a minute.

He nodded and did so. There was no gauging what women would do or ask a fellow to do, and he'd learned that he might as well go along with that, especially where Angel was concerned. She certainly knew her own mind and would do what she wanted. No sense in arguing with her.

Outside he leaned up against a post holding up the porch roof and gazed down the lane, thinking with pleasure of the night before. He sighed.

Women like Sally never knew when some crazy man was going to beat on them for no reason. It was a life many chose, not because they wanted to but because they had so few ways of earning their living if some man didn't come along who would marry them and treat them halfway decent. It was a hateful situation, and one he hadn't pondered much until he met Angel. In a different situation his love could easily have fallen into such a life. He was grateful she hadn't.

Suddenly Angel was shouting out his name. She ran to the door and flung it open. "He's here, in town—Charlie. Oh, Jesse, Charlie did this to her!"

At her words, Jesse was horrified, but he wasn't terribly surprised. He spoke calmly. "We've got to get out of here. He probably followed her. Did he ask about us?"

"I don't know, and she's in no shape to answer questions. We can't leave her here for him to beat on some more, maybe kill."

Sadness filled Jesse, for his brother and the life he led. He wished that somehow things could have been different. Odd how they had turned out like they had, complete opposites, though they'd been through all the same hardships. He could never bring himself to commit some of the horrible deeds that Charlie did as simply a matter of course.

Bringing himself back to the present, he said, "I'll take her to the buggy, and you can ride with her. I'll saddle Buck and bring the other horses. There's no time to pack up our things. Get your riding gear and whatever you can grab and go on out. I'll bring Sally."

"Jesse, be careful. She thinks *you* did this to her. She doesn't know you and Charlie are two different people."

His throat burned. "Oh, God. Well, can't you tell her?"

"I'll try." She leaned over Sally. "Honey, this is Jesse, and he's going to carry you outside. The man who did this to you is his brother. Don't be afraid of Jesse. Let him take care of you. He's a good man."

The woman clung to Angel's hand, but allowed Jesse to pick her up without fighting. Since she wouldn't let go of Angel's hand, she walked to the carriage alongside Jesse, climbing up first, then helping get Sally settled in the seat next to her.

"Stay there, I'll get what stuff I can. I want you to go on ahead. As soon as I saddle up the horses I'll follow. Head on south, don't go back out to the east-west road. If he's coming, that's the direction he'll be riding. Stay on this road. If you find a good place to lay up where he won't find you, wait for me there. If not just keep moving. I'll catch up."

She looked like she was going to defy him. He knew her fears, that if they separated, something might happen and they'd never find each other. But she had to trust him, this was the only way.

"Do it, Angel."

He gave her a steely expression, and she nodded, gathering up the reins. Jesse watched as, her face resigned, Angel slapped leather on the horse's behind. The little mare skedaddled.

He wasted no time. Salvaging what supplies he coul
and snatching up Angel's gold, Jesse hurried across th
clearing toward the meadow. But his plans were cut shor
Charlie came while he was saddling Buck and tying o
the packs.

From the hidden meadow across the creek, Jess
watched Charlie approach the cabin, his gun draw
What was he planning on doing, killing his own brother

Whatever his plans, they were changed abruptly. Cha
lie had scarcely mounted the cabin steps before three ri
ers rode up, hollering and shooting everywhere b
directly at Charlie. They leaped off their horses and rushe
him. He took a couple of wild shots before the huge gi
ger-haired man in the lead was upon him, knocking hi
off the porch where all three quickly overpowered him. H
must have been as surprised as Jesse at their arrival.

Crouching behind the thick undergrowth along th
creek bank, Jesse watched as they kicked Charlie aroun
in the dirt for a while, then trussed his arms behind hi
with a rope. Jesse couldn't help but think, if he let thes
men ride off with his brother, it would solve part of hi
and Angel's problem, yet he couldn't help but imagin
they might kill him. He had to help, somehow.

Torn, Jesse finally decided to follow them for a whil
before deciding what he would do. Angel and Sally wer
out of danger. He would have no trouble catching up t
the slower moving carriage once he finished with thi
business.

To his dismay, the four headed off in the same direc
tion he'd sent the women and were riding as if their tail
were on fire. At this pace they'd soon catch up with th
carriage. Then there would be some showdown. Hir
Angel and Sally against this mess of thieves.

And then, he couldn't help but know, somebod
would die.

Chapter Fifteen

The little mare galloped as if her heart were truly set on escaping, but her valiant efforts to drag the two-wheeled buggy were soon thwarted. The trail grew rougher, narrower. Between the ruts an occasional tree stump jutted from the scarred earth, threatening to rip a wheel off; branches hung low, brushing at its top. Daylight flashed through the overhead canopy as the conveyance crashed along. Beside Angeline, Sally clung to the seat, her features grim.

Hunched forward, Angel gritted her teeth and grappled with the reins. Only pure blind luck would see them through. Abruptly, they broke out of the trees and into the open, a brilliant sun temporarily blinding her. The road hugged the rim of a gentle rise to the west and emerged onto the endless, rolling plains. It was treeless, with no place to hide, not even a shadow in which to rest—just an ocean of grass swaying in a timeless rhythm, brushing the blue of a cloudless sky at the distant horizon. Traveling out there, they'd surely be spotted by anyone in pursuit.

Not sure what to do, Angel pulled up the excited horse, hesitated only a moment, then urged her into the trees as far as they could go. Leaning toward Sally, she touched her arm.

"You okay? I need to get down and look around a bit. I won't be long."

The injured woman nodded, but didn't try to speak through her pitifully swollen lips.

Angel cringed in sympathy, wrapped the leathers

around the brake handle, then leaped down to scout the immediate area. Surely there must be a safe place to hide and wait for Jesse. It looked as if they would have to send the horse and empty buggy off along the trail, for there was nowhere to conceal them. Together she and Sally could hole up in the underbrush. But could the injured woman manage to walk more than a few feet?

Assessing their chances, Angel decided there was no other choice but to get rid of the buggy, much as she hated to be on foot with no means of escape. Soon Jesse would come along with the horses. The important thing was to stay safely hidden until he did, to not let Charlie find them.

The urgency of the situation drove her to act fast. She had to get them both off the road and out of sight. Sally was not a huge woman, but she easily outweighed Angel by twenty or thirty pounds and probably had four or five inches on her.

Angel led the mare deep into the woods, the huge trees nearby scraping at its wide-set wheels. She had spotted an outcropping of rocks, fissures and thick undergrowth, which seemed a good place to hide Sally while she kept a lookout on the trail.

Looping the strap of the water canteen over her head, she quickly explained the situation to the other woman.

"You'll have to climb down. I can help you."

Together they managed the task. Covered with sweat, Angel left the James Crossing fancy woman leaning against a tree. "We've got to get you out of sight, but first I'm sending the horse and buggy off. They should head back to the stables in town, I imagine. Can you wait here?"

Sally nodded grimly. " 'Ere 'ould I go?"

Angel nodded. The woman had grit. They were *going* to make it. And when they did, she would see that Sally had some gold so she could go somewhere and start a fresh life.

* * *

It didn't take long for Jesse to catch up with the men, who
for all their purpose hadn't set a fast pace. Maybe they
couldn't make up their mind where to go or what to do,
now that they finally had their quarry. Their indecision
was a relief to him. It would give the women a chance to
put some space between themselves and these despera-
does. He too would like to put some distance between
them, and had no desire to continue to follow the men,
unpredictable as they were. He was tempted to let Charlie
handle himself, he always had. Somewhere up ahead
were Angel and Sally, and Jesse thought of cutting
through the woods, bypassing the four men to reach them.

So concerned about Angel, he almost rode up on the
men when they stopped to answer the call of nature. He
stopped himself at the last minute, though, hiding in
some brush. From there he observed. Poor Charlie had
been left tied over the saddle of his horse, while the other
three stepped off the trail. When they turned their backs
to do their business, he got a good look at his brother.

They'd beaten him pretty badly, smashed him around
some, and it was evident he was in pain. Probably thirsty
as well. In the shadowy haze of the woods, he imagined
that suffering man as the boy he'd once been, the one who
had taken licks meant for his brother over and over again.

Jesse recalled the boy who'd curled, knees to chin, in
his filthy bed refusing to cry though his back was striped
with crusty blood; the youth who, one night when Zeke
was lashing Jesse, had said it was enough and dragged
the old man off. Jesse had always thought he would have
died that night if not for his brother. Before Angel, Charlie was the only thing Jesse had ever loved. Only together
were either of them truly whole. But that had been ten
years ago.

A lump rose in his throat.

How could he ride away and leave Charlie to his gruesome fate? How could Jesse live with that? There must be something he could do, some way he could set him free. But even then, was his brother in any shape to run? His only choice was to see that Charlie made it away.

At last, that decision made, he swung easily from his horse, pulled his Colt and hailed his opponents. They turned as one, flies still unzipped. It was a comical sight, and one he might have laughed about at any other time. At the moment, though, he wanted only to shoot the bastards and do the world a favor. But he couldn't. Not with them standing there with their pants open, looking confused and then furious, then confused again when they got a good look at him and Charlie.

"God awmighty, they is two of 'em," the giant Fletch said.

"Is that you, little brother?" Charlie asked. A trace of pain laced through the gruffness of his voice.

"It's me."

"Well, do something. Don't just stand there."

"Take off your clothes," Jesse said to the three men.

"Aw, hell. Not again," Rawley said. "I swear one of these days I'm gonna catch you out and you're going to be bare-ass naked the rest of your life. I'll follow you around and see to it."

"Now," Jesse said, motioning with the gun.

"Let me get him," Fletch said. "He cain't shoot all of us."

"You wanta be the one he does?" Cake grumbled and began to unbutton his dirty shirt. "We'll walk out of here alive this way. Live to fight another day. But this time we'll not stop till we catch up to you, whoever the hell you are, and strip your hide."

"Shut up," Rawley said, and began to unbutton his shirt.

Boots thudded into the dust, shirts and pants following. Watching the men, Jesse knew that if these three ever did catch him out, as Rawley put it, they'd get their revenge and then some. None of them would be adverse to providing him with a slow death, laughing all the while. His finger tightened on the trigger, the barrel of his Colt wobbling, but he couldn't kill them, not like this, in cold blood. Jesse had seen the life fade from the eyes of men he'd killed in the war, and he never wanted to look upon that again, not unless he had no other choice.

Charlie was otherwise inclined. "What the hell you doing, little brother? Shoot 'em and be done with it. And get me out of this mess."

"Hold on," Jesse said. He took a lariat off one of the outlaw's saddles and, backing all three up to the trunk of a huge elm tree, walked around and around them until they were safely wrapped. Holstering his gun, he untied his brother. "Now, git, Charlie. Ride out and do whatever it is you want to do. Leave me be."

Instead, what Charlie did was fall off his horse. Surprised, Jesse stared down at his unconscious brother for a moment, then shrugged and knelt beside him.

Only a few seconds passed before Charlie started to come around, his eyes unfocused and dull. Jesse noted the bloody, cracked lips and fetched a canteen. With his bandana he wet his brother's mouth, then raised his head and let him drink. With the familiar head cradled on his arm, a strange emotion went through him, a feeling of connection and yearning.

"Dammit, Charlie. Why didn't you stay dead? Why'd you have to come back and cause all this trouble?"

The golden eyes rolled, tried to focus. An expression of befuddlement settled on the battered face. "I did my best, baby brother, my very best. For me it ain't never been enough, you know that."

It took some time, but he got Charlie aboard his horse, slumped but swearing he could stay in the saddle. Jesse ran off the outlaws' animals then and, leading his brother's mount, the buttermilk and the pack horse, he headed down the trail. Echoing behind him were the curses and shouts of the near-naked men wrapped tight to a tree beside the sparsely traveled trail.

"Ought to have killed them," Charlie said after a while.

Jesse knew he was right, but shook his head. "Wasn't something I could do."

"Always was a scaredy-cat."

Jesse glanced in his brother's direction, the tone of his accusation so like the child he had been and not the man he'd become. And beyond the bruises, the deadly eyes, the tightly stitched lips, the humorless expression, he caught a glimpse of the boy who had become this man. And in the vicinity of his heart, an ache grew—for what had been, for what could never be again.

"We need to be going the other way," Charlie said.

Once again intent on scanning the trail ahead for sign of Angel and Sally, Jesse only grunted.

"I said, let's turn around. I'll take you to the gold, share it with you. Only reason I'm out here running around instead of loading it up right this minute is cause I wanted to give you half."

Jesse wasn't sure he believed his brother. "I don't want your gold. I have to find Angel. Her and me are riding out of this country, to see if we can start a new life where no one knows us or you. And Charlie, I'd appreciate it if you rode in the other direction. You can leave any time you see fit."

Charlie didn't get a chance to answer, for Jesse suddenly spotted Angel ahead. She stepped out of the bushes into the trail, wearing those funny bloomers and a short skirt, her hair in braids so that she almost looked like a child. But what a lovely, endearing child. When she saw Charlie was with him, her face clouded, but Jesse leaped from his horse and took her in his arms, and she melted in his embrace.

232

"I was so afraid something had happened to you," she said against his chest.

"Me too," he said with a grin. "Where's Sally? She okay?"

"I got her bedded down about thirty yards off the trail in some underbrush."

"Let's go get her. We don't want to leave her alone too long."

"Jesse, I want to take her someplace away from here, someplace safe and give her some gold for a new start." Only after she said it did Angel realize that Charlie could hear, and she glanced warily in his direction.

He responded. "Hey, Jesse. You want to share your half with someone, fine by me. Hell, give it back if you want. But I aim to see my brother has what's coming to him. You bring that other whore along, she's your responsibility. And she falls behind, we leave her!"

"What is he talking about?" Angel glanced from Charlie to Jesse with a puzzled frown.

Jesse shook his head and answered her look with one of his own, a warning that it would be best not to discuss their business any more. Feeling her in his arms, he almost forgot he was angry. But Charlie's pained laugh reminded him.

Jesse snarled over Angel's head at his brother. "I told you I don't want the gold. It's bathed in blood."

Charlie snorted. "Ain't you the one? They were just a bunch of renegade soldiers. Probably woulda been hung for what they did if we hadn't killed 'em first. Who cares?"

"The law cares, and they'll hang you if they catch you."

"They won't catch me."

His earlier feelings of sentimentality dispelled, Jesse turned from Charlie in disgust. "No, it'll be me they catch and hang for your crimes. But I don't aim to stick around long enough for them to do it."

233

"It's a lot of gold," Charlie said. "And it belongs to no one. You said you wanted to take her somewhere, make a new start. The two of you could go anywhere, do anything, with that much gold. No one would ever find you."

Temptation crawled into Jesse's mind. For Angel. "How much gold, exactly?" he asked, and swallowed harshly.

She caught at his sleeve. "No, Jesse, don't."

"A dang wagonload, as much as six horses could haul. The axles were buried almost hub deep when we come across the desert with it."

"We've got enough," Angel said.

"And it came from where?" Ignoring Angel, Jesse watched his brother closely. He'd always been able to tell when Charlie was lying if he looked close enough.

"Three soldiers out of Jo Shelby's Iron Brigade stole it down in Texas. Jo would've killed 'em himself if he knew; you've heard tell how he was. Honor and duty-bound." He snarled the words. "Fool could've had all the spoils, way he rode through Texas after the war, but wouldn't take nothing. Hell, he shot up Rabb's Raiders in Austin just to keep 'em out of the Confederate Treasury there—then refused to take any pay for his men, and some of 'em without even a decent uniform to wear. And the war already over. Fool."

Jesse angled his head. "So how'd you and those yahoos come by this stolen gold?"

"Heard it was happening. One of the thieves got too drunk one night in the cantina. Me and Rawley figured if they could steal it, we could take it from them. Let them get away from Shelby first. Danged fools was planning on hauling it all the way to Canada. Can you beat that? Hell, they'd never have made it. So we took it away from them—me and Rawley, Fletch and that madman Cake. He's the one did the actual killing . . . leastways, he started it. Likes it better'n any man I know. Killing, I mean."

Angel plucked at Jesse's sleeve again, but he paid her no mind.

He wet dry lips, thought of all that gold and how he and Angel could live like kings. The law already wanted him, would never believe he hadn't broken the neck of that deputy in Circleville. Why not take a share of this gold if it would mean they could get away from this place?

"You can't spend gold bars," he said to Charlie, a last ditch effort to rid himself of the temptation.

"Ain't gold bars. It come out of a mine in Colorado; it's nuggets and dust. Bags and bags of it. Mined for the dying Confederate cause—a last ditch effort to fund a losing battle. All we gotta do is take it out and spend it a little at a time. No law against that, is there?"

"How do we get it out?"

"No, Jesse. We can't." Angel squinted up into his face.

Not meeting her gaze, he took her arm. "It'll be okay, Angel. I promise it will. This is our chance to break away, once and for all. Neither one of us will have to work doing something we hate. We can just make love and be free. Forever. Just think of all that gold."

Angeline stared into his eyes, shivering. There was something there she'd not seen before, something that frightened her. It was as if, for a moment, Jesse had been in his brother's mind.

Charlie drew his thin lips into a parody of a grin. He had won, and Angel hated him in that moment every bit as much as she loved his twin. He was taking Jesse away from her, and there was nothing she could do. It was either go on alone, or go with them and break the law. She saw that clearly. If she'd had a gun at that moment, she'd have shot Charlie. She loved Jesse with every breath she took, and her heart would shatter if she lost him. But somehow he'd been led astray. Somehow, she had to break the hold his brother had on him, and lead

Jesse back to the light. She had to fight for him, even though Charlie scared her to the bottom of her soul.

"What about Sally?" she asked Jesse, who had busied himself tightening the cinch on the buttermilk. "I had to send the carriage away, couldn't find a place to hide it. She can't ride."

"Then we leave her," Charlie said.

Furious, Angel turned on him. "No, we *won't* leave her. Far as I'm concerned we could leave you—and it'd be good riddance, too."

"Whoa, girl's got spunk," he said snidely to no one in particular.

She caught the glint in his eye, and her hate for him returned. It wouldn't do to turn her back on this one. She feared for Jesse. He was blinded by a love he didn't understand: Love for this brother who would kill him as soon as look at him. Or was it just love of gold that moved him? Maybe she didn't know Jesse as well as she thought.

"I'll get Sally," Jesse said. He didn't like the way Charlie was looking at Angel, and wondered if he was making a terrible mistake. But, if his twin was to be believed, there was much gold to be had, and with it he could assure that he and Angel wouldn't live the life her parents had, poor and starving, struggling to exist in a harsh and unforgiving land. He could give her a life he never could have otherwise.

Those bags of gold she carried would scarcely see them through the trip west especially not with her penchant for generosity. And he'd never learned how to make money except outlawing, and certainly couldn't provide a life for her unless they broke free with money to spend. That was the secret.

He loved Angel more than life itself. He wouldn't let her down. She'd soon see it was the right decision.

They made their way to the Big Blue River, from which they headed south and reached the town of Manhattan on a dusky evening. Boiling up from the southwest was the promise of rain. From there they intended Sally to board a stage for whatever destination she chose.

They rode into town beneath a wall of ominous indigo clouds that crackled with lightning. As if it blew from the very gates of hell itself, the storm's hot wind lent fury to the oppressive heat. Dust devils swirled along the wide streets of the small town, whipping at the traveler's legs and clothing, and sent folks scurrying for cover.

"I could sure use a bath," Angel said, and Jesse silently agreed, tasting grit between his teeth.

"Me too," Sally said. "A good long soak in a hot tub sounds heavenly."

"Let's leave the girls at the bathhouse and hit the saloon," Charlie said.

Jesse took Angel's arm. "Aw, no, not me. And if you're smart you won't either. No sense calling attention to ourselves. Our face is on wanted posters all over Kansas and Missouri. We're going to have to be real careful or we won't live to spend any gold."

Charlie glared at Jesse, but finally nodded. "I'll just wet my whistle real quietlike. One brew and I won't cause a fuss at all. Come on with me."

Jesse clasped Angel's hand. "No, I'll just go with the women. They don't need to be on their own in a town like this."

"Suit yourself." The look Charlie gave him was a familiar one; it was the same as he'd always got whenever he wouldn't do something daring with his wild brother.

"Charlie?" Jesse said, reining up beside him in front of the saloon. "You get yourself in trouble in there, I ain't coming after you. We'll just ride on out. You understand?"

"Oh, yeah. And leave all that gold?"

"You heard what I said, Charlie. No fuss, no bother, or I'm gone."

Angel squeezed his hand and he knew she approved of his handling of the situation, even though she'd been worried about this risky adventure. He was happy to restore some of the faith he feared she'd lost in him.

Without saying another word, Charlie dismounted and disappeared through the bat-wing doors of the saloon. Leaving their horses there, Jesse, Sally and Angel walked toward the bathhouse.

Being with a wanted man, an outlaw, sent shivers of excitement through Angel, made her feel the same way as folks who bragged of having sheltered the James gang.

In the window of the mercantile were several ready-made dresses sewn of plain calico, with high necks, long sleeves and skirts that hung in soft folds; simple frocks made for busy days on the frontier. Sally hung back, gazing through the glass, yearning written on her bruised features.

The outfit she wore, one of gaudy crimson, was what she had worn her last day at the saloon. It made men turn on the street and stare and women lower their heads in disgust. Angel fingered the bag of gold dust she'd transferred to her pocket to pay for their baths.

"Let's go in," she said impetuously.

"Oh, no. I don't have any money to buy that."

"Nonsense. We can look. If you're going to ride the stage, you need something besides what you're wearing. It's dirty and torn."

Jesse didn't try to deter Angel from this little side trip, so she continued. When she looked back, he raised his shoulders and followed them, tilting his wide-brimmed hat forward to shadow his face.

Angel bought Sally one of the dresses, a pair of sensible shoes, some stockings and a small bag.

"I don't have anything to put in that," the woman said, admiring her dainty new reticule.

"Maybe not, but carrying it makes you look dressed proper," Angel said. She then paid for the purchases with some of her gold. She fought the urge to buy herself anything. Her bloomers, skirt and blouse were perfectly serviceable for a time yet, and especially when alternated with the buckskin dress.

Jesse came up behind her when she was paying for the dress. "We might as well replace the supplies we lost at Sally's cabin," he said.

She added a good variety of foodstuffs to her purchases, paid for everything and distributed the packages between herself and him, handing Sally the paper-wrapped bundle of new clothes. After packing the supplies on the horses, they went down the street to the bathhouse.

The storm hit while they were inside, and they came out sometime later to a deserted street, sheets of rain lashing buildings and turning dust to soggy mud.

"We'll need shelter from this," Jesse said.

They'd learned that the west-bound stage wouldn't be in till morning, and so decided to stay overnight in a real hotel with beds. Charlie came out of the saloon reeking of beer and smoke, but otherwise unharmed, and the two men led the horses through the downpour to the livery.

Sally and Angel waited under the sheltering overhang in front of the hotel. The air smelled sweet, and the wind was cool on their cheeks. From inside, Angel heard loud voices, one so familiar it raised the hackles along the back of her neck. It sounded just like her husband. But surely that was only her imagination. What would Prophet be doing over here so far from home? He never traveled.

She licked at dry lips, clearing her throat. "Sally, look inside and tell me who you see."

Peering through the glass doors, Sally replied. "Three men. One is wearing a badge."

"Describe the others." Even before the woman opened her mouth, Angel knew, but she waited for confirmation.

239

"Short, sturdy, bald. The other is tall and thin with a mane of white hair. He's the one doing the ranting. Can't understand what he's saying, though, can you?"

Miserably Angel shook her head, leaning forward and taking a quick peek through the glass. *Prophet!* She knew it. She could hardly breathe. Had they come all this way looking for her? And how in the world had they known she'd be here? Or was it strictly a coincidence? For a moment she froze, couldn't move or say anything.

"Do you know them? Angeline, what's wrong? Say something."

"We've got to warn Jesse, we've got to get out of town. I mean, not you. You can stay, but we have to leave. *Now*."

Pressing the remainder of a pouch of gold into Sally's hand, she gave the woman a quick hug and kiss. "Take care of yourself, and have a happy life. I don't guess we'll see each other again."

Mouth hanging open, Sally regarded the pouch. "I can't take this."

"Yes, yes you can. And be happy. Gotta go."

If Sally had any more objections, they were lost to the battering of the rain and the rumble of thunder. Oblivious to the storm, Angel ran through the downpour toward the livery as if she were fleeing the very devil himself.

Prophet had found her, but she wouldn't—couldn't—go back with him.

Charlie and Jesse stepped from the doorway of the livery into her path, and she bumped into the first, who took her elbows and gave her one of his looks. The touch of his hands made her skin crawl.

Jesse caught at her arm and Charlie let go as if he'd been burned. "Whoa, what's wrong, Angel?" he asked.

Breathless and rain-drenched, she gasped helplessly before she finally got it out. "It's Prophet and Oursler. Down at the hotel. We've got to go. Hurry."

She moved back inside the livery, dragging Jesse, who

still held her. The rain was coming down so hard she could scarcely make out his features. Fear clutched at her chest like fire, and when lightning forked in a savage volley—the noise that of a hundred guns going off at once—she squealed and hunched her head into her shoulders.

"We can't ride in this, Angel. Are you sure it's them?"

She danced around with impatience. "Yes, yes. I saw them. Prophet, Oursler and some other man. A short, squat fellow."

"Probably the local law," Charlie piped in. "Who the hell is this Prophet? I heard tell of him over in Circleville from that sheriff—Oursler was his name, wasn't it? He's the one I heard about her from." He gestured to Angel. "What are they doing over here?"

"They're after me. Me and Jesse," Angel said. "Now come on."

Finally, they stepped into the shelter of the stable, cloaked by the smell of hay and horses and wet earth.

Charlie thought a while as Jesse held Angel close, comforting her.

"Okay, let's think about this. They can't have come here after you. How would they know where you are? Second, if they didn't see you, chances are they won't on a night like this. I say we go check in and get a good night's sleep. If the bastard shows up, we'll kill him, that's all. Or if you want, I can go do that right now. Tell me where you saw him, and the job is done."

"No," Angel cried. "Jesse, don't let him."

"It's okay, don't get upset."

Charlie snorted. "Let me understand this. He came to kill you, the both of you, but you don't want him hurt?" He looked at Angel. "You're as bad as my brother here. So why don't you just go back with him? Then he'll leave your precious Jesse alone."

She glanced up into Jesse's eyes, but couldn't make

241

out any expression there. "I will if I have to, to keep him from hurting you," she said.

"No, no you won't. We're together, all the way. Let's just wait here till this lets up, then we'll ride out, get as far away from this town as we can."

"We can be in Missouri in a few days," Charlie said, "but I still think you ought to let me take care of this problem for you. I don't relish someone on our trail."

Angel tensed, even though Jesse's arms were wound tightly around her. Charlie was much worse of a threat than Prophet. No doubt about it. Prophet might be a stern man, but he was just.

Practically in tears, she waited while Jesse and his brother discussed the situation. Beyond the open door the rain poured down in sheets.

Chapter Sixteen

Because Angel was so distraught, Jesse said they would bed down in the livery. Sleeping alongside their horses, they could ride out as soon as the storm passed, not wait till morning and take a chance that Prophet might see them or get wind they were in town. How had the man followed them here? Why didn't he go home where he belonged?

Strangely, Charlie had little to say about it.

Nestled in the sweet-smelling hay, Jesse held Angel while she slept, afraid to close his burning eyes. He could no more have slept than walked on water. He saw Charlie, though, coiled in a corner snoring, his rifle in his arms as if it were a woman. Still, worrying wouldn't help any, so he readjusted himself and settled in to think about why Prophet might have come out this way.

Though convinced he wouldn't sleep, he must have, for Jesse came awake in the musty darkness with a start. Angel lay curled against him like a puppy, her lithe body entwined within his arms and legs.

Outside the rain had stopped and the night rang with the songs of cicadas, crickets and frogs. The steady, noisy drone was broken only by the occasional hoot of an owl or the far-off call of a lonely coyote.

In those hazy, first-waking moments, Jesse experienced a longing so heartbreaking that tears filled his eyes. All he wanted was this woman, but what with everything that had happened, he feared the worst. She would be taken from him, as surely as darkness filled the night. He sensed it so strongly that he held her even closer, burying his face in the warmth of her bosom, and embracing the rhythmic beat of her heart as if for the last time.

Perhaps he should distance himself, prepare for the day he and Charlie would be caught and hanged, or shot down in some dusty street. If he were harsh to her, maybe that would make it easier on her . . . on him. He'd known that since his brother's rescue.

If only Charlie had been . . . dead? The awful word came to him, but he wasn't sure he'd meant it. He had lived with the notion for so long, perhaps it would have been better than this hard outlaw that had taken his place.

No. Though such an emotion could well mean the end of his life, he loved his brother dearly.

Angeline made a little sound down in her throat and nuzzled against his neck.

"Oh, my Angel, I love you," he whispered. "I'm so sorry for what I've done that may keep us apart."

"Jesse?" she mumbled. "What's happened? What's wrong?"

"Nothing, sweet. The storm is over, I think we ought to go before everyone is up and stirring." Perhaps he should leave her here, end it now . . . but he couldn't.

She raised her head, locked both arms around his neck and gave him a sleepy kiss. "Oh, I had the most wonderful dream. We were together, and there was water everywhere, all around us. It was the ocean I guess, and no one could get to us. The sky was so blue it hurt my eyes. I didn't know you could dream in color, Jesse."

He didn't think he could, unless black and blood-red counted. He shook off the depressing thoughts. Being around Charlie again was taking its toll.

"Come on, we need to get out of here. I'll wake Charlie."

She sat up then picked straw from her hair. "Jesse? About Charlie."

244

"Hush about him. It'll be okay. He's my brother, my twin. I love him. Not like I love you, but I do love him. He needs to make up for what he did. He thinks he can do that by sharing with me. The least I can do is let him." He neglected to tell her what being with Charlie was doing to him, turning him back into a man he didn't much like.

He was up and gone before she could voice her fears, waking Charlie and getting their provisions stowed away.

Without speaking they led the horses into the deserted street. A skiff of clouds streaked across the sky, slicing through the jag of the moon. They rode out quietly, Charlie out front leading the spare animal that carried their supplies; Angel and Jesse rode abreast behind him. Though the streets were empty, Jesse kept a hand on the butt of his revolver, nervously checking every shadow.

From Manhattan the trail followed the Kaw River east to Lawrence and on to Kansas City. There, Charlie told them, they would head south for the foothills of the Ozarks. There was the cave in which he had hidden the wagonload of gold some six years previously.

"Suppose you can't find it, or someone else already has?"

"No chance. It's remote country riddled with caves. And I'll find it, never you fear."

Jesse nodded and didn't argue.

Angel dropped back, watching the two men who now rode side by side chatting amicably, as if they had never had a disagreement in their lives. It was scary how alike they were, yet how unalike.

The devil lived in Charlie, Angeline was convinced of it, and his every glance gave her the chills. But for now, there was no use in causing a fuss. She would not leave Jesse. He needed her now more than ever, what with his brother exercising such influence over him. And she needed him in ways she would never have guessed at only a few months ago. She was no longer the child who'd played games in the dust, but a woman in love with hopes and dreams for a future.

The hours passed easily enough. They rode at a steady pace, neither fast nor slow. Occasionally they met a traveler, sometimes a lone horseman, other times a wagon full of farmers. Yet, far from the emigrant trail, they saw no wagon trains heading west.

They didn't stop all day and it was late before they made camp that night. After a quick supper, Charlie wandered off, and Jesse and Angel cleaned up the dishes. He appeared aloof and cool when she spoke of her hopes for their future, and she finally touched his arm and asked him what was wrong.

"Nothing. Why?" He was still remote.

"It's like you're in another world, one where I'm not allowed to be."

He glanced at her, then quickly away. If the truth was reflected in those golden eyes, Jesse wasn't going to give her a chance to read it. "You're imagining things."

Apprehension nipped at her. "Ever since Charlie came you've acted . . . I don't know . . . sad. Like you were when we first met. Lonely but hidden behind some barrier."

She stepped in front of him, took the clean cooking pot from his hands, clutched like some sort of shield to keep her at bay, set it aside and wound her arms around his neck. Within her embrace he drew himself up and shivered, finally pulling her close.

"I love you, Jesse. What's going on? Is there something between you and Charlie you don't want me to know?"

"Nah, it's not that. I just . . . Oh, God, Angel, I'm so afraid of what's going to happen." Abruptly, he clamped his lips to stop any more words tumbling out.

Leaning back, she touched his mouth with the tips of

her fingers. "When you do that, you look just like Charlie—all drawn up within yourself. We shouldn't have come with him. We can leave, right now, while he's gone. We don't need his gold. Let him have all of it. Please, Jesse, please."

She kissed the tight line of his jaw, felt the muscles quivering there.

Finally he met her gaze, his eyes shimmering as if he might cry, if men did such a thing. The look brought tears to her own eyes.

He kissed the lids. "Aw, Angel, don't cry. Everything will be okay. Don't you see, I have to do this for him? All our lives he was the strongest, protected me from harm. I owe him something for that, and all he's wanted since he went off to prison was to come back and share this gold with me. He thinks he deserted me, feels bad about it."

She didn't think Charlie felt bad about anything he had done in his entire life, but wouldn't argue the issue. Jesse had become so aloof that she feared anything she said would push them further apart.

Together they lay down beside the dying fire, their bedrolls together. Jesse held her close until Charlie returned, then he released her and lay on his back, one arm under his head staring silently into the star-strewn night sky. It was as if he didn't want his brother to know how much he loved her.

With each passing hour, she sensed Charlie silently pulling Jesse away from her. It wasn't something she could actually see, but it was there. As long as they were alone Jesse appeared to care for her, but when his brother was around he acted ashamed of their attraction to each other. She finally gave up trying to sleep and rose quietly, wandering down to sit beside the creek. The sliver of moon that had crossed the daytime sky lay on the horizon to the west, a bright star cradled within its grasp. The gurgling water shimmered with dancing points of light.

She heard a sound, a whimper that at first she thought might be a small animal. It came from thick brush at a bend in the creek. She rose, peered in that direction, but could see nothing. If it were an animal, she needed to leave it be. It came again, sounding more human.

"Hello?" she called softly, so as not to awaken the men back in camp.

The whimpering abruptly cut off. She called out again, then took a few steps.

"Please." It was a voice filled with terror.

"Come out so I can see you."

"Who are you? Will you help me?" It was stronger but still trembling—a woman's, a girl's really, from the sound of it.

Angel moved forward, silently imploring the visitor to come out into the open. It could be a trap of some kind, considering everyone who was searching for her and Jesse, and Charlie too.

"I can't help you if you don't show yourself. I'm going away."

"No, please, no." The brush rattled and a small figure emerged, skin and clothes pale in the night.

"Are you alone?"

"Yes." The child staggered over the rough creek bank toward Angel, and she met her halfway.

Catching the frail girl in her arms, she said, "Where are your people? Are you lost?"

"No . . . not lost. I ran . . . I ran away." The child sobbed in her arms.

"Well, tell me about it." She'd probably got in a fight with her parents and took off. Angel would soon see her back to them. "Poor little thing."

"You won't take me back. You can't. Please."

How familiar the plea, how well she knew what the child might have been through.

"Hush. Hush now, and tell me your name and what happened. Here, let's sit down."

After they had settled on the grassy bank, the creek at their feet, the girl grew very quiet. When she breathed in she hiccoughed, as if she had been crying hard for a very long while. Angel held one tiny, grubby hand in both of hers for a while, then asked for her name.

"I am Monique." Again, she hiccoughed, and rubbed at her eyes. She could have been ten or fifteen, Angel couldn't tell. In a faint voice, heavily accented and somewhat hesitant, she went on. "It is a bad place, there. I . . . I came of age, and he . . . he says I have to be . . . be . . ." The girl couldn't go on, but Angel's imagination filled in the blanks. Much like herself, this child was being asked to become a woman in the most difficult of ways—but where and why? Surely not the same situation as her own.

"What is the name of the place?"

"Valeton, he calls it Utopia sometimes or Silkville."

"Where is it?"

"Far from here, I think. It seems I have walked forever."

Angel couldn't quite place the accent. It was one she had not heard, not Russian or German like those who had settled the town of Catherine or Munjor, but something unfamiliar, less guttural.

"When did you leave there?" Angeline pushed back the hair tangled across the girl's dirty face. "How long have you been running?"

"I left the night before this one, but I was frightened and long-hiding during the day. Then when came the night I could not see well. The moon is not bright."

Angel shrugged. There was really no way of telling how far the girl called Monique had come.

"This Valeton, what do they do there? Is it a town or a farm, what?"

"Worms," she uttered with disgust.

"Worms?" Surely Monique was delirious.

"He . . . Papa Ernest grows silk."

249

"Silk?" Angel began to feel like a fool, repeating what the child said, but it made little sense. "But that isn't why you ran away."

After a big sigh, Monique scooted forward, leaned down and drank deeply from the stream. When she came up, water dripped from her chin and her eyes were droopy with fatigue.

Arising, Angel took her hand and pulled her to her feet. "Come with me, you can sleep in my bedroll tonight and in the morning we'll talk some more. We'll decide then what to do."

"I will not go back. I will run from you as well if you try to make me." Despite the threat, she went willingly with Angel back to camp. There Angel lay, her back curled against Jesse and opened her arms. The girl collapsed and fell asleep immediately.

Jesse shook Angel awake. "Who is this child?"

His voice awoke Monique too, who scrambled to her feet in the light of the morning sun. Only then did Angel get a good look at the girl. She was a plain, bony little thing with birdlike features and sandy-colored hair that looked as if it had been chopped off around the rim of a bowl like a boy's. Her eyes, enormous in her narrow face, were the most beautiful pale violet Angel had ever seen. They revealed her fear better than words could express. The child darted quick glances between Angel and Jesse as if she might bolt at any second.

Angel held out a hand toward her, then spoke to Jesse. "She's lost. I found her down by the creek. I thought she could travel on with us to Kansas City, to see if there isn't someone there who can help her."

"No," Monique screamed. "Do not, do not. Please." She tugged at the hold Angel had on her.

"What's *wrong* with her?" Jesse asked.

"I'm not sure."

"Where is she from?"

"France. I come from France. I would go back there if I only could, but I do not have the ticket money."

"How in God's name did she get here from France?"

Angel shrugged at his question. "You haven't heard the half of it. She says she comes from Valeton and they have worms there that grow silk. Did you ever hear of such a thing?"

Before he could reply, Charlie came out of the trees nearby, adjusting his pants. "What in hell is going on? Who is this?"

Monique dodged, staring for a moment at Charlie, then back at Jesse.

"Mon dieu, sacrilege." She crossed herself with a free hand, then darted behind Angel. There the girl threw her arms around her waist, hugging the breath right out of her.

"Here, here." Angel attempted to soothe Monique, but she was having none of it, babbling in a language they didn't understand. Suddenly she turned loose and ran, so unexpectedly that for a second or two they all stared after her in amazement.

Charlie moved first, racing to scoop her up under one arm and carry her kicking and screaming back to camp. He set her down and slapped her hard across the face.

Jesse caught his upraised arm before he could strike again, but the girl burst into tears, her hand on her cheek. Angel hurried to cradle the child in her arms.

Jesse glared at his brother. "Don't hit her. What's wrong with you? I'd think you'd be tired of hitting, seeing as how we were hit so much. Get her quieted down, Angel. *You*, leave them both alone." The last words, aimed at an amazed Charlie, hit home.

All the same, his brother attempted to explain himself. "She saw us. Both. You saw the look on her face. She knows who we are. She'll tell someone we're here."

"Don't be stupid," Angel said, hugging Monique. "It

was your being twins. That's all. She's upset and seeing you both made her think she was going crazy."

"Oh, and you figured that's all it is, do you?" Charlie asked. *"Well, then. Okay."*

Jesse nudged him. "Don't talk to Angel that way."

"Listen, little brother, I'm getting fed up with your telling me what to do. Especially where this—"

Jesse held up a finger and stared at his brother. "Don't say it."

Charlie's face flushed, but he shut his mouth.

Angel kept an eye on the confrontation between the two while soothing the frightened girl. Sooner or later, she expected they would have it out, no matter what Jesse said about loving his twin. A great anger burned within Charlie that could not be suppressed forever. She wondered why Charlie could focus any of it on his brother. Jesse was by far the more gentle and caring of the two. She couldn't imagine him doing anything to foster such rage.

"I'm going to build up the fire and put on some coffee. We'll eat breakfast, then figure out what to do with her. We better be on the move."

As Jesse squatted to start the fire, Angel caught Charlie shoot her a vicious look. He would destroy her, even if he had to go over his brother's body to do it. And, she realized, it was all a vicious game to him. A game he intended to win.

Over a breakfast of the last of the fatback, johnnycakes and black coffee they had, Monique told her story. It was surely an effort to prevent them from taking her to Kansas City. For from there she would probably be sent back to Valeton where her parents worked and lived, but Angel listened intently. The girl spoke around great mouthfuls of food that she gulped as if half-starved.

"There is a big house made of rocks, with many rooms. Our families came from France to join Papa Ernest.

252

There love is free. Papa Ernest says he is free to practice such a thing as are they all. He forbids marriage between any of us, we must lie with each other at his will." Here she paused, staring into her empty plate. Angel forked another slab of the fatty meat from the skillet. The girl grabbed it, shifting it back and forth between both hands to cool while she went on.

"And he enjoys their favors too, whenever he wishes. Many of the women carry his children, and he boasts that all will someday bear him at least one child. I was to be next, so I ran away."

"My God," Jesse said.

"No worse than other stuff that goes on all the time," Charlie said.

Despite the scoffing tone of voice, Angel saw him blush with rage. Did he feel something for this girl's plight after all? Could goodness linger somewhere deep in his soul?

As for Angel, she couldn't help but compare Monique's situation with her own. The poor girl probably had it much worse, for Valeton sounded like a den of iniquity, a place where orgies were a normal occurrence. Prophet often spoke of such wicked cities when he read from the Bible.

"Monique, what do your parents think of this?" she asked.

"We seldom see each other. He puts us, the young girls ready to . . . to breed, in rooms shut away from our parents. Even my dear brother I don't see."

"Isn't this against the law?" Angel asked.

He shook his head, laughing with disgust. "Plenty of things are against the law. Not much is done about it, though. He probably has plenty of money."

Monique nodded vigorously. "Oh, yes. He charges each one who comes and they bring all their worldly goods with them. We plant trees all day. He says they are for the worms he will bring in from Japan to make silk."

Angel had never heard of such a thing. "What kind of trees? I don't understand how worms can be forced to make silk."

"Last year, the first year we were there, Papa said we would plant twenty thousand trees, and I'm sure we did. They are a berry . . . mulberry? I do not know. This year we planted bigger ones, but not so many. It is so the worms will have something to eat."

"How does the old fart have time to bed those women, and keep all those worms working at the same time? She's making this up." Charlie said.

Everyone ignored him.

After a while, Angel said, "Just because we don't understand doesn't make it untrue. No one could make up such a story. I don't think we should send her back, Jesse."

"Okay, but what do we do with her?"

Charlie slammed down his empty plate. "Well, we sure as hell ain't taking her with us."

"We're not turning her loose alone either," Angel said. "How old are you, honey?"

"I am fifteen," Monique said, her chin quivering and head high.

Charlie rose, a palm cupped over his holstered revolver. "You know, I'm good and sick and tired of her talking to me like that."

"What're you going to do, Charlie, shoot me?" Angel taunted, then immediately wanted to bite her tongue. He might very well do just that, and no matter what Jesse did about it, it'd be too late.

"I tell you what," Charlie said, grabbing up his saddle. "While you palaver and decide what you're going to do with the little princess here, I'm going to check out our back trail. If it turns out someone sent her in here to spy on us, they'll be back there somewhere waiting on her. And if they are, why then I'll just put a bullet in them."

Jesse grabbed his arm, but Charlie shoved him away. "You do something about this while I'm gone, 'cause when I get back I'm heading out and I expect you to come with me. You know you owe me that much, Jesse. I think you should leave both of these whores behind. One or both of them could get killed if they go with us. You know that."

"Damn you, Charlie, I told you—"

Angel grabbed Jesse's shirttail. "Let him be, Jesse, please. Just let him be. It doesn't matter what he calls us, they're just names, that's all."

Chatting, Jesse and Angel finally decided to take Monique with them to a mission Jesse had heard of. There nuns would happily take in the young girl. Monique agreed that she would like that very much, at least until she could decide what to do. Angel suggested they give the nuns a bag of gold dust for her keep, and Jesse agreed. It was her gold, after all.

Away from Charlie, Angel found Jesse returned to his former self. He was kind and loving, and spoke of their future wistfully, as if it might happen after all.

When Charlie returned, he grudgingly agreed to the plan, but Jesse had to promise solemnly that they would arrive at the mission by late the next day. There they could leave the girl and ride on.

"It'd be best if we left Angeline there, too. She'd be safe. You could come back after her later."

Angel grabbed at Jesse's arm. "No, I'm not staying there. Don't listen to him."

Jesse patted her hand, staring off into space. "Of course not, Angel. Of course not." But she could tell he was thinking about something, and her heart trembled with fear until she thought it might crack.

That night, long after they bedded down—Monique, Angel and Jesse on one side of the fire, Charlie on the other—a noise awoke her. A group of high clouds frosted

255

the moonless night, revealed Charlie digging around in their packs. She peeked through half-closed lids while he rummaged about for a while longer, then took out something and crept off in the direction of the creek.

What could he be doing? Curiosity got the better of her after a while, and silently she slipped from her bedroll and followed the narrow path. It led to a nearby stream.

A zephyr from the day's brisk wind lifted her loose hair. The night was cool, the grass moist with mist off the water. It wet her toes and tickled the bottoms of her bare feet. Under the thick canopy of trees, splashes from the cloudy sky cast a cold light on her cheeks and illuminated Charlie, immersed waist-deep washing his hair with a bar of soap.

She caught her breath and slipped behind a tree. If he'd looked up at that moment, he'd have seen her plain as day. But he didn't. Mesmerized, she gazed at him. Many times she'd spied on Prophet. Sometimes one could get to know hidden secrets about a person by watching them while they were unaware. Especially someone as mysterious as Jesse's brother.

He finished lathering his hair and ducked under the water to rinse off the soap. He surfaced with his head thrown back, droplets streaming off his long, dark hair, and he began to scrub under both arms and across his belly. When he turned, the night light caught at white scars slashed like ribbons across his back. A stab of pity shot through her. As children, this man and Jesse had been helplessly caught in a web of adult violence they couldn't prevent. For a moment, she could almost understand the rage he felt—she, too, had felt anger at being in a situation that seemed beyond her control.

But it hadn't been beyond his control, not entirely. Jesse said Charlie had finally put an end to his torture and left Jesse to face it alone. Yet maybe the guilt of doing so had caused his soul to shrivel and die. For an instant she wondered what might have become of this man had someone loved him like she loved Jesse. But there was certainly more to it than that. Jesse had endured the same punishment and grown stronger. It was dangerous to think anyone could help Charlie.

Once more she concentrated on the man taking a bath in the creek. Silver moonlight streaked over his muscular torso and kissed his face, so like Jesse's. His features, though partly in shadow, appeared more relaxed than when he was in public. As if he himself were two people. It was a scary thought. Could the goodness of his brother be buried under that face he put on for others? And likewise, could his own evil lurk within Jesse?

Without warning he lunged up the bank, moving so close to the brush she was hiding in that she could have reached out and brushed fingertips over his skin. Could he hear her breathing, the loud thumping of her heart?

Standing naked in the lacy shadows cast by drooping tree limbs, he could have just as easily been Jesse as Charlie. Her gaze lingered for an instant on his face, relaxed in the privacy of the moment, as if he had tamped down the hatred he lived with. He was almost as beautiful as Jesse—would be if he could let go of the meanness.

Her eyes swept downward over his bare chest, along the trail of dark hair. She wanted to stop there, but couldn't. What a sinful need she possessed, to see all of him, to compare him to Jesse. There, just below his belly button was the birthmark Jesse had told her about. Maybe the size of the end of his thumb, it resembled an animal's paw print. There was, of course, something different about these two identical men, for Jesse had no such mark. Was it a mark of the devil? Without thinking, she gasped, then covered her mouth with both hands.

"Why don't you join me?" Charlie asked softly. He reached out and caught her wrist in a tight grip.

Her heart threatened to stop and all the breath went out of her.

Chapter Seventeen

With Charlie's fingers clamped over her wrist, his steely gaze burning into her, Angel swallowed a scream. Eyes squinched tightly to shut out even a glimpse of his naked body, she took several deep breaths, smelling soap in his wet hair, the damp earth around them, and a sprinkling of the day's heat from the leaves fanned overhead. But most of all she sensed the danger of being alone with this man.

With the tip of one finger he gently touched her lips. "That's a good girl. You don't want him down here to see this."

Her heart leaping in her breast, she shook her head. "Let me go. If you hurt me he'll kill you."

"Oh, I don't think so. He doesn't have it in him. But I do. Think about that." His warm breath flowing over her face, he tapped her lips hard. Tears sprung to her eyes and she opened them a little. The threat of this wicked man grew into a live thing that made her nerves tingle.

His smile, lips drawn tightly into a grimace, set those nerves afire. "Or maybe we'll share you," he said softly. "My brother might wonder what you were doing spying on me from the bushes while I took a bath. Oh, but don't worry none. I won't hurt you . . . this time."

He leaned forward and captured her mouth beneath his. Harsh and demanding, his tongue darted out and he drew her close; his damp flesh wet her bodice, the heat of his naked desire throbbed against her. It was an unspoken challenge that sent fingers of wicked hunger through the pit of her stomach.

Ashamed of the feeling, she struggled in silence, shoving frantically at him. Without strain, he easily held her captive for a moment longer. In that instant she felt totally helpless, at his mercy. He could do anything to her and she couldn't stop him. What would it be like to let this evil opposite of Jesse make love to her? Though her mind was repelled by the idea, flames of lust licked at her loins. This was a man who looked just like the man she loved; how could she remain entirely immune to him?

To kill the unwanted desire, she imagined her ravaged dead body sprawled in the brush, clothes ripped away, her intimate secret self revealed. Charlie would tell Jesse he had found her that way, and he might believe him. They were brothers, after all. *Twins.* Renewed efforts to loosen his grip gained her nothing. Even a kick aimed at his shin missed its target.

With a demonic smirk he pushed her away, sent her staggering into a tree. Wiping his mouth with the back of one hand, he spat at her feet and aimed an intense bright stare at her.

"Isn't that what you came down here for?"

Backed against the rough bark, she rubbed at wrists that smarted. "No, no, that's not true. I just wanted . . . I thought you . . . I saw you leave, and oh, darn it, I love Jesse."

His mocking laughter shamed her.

The way he held himself, legs apart, shoulders back, he might have been dressed like a soldier going into battle instead of naked and vulnerable. He continued to stare at her, and despite it all, she couldn't look away.

He was so much like Jesse the first time she'd met him: wary, bitter, defensive and expecting the worst. Something else ruled this man, though. Something she'd never seen in Jesse. It was a base cruelty. And while there were things she found attractive in this man, they were his similarities to his brother. The rest was foul.

259

Charlie interrupted her reveries. "Oh. Well, don't worry. I don't want anything you have. I just wanted to show you how easily I could take it if I was of a mind to. Suppose I tell him you followed to watch me take a bath? Don't think for a minute he would listen to anything you had to say. He might even agree to leave you in that convent if I want him to—then probably wouldn't come back after you either. What with all that gold and women willing to do anything to share it, what would he want with a plain little thing like you?"

"Shut up." Her voice cracked, dry panic almost choking her. "You wouldn't tell him. He'd kill you if I said you touched me!"

Charlie chuckled low. "Haven't you noticed? Jesse can't kill anyone, least of all me. It'd be like killing himself. No, there's nothing you can do, no matter what I decide. That's simply the way it will be."

An unspeakable hatred filled her, but she could think of no reply. All she could do was trust Jesse.

Charlie scrubbed at his lips as if to rub away her taste, gazing at her with an unreadable expression. "You've caused enough trouble between the two of us. Throwing yourself at me won't help your standing with my brother. I don't think you'll run to him about this, will you?"

"You are a terrible man. I won't say anything—but if you touch me again, or if you do anything to hurt Jesse, I'll kill you. I promise I will." At that moment she believed her vow, even though she had no idea if she could do such a thing or how to go about it.

He laughed, then covered his mouth. "Whoops, mustn't wake good old Jesse. But see, there's so many people want to kill me, you'd have to stand in a line a mile long. And when it came your turn, you couldn't do it, not anymore than they could. All my enemies are weak and stupid."

"They don't have you in front of them for incentive."

He cast her a glance she would have sworn carried a tiny shred of admiration, but it quickly passed and he became his old self, unhappily devoid of any live spark. With a small noise, Angel turned and fled back to the camp. There, she was a long time in falling asleep.

They left early the next morning, Monique riding the pack animal, their supplies divided amongst them. Because Angel rode with Monique, the two chattering animatedly, Jesse dropped back to keep Charlie company. For three days they had ridden east, an uneasy peace existing between them. Something was up, but he waited for his brother to speak.

"Didn't have these women with us we'd be nearly there by now," Charlie finally said.

"Don't start with that. I'm not leaving Angel."

"Warms your bed, is that it?"

"You been with us, you know better. I love her."

Charlie made a rude sound down in his throat. "Love. You can't tell me you haven't bedded the wench. Besides, if you loved her, you'd want to protect her. You'd leave her someplace safe, not drag her along with us. No telling who'll be after us 'fore this is over. Probably a posse or two as well as Rawley and them. And what about that Prophet? He must be mad enough to kill her himself, else why is he off here instead of taking care of his place? You'd think he'd just let her go, the dumb old fart."

"Angel wouldn't stay at the convent, even if I did agree to leave her," Jesse said, and realized for the first time that he had been seriously considering doing such a thing. Everything Charlie said about the danger around them was true. But if he went off and left her at the convent with Monique, Angel would be furious and probably escape the first chance she got. It was safer to keep her with him. And then he could have her by him too.

"You could talk her into it. She loves you. Tell her you'll be back for her on your way out west."

Jesse shook his head. "Can't. Won't."

261

Charlie was quiet for a while. "She's just another woman, brother."

"I told you—"

Charlie held up a hand. "Now don't get hot. Let me tell you something about your precious Angel, then let's see what you think."

"I'm not going to listen. What could you possibly know about her?"

Jesse eyed Charlie closely to see if he was lying. Their eyes met, held.

"Brother?"

"No."

"In the middle of the night while you were sleeping, I went to take a bath—"

"Goddammit, I said no. Now let that end it."

Defeated, Charlie glared. "Okay, be a fool. But she followed me down there, and she must've had a reason. She'll do to you what our mama did to us, you give her the chance. She'll abandon you the first time someone better comes along."

"Not Angel." In spite of the denial, Jesse's heart fluttered with terror. Would Angel leave him? He'd be lost, if she did. Completely and totally worthless. Surely he'd go back to the way he was before he met her: robbing, riding with a gang, sooner or later killing. He had no other woman but his mother on which to base the behavior of the female of the species, and Charlie was right—she had thrown her little boys away like trash, discarded them without a backward glance.

Why would Angel follow Charlie to the creek? Pushing away a growing jealousy, he studied her: the long golden hair in plaits down her back, the goofy bloomers and skirt she wore. He thought of how she snuggled up against him, her warm, sweet kisses. No, she would not betray him. Never. He would not listen to his brother.

After riding in silence for a while, Charlie asked how much farther it was to the convent.

Grateful for the change of subject, Jesse said, "It's just before the trail we'll take south to miss Kansas City. It sits in the crook of the river."

"What's the name of this place?"

"The Convent of the Seven Angels."

Jesse smiled at *his* Angel and urged Buck forward to ride beside her, taking comfort in being close and his decision to keep her so. Glancing into her face, seeing the comforting look she gave him, he wished fervently that he had her all to himself. Somewhere far away from Charlie's lies and the timid little girl with the big eyes who stared at him and his brother like they were madmen.

Something was going on between Charlie and Angel. He didn't know what, but it wasn't what Charlie implied. He longed to hold her in his arms, something he had not dared to do even late at night with Charlie sleeping right across the campfire. Wanting her so much kept him in a turmoil.

He glanced at her again, and she smiled so sweetly that he almost melted in his saddle. How had he found such a beautiful girl to love? Much as she hated what they were doing, she had stuck with him too. He would never let her down, no matter what! If Charlie broached the subject again, he'd shut him up for good. And tonight, somehow, someway, they'd be alone together—him and his beautiful Angel.

They camped in a secluded spot along the banks of the Kaw River where he and Angel could slip off to a little hideaway Jesse had spotted a ways back down the trail. All he needed to do was to hold her, love her, and everything would be fine once more. It would only be a little while until dark.

Monique, child that she was, complained all through dinner about her discomforts, her voice whiny and repetitious.

Apparently, Charlie finally had enough. "For God's

sake, shut up! Why don't you run off, do us all a favor?" He took a step toward her, lifting a hand. As Monique cringed, Angel cried out.

"Don't do that, Charlie," Jesse said. "Don't hit her. I swear I don't see how you can think that solves anything, after what we've been through."

Charlie's eyes flared and he swung around, his hands balled into fists at his sides. "You shut up, or it'll be you I'll hit."

Without flinching, Jesse stood his ground, holding Charlie's gaze until it faltered. Angel watched the two square off and wondered how much more it would take before they lit into each other. Which one would be the victor, she had no idea. Would it be Charlie? If it came down to a real fight, Jesse didn't have the meanness to stand up to someone like his twin. Then where would she and Monique be?

Obviously frightened, the young teenager stopped her griping and sat staring into the dying fire. Charlie went for a walk to cool off and Jesse put an arm around Angel. For a while they stood together, gazing at the flames. Slowly, the sun slipped beyond the hills and darkness claimed the riverbank.

Jesse held Angel from behind, his arms wrapped around her, his chin rubbing the top of her head. Leaning back against his shoulder, Angel embraced the moment of tenderness. She missed sleeping in his arms, which they hadn't done since falling in with Charlie. And then there was Monique, who clung to her like a cockle burr. Even now, the girl stared in their direction, her big eyes reflecting the flickering flames.

Jesse whispered in her ear. "Stay awake a while. When Charlie and Monique fall asleep, we'll move our bedrolls yonder." He gestured with the lift of a shoulder.

He turned her, and his hands cupped over her breasts. It sent tiny shivers of delight through her. She imagined his lips there, the illusion so bewitching she almost swooned with delight. A cool breeze picked up, adding gooseflesh to her tingling skin. Pressed against Jesse, the tight muscles of his flat belly, the hardness of his loins and tense thighs, brought her a thrill of desire. Her lips ached for his, her nipples hardened under his touch, and if Monique hadn't been nearby, she would have caressed him in all the places that sent him wild—would have kissed him, pulled his mouth to her breasts right there, right then.

His suggestion, his promise for tonight, kept her from doing that, but she could hardly wait.

There would be no moon, and she wondered how they would find their way. But once Charlie and Monique quieted down, Jesse built up the fire so that its flickering light licked at the dark shadows of the night. He led her through the dense forest until they came upon a tiny clearing through which they could barely see the distant flames. The whisper of the nearby river provided a babbling serenade.

In that tiny dark pocket, removed from the world, she soon forgot all but the two of them.

Breathing heavily, Jesse sat her in a patch of mint, then knelt to remove her blouse and shift. He bent to taste each erect nipple and trailed fingertips over her flesh until she shuddered and moaned. In the darkness, she reached out, brushing at his bare chest. The contact sent a jolt up her arms. Every inch of her being quickened.

He laid her down, lifted her hips and removed her bloomers oh, so slowly, nipping and licking along her thighs. Drunk with desire, she fisted both hands in his thick hair, and let out a cry of pleasure when he moved to the warm dark curls between her legs. He laved her there.

Crushed mint tinged the air and a soft breeze kissed her naked flesh as she writhed beneath his knowing touch. Then he pulled away.

Hovering above her, Jesse put a knee on either side and

found her tiny throbbing heart. With tender fingers, he made her squirm with anxiousness until at last he softly maneuvered and she felt his hot flesh pushing itself inside. Moaning, she arched her back, pushing against him. She wanted more, *needed* more.

"Tell me if I hurt you," he said deep in his throat, emotion thickening his voice. He thrust deeper and she caught him by the hips urging him faster. "Don't let me hurt you," he pleaded, gasping between each word. His body was pounding against hers now, taking her to the place where only the ecstatic, exquisite pain of passion existed.

Angeline couldn't speak, her cries incoherent and wild in the night. The world spun until she grew dizzy, everything within expanded and brightened, throbbing, and together they sailed off into the darkness. No longer of this earth, she soared past the night sky and beyond the stars, tumbling free into a shimmering place. She and Jesse became one being, together forever.

Then, from out of the darkness, someone screamed. Had it been her? Her body had been reacting without conscious thought, so the idea did not surprise her. She cried with joy when at last they returned to earth, their bodies heaving. Exhausted, sated, limbs limp, they settled at last back into reality.

Though Jesse begged her not to cry, Angeline did, and he cried with her. At last she fell asleep with his mouth against her bare flesh, the taste of his kisses still intoxicating her.

Before the sun came up, Jesse and Angeline made their way to the water's edge to bathe. In the lavender dawn they could see the camp, a shadowy, blanket-covered mound on either side of the dead fire.

They returned to camp, acting as if nothing had happened. Jesse stirred up the coals and built a fire, then put water in the coffee pot to boil. Angel dragged out a skillet

266

to cook thin slices of ham and fry johnnycakes in the grease. The aroma awoke Charlie and he grumbled his way into the woods and back out again before speaking.

"I think Monique ran off last night," he said with a casualness that sent shivers through Angel.

She shot him a glance and saw what she'd seen that night on the creek bank: deceit and a dreadful sly humor that dared anyone to challenge his word.

"Well, hell," Jesse said, then walked over and threw back the girl's blanket. It had been stretched cleverly over one of their saddles to look as if she slept there.

"Did you hear her leave?" he asked Charlie.

His brother shrugged. "How do I know? You all were making so danged much noise. She must be good, brother, to make you carry on like that."

Angel flushed and busied herself with the cornmeal cakes, which had browned around the edges.

"That's none of your business. And you'd better watch your mouth. I think we ought to look for her."

Angel kept her silence, grateful that Jesse did the same. They needed to find Monique. She couldn't imagine that frail little waif on her own for very long without running into terrible trouble. And Jesse and Charlie fighting wouldn't help find her.

Charlie kicked at the dirt. "Hell, let her be. She didn't want to go to that convent, that's all, so she took off. It's not our concern."

"Jesse?" Angel said, glancing quickly at him.

He nodded. "I'll look around. Did she take a horse?"

Charlie shrugged. "Maybe I'll stay here and help Angel fix breakfast, if you're gonna go traipsing around the countryside."

Angel dropped the lid on the skillet with a clatter. Coffee boiled out of the spout, hissing in the hot fire. She ignored it and rose. "I'll help you look for her. Charlie can finish making breakfast."

267

Charlie laughed humorlessly. "Fine by me if you want burned meat and johnnycakes."

Moving the overflowing coffeepot from the center coals, Jesse reached out a hand to Angel. "You can manage not burning them." While his tone sounded unusually sharp and commanding, his expression showed he understood. She thanked heaven. She would not remain alone with Charlie. Ever.

She glanced over at him, but he was glaring at her, and she shuddered. She turned away to follow Jesse.

"How far could she have gone?" she asked.

"On foot in the dark? I can't see her getting even a mile. You know how dark it was last night. She'd be off the trail and lost in no time. I don't know what to think."

Jesse knelt and studied the soft earth, then moved and did so again. "No prints. That's funny. She'd have gotten this far, you'd think."

Puzzled, he moved along the edge of the trail in one direction then retraced his steps, Angel watching him.

"Maybe she decided to go through the woods."

"I don't think so. Not in the dark." Nevertheless he moved off the beaten path and studied the thick underbrush. When they found nothing, they made their way back to camp.

Struck suddenly by a memory of their night together, and the strange scream she'd heard, Angel glanced toward the place where they had made love. She glimpsed something white hanging low to the ground in some brush.

Angel nudged Jesse and moved off in that direction. With dread, she retraced their steps of the night before, and there, not twenty feet from where they'd savored each other and slept the night away in each other's arms, a tiny foot protruded from a pile of leaves. Nausea boiled in her throat, for she knew that it was Monique—and knew that she was dead. She cast a pleading look at Jesse, as if he could all make it all go away.

He dropped to his knees and raked back the leaves, uncovering another thin leg, a torso, and finally a head. Monique's face carried several bruises, purple marks encircled her throat, and long scratches marked her bare breasts. Shreds of clothing lay partway buried beneath the pitiful body.

Angel clutched her mouth, then turned and ran. She fell to her knees gagging. All the while, from the corner of her tearing eyes, she could see Charlie, bent over the fire, calmly turning the ham and johnnycakes.

Heart filled with despair Jesse gazed at the dead girl, and felt sure his brother had done this despicable thing. It made him sick—so sick he wanted to join Angel and puke up his guts. But he didn't know what to do about it.

Within his soul a dread dark beast raised its horrible head, nudged at him. Fury, anger, retribution, all hammered to be released. Evil was in the blood; he'd heard it said, and it was at moments like this he knew it to be true. Only with a great deal of effort could he restrain the lurking creature within him that bade him to kill his own kin.

He knelt there, sucking in deep breaths, his hands clenched until the knuckles turned white. Muscles along his arms and legs trembled. He *should* kill Charlie for what he'd done, destroy him so that he would no longer have to worry about the terrors that he could do. His brother was irredeemable. But he could not kill him, he could only mourn the death of this innocent child. He must keep his beast in check; if it escaped he feared he would be no better than Charlie. Because of the power of his blood, if he destroyed one evil—Charlie—he would unleash another.

Realistically, he could turn Charlie in to the law. But then he too would be hung.

He could try to run him off. Or he and Angel could disappear in the middle of the night so Charlie could never find them again. But then what about this poor girl?

269

Where was her justice? Like so many in this unforgiving land, she would find none.

He knelt once again at her side, brushing leaves and dirt from her face, then closed the staring eyes. He rose.

They would have to bury her, and he toyed with the idea of forcing Charlie to do it, but even beginning to confront his brother made his blood boil. He might as well do it himself. The business of hacking away at the earth might still his demons.

He soon saw that without a shovel, he could never dig deep enough, so he gathered rocks and began to pile them over her pale still form. A cairn would have to be enough.

Without speaking, a wan-faced Angeline came to help him, an occasional sob jerking from her throat all the while they covered the poor girl.

Chapter Eighteen

The rich green of the foothills of the Ozarks rose into a cloudless blue sky. The trail grew more difficult, rising and falling, then curving along one rise and another, fording streams that roared deep and crystalline blue. They'd continued on as if Monique's death had never happened.

Charlie told them about the country where he'd hidden the wagonload of gold, of the caves and underground springs, the bottomless holes within the caverns. They'd be there in two or three days, he said.

Jesse could hardly meet his twin's gaze. By killing Monique Charlie had changed their kinship forever. And it had made him realize that no matter what, he would protect Angel from this monster that was his brother.

Soon this would be over, and he and Angeline could live like humans again. He longed to belly up to a table filled with platters of ham and beef, dishes of potatoes and gravy, biscuits and apple pie hot from the oven. He ached to take Angel's hand and lead her into a dark room with a real bed and sheets and pillows.

In the last few days, when his thoughts had been so dark with Monique's death, memories of the last night they'd had together were all he had to retain his sanity. Still, he—they—needed to make new memories, away from all this.

A few miles south of Blue Springs, Charlie led Jesse and Angel off the trail, obviously following his own instincts, for Angel could see nothing to mark the way.

271

Soon their horses traveled nose to tail along a narrow path that skirted a ridge, Charlie out front, Angel in the middle, Jesse bringing up the rear and leading the pack horse. Angeline had never been a confident rider, though she felt assured with her gentle, sweet buttermilk mare, Jezebel. They fit together. This camaraderie was all that kept her from panicking as they worked their way deeper into the rugged foothills. To the right the terrain fell away steeply, the incline thick with huge trees and tumbled boulders.

As the sun climbed higher into the sky, a distant roar grew louder and louder, until it was all she could hear. Afraid to look back for reassurance from Jesse, she strained to see beyond Charlie. Ahead, streams of brilliant light flashed in rainbow hues, then disappeared within the thick woods, then flashed again. The hot air cooled, an icy mist wet her face, then lay like dew across Jezebel's withers.

Charlie twisted in his saddle and shouted something she couldn't hear. Abruptly they broke out into the open. From far above, water cascaded off the mountain, filled a huge bowl, then left it to tumble on down the slope. Her skin grew wet and cold from the spray, and soon her hair and clothing dripped.

A rainbow arced over the falls, caused by errant rays of sunlight. The narrow trail widened at the rock-strewn, gently sloping bank along one side of the pool. Charlie and Jesse dismounted and she gratefully did the same. Tilting her face into the spray, she gasped with wonder at the beauty of the waterfall.

Hands cupped around his mouth, Charlie shouted at Jesse. "We'll camp here the night. It's another day's ride yet."

Angel stared back along the treacherous way they had come. He had not brought a wagonload of gold along this trail. Had he been lying all this time? Did he have them up here for some other awful reason? He had killed Monique without a pang, she felt sure, would he not do the same to her and his own brother?

She suppressed an urge to run to Jesse and shout a warning, but he came nearer to her instead, and voiced the doubts she had felt.

"What're you trying to pull, Charlie? You didn't bring any wagon along this trail."

"We're going in from the other way. The way I came out. We brought it up from the south down in Texas, brother, remember?"

The tone was so derisive that Angel wanted to slap him as she would a misbehaving child. It didn't help that he smirked at her as if they were in cahoots. Quickly she turned, clutching Jesse's hand.

Moisture beaded in his hair and over his face. He looked so gloomy that she flashed a reassuring smile. "Well, I'd like to take a bath if I could have some privacy."

"Time enough for that after we get settled in," Charlie said. "We'll need a drier place to set camp. Let's move off yonder, get out of this noise and spray. Hell, I can't even hear myself think."

After they unpacked the horses and hobbled them near a clearing a few hundred feet away from the falls, Charlie tried to send Jesse off after wood.

To her relief, Jesse didn't buy it. "Either Angel and I go for wood, or you and I go. She isn't staying here alone with you."

Charlie made a face, then winked at Angel. "Why, you make it sound like I'd hurt her. You know I wouldn't do that, what with you loving her and all. But that's okay. It's whatever you want, kid brother. I've had my fill of violence for the week."

Jesse's head snapped around, his eyes hard as agates. Tension charged the air. Charlie watched his brother like

273

a wolf would a rabbit, and Angel held her breath. He was deliberately baiting Jesse. Why? And why now, when they were almost within reach of the gold? Did he really intend to share it with Jesse, or was he just leading his brother off into the wilderness to kill him? And what of her? A memory of the ravaged body of Monique chilled her to the bone.

How she wished they had never come here.

After the two men went off to gather wood for the fire, she fetched the buckskin dress Twana had given her and the sweet soap she had bought, and picked her way from the camp to a spot where water overflowed the basin. She washed her soiled dress first, rubbing at the stains.

The incessant roar of the tumbling water shut out some of her worst thoughts, her fears of what Charlie really had in mind. Soon the tranquil surroundings gentled her spirit and she hummed a tune as she worked.

Once the lovely dress was draped across a bush to dry, she glanced quickly around, then stripped off the bloomers and blouse. Naked in the late afternoon light, she repeated the process of scrubbing the fabric clean and spreading it out. Then, removing her moccasins, she padded to the edge of the pool and slipped into the cold, crystalline water. Careful not to wade too far from shore and get in deep water, she fingered the braids loose, soaped and rinsed her hair, then rubbed her body all over with the fragrant bar. Bubbles shimmered on the surface of the pool, then danced downstream. After rinsing off, she waded toward shore.

"I think it's high time I taught you how to swim," Jesse called from nearby.

Laughing, she took another step, then caught sight of his wavering image in the heavy mist off the falls. His bare chest and arms were gleaming, and his pants were unbuttoned at the waist. His feet were bare. Seeing his hair long and whiskers dark, she realized how scruffy

274

he'd become during the trip. As had they all, she supposed.

She studied him closely. He held out a hand, laughing with her, his eyes sparkling as only they could.

"No time like the present," she told him, and backed into the pool. Water hugged her waist and she remained there, her breasts bared while he approached.

Without taking off his pants, Jesse waded in, then gestured with a laugh. "We can get them and me clean at the same time."

The birthmark. Charlie wouldn't dare take off his pants. Fright locked her tongue and she scampered backward. Was this Charlie? Underfoot the bottom sloped quickly away, and suddenly she was going under, clawing frantically as if she could grab air and save herself.

He lifted her easily under the arms, his fingers spread across her breasts.

Choking, she peered at him through streaming hair. Was it Charlie or Jesse, and why couldn't she tell? If she kicked free of him she'd go under. Should she take a chance and drown, on become another of Charlie's victims?

"Angel, stop struggling. I've got you. Come on, take it easy." He kissed her tenderly.

Temporarily appeased, she stopped struggling and rested her hands on his shoulders. "Jesse?"

"It's okay," he soothed and covered her mouth with his.

It was the warm, moist gentle mouth she knew so well. She locked both arms around his neck, and he pulled her closer so that her bare breasts pressed against his chest. His tongue played along the inner sensitive flesh; his teeth bit at her lower lip.

As they kissed he waded deeper into the water. She was barely conscious of the movement, too lost in his touch to object. He'd kindled the fire that had proven so powerful within her, made it glow in anticipation. She hungered for his love. This was Jesse, of course it was.

She would have known the difference immediately, wouldn't she? Having been kissed by both. Still, why hadn't he taken off his pants before coming in?

Because he was afraid she'd see the birthmark and know the truth. He tightened his grip, the kiss suddenly going deeper, more savage.

She kicked out, scratching at him, then broke free from his insistent mouth and screamed.

"Don't do that, Angel, my sweet," he said softly in her ear, holding her easily out of the water. "If I let you go, you'll drown. Remember you can't swim."

Her heart fluttered and it cut off her breathing. "Charlie, damn you, let me go."

He instantly released her, and she sank, kicking and flailing. She gulped in a mouthful of water that gagged her. The last thing she saw before going under was the flare of bestial eyes. They were not Jesse's. She was about to die.

Hands under her arms, the beast dragged her to the surface. She peered into his face and saw herself reflected in Charlie's cruel eyes.

"Where's Jesse?" she choked out.

"If I were to let you go, do you think you would drown or figure out how to swim?" He tilted his head, contemplating the question. "I always knew I'd learn to swim."

"Where's Jesse? Let me go, Charlie."

"Oh, okay," he said, and turned her loose once again.

As the cold water closed over her head she tried not to panic, holding her breath and keeping her eyes open. Every instinct told her to flail, but instead she searched her blurry underwater surroundings until she saw the rocks protruding from the shore and the slope of the bottom. If she could reach them, she'd be safe. Kicking both feet and paddling awkwardly as she'd seen Jesse do, slowly in the right direction. Off to her left she saw Charlie, or at least his clothed legs moving along beside her. If she made shore, would he hold her under? What terrible games he liked to play.

Her outstretched arms touched the sloping bottom, and she pushed upward, her lungs aching for air. Just as she thought she would surely have to breathe in a mouthful of the deadly water, her head popped out and she sucked in oxygen. Choking and gasping, she clambered onto the bank, then coughed and spat fluid.

He waded out and stood alongside her. Water poured from his wet pants down next to her. "Angel, how did you like your first swimming lesson? You did mighty fine, mighty fine. Old Jesse would be proud of you."

"You bastard," she snarled weakly.

His mocking laughter rose above the roar of the cascade. "Next time, you might ask me to take off my pants, otherwise it'll be mighty hard to tell us apart."

Leaving her there, naked and spitting, he strode back to camp.

He could have killed her, or let her die. She wondered what he would do the next time, but feared telling Jesse what had happened. He'd been so strange since Monique's death, so silent. Was he only a hair away from snapping himself? Was it better for her to deal with his brother alone?

She slipped into her wet bloomers and blouse, and found a golden rock warmed by the last dying rays of the sun. There she sat alone with her thoughts while dusk grew around her. Where was Jesse and why had he let Charlie out from under his watchful eye?

As if the thought had summoned him, Jesse emerged from the woods. He called out to her, then strode over.

"Did you get your privacy? Charlie said you were taking a bath."

"Oh? How did he know that?" Her jaw clenched with the question, and she was furious that Jesse still innocently trusted his brother, after all that had happened. On

277

the verge of blurting out the truth, she rushed past him without speaking.

If she opened her mouth, the words would fall out; she wouldn't be able to help it. Then what? She could tell that Jesse had bottled up his own rage, much as Charlie had. What would happen when it came out?

For now, she would keep her silence, and be more careful. She did not want Jesse to fight with his brother over her. Whatever happened, no good would come of that. She *would* have to handle this matter herself.

She was able to contain her rage until late that night, after they'd eaten and cleaned up. It was then that Charlie said in a congenial voice, "I'd be glad to bed down out in the woods if you two need some privacy."

Refusing to look at him or Jesse, Angel spat, "You can sleep in the bottom of the canyon for all I care. All I want to do is go to bed. You can *both* leave me be."

"Well, brother, I guess that leaves you out in the cold, doesn't it?" Charlie asked.

With a puzzled expression, Jesse glanced at his brother, then moved to Angel's side. "What's wrong? What happened?"

She shook free, suddenly miserable and hurt. Why hadn't he watched Charlie better? If they had to come on this godforsaken trek, the least he could do was protect her from his crazy brother.

"You put a leash on him, Jesse. Keep him away from me, or so help me . . ." Having not meant to say anything, she was immediately contrite.

Jesse's eyes flamed, the muscles along his jaw rippled. "What did he do?"

Laying a hand on his arm, she tried belatedly to calm him down. "Nothing, it's okay. Nothing happened, he just made me mad, that's all."

Charlie didn't let it be, though, and added, "Why, brother, I just did what you ought to've done. I tried to teach her how to swim, but she was having none of it. Almost drowned me and her both. All I wanted to do was give her a swimming lesson."

The expression in Charlie's amber eyes sent a gust of dread through Angel. Under her grip, Jesse's arm muscles hardened to steel. He turned to face his brother.

"Please, Jesse, don't," she whispered, fearing what would happen when the dam of Jesse's emotion burst. But it was too late.

"It was bad enough what you did to that poor little girl, but I told you never to mess with Angel." His voice was so thick with fury Angeline hardly recognized it.

Brushing her aside, Jesse exploded with rage, leaping on his brother and driving him backward into a tree. Charlie, who obviously had not expected such a reaction, finally recovered and hammered at his assailant's hunched back, doing little damage. Though Angel yelled at them to stop, they ignored her.

It was like watching a man fight himself in some dreadful nightmare. Had they not worn different shirts, she might not have been able to tell them apart. The pensive expression Jesse usually carried had turned bitter and ugly, and in its spell, his face matched Charlie's. Her fears had come true: His demon was loose, perhaps never to be imprisoned again.

Both men fought like animals, oblivious to the pain of the horrendous blows they dealt each other. Patches of blood soon bloomed on their identical faces. Neither wore the guns they usually carried, and for that she was grateful, but it still began to look as if this could only end in death.

Twice she waded into the melee, only to be knocked aside. An elbow hit her in the stomach the second time, and she fell to her butt, gasping for air, tears of pain and frustration flooding her cheeks. She couldn't stop them short of killing one.

279

She turned for an instant, regarding Jesse's Colt in its holster next to his saddle nearby on the ground. She went to her knees to crawl after it. Grasping it in both hands, she raised the weapon to point at the struggling twins. The barrel wavered, catching the last rays of sunlight filtering into the clearing. But she couldn't shoot at them. It wasn't in her. And no matter the beast he had become, she still loved Jesse.

Instead, she pointed the weapon skyward and pulled the trigger. The report slammed into her eardrums, but did nothing to deter Charlie or Jesse. They were beyond consciousness of anything but their fierce struggle.

Helpless, hopeless, she knelt there, the gun hanging from her fisted hands, and watched the battle, tears running down her face. If Charlie won she would *have* to shoot him. She only hoped she could do it, then.

At last Jesse slammed a fist hard into Charlie's temple, staggering him to his knees. Shaking his head, he tried to rise, but Jesse hit him again, a long wicked undercut that lifted him in an arc, sent him flying backward, a stream of blood stringing through the moist air. On impact his head snapped back and smashed into the ground with a solid whack. Rolling over twice, he stayed down for a moment, then pulled his knees up and began to rise.

Angel closed her eyes, praying as she never had before that he not get up. Jesse would kill him if he did.

Charlie's pitiful struggle broke the spell under which Jesse had fallen. He turned away from the sight of his battered sibling, his eyes searching frantically. His gaze alit on her, and he staggered a few steps, then fell to his knees and onto his face, as if being dragged to the earth.

Quickly, she recovered and half-ran, half-crawled to him. Laying aside the Colt, she rolled him over. As he came to rest, she heard an animal-like noise somewhere between a grunt and a roar, and looked up to see Charlie moving toward them, shrieking. His boot toes dragging, he lumbered closer, looking as if he might crash to the ground at any moment.

Which he proceeded to do. There the two brothers lay, side by side, bloodied, cut, bruised and half-conscious.

Angel climbed to her feet and stared down at them for a good long while, before her pity turned to anger. It was an anger that grew until she had to do something besides railing at the men; they couldn't hear her anyway. Turning her back, she fetched the cooking vessel from camp, marched through the woods to the pool of water, then filled it and returning to their inert forms, dumped it on Jesse. Without pause she did the same thing again, only this time Charlie got a face full of water.

Both sputtered and moaned and dragged themselves to a sitting position.

"Now, why don't the two of you go take yourselves a bath," Angel said. "And I hope you haven't broken any bones, 'cause this would be a heck of a place to be stranded."

"I wasn't going to hurt her," Charlie declared, and he peered at Jesse from the eye that was less swollen. "I wouldn't do anything to her. She loves you, anyone can see that. Hell, one of us ought to get that lucky."

"She can't swim, she could've drowned." Jesse said. "You killed that poor girl, Monique—"

"It was an accident."

Jesse squinted at him. "Sure, and pigs fly."

"She got scared, started fighting me. I didn't want her to make noise and bother you and Angel. You were . . . well, going at it. And so I put a hand over her mouth, just to quiet her down till I could explain I didn't want none of what she had."

"I saw the marks on her throat, Charlie. Tell the truth for once."

281

"The only time I never told the truth was when Zeb wanted to light into you and I lied and said it was me."

Jesse massaged his bruised shoulder, worked the arm up and down, and grimaced. "I can't play that game any more, Charlie. I know all you did for me when we were kids, but that don't make everything all right. And you left me there, too. For a long time I didn't know if I loved you or hated you, just knew you were gone and I was alone to deal with that old man."

"I thought I killed him, truly I did," Charlie muttered, then glanced away. "Damn, I think you loosened all my teeth."

"And what did you think would happen to me if he was dead?"

"Someone'd take you in. Everyone always thought you were the sweetest thing; they were always mooning over you. It was never that way for me. They must've seen the devil in me. I could get in trouble without even waking up in the morning." Charlie paused. "Besides, it was time you learned to take care of yourself."

Jesse gazed at his brother, wished Charlie would return the look. "But why didn't you take me with you?" The plea came out in a small voice, sounding much like that grieving thirteen-year-old who'd wept himself sick when he'd found his twin gone.

"Because you could never have gone where I was going. You didn't have the guts for it. You'd have been dead in six months, doing what I've done." Charlie met his stare then, one visible eye muddy with sorrow.

"I've always loved you, Jesse. Always. And all these years I've known you loved me too, no matter the anger you might've felt. Most boys have *mothers* to love them, all we had was each other."

Grief swelled in Jesse's throat until he thought he couldn't swallow. Every inch of his body ached from the beating he'd been given, and looking at his brother he knew Charlie felt the same. But a different kind of pain swallowed him up. It was a feeling of loss and desolation that made him want to throw back his head and howl.

He loved Angel. But the connection he felt for his twin was just as powerful. It held he and Charlie together despite anything either of them did. Jesse would not, could not, choose between them. Both were as necessary to his existence as air and water. Somehow, he had to find a solution. He knew the danger Charlie posed, but at the same time, could not betray or abandon him. Was there an agreement they could come to that could protect everyone?

Shaking, he opened his arms and put them tenderly around his brother's battered shoulders.

For a long moment, Charlie remained inert, then he lifted his arms and returned the hug. Jesse felt him cringe within his embrace, and he did so too. His brother—this venomous, murderous bastard—was in as much pain as he was. But Charlie had developed his own way of dealing with that anguish, that was how they differed.

Sharing his brother's embrace, Jesse experienced a dread beyond his own understanding. Charlie would soon be taken from him, violently, and it seemed there was nothing that could be done. His brother had started down the dark path, soon it would swallow him.

He closed his eyes tight to block out the dark premonition. Perhaps it was just the night closing in as the sun fell behind the peaks to the west. All the same, anxiety set his heart to thudding.

Against his chest, his brother's galloped to match its pace.

Chapter Nineteen

After riding alongside a rock bluff most of the morning, Charlie reined in ahead of Jesse and dismounted. Ahead, remnants of a wide trail meandered along a bench and out of sight. Though overgrown with saplings, it had obviously once been a road or trace. Likely it had been blazed by Indians centuries ago.

Jesse shifted uncomfortably in the saddle, his only consolation that his brother suffered as much as he from yesterday's fight. A rapport of sorts had been reached between them, and though he could never forget the terrible things Charlie had done, he held no more resentment or guilt for his brother's abandonment when they were young. For that he was grateful.

From the back of his restless gelding, Jessie checked their surroundings and saw nothing but heaped boulders, a mass of persimmon sprouts hung thickly with small golden fruit, and sumac. The air held motes of dust and tiny bugs caught in beams of errant sunlight, a damp smell of rotting leaves and rich soil.

Indicating the mass of new growth, Charlie announced, "This is it."

"I don't see anything."

"It's been six years. Everything's grown up around it." Charlie took a hatchet from his saddlebags and went to work. He hacked at the finger-sized scrub, grunting from the exertion, and soon he had uncovered an opening in the bluff about the size of a small shed. A wagon could easily have passed through.

284

Up until that moment, Jesse hadn't truly believed Charlie. Part of him had feared his brother leading them around on a wild goose chase as an excuse to remain together, though for what dark purpose he couldn't fathom. Yet, considering the remoteness of this place, his brother had to have previous knowledge about this cave. It certainly hadn't been visible when they had ridden up. Did that mean the gold was real too? Was he really so close to a new life for himself and Angel—and maybe Charlie too? Suddenly, all of his dreams seemed within reach.

Grateful they had reached their destination, Angel slid from Jezebel's back. Though finally accustomed to riding for long periods of time, the stress of following the hazardous mountain trail over the past few days had left her stiff and uncomfortable. Rubbing at the small of her back, she studied Jesse's bruised, swollen features and his expression of hope.

For the last few days, she had done nothing but pray there would be no gold. Then she and Jesse could be on their way and not owe Charlie anything. If he divided a fortune between them, then what might he want in return? They might *never* be rid of him.

All she wanted was for her and Jesse to go somewhere and be safe, but that wouldn't happen until this business with Charlie was settled. One last time she damned the Confederate gold and all it stood for, then went to stand beside Jesse while Charlie cleared the last of the growth from the opening of the cave.

Tying the horses outside they all went into the yawning mouth, Jesse and Angeline holding hands and following Charlie. Their footsteps echoed into the darkness that soon swallowed them. At their backs, the bright sunlight grew dim.

"How are we going to find it in the dark?" Jesse asked, and his voice bounced all around them.

285

"Just wait. Come on, and watch your footing, the floor drops up ahead."

Angeline clung to Jesse's arm as they started down the incline, fearing that with every step the floor might fall out from under her. Placing each foot carefully ahead of the other, she didn't notice the light until it struck her full in the eyes. Far above their heads, small crevices let in long fingers of sunlight to expose a huge domed chamber. And pushed to one side of that room was a wagon. A wheel had fallen off, leaving the wagon lopsided and dumping out large canvas bags which lay where they had fallen.

Charlie ran to grab one, then struggled to untie the drawstring. "It's here, it's still here, just like I left it. My God, we're rich." He breathed the last like a prayer.

"You weren't sure it would be?" Jesse accused, but joined his brother to work at the fasteners of another bag.

With a dark dread in her heart, Angeline watched them claw at the bags. This gold would only bring disaster. Every fiber of her being told her to turn around and flee as fast as she could, but she didn't—she couldn't. Whatever happened, she would not leave Jesse. If she could do it at all, this would be her last chance to save him from the influence of his brother. No matter the evil that surrounded him, Jesse was the only man she could ever love. He had taught her how—both to love and be loved, both by touch and example. She would not desert him now.

Each of the brothers had a bag of gold open, their hands filled. The precious metal seemed to gleam with a life of its own.

She moved slowly toward them, staring down at the shining ore running through Jesse's fingers. "All I want is you, Jesse. Just you."

He met her gaze. "And I want you, my Angel. But with

this we can have everything you've ever wanted. Don't you see? This is our gold. This is yours!"

She shook her head, then moved away from them. At the front of the wagon, she stumbled over something, heard it clatter, then reached down and picked up a large bone. A bit of hair clung to one end of it. Letting out a screech, she dropped it.

"What is this?"

Charlie's glance dismissed her concern. "The horses. The wagon ran away coming down the incline, and the damn animals got tangled in the traces. It rolled up over them, busted 'em all up. Had to shoot 'em."

His lack of compassion brought tears to her eyes, and overpowered Angel with the most terrible feeling of loneliness and despair. Jesse would not leave and she couldn't go without him. What was she doing here? She didn't have an answer. She glanced over at him.

One of his hands was buried in the bag of gold, and Jesse gave her a look of joy. His eyes were warm, but the emotion was lost on her, for he turned to his twin. "How we supposed to get it out of here?"

Charlie answered as if he were just coming up with a plan. "We need to buy a wagon, two would be better, and some horses—and we'll have to use some of the gold to do it. But it will call attention to whoever is doing the buying. I didn't count on our face being plastered on wanted posters all over the country."

They both turned toward Angel, but she was relieved when immediately Jesse said, "No."

"Hell. Why not? She's smart. She can buy a wagon and a team, and drive 'em back here. And while we're loading up she can go back and buy another. It'll be easier to haul all of this out of here in two."

"Easier to divide when we go our separate ways too," Jesse agreed.

Was this the only way out of this godforsaken situation? Fine, then. She moved to Jesse's side. "If you want me to do it, I will," she said. Her eyes welled with tears, but she took his hand and held it firmly.

Cupping the side of her face with one hand, Jesse leaned down and kissed her. She felt her lips tremble under his. A love so all consuming she nearly cried out with the joy of it, filled her being.

One arm wrapped around her, and Jesse pulled her close; she fed on the warmth of his body. He had vowed to protect her, no matter what, and she had to believe he would do that. Otherwise, would life be worth living? He must have sensed her fear, for suddenly a shudder rippled through him.

"No," he said, then. "She's not doing it. It's too dangerous. If Prophet is still out there looking for her, he could be nearby. It's possible he's tracked us. This would be the perfect opportunity for him, what with her on her own. You'll have to come up with something else."

Jesse's words filled her with joy and lent her strength. "Why don't we haul what we can carry on our horses and be done with it?" she asked. "It's more than enough. What do we need with all of it?" They didn't need any of it. Men had died protecting this gold, others had killed to get it. It was bathed in blood.

Charlie threw his hands up in disgust. "You're crazy. I knew women didn't have much sense, but I thought they all had a hunger to be rich. Just think, girl, what you could have with all this. Think of the fancy house and clothes and baubles. Diamonds and rubies. Carriages. Be reasonable. Talk to her, Jesse. Make her see reason. Make her go buy the wagon."

"I said no, dammit," Jesse said. "I won't put her in jeopardy for this."

"Then one of us will have to do it, cause I ain't leaving this here." Charlie swept his arm around, a ray of sunlight catching the expression of greed on his face.

"Then we'll *all* go," Jesse said.

"And leave the gold unguarded?"

Jesse snorted. "For God's sake, it's been here more than six years, what difference are another few days going to make?"

"The two of you go. I want to stay here with it."

Jesse picked up two of the heavy bags. "Tell you what, Charlie. Angel and I will take this and be gone. You can do what you please about the rest."

Charlie yanked at his brother's sleeve. "Don't be a fool. You can have half of *all* of this." Again the sweep of a hand. "How can you just walk away with such a measly sum?"

Suddenly Jesse dropped the gold. One of the rotting bags split open and nuggets scattered across the floor with an echoing clatter. "You know how? Like this. Because I think the price is too high. I just realized it, and I think Angel did a long time ago. This wealth is only that—wealth. And I have all I need with her. All we want is to get free of the law. I don't know why you're trying to cinch us up tight here, but if you want it, you get this gold out of here any way you can. Leave us out of it. Come on, Angel, let's go."

A feeling of exquisite relief passed through her. She moved with him, hanging on to his hand, toward the mouth of the cave. They hurried into the darkness.

"Don't be a damn fool," Charlie shouted from behind them in the darkness. The cave vibrated with his rage. "... *damn fool* ... damn fool ... damn fool" echoed off to nothing, followed shockingly by a gunshot and the whine of a bullet ricocheting off the stone walls. Another shot followed.

She shouted and tried to run, though Jesse held her back. "Come on, he's *shooting* at us, Jesse." She tugged fiercely at him, but he didn't budge.

Instead he pulled out his Colt, then shoved her down

289

against the wall. "No. He's not shooting at us. Stay here, I'll be back."

"No, don't. Please." Terror gripped her. Why was he going back? He wouldn't shoot his own brother, she knew that. But Charlie wouldn't hesitate to kill Jesse. She snatched at him, screaming for him not to go, but he slipped away into the darkness. After a while she could no longer hear anything but the furtive scrape of his boots against the rock. The silence dragged on, but then something distracted her, sounds from the cave's entrance: men's voices, horses whinnying, footsteps scraping along the stone floor.

Frantic, she ran after Jesse. Forgetting about the sudden incline she stumbled and fell, then rolled and skidded painfully. Finally she fetched up against a boulder with a thud that nearly knocked her silly. Elbows and knees burning, head thumping, her breath coming in gasps, she crouched still as a statue, listening for some sound—anything. She could not hear either Jesse, Charlie or the men. Had she imagined someone entering the cave? Half-hysterical with fear, it was possible. What she did know was that Jesse and Charlie were somewhere up ahead, facing off. Would they at last end this long feud by gunning each other down? She hated Charlie, but she couldn't bear the thought of Jesse having to kill him. He would never get over that.

She had to know what was going on.

"Jesse?" she called in a low voice.

"Hsst, be quiet," came a reply in the same tone. "Come on down, but carefully."

Afraid to stand, she scooted along on her butt, knowing nothing but to continue skidding downhill until she reached the place where the wagon had wrecked. At last she spotted the rays of sunlight, though they were fading. It must be getting late, the sun moving lower in the sky. Soon it would be pitch black in the cave.

From outside of the entrance came a clatter of rolling rock. Someone had kicked something! She froze, remained where she was, and gazed around the dimly lit room. Afraid to call out for fear she'd be heard by the people outside, she moved slowly toward the dark hulk of the gold wagon. It seemed to take forever.

"Angel?" The voice came out of the deep shadows.

"Jesse?"

"Yeah. Come around the wagon."

"Where's Charlie?"

"Don't talk any more. Someone's coming."

"I know."

"Hsst."

She obeyed and worked her way slowly and carefully into the sheltered vee formed by the cave wall and the wrecked wagon.

An arm eased around her shoulders, and breath beat against the back of her neck. Lips against her ear whispered, "Could you see who it was outside?"

"No."

"Dammit. It must be that bastard Rawley."

"Jesse?"

"What?"

"You're Charlie."

He let out a big sigh.

"Where's Jesse?"

"Don't know. He came back, I saw the glint of his gun barrel and—"

"You shot him." The accusation shut him up briefly.

He clamped a sweaty hand over her mouth. "Hush up. You want to get us killed? I didn't shoot him. He went down out of sight yonder in the shadows."

His damp palm smelled and tasted of the gold, metallic and bitter—something she'd grown used to while mining her own meager supply of the valuable ore. She tried to twist free, jabbing at him with an elbow.

291

He let out an "oof," then tightened his grip. "Caln down, Angel, or I'll club you and then you'll be stil Don't move again, got it?"

She bobbed her head up and down, hoping he woul then let her go, but he didn't. His other hand, which hel a revolver, settled over her breast, the hard feel of the gu butt surrounded by his fingers pressed into her flesh Silently cursing him, she remained very still.

From outside, they heard muffled voices. Were the going to come inside? All she and Charlie could do wa wait and see what happened and who appeared.

The rays of light from above were growing dimme and dimmer. With luck the room would be plunged int total darkness before the newcomers stumbled across them, then all they had to do was remain so quiet they wouldn't know they were there.

Angel wished she knew where Jesse was and if he was okay. Charlie could be lying to her; perhaps his brother was already dead somewhere in the dark.

An interminable amount of time crept by as they waited, helpless to do anything. Occasionally sounds would echo nearby and she would listen until her ears rang with the silence. Was there an animal of some kind in here, a small bear perhaps?

Slowly the beams of light faded. It was like going gradually blind.

Charlie uttered whispered curses in her ear, foul things she hardly comprehended. Were they directed at her or the circumstances?

Something touched her leg, but Charlie's hand muffled her squeal.

"Shut up," he said, his breath wet in her ear.

She kicked, trying to pry his hand away from her mouth. He shifted, covering her nose as well. Unable to breathe, she bucked and tore at his arm. Oh God, was he going to kill her now, after all she'd survived?

Suddenly Charlie stiffened and his hand loosened over

ıer mouth. Turning, Angeline saw Jesse. He shoved the
barrel of his colt against Charlie's side with a great deal
of force.

"You feel that, Charlie?" he whispered. "Now, let her
go."

The hand came off her mouth, the other released her,
and she pawed at the darkness. When she felt Jesse's
shoulder, she threw both arms around his neck. A steady
pulse pounded against her cheek. She almost cried out
with joy.

A shout broke her elation. "Cole, you in there?"

"Dammit, that's Rawley," Charlie said.

His voice must have carried, for soon a reply came.
"Yep, it's me all right. Me and Fletch and Cake. You
remember us, don't you? The same ones that helped you
get the gold. The ones you turned around and stole it
from. Slick, Cole. That was slick. But we found you, and
that was slicker."

"Jesse?" Angel said.

"Don't worry, we'll get out of this. Won't we, Charlie?
We will, 'cause brother Charlie here is gonna give those
yahoos their share of the gold—aren't you, Charlie?"

"Why should I do that?" he hissed. "I paid for this with
jail time, they didn't."

"You haven't paid half what you could if the law
catches you. You killed three men. They'll hang you."

Charlie was silent for a moment.

Rawley shouted again, somewhere nearby, then waited
until the echo died down.

"And you right beside me, little brother. You right
beside me."

"You'd let them blame him too, wouldn't you?" Angel
asked. "He's your brother. You're supposed to *love* him.
How can you—?"

"Having a little fuss in there, are you?" Rawley called.
"Tell you what, Cole. We're coming on in. Goddamn, it's
dark as the hubs of hell in there. But I guess that just

293

means you can't see us to shoot us, doesn't it?"

Charlie fired off several quick shots toward the mouth of the cave. The bullets ricocheted in an eruption of hellacious noise. The men shouted, and even Jesse and Angel cried out.

"You damn fool, you'll kill us as well," Jesse told him when the noise died down.

"They aren't getting our gold."

"Be reasonable. We can't get out of here, and when daylight comes, they'll be able to see us."

"And we'll be able to see them. Until then, they can't."

Jesse seemed to consider that for a moment, then rose and pulled Angel to her feet as well.

"Rawley? Is that your name?" he called.

"Yeah. Who's that?"

"Jesse Cole. Charlie's brother. Me and Angel are coming out. Don't shoot."

Laughter filled the cavern. "And why in the hell should I not shoot you? I recall what you did to us." He paused, then before Jesse could reply, added, "Twice."

"Well, yeah, but you were kicking me around. You'd a done the same."

"Make your brother give us our share of the gold and you all go free."

"Charlie?" Jesse turned to his brother.

"No. They'll have to kill me to get it."

"And that's exactly what they'll do too."

"Charlie, please," Angel said. "Let us all get out of here. Then we can all go our separate ways."

He didn't reply for a moment, then said softly, "You don't understand. They're going to kill us, one way or the other. And what Fletch'll do to you before you're dead, you don't want to think about. He's a monster who loves to torture women. It's how he gets his kicks. We have no choice but to kill them before they can kill us."

"Not much different from you, then, is he?" Angel spat

Even now the man was trying to manipulate them. Why had she bothered ever trying to understand?

Before Charlie could reply or react the voice came once more out of the darkness.

"Well, Jesse Cole? Have y'all come to an agreement?" Rawley laughed again, and suddenly Angel had a terrible fear that Charlie was right.

Chapter Twenty

"It's a standoff. Someone's got to do something," Charlie said.

"In the dark?" Jesse asked. "Let's stall, wait till daylight so we can see. We'll have a better chance."

"You don't get it. We don't have any chances but those we make ourselves. I'd rather go out blazing than be shot like a dog without a fight. And either of those is better than being hung."

Angel shivered, snuggling closer to Jesse. He brushed hair away from her face and wiped the tears from her cheeks.

"I'll get you out of here, I will," he said.

Charlie laughed. "How? How you going to do that?"

Jesse thought for a while, then touched his lips to the heartbeat at her temple. He'd made up his mind. "If you won't make a deal with them, then I will. I'll pretend I'm you."

"No, Jesse," she said, hanging on to his arm. "They'll kill you."

"I don't see what good that will do anyway," Charlie said.

"No, listen. If they think we're making a deal . . . if they have us, then maybe I can talk them into letting *her* go."

"That doesn't do anything for us. I don't get it."

Sorrow grew in Jesse's chest. "No, I don't suppose you do. The most important thing is to save Angel. If she's safe, I can die happy."

"No, no. I won't go." Angel clung even tighter to him. "You can't make me leave without you."

"*You* might be willing to die for some woman, but I'm not," Charlie said. His words made Jesse only that much more aware of how different they'd grown.

Rawley's voice reached out to them. "What's all the fuss down there? You'all fighting over who gets to die first?"

"Hey, this is Charlie. I want to make a deal," Jesse shouted before either Charlie or Angeline could stop him.

"Go on." The words echoed out of the darkness.

"To show my good faith, I'll carry out two bags of gold to you. And I'm bringing the woman with me. You let her go and you can come down and get your share in the morning, as soon as the sun comes back up and we can see."

"It's dark down there. Why do we need to wait?"

"Sunlight comes in. You'll see. We won't be able to find our way until morning."

Angel clung to him. "Jesse, don't do it, please. I won't leave you here. They'll kill you." Her tears came in earnest now, and he felt them running down her cheeks as he kissed her.

He held her close, heart as near breaking as it had ever been. Nothing in his life had prepared him for the way he felt about this woman. He realized that now. Not the childhood love for his brother, nor the unfulfilled yearning for a mother and father. That lonely little boy, all his fears and hatred of his youth, they had found a balm: the love of this woman.

She continued to sob wildly and he hardened himself against it, prying away her arms. "I'll get the bags. Come on, Angel, let's go."

"I can't, I won't." When he didn't respond, Jesse saw her eyes widen in desperation. "Charlie, don't let him do this. I won't live without him. I can't. Please help us. If you love him, help us."

Jesse ground his teeth and felt his own eyes fill with tears. Encircling her in his arms once again, he said,

"This is for you, Angel. I love you. They won't kill us. I need you safe. Just come and wait outside. That's all I ask. Come outside and wait. We'll make the deal and then everything will be okay. We'll go away together, I promise. Now, do as I ask."

"You're a damned fool, Jesse," Charlie muttered. "They're not honorable men. They will kill you, grab her, and come on down here for the gold and for me."

"I don't think they will. Without me they don't know what's down here. I think they'll let me lead them down. Afterward, they may try to get us both, but if they do, we can handle that." He paused, the eerie silence broken only by their breathing. "Can't we?" It was a challenge he tossed to his brother, the man who claimed to fear nothing. They would see.

Clearly, Jesse would not be deterred, and so Angel let him believe she had surrendered to his wishes. The courage to do something herself to assure their survival grew within her, like a flame from a spark. This would not end with her running away and leaving him. She was tired of running—first from Prophet, next from Charlie, now from this. Things were going to change.

Jesse's voice interrupted her. "Okay, I've got the gold. Come on, Angel, let's go."

"Jesse?"

"What, Charlie? Don't try to stop me. I'm getting her out of here. You do what you please."

"Fine, Jesse. You can bet I will."

Angel lost touch with Jesse, felt him jerk away, then heard a scuffle and a hollow thunk followed by a groan.

"What is it, what happened?"

"Nothing. Angel." Suddenly he was back, and he grabbed her arm. "Come on, let's take the gold to our friends out there and get you out of here."

"What happened?" she insisted into the shadows.

"Charlie tried to stop me. I knocked him out, that's all. He'll be okay. Come on, let's make our deal. We'll let those sons of bitches have their gold so we can get out of here."

"I can't see anything, Jesse. I've never been in a place so dark before."

"Let's go. Take my hand and follow me."

She did as he bid and moved quietly behind him. Moving about in utter darkness created a feeling of detachment from reality. Each footfall against the hard rock floor jarred her senses.

Beside her, Jesse shouted at the men that he was coming out, and the sharp sound of his voice in the silence made her jump and squeeze his hand. She couldn't wait too long to act. Following closely on his heels she gradually loosened her hand from his. Finally, she took a deep breath, then yanked free and ran. Hands held out in front of her, she bumped up against the wall with a jolt, then felt her way down to the floor. There she curled into a tiny ball, trying to muffle her ragged breath.

"Angel? Angel, dammit where are you? Answer me?" It was Jesse yelling, and he was mad—furious, in fact. Well, if they lived through this, he could give her hell, then. She'd welcome it gladly. But this way he wouldn't be tempted to trade his life for hers.

"Angel, oh, Angel my sweet," called another voice, mocking. It was one she knew, that of the huge man who had tried to drag her off into the woods, the one they had called Fletch. Fear crawled into her throat, nearly choking her. If he found her . . . She refused to let the thought continue.

"What the hell is going on?" the man called Rawley shouted.

"I don't know. Angel, dammit, come on out. I want you out of here, now."

Tempted to shout that it was just too bad what he

299

wanted, she kept her mouth clamped shut. They'd find her, then, and ruin everything.

"Okay, do as you please. I was only trying to help, but you had to go and mess it up. Women think they know everything. Goddammit, Jesse, I tried, I really did."

Oh, dear God. That was Charlie out there. So it must be Jesse lying back there at the wagon. That's what the struggle had been about. Charlie had hit Jesse, not the other way around, and now Charlie was out there with those three men, no doubt going to kill them. And Jesse . . . well, he had to be lying down there hurt and alone in the dark.

She had to get him. All that mattered was being with Jesse.

Inching away from the wall, she crawled on hands and knees along the uneven stone floor. It would be downhill all the way, but at this point she was so confused up could seem like down. She had to be very careful or she might walk right into the arms of those horrible men.

Their voices murmured off to her right, and though she couldn't understand but a few words, it did help her get her bearings. She had only crawled a few feet when she heard one of them say clearly, ". . . Let's take it outside where we can see better."

She stopped, listened. Their voices carried clearly. Had she moved nearer them? She didn't think so. It was the oddity of the caverns.

"Hell, man, it's night out there too, and no moon. I told you to wait till daylight," Charlie said.

"Oh, sure, and let you slip away."

"I'm not going anywhere without the gold. This is the only way out. And what would you care anyway? I couldn't carry more than a couple of bags, you'd have all the rest."

"Say, Charlie, where's that brother of yours? What'd you do, kill him?"

"I might have. What difference does it make?"

300

The rough-voiced man called Fletch joined in. "I want to know what happened to the woman."

"Forget the woman," Rawley said. "It's Charlie here we got to keep track of. And he's right, let's wait till morning. It'll be much less work if we can see what we're doing. Besides, I'm tired. This has been one hell of a goose chase you led us on, Charlie."

"That's right. So why don't we just settle down and wait. When the sun comes up, we'll go on down and split up the gold." His voice was soft, and Angel had to admit that Charlie could be such a charmer when he wanted to. She hoped he convinced them, though she didn't believe him at all. He had something else in mind besides splitting his precious gold with these three outlaws.

While the men rattled and banged around outside, getting settled for the night, she worked her way inch by careful inch down the incline. It was slow going and nerve-wracking—at any moment she could dislodge a pebble and give away her presence, or trip over something and fall—but after what seemed a lifetime the slope leveled out. She knew she had reached the domed cavern. The wagon would be off to her right. All she had to do was follow the wall until she found it, and hopefully Jesse. Then, no matter how this ended, they would be together.

Jesse groaned and stirred. A hammer thumped monotonously on his head—hard. Fingering the spot, he opened his eyes to total blackness. For an instant he didn't know where he was or what had happened. The memory of the last few minutes came back slowly, fuzzily. The cave, his brother, the gold and . . . Angel.

My God, Angel. He dared not call her name. What had happened? Could he still save her? Where was his brother? An initial effort to rise totally failed. The world tilted and he fell onto his back again. Rolling over on his stomach he tried again and managed to crawl to his hands and knees.

From off in the distance came an indistinct murmur he finally realized were men's voices. And nearby came a scuffling sound and then a whisper. It was his name, and it was repeated over and over, softly and fearfully.

"Jesse." A long pause. "Jesse."

It was like when he was a kid and he would imagine his mother calling him in the darkness of the night, whispering so Zeke wouldn't hear and banish her. It was a sweet, loving voice, not the voice of a woman who would throw her babies away.

"Jesse, please."

"Angel?"

"Oh God, yes. Jesse."

Hot tears filled his eyes. He'd wanted her safe, but she'd come back for him. They would both surely die. Yet she hadn't deserted him.

Emotions in a turmoil, he reached out. "Oh, my Angel."

"I'm here, Jesse."

A hand touched his back, then fingers trailed through his hair.

"What are you doing, Jesse? Are you hurt?"

"No, I'm trying to get up."

Her soft touch found a goose egg, but he barely felt the pain. He lifted one arm and traced the length of her body, then grasped her around the waist. She helped him sit up, leaned him tenderly against the stone wall.

"Why did you come back? I wanted you to get away. Where's Charlie? He hit me," he added as an afterthought.

"I'm not safe without you. Or if I am it doesn't feel that way." She found his mouth with her own and kissed him long and deep, as if taking sustenance.

The thundering of his heart increased the ache in his

302

head, made him dizzy. He wrapped her up close, hung on to keep from spiraling away. He would never let go again. Somehow they would get out of this.

"They're planning to wait till daylight before coming down to divide the gold. Charlie's with them. But I think he is going to kill them when they get down here." She spoke low but distinctly near his ear.

"Probably," he said sadly. "Charlie won't ever stop killing. I know that now. I'm sorry I got you into this, I should've ridden away from him fast as I could, never let him near you."

"If he'd been my brother I'd have wanted to save him too." She rubbed a hand along his chest, down across his stomach, and he reveled in her touch. This was the only person in the world who truly cared for him, and he was glad that he'd been lucky enough to find her—even for such a short time.

"Are we going to die here, Jesse?" Angel's voice echoed his thoughts.

A beat went by before he answered, and he forced himself to tell her the truth. "Maybe, yeah, I guess we could."

"Then let's make love."

His hand stopped its gentle rubbing of her back. He gathered his breath, held it for a moment, then let it out slowly.

"Now?" They were in mortal danger, and yet . . .

In reply, she guided his other hand to her breast, began to unfasten his pants. "Right now," she whispered. "When I die, I want to be in your arms."

Jesse's trembling fingers caressed her. Angeline felt the heat of his desire, sensed his underlying fear. But her words had been true. This could be the last time she would ever experience such ecstasy. Passion surged through her at his touch. He joined her frenzy, hungrily tearing at her shirt and bending to taste her bared flesh.

Samantha Lee

In the absolute and total darkness, all sensations seemed twice as powerful. The smoothness and warmth of his skin, the woodsy flavor as she nibbled along his belly, the smell of his maleness and the cavern's damp earth: they all set her senses to zinging, shooting off in all directions until she reeled with mindless desire. She wanted his hands and mouth everywhere, ached to feel him inside her, yearned to howl with pure rapture. Yet she dared not cry out.

Passion consumed Angeline's dread as she lay back on the floor of the black cave with Jesse. His hands, his mouth, his very breath set her ablaze. Every act might be for the last time, and it had to be the best. His fingertips tingled over her satiny skin, his mouth pulsed at her nipples and lips, and she felt the fiery heat of his hardened arousal burning against her skin.

Yanking, ripping and tearing away clothing, they went at each other in an eerie silence. In spite of their avid needs, they did not hurry the act. Jesse spent long, breathless moments at her breasts—left them only to return once more, as if they were what sustained him. All the while his hands roamed along her thighs, across her belly, teasing the moist flesh between her legs. She needed him inside her, wanted him filling her all at once, but also wanted to make this last forever.

At last, neither could resist a moment longer. Angel throbbed with a painful desire, and she guided him to her. He pushed inside, thrusting deep to join with her "tiny beating heart," and it was too much.

Their gasps and shrieks of pleasure exploded around them, and for a moment she forgot where she was. Surrounded by the exuberant echoes of their ecstasy, exhausted and sweaty, she pleaded and begged for it to go on. Moving against him in a tantalizing dance, she found her skin slick against his.

He groaned beneath her, and though it had been only moments since their culmination, she felt him growing once more inside her.

304

Once more, once more, and then we die. He rose and fell in exquisite slow motion above her, driving her to a precipice, dangling her there ever so long, threatening to cast her into joyous oblivion. The fall, when it came, was both torture and delight—and it seemed to last for an eternity.

Tumbled at last from the peak, she clung to him. Crushed in his arms, she had the final, muted hope that together they would soar off into infinity. Leave this evil for a place of dreams and promises come true. With that, she drifted into slumber.

Chapter Twenty-one

Early rays of golden sunlight filtered through the openings in the roof and awakened Angel. Jesse still slept, coiled around her like a cocoon. In the shadows the tip of his nose, cheek bones, forehead and chin caught the light, his eyes and his mouth smudged. Curls of dark hair lay along his temples. She gazed into that familiar, dear face, picturing the children they could have had together. The child they might have conceived this very night.

They *had* to survive, if only to right the wrongs of the generation that had come before, to avenge children abandoned by their parents. She and Jesse would cherish each and every child they brought into this world. If only God would allow them to live.

Jesse stirred, pulled her closer. He murmured something soft and woozy, content in the safety of his dreams.

She kissed him gently. Nearby she heard men talking, moving noisily. That brought her back to reality.

In a panic, she shook him. "Jesse, wake up. They're coming."

His initial movements brought a groan and he fingered the lump on his head.

"You okay?"

"Yes."

"Hurry, then. We have to hurry."

Still seeming dazed, he struggled to his feet. "We've got to get away from here before they see us."

"I know. Down there, out of sight." They fumbled into their clothes.

"Come on," he urged. They were near the wagon, and minute by minute the light spilling through the openings above grew brighter. As the men came in sight, Jesse and Angel slipped into a darkened alcove opposite where they had lain.

Jesse pulled his Colt from its holster. "I have enough bullets for all of them, even Charlie—if it comes to that." He spoke quietly and Angeline saw that his eyes were wet as he thumbed back the trigger. Then he shoved Angel behind him and she couldn't see his face.

The big man called Fletch came into sight first. He had hold of Charlie, shoving him along each time he slowed his pace. Apparently he hadn't been as charming as he should have, Angel found herself thinking. Rawley and Cake brought up the rear.

The trio stepped into the light at precisely the same moment that additional footsteps echoed at their backs.

"Hold it!" a voice rang out.

Angel watched Rawley whirl and pull his gun.

A tall, angular white-haired man stepped into the light, carrying a rifle.

It was John Prophet! Angel whimpered and stuffed a fist in her mouth.

Before he could raise the weapon, though, Rawley pulled off a shot. It missed, and slammed from wall to wall until its whine died away. Shouting, two other men suddenly appeared behind Prophet. It was Oursler, and— someone who looked mighty familiar. They began to return fire. Everything became a madhouse, with everyone shooting and yelling. The noise was deafening. The cavern filled with the acrid smell and taste of gun smoke.

Behind Jesse, Angel covered her ears and closed her eyes. The stench of blood and gunpowder filled her nostrils, brought tears to her eyes; the terrible noise pummeled her. Suddenly Jesse leapt from his hiding place, and she screamed his name. With him out of the way, she saw clearly what was going on. Caught sight of Prophet's white hair. He was still standing, though in the growing light, bodies littered the floor, some still twitching. Nausea rocketed up from her stomach and she turned away momentarily to control it.

Prophet bellowed. Somehow, his booming, authoritative voice managed to get the others' attention.

"Hold your fire! Damnation, this is going to get us all killed."

Only Charlie, Jesse, Prophet and the sheriff were left to obey the demand. The others had been in the middle of the crossfire, Angel supposed. The three outlaws certainly appeared to be dead. She gagged.

"Where's Angeline? What have you done with her?" Prophet yelled.

Jesse was in front of her, and spoke over his shoulder. "Stay right where you are. I'll shoot him if I have to."

"No, don't," she cried and moved out to stand beside Jesse. "I don't *want* him dead, and I don't want you to kill him."

He studied her closely, then gently thumbed the hammer down and lowered the Colt.

Prophet eyed her for a long beat, then raised his rifle and pointed it at Jesse.

Calmly, she stepped in front of him. "John, I'll go back with you if you let him go," she said. Fear palpated her heart like a huge hand. She could hardly breathe, but she stood her ground.

At her back, Jesse said, "She's not going back with you. I'll kill you."

Prophet laughed bitterly. "So you have ruined my Angeline. I feared as much."

Glancing around, Sheriff Oursler appeared. He seemed to have escaped injury. He took in the scene calmly, then jerked his attention to Charlie and Jesse. "All I want to know is which of you killed my deputy?"

When neither answered, his composure slipped. "I asked which of you sons a bitches murdered my friend? I don't much care 'cause you're *both* going to hang. But I'd just like to know."

Jesse didn't say a word, just put a protective arm around Angel. "At least you'll be safe. It's time this ended."

She put her arms around him. "No."

"They're going to hang us both if we don't kill them right here. And then Charlie and I will be on the run the rest of our lives. Which I doubt will be very long with half the marshals in the country looking for us."

Angel chose instead to address her husband. "John, please. Jesse didn't do anything wrong. It was his brother. You can stop this if you want. If you ever loved me, please let Jesse go. I'll go home with you, then."

The white-haired man's eyes slitted, and she expected fire to come from his mouth when he spoke. "Do you think I want you now? After you've lain with this heathen?" He turned his head, obviously torn.

Out of the corner of her eye Angel caught a slight movement; Charlie was slowly inching his way around the front of the wagon. It looked as if he had lost his gun. The man knelt slowly, so that neither Oursler or Prophet noticed, caught up as they were in their conversation with Jesse and Angel.

To her side, Angel saw Jesse ever so slowly thumb back the hammer of his Colt. He knew what his brother had planned.

With a roar Charlie came up and flung one of the large bones of the horses who had died here so many years before. It caught Oursler on the temple, staggering the lawman so that he dropped his weapon. Prophet swung and pointed the rifle from his hip but Charlie was on the move, scooting across the floor to retrieve Oursler's gun. The first bullet from Prophet's rifle cut rock at his feet and whined away.

Jesse raised his own weapon, and Angeline wondered what he would do. He swung the barrel past Prophet until it pointed at his brother. Charlie stood over the sheriff, ready to shoot him with his own gun.

"This ends now," Jesse cried.

"All the hell I ever wanted was the goddamned gold," Charlie shouted. All went still.

Out of the pall of silence that followed, a single booming shot echoed out.

Everyone froze in horror. Charlie was aiming at the helpless Oursler, but he hadn't fired. Angel swung her gaze between Jesse and Prophet, then back to Charlie. Then she noticed the blood blooming in the center of his chest. Her gaze suddenly went to the man on the floor, it was the man who had come with Oursler and Prophet. With his dying strength he had shot Charlie.

The outlaw staggered several paces, then fell with one arm outstretched, reaching for the treasure he had come all this way to reclaim. No one moved as he crawled toward the scattered bags of gold. His fingers clutched a few of the spilled nuggets, then he lay still.

Jesse ran to his brother, knelt and turned him over. He began to cry.

Angel knelt behind him, putting her arms around him. Charlie stared up into Jesse's eyes, but the light had gone out of his own, his fist clutching the precious nuggets for which he had died.

"I'm so sorry, Jesse. I'm so sorry," Angel murmured. She rocked him, his tears hot against her shoulder.

After a while she looked up. Prophet stood over them, a strange, resigned expression on his face.

"Please, please, John, let us go. I love him. He's my world. I'll never be happy with anyone else. Do this for us, please. For me." Her tears flowed freely until she could no longer see the face of her husband.

Slumped, he studied her for a long time, no longer the

310

self-righteous man she remembered. He was just sad and old. Maybe that's all he'd ever been.

"Oursler," Prophet said, clearing his throat and trying again. "Sheriff, I think we've got our man."

"No, oh, no." Angel sobbed and clung to Jesse, who continued to stroke his brother's face. She touched his shoulder and he looked up at her. There was sadness in his eyes, but he looked different too. Stronger. Had his brother's death made him whole only in time to be hanged?

Prophet went on. "I'm sorry Charlie Cole is dead. You'll get cheated out of hanging him. This here's the man who killed your deputy, isn't he?"

Still woozy from being hit in the head with the bone of a horse, Oursler shook his head. "What?"

"Well?" Prophet roared, some of his bravado returning.

"Yeah, sure. I reckon that's him. It was one of them."

"And you'll notify everyone he's been killed? Get the posters taken down, the reward rescinded?"

Angel listened in disbelief. As much as she had hoped and prayed for Prophet's understanding, she had never thought it would happen.

"And these other three. Isn't there a reward for capturing these outlaws? I don't see why we can't take some of this here recovered bounty, do you? How much was that reward, sheriff?"

Angel untangled herself and stood to face the man she had lived with as a daughter for six years. Her respect for this man had grown. "Thank you," she whispered. "Thank you so much."

Prophet sighed. "I always did love you, Angeline, but I think you know that," the old man said. "Now, get your man out of here before we change our mind. And on your way pick up a couple bags of gold. It'll see you to where you're going and then some."

She bent and touched Jesse's arm. He raised his face to

311

gaze at her. The sorrow in his golden eyes had mostly cleared. His love for her shined through. He turned to the white-haired man, but was cut short.

"Don't thank me, young man, just see you take good care of her, or I'll be coming after you." Prophet turned away.

Angel thought she caught a glimmer in the man's eyes, but she wasn't sure.

Jesse spoke up then, anyway. "I *do* thank you, sir. And we're going to take real good care of each other," Jesse said. He took her by the hand.

Because he walked right on past the gold without sparing it a glance, Angeline stooped and picked up two of the heavy bags, then followed him out of the cave into the brilliant morning sunlight.

Author's Notes

During the westward movement, particularly after the Civil War, many young girls like Angeline Prophet were purchased by men who wanted to homestead additional land. In most cases the girls remained wives to the men who had bought them, for once they settled in some remote soddy, there was little else they could do. Not much has been written about this particular type of "slavery," in which everyone had something to gain except possibly the unwilling bride. Unlike most of these girls, Angeline was able to escape her fate.

The gold mine which Angel visited before her escape actually exists, but it is located on private property and is not open to the public. A brochure published by the Jackson County Tourism Council in Holton, Kansas, states that a vein of gold was discovered south of the town site in a hillside along Elk Creek in 1863. The mine finally shut down because the ore was thought not to be valuable enough to continue operations, but no date of that closure is known. The Jackson County Historical Museum in Holton has on exhibit three small sections of the mine's narrow gauge rail track and two small ore-bearing rocks.

In 1867 Joseph Geiting McCoy went in search of a town to which cattle could be driven into Kansas from Texas. After investigating several that turned out not to be suitable, he found the settlement of Abilene. It wasn't much of a town with its twelve log houses, only one with a

313

shingle roof, but there was sufficient water and grass to support large herds of cattle. After many setbacks and extensive work with the railroad, McCoy's dream finally came true. The year of 1867 saw thirty-five thousand cattle trailed to Abilene. Soon hundreds of thousands of head followed the Chisholm Trail to Abilene. At one time there were thirty-five active saloons in the city limits. In 1871 Wild Bill Hickok was hired to keep order in the rowdy cow town. As a direct result of residents' complaints about the wild Texas cowboys, Abilene was deserted by 1873, the cattle and punchers moving on to where they were more welcome.

Silkville, from which Monique escaped, is not fictitious. Such a place did exist in Kansas and orgies were said to be commonplace. Frenchman Ernest Valeton de Boissiere founded what he originally called Valeton, and referred to it as a Utopia. He planned that all his people would live in perfect harmony in Silkville's sixty-room mansion. All they had to do was give up all their worldly possessions.

In the spring of 1870, twenty thousand mulberry seeds were planted, and the following spring eight thousand yearling mulberry trees were set out. A large limestone building housed a factory equipped with looms and other machinery brought over from France to produce silk ribbon. Silkworms from Japan were shipped in to spin the silk. The complex eventually consisted of the chateau, the factory, a barn, winery, ice house, assorted other buildings and a school for the workers' children. The grand and successful experiment came to an end when Boissiere, then an old man, gave the farm to the Odd Fellows Lodge and returned to France in May of 1892.

In a long court battle in which two women claimed to be illegitimate children of Boissiere, testimony revealed that Silkville had indeed been a place of free love where marriage was strictly forbidden and Boissiere took his pick of the women.

And finally, though Oursler is a common name around Circleville, there was never, to my knowledge, a sheriff by that name. He is entirely fictional, as is John Prophet. As for the wagonload of gold, such tales continue to circulate of undiscovered treasures hidden deep in the many caves throughout the Ozarks. None have ever been found, or if they have, the secret has been well kept.

IMAGES IN SCARLET

SAMANTHA LEE

Allison Caine hardly imagined the road to Santa Fe to be picture perfect, but the headstrong photographer has to admit that she never expected a man sleeping in the middle of the road to bar her path. And for a man with no memories, the virile "Jake" sure seems built to make a few worth remembering. Snatches of his life are all Jake can summon of his fragmented past: swirling images of sheets of scarlet and a woman beneath. But now—a beauty that consorts with outlaws and whose lips promise passion untold— Allie makes him ache for the truth which is just beyond reach. Deep in his heart he knows that he is the man of her dreams and not the killer his flashbacks suggest. All he has to do is prove it.

___4578-8 $4.99 US/$5.99 CAN

Love, Cherish Me

Rebecca Brandewyne

The man in black shows his hand: five black spades. Storm Lesconflair knows what this means—she now belongs to him. The close heat of the saloon flushes her skin as she feels the half-breed's eyes travel over her body. Her father's plantation house in New Orleans suddenly seems but a dream, while the handsome stranger before her is all too real. Dawn is breaking outside as the man who won her rises and walks through the swinging doors. She follows him out into the growing light, only vaguely aware that she has become his forever, never guessing that he has also become hers.

__52302-7 $5.99 US/$6.99 CAN

A Gentle Magic

EMMA CRAIG

When cattleman Cody O'Fannin hears a high-pitched scream ring out across the harsh New Mexico Territory, he rides straight into the heart of danger, expecting to find a cougar or a Comanche. Instead, he finds a scene far more frightening—a woman in the final stages of childbirth. Alone, the beautiful Melissa Wilmeth clearly needs his assistance, and although he'd rather face a band of thieving outlaws, Cody ignores his quaking insides and helps deliver her baby. When the infant's first wail fills the air, Cody gazes into Melissa's bewitching blue eyes and is spellbound. How else can he explain the sparkles he sees shimmering in the air above her honey-colored hair? Then thoughts of marriage creep into his head, and he doesn't need a crystal ball to realize he hasn't lost his mind or his nerve, but his heart.

___52321-3 $5.50 US/$6.50 CAN